# HAUNTED NEW ENGLAND

# HAUNTED NEW ENGLAND

*Classic Tales of the Strange and Supernatural*

Edited by
Charles G. Waugh, Martin H. Greenberg &
Frank D. McSherry, Jr.

Foreword by Rick Hautala

*Illustrated by Peter Farrow*

## YANKEE BOOKS

A division of Yankee Publishing Incorporated
Dublin, New Hampshire

Designed by Jill Shaffer
Yankee Publishing Incorporated
Dublin, New Hampshire 03444

First Edition
Second Printing, 1989

SKU 02

*Library of Congress Cataloging-in-Publication Data*

Haunted New England / edited by Charles G. Waugh, Martin H.
Greenberg
    & Frank D. McSherry, Jr. ; illustrated by Peter Farrow.
        p.        cm.
    1. Ghost stories, American — New England. 2. New En-
gland — Fiction.
I. Waugh, Charles. II. Greenberg, Martin Harry. III. McSherry,
Frank D.
PS648.G48H27    1988                                    88-17097
813'.0872—dc19                                             CIP

# TABLE OF CONTENTS

# ACKNOWLEDGMENTS

"The Trap" by Henry S. Whitehead. Copyright 1932 by Henry Whitehead. Reprinted by permission of the Scott Meredith Literary Agency, Inc., 845 Third Ave., New York, NY 10022.

"The Island" by Elizabeth A. Lynn. Copyright 1977 by Mercury Press, Inc. From *The Magazine of Fantasy and Science Fiction.* Reprinted by permission of Richard Curtis Associates, Inc.

"The Woman at Seven Brothers" by Wilbur Daniel Steele. Copyright 1917 by *Harper's Magazine.* Copyright renewed. Reprinted by permission of Harold Matson Agency, Inc.

"Mr. Murdoch's Ghost" by Richard Frede. Copyright 1977 by Richard Frede. Reprinted by permission of International Creative Management, Inc.

"The Summer Rebellion" by Hortense Calisher. This story appeared in another form under the title "The Summer Psychosis" in *Harper's Ba-*

# FOREWORD

L ET'S TAKE A little stroll around the barn. I've got a few things I want to say to you before you dive into *Haunted New England* . . . just a little something to ease you into it, you understand. I'll try to be brief.

First of all, a quick glance at the list of stories and authors represented here should tell you one thing right away — this is not your ordinary anthology of ghost stories, New England or otherwise. When I saw Sarah Orne Jewett listed with H. P. Lovecraft, and Edith Wharton with Jack Finney and Tom Easton, I knew this anthology had its heart (cold though it might be) in the right place and its vision set on the wide vista of New England writing. Of course, there's no doubt that New England has inspired a whole range of stories — even within such a rather limited scope as ghost stories set in the area. Any anthology, though, that can pull together such apparently disparate authors and not become an architectural nightmare like, say, the house in "Mr. Murdoch's Ghost," is simply a wonder.

Perhaps all writers of horror fiction get tired, after a while — quite a *short* while, actually — of feeling they have to defend what they do. I know *I* certainly do, and this is never more painfully evident than when, in the course of an interview or conversation, the question comes up: "When are you going to write something *serious?*" . . . as if the situation the little girl narrator faces in "Lady Ferry" isn't *serious!* . . . as if the grief the protagonist suffers in "The Island" isn't *serious!* Okay . . . enough of that! Point made. I'll get out of my Larry Holmes crouch and put my fists down.

Recently, I've been getting a new question. Well, kind of new — a variation on the *serious* question. I've been asked more than once recently if I consider what I write to be "art." I'm sure this question has its origin in the commercial success of Stephen King and the questioner's attempts to harness those two apparently incompatible beasts — art and commerce. Any reasonable critic must see that they aren't mutually exclusive.

From now on, though, whenever I'm asked that question, after I stammer through my answer (which usually descends to begging the question: "What else would you call it . . . experimental biology? . . . mechanical engineering?"), I'm going to hand the questioner a copy of *Haunted New England.* If these stories aren't *art* (you have my permission to use a capital A in *art* if you'd like), then what are they? Still they were all written, primarily, to *scare* you! Each story sets out to send chills rippling up and down your spine like a xylophone, if not actually give you a terminal case of the willies — and I think these stories achieve just that.

Sometime in mid-January, I received a phone call from Clarissa Silitch at *Yankee,* asking if I was interested in writing the foreword to this anthology. After a brief discussion about the theme and stories included, I accepted; and after a week or so, I received a manuscript copy of the stories . . . rather hefty, I might add. A few nights later, I sat down and read (or re-read) the stories. But as I read, I found myself getting . . . well, a bit frustrated.

I envy you readers. You don't have to charge through this anthology the way I did. I had to get an impression of how all of these stories hung together, and I had to get my foreword done so I wouldn't throw the production schedule out the window. But — like a box of expensive chocolates you receive for Christmas, and which you tell yourself you will sample only once a day until they're gone — you can linger with this book. You could read one story a night until they're gone . . . preferably just before tucking in. See what dreams . . . or *nightmares* . . . come. Or you could drag it out a bit more. Read, say, one a week just to see how much psychic indigestion you can take.

But I have something a bit more elaborate in mind. As I read through this anthology, I was struck by the variety of times and places and seasons in the book. Like New England weather, the inspiration for each particular story seemed . . . well, changeable. Just as there is no easily definable "typical" New England day, there is no "standard" New England ghost story. The range here is as far as it is from Bangor to Providence . . . further, even, because these stories also span quite a bit of time, both in their composition and in their settings. Ghosts may be very specifically "place-tied," but they certainly are not bounded by time.

If you can restrain yourself from taking the whole book down in a one- or two-sitting gulp, you might want to take your time over *Haunted New England,* saving certain stories for certain "appropriate" situations.

Try this, for instance: Several of these stories are set on or near the coast (usually the Maine coast). Hold off from reading "The Woman at Seven Brothers," "Summer Rebellion," "The Island," "Fog," and "Mr. Arcularis" until you take a day off and hit the beach . . . a nice, languid August afternoon, when the ocean water and the iced tea just aren't enough chill for you. I suspect you just might succeed in raising a few goosebumps in spite of the ninety-degree temperature.

Or how about this: the standard fare of all ghost stories is the dimly lit, draughty old house. Hold off from reading "The Challenge," "The Shunned House," "Roll Them Bones," and "Hour After Westerly" until some rainy, windy autumn night. Turn off every light in the house except your reading light, and make sure you're sitting by a window. . . one with a loose pane that rattles with the wind would be just fine.

And then, once autumn blends into winter, stoke up the fire in the fireplace, wait until there's a knife-edged blizzard howling in the dark outside your house, get a mug of mulled cider, and dip into "The Triumph of Night," "Old Woman," "Mr. Murdoch's Ghost," and "Haunted Ground."

Once spring comes, and lengthening days and soft showers lull you into thinking everything's "safe" once again, try sitting outside, toward evening, when there's the heavy scent of lilac in the air, and read "Lady Ferry," "Carrion Crypt," and "Where the Cluetts Are." You just might find yourself lying wide awake well past midnight, watching the curtains waft gently in the spring breeze.

These are just suggestions, you understand. I realize most of you will — like me — wait until everyone else is in bed, bolt the door, draw the shades, and settle down to read these stories one right after the other. While you're at it, take that box of Christmas chocolates and chomp through it, piece by piece until they're gone! You don't *have* to read *Haunted New England* in one sitting, though I suspect you will . . . but then just *try* to get a good night's sleep!

Happy reading . . .

Rick Hautala
Westbrook, Maine
February 7, 1988

*Henry S. Whitehead*

# THE TRAP

I T WAS ON A certain Thursday morning in December that the whole
thing began with that unaccountable motion I thought I saw in my
antique Copenhagen mirror. Something, it seemed to me, stirred —
something reflected in the glass, though I was alone in my quarters. I
paused and looked intently, then, deciding that the effect must be a pure
illusion, resumed the interrupted brushing of my hair.

I had discovered the old mirror, covered with dust and cobwebs, in an
outbuilding of an abandoned estate-house in Santa Cruz's sparsely settled
Northside territory, and had brought it to the United States from the Virgin
Islands. The venerable glass was dim from more than two hundred years'
exposure to a tropical climate, and the graceful ornamentation along the top
of the gilt frame had been badly smashed. I had had the detached pieces set
back into the frame before placing it in storage with my other belongings.

Now, several years later, I was staying half as a guest and half as a tutor
at the private school of my old friend Browne on a windy Connecticut
hillside — occupying an unused wing in one of the dormitories, where I
had two rooms and a hallway to myself. The old mirror, stowed securely in
mattresses, was the first of my possessions to be unpacked on my arrival;
and I had set it up majestically in the living-room, on top of an old
rosewood console which had belonged to my great-grandmother.

The door of my bedroom was just opposite that of the living-room, with a hallway between; and I had noticed that by looking into my chiffonier glass I could see the larger mirror through the two doorways — which was exactly like glancing down an endless, though diminishing corridor. On this Thursday morning I thought I saw a curious suggestion of motion down that normally empty corridor — but, as I have said, soon dismissed the notion.

When I reached the dining-room I found everyone complaining of the cold, and learned that the school's heating-plant was temporarily out of order. Being especially sensitive to low temperatures, I was myself an acute sufferer; and at once decided not to brave any freezing schoolroom that day. Accordingly I invited my class to come over to my living-room for an informal session around my grate-fire — a suggestion which the boys received enthusiastically.

After the session one of the boys, Robert Grandison, asked if he might remain; since he had no appointment for the second morning period. I told him to stay, and welcome. He sat down to study in front of the fireplace in a comfortable chair.

It was not long, however, before Robert moved to another chair somewhat farther away from the freshly replenished blaze, this change bringing him directly opposite the old mirror. From my own chair in another part of the room I noticed how fixedly he began to look at the dim, cloudy glass, and, wondering what so greatly interested him, was reminded of my own experience earlier that morning. As time passed he continued to gaze, a slight frown knitting his brows.

At last I quietly asked him what had attracted his attention. Slowly and still wearing the puzzled frown, he looked over and replied rather cautiously:

"It's the corrugations in the glass — or whatever they are, Mr. Canevin. I was noticing how they all seem to run from a certain point. Look — I'll show you what I mean."

The boy jumped up, went over to the mirror, and placed his finger on a point near its lower left-hand corner.

"It's right here, sir," he explained, turning to look toward me and keeping his finger on the chosen spot.

His muscular action in turning may have pressed his finger against the glass. Suddenly he withdrew his hand as though with some slight effort, and with a faintly muttered "Ouch." Then he looked at the glass in obvious mystification.

"What happened?" I asked, rising and approaching.

"Why — it — " He seemed embarrassed. "It — I — felt — well, as though it were pulling my finger into it. Seems — er — perfectly foolish, sir, but — well — it was a most peculiar sensation." Robert had an unusual vocabulary for his fifteen years.

I came over and had him show me the exact spot he meant.

"You'll think I'm rather a fool sir," he said shamefacedly, "but — well, from right here I can't be absolutely sure. From the chair it seemed to be clear enough."

Now thoroughly interested, I sat down in the chair Robert had occupied and looked at the spot he selected on the mirror. Instantly the thing "jumped out at me." Unmistakably, from that particular angle, all the many whorls in the ancient glass appeared to converge like a large number of spread strings held in one hand and radiating out in streams.

Getting up and crossing to the mirror, I could no longer see the curious spot. Only from certain angles, apparently, was it visible. Directly viewed, that portion of the mirror did not even give back a normal reflection — for I could not see my face in it. Manifestly I had a minor puzzle on my hands.

Presently the school gong sounded, and the fascinated Robert Grandison departed hurriedly, leaving me alone with my odd little problem in optics. I raised several window-shades, crossed the hallway, and sought for the spot in the chiffonier mirror's reflection. Finding it readily, I looked very intently and thought I again detected something of the "motion." I craned my neck, and at last, at a certain angle of vision, the thing again "jumped out at me."

The vague "motion" was now positive and definite — an appearance of torsional movement, or of whirling; much like a minute yet intense whirlwind or waterspout, or a huddle of autumn leaves dancing circularly in an eddy of wind along a level lawn. It was, like the earth's, a double motion — around and around, and at the same time *inward,* as if the whorls poured themselves endlessly toward some point inside the glass. Fascinated, yet realizing that the thing must be an illusion, I grasped an impression of quite distinct *suction,* and thought of Robert's embarrassed explanation: *"I felt as though it were pulling my finger into it."*

A kind of slight chill ran suddenly up and down my backbone. There was something here distinctly worth looking into. And as the idea of investigation came to me, I recalled the rather wistful expression of Robert Grandison when the gong called him to class. I remembered how he had looked back over his shoulder as he walked obediently out into the hallway, and resolved that he should be included in whatever analysis I might make of this little mystery.

Exciting events connected with that same Robert, however, were soon to chase all thoughts of the mirror from my consciousness for a time. I was away all that afternoon, and did not return to the school until the five-fifteen "Call-Over" — a general assembly at which the boys' attendance was compulsory. Dropping in at this function with the idea of picking Robert up for a session with the mirror, I was astonished and pained to find him absent — a very unusual and unaccountable thing in his case. That evening Browne told me that the boy had actually disappeared, a search in his room, in the gymnasium, and in all other accustomed places being unavailing, though all his belongings — including his outdoor clothing — were in their proper places.

He had not been encountered on the ice or with any of the hiking groups that afternoon, and telephone calls to all the school-catering merchants of the neighborhood were in vain. There was, in short, no record of his having been seen since the end of the lesson periods at two-fifteen; when he had turned up the stairs toward his room in Dormitory Number Three.

When the disappearance was fully realized, the resulting sensation was tremendous throughout the school. Browne, as headmaster, had to bear the brunt of it; and such an unprecedented occurrence in his well-regulated, highly-organized institution left him quite bewildered. It was learned that Robert had not run away to his home in western Pennsylvania, nor did any of the searching parties of boys and masters find any trace of him in the snowy countryside around the school. As far as could be seen, he had simply vanished.

Robert's parents arrived on the afternoon of the second day after his disappearance. They took their trouble quietly, though of course they were staggered by this unexpected disaster. Browne looked ten years older for it, but there was absolutely nothing that could be done. By the fourth day the case had settled down in the opinion of the school as an insoluble mystery. Mr. and Mrs. Grandison went reluctantly back to their home, and on the following morning the ten days' Christmas vacation began.

Boys and masters departed in anything but the usual holiday spirit; and Browne and his wife were left, along with the servants, as my only fellow-occupants of the big place. Without the masters and boys it seemed a very hollow shell indeed.

That afternoon I sat in front of my grate-fire thinking about Robert's disappearance and evolving all sorts of fantastic theories to account for it.

By evening I had acquired a bad headache, and ate a light supper accordingly. Then, after a brisk walk around the massed buildings, I returned to my living-room and took up the burden of thought once more.

A little after ten o'clock I awakened in my armchair, stiff and chilled, from a doze during which I had let the fire go out. I was physically uncomfortable, yet mentally aroused by a peculiar sensation of expectancy and possible hope. Of course it had to do with the problem that was harassing me. For I had started from that inadvertent nap with a curious, persistent idea — the odd idea that a tenuous, hardly recognizable Robert Grandison had been trying desperately to communicate with me. I finally went to bed with one conviction unreasoningly strong in my mind. Somehow I was sure that young Robert Grandison was still alive.

That I should be receptive of such a notion will not seem strange to those who know my long residence in the West Indies and my close contact with unexplained happenings there. It will not seem strange, either, that I fell asleep with an urgent desire to establish some sort of mental communication with the missing boy. Even the most prosaic scientists affirm, with Freud, Jung, and Adler, that the subconscious mind is most open to external impression in sleep; though such impressions are seldom carried over intact into the waking state.

Going a step further and granting the existence of telepathic forces, it follows that such forces must act most strongly on a sleeper; so that if I were ever to get a definite message from Robert, it would be during a period of profoundest slumber. Of course, I might lose the message in waking; but my aptitude for retaining such things has been sharpened by types of mental discipline picked up in various obscure corners of the globe.

I must have dropped asleep instantaneously, and from the vividness of my dreams and the absence of wakeful intervals I judge that my sleep was a very deep one. It was six-forty-five when I awakened, and there still lingered with me certain impressions which I knew were carried over from the world of somnolent cerebration. Filling my mind was the vision of Robert Grandison strangely transformed to a boy of a dull greenish dark-blue color; Robert desperately endeavoring to communicate with me by means of speech, yet finding some almost insuperable difficulty in so doing. A wall of curious spatial separation seemed to stand between him and me — a mysterious, invisible wall which completely baffled us both.

I had seen Robert as though at some distance, yet queerly enough he seemed at the same time to be just beside me. He was both larger and smaller than in real life, his apparent size varying *directly* instead of *inversely,* with the distance as he advanced and retreated in the course of conversation. That is, he grew larger instead of smaller to my eye when he stepped away or backwards, and vice versa; as if the laws of perspective in his case had been wholly reversed. His aspect was misty and uncertain — as if he lacked sharp or permanent outlines; and the anomalies of his coloring and clothing baffled me utterly at first.

At some point in my dream Robert's vocal efforts had finally crystallized into audible speech — albeit speech of an abnormal thickness and dullness. I could not for a time understand anything he said, and even in the dream racked my brain for a clue to where he was, what he wanted to tell, and why his utterance was so clumsy and unintelligible. Then little by little I began to distinguish words and phrases, the very first of which sufficed to throw my dreaming self into the wildest excitement and to establish a certain mental connection which had previously refused to take conscious form because of the utter incredibility of what it implied.

I do not know how long I listened to those halting words amidst my deep slumber, but hours must have passed while the strangely remote speaker struggled on with his tale. There was revealed to me such a circumstance as I cannot hope to make others believe without the strongest corroborative evidence, yet which I was quite ready to accept as truth — both in the dream and after waking — because of my former contacts with uncanny things. The boy was obviously watching my face — mobile in receptive sleep — as he choked along; for about the time I began to comprehend him, his own expression brightened and gave signs of gratitude and hope.

Any attempt to hint at Robert's message, as it lingered in my ears after a sudden awakening in the cold, brings this narrative to a point where I must choose my words with the greatest care. Everything involved is so difficult to record that one tends to flounder helplessly. I have said that the revelation established in my mind a certain connection which reason had not allowed me to formulate consciously before. This connection, I need no longer hesitate to hint, had to do with the old Copenhagen mirror whose suggestions of motion had so impressed me on the morning of the disappearance, and whose whorl-like contours and apparent illusions of suction had later exerted such a disquieting fascination on both Robert and me.

Resolutely, though my outer consciousness had previously rejected what my intuition would have liked to imply, it could reject that stupendous conception no longer. What was fantasy in the tale of "Alice" now came to me as a grave and immediate reality. That looking-glass had indeed possessed a malign, abnormal suction; and the struggling speaker in my dream made clear the extent to which it violated all the known precedents of human experience and all the age-old laws of our three sane dimensions. It was more than a mirror — it was a gate; a trap; a link with spatial recesses not meant for the denizens of our visible universe, and realizable only in terms of the most intricate non-Euclidean mathematics. *And in some outrageous fashion Robert Grandison had passed out of our ken into the glass and was there immured, waiting for release.*

It is significant that upon awakening I harbored no genuine doubt of the reality of the revelation. That I had actually held conversation with a transdimensional Robert, rather than evoked the whole episode from my broodings about his disappearance and about the old illusions of the mirror, was as certain to my utmost instincts as any of the instinctive certainties commonly recognized as valid.

The tale thus unfolded to me was of the most incredibly bizarre character. As had been clear on the morning of his disappearance, Robert was intensely fascinated by the ancient mirror. All through the hours of school, he had it in mind to come back to my living-room and examine it further. When he did arrive, after the close of the school day, it was somewhat later than two-twenty, and I was absent in town. Finding me out and knowing that I would not mind, he had come into my living-room and gone straight to the mirror; standing before it and studying the place where, as we had noted, the whorls appeared to converge.

Then quite suddenly, there had come to him an overpowering urge to place his hand upon this whorl-center. Almost reluctantly, against his better judgement, he had done so; and upon making the contact had felt at once the strange, almost painful suction which had perplexed him that morning. Immediately thereafter — quite without warning, but with a wrench which seemed to twist and tear every bone and muscle in his body and to bulge and press and cut at every nerve — he had been abruptly *drawn through* and found himself *inside.*

Once through, the excruciatingly painful stress upon his entire system was suddenly released. He felt, he said, as though he had just been born — a feeling that made itself evident every time he tried to do anything; walk, stop, turn his head, or utter speech. Everything about his body seemed a misfit.

These sensations wore off after a long while, Robert's body becoming an organized whole rather than a number of protesting parts. Of all the forms of expression, speech remained the most difficult; doubtless because it is complicated, bringing into play a number of different organs, muscles, and tendons. Robert's feet, on the other hand, were the first members to adjust themselves to the new conditions within the glass.

During the morning hours I rehearsed the whole reason-defying problem; correlating everything I had seen and heard, dismissing the natural skepticism of a man of sense, and scheming to devise possible plans for Robert's release from his incredible prison. As I did so a number of originally perplexing points became clear — or at least, clearer — to me.

There was, for example, the matter of Robert's coloring. His face and hands, as I have indicated, were a kind of dull greenish dark-blue; and I may add that his familiar blue Norfolk jacket had turned to a pale lemon-yellow while his trousers remained a neutral gray as before. Reflecting on this after waking, I found the circumstance closely allied to the reversal of perspective which made Robert seem to grow larger when receding and smaller when approaching. Here, too, was a physical *reversal* — for every detail of his coloring in the unknown dimension was the exact reverse of complement of the corresponding color detail in normal life. In physics the typical complementary colors are blue and yellow, and red and green. These pairs are opposites, and when mixed yield gray. Robert's natural color was a pinkish-buff, the opposite of which is the greenish-blue I saw. His blue coat had become yellow, while the gray trousers remained gray. This latter point baffled me until I remembered that gray is itself a mixture of opposites. There is no opposite for gray — or rather, it is its own opposite.

Another clarified point was that pertaining to Robert's curiously dulled and thickened speech — as well as to the general awkwardness and sense of misfit bodily parts of which he complained. This, at the outset, was a puzzle indeed; though after long thought the clue occurred to me. Here again was the same *reversal* which affected perspective and color-ation. Anyone in the fourth dimension must necessarily be reversed in just this way — hands and feet, as well as colors and perspectives, being changed about. It would be the same with all the other dual organs, such as nostrils, ears, and eyes. Thus Robert had been talking with a reversed tongue, teeth, vocal cords, and kindred speech-apparatus; so that his difficulties in utterance were little to be wondered at.

As the morning wore on, my sense of the stark reality and maddening urgency of the dream-disclosed situation increased rather than decreased. More and more I felt that something must be done, yet realized that I could not seek advice or aid. Such a story as mine — a conviction based upon mere dreaming — could not conceivably bring me anything but ridicule or suspicions as to my mental state. And what, indeed, could I do, aided or unaided, with as little working data as my nocturnal impressions had provided? I must, I finally recognized, have more information before I could even think of a possible plan for releasing Robert. This could come only through the receptive conditions of sleep, and it heartened me to reflect that according to every probability my telepathic contact would be resumed the moment I fell into deep slumber again.

I accomplished sleeping that afternoon, after a midday dinner at which, through rigid self-control, I succeeded in concealing from Browne and his wife the tumultuous thoughts that crashed through my mind. Hardly had my eyes closed when a dim telepathic image began to appear; and I soon realized to my infinite excitement that it was identical with what I had seen before. If anything, it was more distinct; and when it began to speak I seemed able to grasp a greater proportion of the words.

During this sleep I found most of the morning's deductions confirmed, though the interview was mysteriously cut off long prior to my awakening. Robert had seemed apprehensive just before communication ceased, but had already told me that in his strange fourth-dimensional prison colors and spatial relationships were indeed reversed — black being white, distance increasing apparent size, and so on.

He had also intimated that, notwithstanding his possession of full physical form and sensations, most human vital properties seemed curiously suspended. Nutriment, for example, was quite unnecessary — a phenomenon really more singular than the omnipresent reversal of objects and attributes, since the latter was a reasonable and mathematically indicated state of things. Another significant piece of information was that the only exit from the glass to the world was the entrance-way, and that this was permanently barred and impenetrably sealed, so far as egress was concerned.

That night I had another visitation from Robert; nor did such impressions, received at odd intervals while I slept receptively-minded, cease during the entire period of his incarceration. His efforts to communicate were desperate and often pitiful; for at times the telepathic bond would weaken, while at other times fatigue, excitement, or fear of interruption would hamper and thicken his speech.

I may as well narrate as a continuous whole all that Robert told me throughout the whole series of transient mental contacts — perhaps supplementing it at certain points with facts directly related after his release. The telepathic information was fragmentary and often nearly inarticulate, but I studied it over and over during the waking intervals of three intense days; classifying and cogitating with feverish diligence, since it was all that I had to go upon if the boy were to be brought back into our world.

The fourth-dimensional region in which Robert found himself was not, as in scientific romance, an unknown and infinite realm of strange sights and fantastic denizens; but was rather a projection of certain limited parts of our own terrestrial sphere within an alien and normally inaccessible aspect or direction of space. It was a curiously fragmentary, intangible, and heterogeneous world — a series of apparently dissociated scenes merging indistinctly one into the other; their constituent details having an obviously different status from that of an object drawn into the ancient mirror as Robert had been drawn. These scenes were like dream-vistas or magic lantern images — elusive visual impressions of which the boy was not really a part, but which formed a sort of panoramic background or ethereal environment against which or amidst which he moved.

He could not touch any of the parts of these scenes — walls, trees, furniture, and the like — but whether this was because they were truly non-material, or because they always receded at his approach, he was singularly unable to determine. Everything seemed fluid, mutable, and unreal. When he walked, it appeared to be on whatever lower surface the visible scene might have — floor, path, greensward, or such; but upon analysis he always found that the contact was an illusion. There was never any difference in the resisting force met by his feet — and by his hands when he would stoop experimentally — no matter what changes of apparent surface might be involved. He could not describe this foundation or limiting plane on which he walked as anything more definite than a virtually abstract pressure balancing his gravity. Of definite tactile distinctiveness it had none, and supplementing it there seemed to be a kind of restricted levitational force which accomplished transfers of altitude. He could never actually climb stairs, yet would gradually walk up from a lower level to a higher.

Passage from one definite scene to another involved a sort of gliding through a region of shadow or blurred focus where the details of each scene mingled curiously. All the vistas were distinguished by the absence of transient objects, and the indefinite or ambiguous appearance of such semi-transient objects as furniture or details of vegetation. The lighting of every scene was diffuse and perplexing, and of course the scheme of reversed colors — bright red grass, yellow sky with confused black and gray cloud-forms, white tree-trunks, and green brick walls — gave to everything an air of unbelievable grotesquerie. There was an alteration of day and night, which turned out to be a reversal of the normal hours of light and darkness at whatever point on the earth the mirror might be hanging.

This seemingly irrelevant diversity of the scenes puzzled Robert until he realized that they comprised merely such places as had been reflected for long continuous periods in the ancient glass. This also explained the odd absence of transient objects, the generally arbitrary boundaries of vision, and the fact that all exteriors were framed by the outlines of doorways or windows. The glass, it appeared, had power to store up these intangible scenes through long exposure; though it could never absorb anything corporeally, as Robert had been absorbed, except by a very different and particular process.

But — to me at least — the most incredible aspect of the mad phenomenon was the monstrous subversion of our known laws of space involved in the relation of various illusory scenes to the actual terrestrial regions represented. I have spoken of the glass as storing up the images of these regions, but this is really an inexact definition. In truth, each of the mirror scenes formed a true and quasi-permanent fourth-dimensional projection of the corresponding mundane region; so that whenever Robert moved to a certain part of a certain scene, as he moved into the image of my room when sending his telepathic messages, *he was actually in that place itself, on earth* — though under spatial conditions which cut off all sensory communication, in either direction, between him and the present tri-dimensional aspect of the place.

Theoretically speaking, a prisoner in the glass could in a few moments go anywhere on our planet — into any place, that is, which had ever been reflected in the mirror's surface. This probably applied even to places where the mirror had not hung long enough to produce a clear illusory scene; the terrestrial region being then represented by a zone of more or less formless shadow. Outside the definite scenes was a seemingly limitless waste of neutral gray shadow about which Robert could never be certain, and into which he never dared stray far lest he become hopelessly lost to the real and mirror worlds alike.

Among the earliest particulars which Robert gave, was the fact that he was not alone in his confinement. Various others, all in antique garb, were in there with him — a corpulent middle-aged gentleman with tied queue and velvet knee-breeches who spoke English fluently though with a marked Scandinavian accent; a rather beautiful small girl with very blond hair which appeared as glossy dark blue; two apparently mute Negroes whose features contrasted grotesquely with the pallor of their reversed-colored skins; three young men; one young woman; a very small child, almost an infant; and a lean, elderly Dane of extremely distinctive aspect and a kind of half-malign intellectuality of countenance.

This last named individual — Axel Holm, who wore the satin small-clothes, flared-skirted coat, and voluminous full-bottomed periwig of an age more than two centuries in the past — was notable among the little band as being the one responsible for the presence of them all. He it was who, skilled equally in the arts of magic and glass working, had long ago fashioned this strange dimensional prison in which himself, his slaves, and those whom he chose to invite or allure thither were immured unchangingly for as long as the mirror might endure.

Holm was born early in the seventeenth century, and had followed with tremendous competence and success the trade of a glass-blower and molder in Copenhagen. His glass, especially in the form of large drawing-room mirrors, was always at a premium. But the same bold mind which had made him the first glazier of Europe also served to carry his interests and ambitions far beyond the sphere of mere material craftsmanship. He had studied the world around him, and chafed at the limitations of human knowledge and capability. Eventually he sought for dark ways to overcome those limitations, and gained more success than is good for any mortal.

He had aspired to enjoy something like eternity, the mirror being his provision to secure this end. Serious study of the fourth dimension was far from beginning with Einstein in our own era; and Holm, more than erudite in all the methods of his day, knew that a bodily entrance into that hidden phase of space would prevent him from dying in the ordinary physical sense. Research showed him that the principle of reflection undoubtedly forms the chief gate to all dimensions beyond our familiar three; and chance placed in his hands a small and very ancient glass whose cryptic properties he believed he could turn to advantage. Once "inside" this mirror according to the method he had envisaged, he felt that "life" in the sense of form and consciousness would go on virtually forever, provided the mirror could be preserved indefinitely from breakage or deterioration.

Holm made a magnificent mirror, such as would be prized and carefully preserved; and in it deftly fused the strange whorl-configured relic he had acquired. Having thus prepared his refuge and his trap, he began to plan his mode of entrance and conditions of tenancy. He would have with him both servitors and companions; and as an experimental beginning he sent before him into the glass two dependable Negro slaves brought from the West Indies. What his sensations must have been upon beholding this first concrete demonstration of his theories, only imagination can conceive.

Undoubtedly a man of his knowledge realized that absence from the outside world if deferred beyond the natural span of life of those within, must mean instant dissolution at the first attempt to return to that world. But, barring that misfortune or accidental breakage, those within would remain forever as they were at the time of entrance. They would never grow old, and would need neither food nor drink.

To make his prison tolerable he sent ahead of him certain books and writing materials, a chair and table of stoutest workmanship, and a few other accessories. He knew that the images which the glass would reflect or absorb would not be tangible, but would merely extend around him like a background of dream. His own transition in 1687 was a momentous experience; and must have been attended by mixed sensations of triumph and terror. Had anything gone wrong, there were frightful possibilities of being lost in dark and inconceivable multiple dimensions.

For over fifty years he had been unable to secure any additions to the little company of himself and slaves, but later on he had perfected his telepathic method of visualizing small sections of the outside world close to the glass, and attracting certain individuals in those areas through the mirror's strange entrance. Thus Robert, influenced into a desire to press upon the "door," had been lured within. Such visualizations depended wholly on telepathy, since no one inside the mirror could see out into the world of men.

It was in truth, a strange life that Holm and his company had lived inside the glass. Since the mirror had stood for fully a century with its face to the dusty stone wall of the shed where I found it, Robert was the first being to enter this limbo after all that interval. His arrival was a gala event, for he brought news of the outside world which must have been of the most startling impressiveness to the more thoughtful of those within. He, in his turn — young though he was — felt overwhelmingly the weirdness of meeting and talking with persons who had been alive in the seventeenth and eighteenth centuries.

The deadly monotony of life for the prisoners can only be vaguely conjectured. As mentioned, its extensive spatial variety was limited to localities which had been reflected in the mirror for long periods; and many of these had become dim and strange as tropical climates had made inroads on the surface. Certain localities were bright and beautiful, and in these the company usually gathered. But no scene could be fully satisfying; since the visible objects were all unreal and intangible, and often of perplexingly indefinite outline. When the tedious periods of darkness came, the general custom was to indulge in memories, reflections, or conversations. Each one of that strange, pathetic group had retained his or her personality unchanged and unchangeable, since becoming immune to the time effects of outside space.

The number of inanimate objects within the glass, aside from the clothing of the prisoners, was very small; being largely limited to the accessories Holm had provided for himself. The rest did without even furniture, since sleep and fatigue had vanished along with most other vital attributes. Such inorganic things were present seemed as exempt from decay as the living beings. The lower forms of animal life were wholly absent.

Robert derived most of his information from Herr Thiele, the gentleman who spoke English with a Scandinavian accent. This portly Dane had taken a fancy to him, and talked at considerable length. The others, too, had received him with courtesy and good-will; Holm himself, seeming well-disposed, had told him about various matters including the door of the trap.

The boy, as he told me later, was sensible enough never to attempt communication with me when Holm was nearby. Twice, while thus engaged, he had seen Holm appear; and had accordingly ceased at once. At no time could I see the world behind the mirror's surface. Robert's visual image, which included his bodily form and the clothing connected with it, was — like the aural image of his halting voice and like his own visualization of myself — a case of purely telepathic transmission; and did not involve true inter-dimensional sight. However, had Robert been as trained a telepathist as Holm, he might have transmitted a few strong images apart from his immediate person.

Throughout this period of revelation I had, of course, been desperately trying to devise a method for Robert's release. On the fourth day — the ninth after the disappearance — I hit on a solution. Everything considered, my laboriously formulated process was not a very complicated one; though I could not tell beforehand how it would work, while the possibility of ruinous consequences in case of a slip was appalling. This process depended, basically, on the fact that there was no possible exit from inside the glass. If Holm and his prisoners were permanently sealed in, then release must come wholly from outside. Other considerations included the disposal of the other prisoners, if any survived, and especially of Axel Holm. What Robert had told me of him was anything but reassuring; and I certainly did not wish him loose in my apartment, free once more to work his evil will upon the world. The telepathic messages had not made fully clear the effect of liberation on those who had entered the glass so long ago.

There was, too, a final though minor problem in case of success — that of getting Robert back into the routine of school life without having to explain the incredible. In case of failure, it was highly inadvisable to have witnesses present at the release operations — and lacking these, I simply could not attempt to relate the actual facts if I should succeed. Even to me the reality seemed a mad one whenever I let my mind turn from the data so compellingly presented in that tense series of dreams.

When I had thought these problems through as far as possible, I procured a large magnifying glass from the school laboratory and studied minutely every square millimeter of that whorl-center which presumably marked the extent of the original ancient mirror used by Holm. Even with this aid I could not quite trace the exact boundary between the old area and the surface added by the Danish wizard; but after a long study decided on a conjectural oval boundary which I outlined very precisely with a soft blue pencil. I then made a trip to Stamford, where I procured a heavy glass-cutting tool; for my primary idea was to remove the ancient and magically potent mirror from its later setting.

My next step was to figure out the best time of day to make the crucial experiment. I finally settled on two-thirty A.M. — both because it was a good season for uninterrupted work, and because it was the "opposite" of two-thirty P.M., the probable moment at which Robert had entered the mirror. This form of "oppositeness" may or may not have been relevant, but I knew at least that the chosen hour was as good as any — and perhaps better than most.

I finally set to work in the early morning of the eleventh day after the disappearance, having drawn all the shades of my living-room and closed and locked the door into the hallway. Following with breathless care the elliptical line I had traced, I worked around the whorl-section with my steel-wheeled cutting tool. The ancient glass, half an inch thick, crackled crisply under the firm, uniform pressure; and upon completing the circuit I cut around it a second time, crunching the roller more deeply into the glass.

Then, very carefully indeed, I lifted the heavy mirror down from its console and leaned it face-inward against the wall; prying off two of the thin, narrow boards nailed to the back. With equal caution I smartly tapped the cut-around space with the heavy wooden handle of the glass-cutter.

At the very first tap the whorl-containing section of glass dropped out on the Bokhara rug beneath. I did not know what might happen, but was keyed up for anything, and took a deep involuntary breath. I was on my knees for convenience at the moment, with my face quite near the newly made aperture; and as I breathed there poured into my nostrils a powerful *dusty* odor — a smell not comparable to any other I have ever encountered. Then everything within my range of vision suddenly turned to a dull gray before my failing eyesight as I felt myself overpowered by an invisible force which robbed my muscles of their power to function.

I remember grasping weakly and futilely at the edge of the nearest window drapery and feeling it rip loose from its fastening. Then I sank slowly to the floor as the darkness of oblivion passed over me.

When I regained consciousness I was lying on the Bokhara rug with my legs held unaccountably up in the air. The room was full of that hideous and inexplicable dusty smell — and as my eyes began to take in definite images I saw that Robert Grandison stood in front of me. It was he — fully in the flesh and with his coloring normal — who was holding my legs aloft to bring the blood back to my head as the school's first-aid course had taught him to do with persons who had fainted. For a moment I was struck mute by the stifling odor and by a bewilderment which quickly merged into a sense of triumph. Then I found myself able to move and speak collectedly.

I raised a tentative hand and waved feebly at Robert.

"All right, old man," I murmured, "you can let my legs down now. Many thanks. I'm all right again, I think. It was the smell — I imagine — that got me. Open that farthest window, please — wide — from the bottom. That's it — thanks. No — leave the shade down the way it was."

I struggled to my feet, my disturbed circulation adjusting itself in waves, and stood upright hanging to the back of a big chair. I was still "groggy," but a blast of fresh, bitterly cold air from the window revived me rapidly. I sat down in the big chair and looked at Robert, now walking toward me.

"First," I said hurriedly, "tell me, Robert — those others — Holm? What happened to *them,* when I — opened the exit?"

Robert paused half-way across the room and looked at me very gravely.

"I saw them fade away — into nothingness — Mr. Canevin," he said with solemnity; "and with them — everything. There isn't any more 'inside,' sir — thank God, and you, sir!"

And young Robert, at last yielding to the sustained strain which he

had borne through all those terrible eleven days, suddenly broke down like a little child and began to weep hysterically in great, stifling, dry sobs.

I picked him up and placed him gently on my davenport, threw a rug over him, sat down by his side, and put a calming hand on his forehead.

"Take it easy, old fellow," I said soothingly.

The boy's sudden and very natural hysteria passed as quickly as it had come on as I talked to him reassuringly about my plans for his quiet restoration to the school. The interest of the situation and the need of concealing the incredible truth beneath a rational explanation took hold of his imagination as I had expected; and at last he sat up eagerly, telling the details of his release and listening to the instructions I had thought out. He had, it seems, been in the "projected area" of my bedroom when I opened the way back, and had emerged in that actual room — hardly realizing that he was "out." Upon hearing a fall in the living-room he had hastened thither, finding me on the rug in my fainting spell.

I need mention only briefly my method of restoring Robert in a seemingly normal way — how I smuggled him out of the window in an old hat and sweater of mine, took him down the road in my quietly started car, coached him carefully in a tale I had devised, and returned to arouse Browne with the news of his discovery. He had, I explained, been walking alone on the afternoon of his disappearance; and had been offered a motor ride by two young men who, as a joke and over his protests that he could go no farther than Stamford and back, had begun to carry him past that town. Jumping from the car during a traffic stop with the intention of hitch-hiking back before Call-Over, he had been hit by another car just as the traffic was released — awakening ten days later in the Greenwich home of the people who had hit him. On learning the date, I added, he had immediately telephoned the school; and I, being the only one awake, had answered the call and hurried after him in my car without stopping to notify anyone.

Browne, who at once telephoned to Robert's parents, accepted my story without question; and forbore to interrogate the boy because of the latter's manifest exhaustion. It was arranged that he should remain at the school for a rest, under the expert care of Mrs. Browne, a former trained nurse. I naturally saw a good deal of him during the remainder of the Christmas vacation, and was thus enabled to fill in certain gaps in his fragmentary dream-story.

Now and then we would almost doubt the actuality of what had occurred; wondering whether we had not both shared some monstrous delusion born of the mirror's glittering hypnotism, and whether the tale of the ride and accident were not after all the real truth. But whenever we did so we would be brought back to belief by some monstrous and haunting memory; with me, of Robert's dream-figure and its thick voice and inverted colors; with him, of the whole fantastic pageantry of ancient people and dead scenes that he had witnessed. And then there was that joint recollection of that damnable dusty odor.... We knew what it meant: the instant dissolution of those who had entered an alien dimension a century and more ago.

There are, in addition, at least two lines of rather more positive evidence; one of which comes through my researches in Danish annals concerning the sorcerer, Axel Holm. Such a person, indeed, left many traces in folklore and written records; and diligent library sessions, plus conferences with various learned Danes, have shed much more light on his evil fame. At present I need say only that the Copenhagen glass-blower — born in 1612 — was a notorious Luciferian whose pursuits and final vanishing formed a matter of awed debate over two centuries ago. He had burned with a desire to know all things and to conquer every limitation of mankind — to which end he had delved deeply into occult and forbidden fields ever since he was a child.

He was commonly held to have joined a coven of the dreaded witch-cult, and the vast lore of ancient Scandinavian myth — with its Loki the Sly One and the accursed Fenris-Wolf — was soon an open book to him. He had strange interests and objectives, few of which were definitely known, but some of which were recognized as intolerably evil. It is recorded that his two Negro helpers, originally slaves from the Danish West Indies, had become mute soon after their acquisition by him; and that they had disappeared not long before his own disappearance from the ken of mankind.

Near the close of an already long life the idea of a glass of immortality appears to have entered his mind. That he had acquired an enchanted mirror of inconceivable antiquity was a matter of common whispering; it being alleged that he had purloined it from a fellow-sorcerer who had entrusted it to him for polishing.

This mirror — according to popular tales a trophy as potent in its way as the better-known Aegis of Minerva or Hammer of Thor — was a small oval object called "Loki's Glass," made of some polished fusible mineral and having magical properties which included the divination of the immediate future and the power to show the possessor his enemies. That it had deeper potential properties, realizable in the hands of an erudite magician, none of the common people doubted; and even educated persons attached much fearful importance to Holm's rumored attempts to incorporate it in a larger glass of immortality. Then had come the wizard's disappearance in 1687, and the final sale and dispersal of his goods amidst a growing cloud of fantastic legendry. It was, altogether, just such a story as one would laugh at if possessed of no particular key; yet to me, remembering those dream messages and having Robert Grandison's corroboration before me, it formed a positive confirmation of all the bewildering marvels that had been unfolded.

But as I have said, there is still another line of rather positive evidence — of a very different character — at my disposal. Two days after his release, as Robert, greatly improved in strength and appearance, was placing a log on my living-room fire, I noticed a certain awkwardness in his motions and was struck by a persistent idea. Summoning him to my desk I suddenly asked him to pick up an ink-stand — and was scarcely surprised to note that, despite lifelong right-handedness, he obeyed unconsciously with his left hand. Without alarming him, I then asked that he unbutton his coat and let me listen to his cardiac action. What I found upon placing my ear to his chest — and what I did not tell him for some time afterward — was that *his heart was beating on his right side.*

He had gone into the glass right-handed and with all organs in their normal positions. Now he was left-handed and with organs reversed, and would doubtless continue so for the rest of his life. Clearly, the dimensional transition had been no illusion — for this physical change was tangible and unmistakable. Had there been a natural exit from the glass, Robert would probably have undergone a thorough re-reversal and emerged in perfect normality — as indeed the color-scheme of his body and clothing did emerge. The forcible nature of his release, however, undoubtedly set something awry; so that dimensions no longer had a chance to right themselves as chromatic wave-frequencies still did.

I had not merely *opened* Holm's trap; I had *destroyed* it; and at the particular stage of destruction marked by Robert's escape some of the reversing properties had perished. It is significant that in escaping Robert had felt no pain comparable to that experienced in entering. Had the destruction been still more sudden, I shiver to think of the monstrosities of color the boy would always have been forced to bear. I may add that after discovering Robert's reversal I examined the rumpled and discarded clothing he had worn in the glass, and found, as I had expected, a complete reversal of pockets, buttons, and all other corresponding details.

At this moment Loki's Glass, just as it fell on my Bokhara rug from the now patched and harmless mirror, weighs down a sheaf of papers on my writing-table here in St. Thomas, venerable capital of the Danish West Indies — now the American Virgin Islands. Various collectors of old Sandwich glass have mistaken it for an odd bit of that early American product — but I privately realize that my paper-weight is an antique of far subtler and more paleologean craftsmanship. Still, I do not disillusion such enthusiasts.

*Elizabeth A. Lynn*

# THE ISLAND

> *Cape Cod girls they have no combs*
> *Heave away, haul away,*
> *Comb their hair with codfish bones*
> *We are bound for Australia.*
> *Heave away my bully bully boys*
> *Heave away, haul away,*
> *Heave away and don't you make a noise*
> *We are bound for Australia . . .*
>
> TRADITIONAL SEA CHANTY.

T HE ISLAND sat in a ring of stone and a nest of fog.

It was a flat and sandy land, treeless, silent, smooth and white. Its toothy wet escarpment looked like a good place to lay lobster pots, but the fishermen never did. The way to it was treacherous. Once there had been a bell-buoy marking where the secret rocks began their rise, but something had happened to it. Fog lingered round the island. Its name on the sea charts was variously rendered as Seal Island or Silk Island. On some charts it was not named at all.

Douglas Murdoch saw it from the bedroom window.

He leaned out the window feeling the foggy wind on his cheek, cool with the promise of winter. The Labor Day crowds were gone. The Turrets had hosted a few tourists, but most people didn't want to have to climb the paths from the ancient cupola'd guest house to the beach and the shops. Mrs. Alverson was negative about cars. There was no driveway up to The Turrets, just the rutted tracks laid down by Sally Ives' jeep. He heard from the kitchen below the sound of his seven-year-old daughter singing. It had been a good idea to stay here, he decided. They had almost stayed in a slick hotel in the village. But the peace and isolation felt good to him; and Janna seemed happy. They were going sailing today, the second time. He gazed north at the boulder-strewn coast.

And saw the island for the first time as it floated in the morning fog.

He went, slowly, down the steep old stairs.

Janna said, "Mrs. Alverson had to leave and she said for you to get your own breakfast. I had eggs."

He opened the capacious refrigerator. Eggs, bacon, milk, butter. Salt, pepper, garlic. Onions. He took the smallest cast-iron skillet from the wall.

"Did you fold the quilts?" she asked him.

"I forgot."

"I'll do it." She slid off her chair. He could not get it through her head that Mrs. Alverson would do that, or else she did not want to relinquish the habit that her mother had taught her . . . Laura. He pushed the weight and pain of memory away — the eggs. Look at the eggs, stir the eggs. They'll burn. *I hate burned eggs.*

In his head the voice was Laura's.

No, this would not be one of those days. Would *not* be. Would NOT.

Janna came down the stairs. "Da, where are we going today?"

"Sailing."

"*Where* sailing?"

Janna was important. Think of Janna. "I thought maybe north today."

"I want to see the windmill again."

On the first excursion they had gone south and seen an old battered mill, vanes still turning, though three of them were splintered stubs. A relic. God that's an ugly word. That was Laura now, a relic.

The windmill, think about the windmill. He had asked Sally Ives about it.

("The old Bigelow mill. It's been empty for years. It never worked well, the vanes kept breaking. The wind's too strong.")

"Wouldn't you like to see a new thing?" he asked Janna.

"*What* new thing?"

"Um. I don't know. . . . I saw a little island out in the fog, a little baby island, just right for two people to picnic on. We could go there." That was good, that was better. Janna nodded so hard that her black braids flew. He levered the eggs out of the pan and sat at the long wood kitchen table to eat. She brought him a napkin. "Thank you, lovey."

She leaned into him shyly. It hurt him that she was still so shy of him. *You lay four months in a hospital ward bandaged like a mummy, and she got to see you twice a day for five minutes; how could she be anything but shy of you?* "Let's go to the island," she whispered.

THEY climbed down the steep cliffside path to the village. Janna ran ahead. Douglas took his time. The accident had left him with shattered legs. The doctors had rebuilt them, but the left was an inch shorter than the right, and both were full of metal bits and pins that ached when it rained, like shrapnel. He had spent a month learning how to walk at the rehabilitation hospital in Boston. He had only been out three weeks.

He caught up with Janna. She was sitting on a rock singing with great energy: "Fifteen men on a dead man's chest, Yo-ho-ho and a bottle of rum!"

Sally grinned at them when they came into the store. "Where you goin' today?" she asked Janna. She was an immense woman, six feet tall, 180 pounds and none of it fat. She ran the Emporium, the grocery and goods store in the village of Kennequit. She was forty, unmarried; she lived with her seventy-year-old parents in a small old house on a cliff. Mrs. Alverson had told Douglas that, and more, when she had told him that Sally Ives could rent him a boat. ("She owns two of them. She'll rent them to you — *if* you can sail.")

"To an island," said Janna. "Can I have a jelly bean, Sally?" There was a jar of jelly beans on the counter. Sally tipped it down. Janna hunted with concentration for a green one. She only liked the green ones.

"Which island?" Sally asked.

"I saw it from The Turrets window," said Douglas. "North of here, small and round and very flat, almost like a Pacific island. You know the one I mean?"

"Seal Island. I wouldn't go there. It takes some pretty fancy sailing."

"I'm not a novice."

"I know. You're renting my boat. The channels to it aren't marked and there are a lot of rocks around it. The water's shallower there than you might think."

"All right."

Janna was listening. "We can't go?" she said.

"Sorry, lovey. Sally says we better not."

"Have you been there?" Janna asked Sally.

"No." The woman's voice was almost gruff.

"There'll be other islands, lovey," Douglas said.

Janna nodded. Another child might have argued or wheedled. Janna accepted, stoic.

So she had looked at him, expressionless, shoulders set, when he told her Laura was not getting better, was not coming home, was dead.

"Come on, lovey," he said to his strange girl, his bleak baby. "Let's go to the dock."

KENNEQUIT harbor was famous. There were half a dozen picture post-cards of it — at sunrise, at sunset, in fog — and one Early American painting which hung in a Boston museum. Sally's boats were named the *H2* and the *O*. The *O* was the small one. They raised the sails. Janna was serious and careful as she strapped herself into her life-vest. Douglas hated the bulky things.

He stowed his under the seat, close to hand. "Shall I untie the lines?" asked Janna. She loved nautical words and now called all ropes *lines*, even pieces of string that had never touched water. They maneuvered slowly out of the marina. The wind was just right. It belled the sail. When they were clear of the other boats, Douglas handed the tiller to Janna. She steered lightly and surely, she was a natural sailor, better than he would ever be. He wished that Laura could see her.

His nerves knotted. Janna was singing. "Cape Cod girls they have no combs, Heave away, haul away, Comb their hair with codfish bones. . . ." Laura had taught her the song, sung it with her. The lonesome thin soprano rose again. "Cape Cod boys they have no sleds, Heave away, haul away. . . ." They had told him at the hospital that he had to forget, that he would forget. How *could* he forget?

"Janna!" he said.

She stopped.

No, he thought, you mustn't stifle her. You came here to make barriers dissolve, not reinforce them. Praise her. Tightly he said, "Go ahead, Jan. I like it when you sing."

She shook her head. She was watching his face. Her eyes were blue, like her mother's, just like her mother's. She had seen his pain and was guarding her tongue.

"I remember when mother used to sing that with you," he said.

---

"Other songs too. You remember the Greenland whale song?" He tried to sing. "Oh, Greenland is a dreadful place, it's a place that's never green. Where there's ice and there's snow and the whale fishes blow — "

"That's the end," Janna said.

"Sing it."

She shook her head again. "Can we go look at the island?" she asked.

"Yes. We'll do that."

They nosed up the coast.

For no good reason, it was hard to find. Finally Janna steered straight at a blowy patch of fog, and there it was. Douglas caught the tiller. They zigzagged around the island. It looked a perfect place to picnic. The fog stayed just offshore of it, and the bright autumn sun made the white beach glitter. There was an ethereal quality about the place. But except for the clinging fog there was nothing soft about it. It was white and sharp and as unshadowed as a piece of paper.

Then he saw her.

She was sitting on a rock, her feet in the spray. She wore a long thing like a caftan, and her hair fell around it, black and thick and long. She was not looking at him. He knew how her hair would feel. . . . His breath clogged in his throat. *No.*

She stood up. He slammed his fist on the gunnel. *She* — ! She walked into the center of the island.

Her walk was a stranger's.

"Da!" said Janna.

Douglas wrenched his mind back to his daughter, the boat, the sea — they were too close. He tussled the boat away from the island. He kept wanting to look away, to look at the beach. The boat balked, it would not come.

"Let me," said Janna. She closed her hand round the stick. The boat turned like an obedient dog.

The fog blew in, hiding the island.

Douglas sweated. Laura was five and a half months dead; he had lain beneath a car a foot from her, helpless, trapped, and heard her die — but he had seen her, there! He hit the gunnel again to make it stop. So there was another woman in the world with hair like thick and inky rain. . . . That someone, not Laura, was on the island. A local woman, with a knowledge of the rocks and tides.

"Let's go back now, lovey," he said to his daughter.

"Well," said Sally, "did you have fun?" She tipped the jelly bean jar for Janna.

"Where'd you go today?"

"To the island," said Janna.

Sally looked at Douglas. "We just sailed around it," he said hastily. "We didn't land. Janna really wanted to see it. There was someone on it."

"Oh?" She was annoyed.

"A woman. With black hair. Tall woman. Do you know who it might be?"

"Could be anyone. Some tourist."

She was not going to help him. He would have to ask Mrs. Alverson. He collected Janna. "Come on, Captain."

Sally relented as they neared the door. "You want to take the boat out tomorrow?"

"We'd like to," Douglas said.

"Not that many more days of good weather. You might as well take advantage of them while you're here."

"Thank you."

He had his hand on the door when she said, "What kind of a boat did she have?"

"Boat." He thought. "I didn't see it."

*HE WAS driving. His eyes felt like sand and his arms like lead. He had been driving for four hours. Laura sat beside him, frowning at the dark road, hands knotted in her lap. Her tension reproached and irked him. "Janna's all right," he said. She glanced at him, eyes like blue ice. The babysitter had called. Janna was feverish. They had been out on Cape Cod for a rare three-day vacation, just the two of them —*

*"All kids get fevers. Let's stay and call in the morning. It's a six-hour drive."*

*"No. I want to go home."*

*The road was a monotonous strip of white, leading nowhere. Douglas rubbed his eyes.*

*The truck lurched out in front of them from the right. He had not seen the crossroads. The big sluggish station wagon squealed as he fought to turn the wheel. He smelled rubber. Laura screamed. Under his hands the wheel spun and the car seemed to leap at the wallowing whalelike tanker. They hit it. . . .*

*"I want to go home," she whispered to him. He could hear the drip, drip — reason and his senses told him it was the gasoline running from the car, not blood, not her blood. Her voice got fainter. "I want to go home, Doug."*

*"Laura!"*

He clawed out of the dream. "Laura," he said. She was not there to hear him. She would never hear him. The pills were in the dresser drawer; they would put him out. Sweat coated him. He made himself stop shaking. He felt his way through the dark round room to the dresser. From the dresser to the door, from the door to the hall, to the bathroom, pills in hand — he took two. He would never forget. The doctors in Boston were crazy to think that he ever would, or could.

His dreams would see to that.

He went back to bed. He didn't try to sleep. The pills would make him sleep. He lay beneath the quilt and listened to the sea sound, rhythmic as the susurrus of cars on a highway.

In the next bed, his daughter slept, her breath even and untroubled.


THE NEXT day Douglas took the tiller. "Da, where are we going?" Janna asked.

"Oh, around."

They went north.

Douglas had no trouble finding the island.

She was there. She sat in the same place, maybe on the same rock. The sea surged roughly up. She seemed oblivious of the chill spray on her long legs. Maybe she owned the island. She sat there as if she owned it. He waited for her to see the sails and the tossing boat, to see him. He waited to see her face. She bent her head so that her hair hid her features wholly. She combed her hair.

"Janna."

"Um?"

"Look."

"What?"

"Do you see her? The woman?"

"I don't see anybody," she said. "Where is she, is she swimming?"

"No — there. On the island."

"No." She shook her head.

"Janna, look!" He didn't want to point. He caught her thin shoulder with one hand. "Look, there she is. She's combing her hair."

"I don't see anybody. There isn't anybody." Janna looked from him to the island. "Da, I don't like this game."

"Janna, this isn't a game. There's a woman sitting on the rock — she looks like mother! Can't you see her?" He couldn't believe her look of fright, confusion, innocence. He wanted to shake her. The denial seemed pointless. Was it because the woman looked so like Laura?

He would be patient. "Janna, honey, look there. Look again." The hands still moved, softly stroking. "She has black hair, she's sitting on that rock — "

"No!" said Janna, and burst into wild tears.

He had to turn the boat in order to comfort her.

"All right. All right, lovey, never mind. Never mind."

The psychiatrists in Boston would have fancy names for what she was doing. He cuddled her. Suppression, repression, avoidance. "I want to go home," she said into his knees.

"All right, lovey, we'll go home," he said. "Listen, we won't tell Sally we were at the island again today, okay. It will be our special secret. When she asks where we went, let's just say 'North'. Okay?"

"Okay."

"Well," said Sally, "where'd you go today?"

Janna's eyes were red and her nose was swollen, but she answered calmly, "North. Can I have two jelly beans, Sally?"

"Just north?" said Sally. She tipped the jar and looked at Douglas. *Nosey,* he thought.

"Just north," he said.

After dinner he spoke with Mrs. Alverson. "I think we'll go back tomorrow," he said. "We'll take off around noon. Maybe we'll come back next year in the summer."

She was stirring batter. "You do that. It's been good having you here, not like some. I'm making brownies. You want some to take with you on the road?"

"Oh, no, that's — "

"I'm making them anyway," she said. "For my grandkids. The youngest of them, Arabella, is three tomorrow."

He imagined her surrounded by grandchildren. She was all angles and bones, like her tall gaunt house. "Do they live here? In Kennequit?"

"My family's been fishing the Maine coast for 150 years, Mr. Murdoch."

"Then you must know just about everybody."

"They call me the Recorder," she said and grinned slyly. "Like the Recording Angel, you know? They call me that in church."

"Who is there in Kennequit with long black hair? A woman, I mean."

She shook her head, stirring, stirring. "Nope. Nobody I can think of. We're mostly blonds here. Swedes and Danes and Celts settled this part of the coast. Lots of Scots folks. Even a few Murdochs. Got any cousins in Maine?"

"No," he said. "The island? Seal Island?"

"Silk Island, we call it," she said. "I know it."

"It looks like a good place to fish."

"It isn't," she said. "Don't go there."

"Do you know who owns it?"

"Nobody owns it, Mr. Murdoch. It isn't a safe place. Nobody owns it."

HE WOKE at dawn.

The house stayed compliantly still and silent as he dressed and limped down the stairs. The fog was thick and cold along the coast. Somewhere out on the sea the sun was rising. He walked down to the docks. Fishermen on their boats handling their traps watched him as he freed the *O* from her moorings and coaxed her out into the icy bay. He didn't know any of them.

Janna was asleep. He would go and come back so quietly that no one would know he had been out. . . . He had to do it.

The fog twitched aside for him like a velvet gray curtain. He saw the island plainly: a white and shadowless space, glittery with quartz sand. He sailed around it. There seemed to be no good place to land. There had to be. He went round once more, looking for it. The fog smelled of salt and rain.

He saw her.

She was combing her hair. Her robe was green, like the sea. She was looking straight at him at last — he strained to see her face. The rising sun beat in his eyes.

He urged the boat a little closer.

She was singing.

"Cape Cod girls they have no combs. . . ." Clear and sweet and thin, it mingled with the ocean rush dinning at his ears. She stood up. "Comb their hair with codfish bones. . . ." She saw him at last. She waved, a curl of her hand. "Doug!" she called.

"Laura?" he said. He pointed the prow of the boat forward into the sun. "Laura!" Under his hands, the tiller bucked, the boat seemed to leap at the island. He felt beneath his keel the scrape and tear of the rocks. She was smiling. Water surged through the planking. He was close enough to see her eyes.

They were green as the seawrack, green as the beckoning sea.

At her feet lay the flotsam and jetsam driven up by the sea: wooden planks, a torn sail like feathers, rusty bolts, half hidden in the sand. A bleached shard of something that might once have been a shirt.

*Why?* he thought.

He tried to hold on to the rocks. *Why did I do this?*

THE ISLAND sat in a ring of stone and a nest of fog.

It was a flat and sandy land, treeless, silent, smooth and white. Its toothy wet escarpment looked like a good place to lay lobster pots, but the fishermen never did. The way to it was treacherous. Once there had been a bell-buoy marking where the secret rocks began their rise, but something had happened to it. Fog lingered round the island. Its name on the sea charts was variously rendered as Seal Island or Silk Island. On some charts it was not named at all.

*Wilbur Daniel Steele*

# THE WOMAN AT SEVEN BROTHERS

I TELL YOU SIR, I was innocent. I didn't know any more about the world at twenty-two than some do at twelve. My uncle and aunt in Duxbury brought me up strict; I studied hard in high school, I worked hard after hours, and I went to church twice on Sundays, and I can't see it's right to put me in a place like this, with crazy people. Oh yes, I know they're crazy — you can't tell *me*. As for what they said in court about finding her with her husband, that's the inspector's lie, sir, because he's down on me, and wants to make it look like my fault.

No, sir, I can't say as I thought she was handsome — not at first. For one thing, her lips were too thin and white, and her color was bad. I'll tell you a fact, sir; that first day I came off to the light I was sitting on my cot in the storeroom (that's where the assistant keeper sleeps at the Seven Brothers), as lonesome as I could be, away from home for the first time and the water all around me, and, even though it was a calm day, pounding enough on the ledge to send a kind of a *woom-woom-woom* whining up through all that solid rock of the tower. And when old Fedderson poked his head down from the living room, with the sunshine above making a kind of bright frame around his hair and whiskers, to give me a cheery, "Make yourself to home, son!" I remember I said to myself: "*He's* all right. I'll get along with *him*. But his wife's enough to sour milk." That was queer, because she was so much under him in age — 'long about twenty-eight or so, and him nearer fifty. But that's what I said, sir.

Of course that feeling wore off, same as any feeling will wear off sooner or later in a place like the Seven Brothers. Cooped up in a place like that you come to know folks so well that you forget what they *do* look like. There was a long time I never noticed her, any more than you'd notice the cat. We used to sit of an evening around the table, as if you were Fedderson there, and me here, and her somewhere back there, in the rocker, knitting. Fedderson would be working on his Jacob's ladder, and I'd be reading. He'd been working on that Jacob's ladder a year, I guess, and every time the inspector came off with the tender he was so astonished to see how good that ladder was that the old man would go to work and make it better. That's all he lived for.

If I was reading, as I say, I daren't take my eyes off the book, or Fedderson had me. And then he'd begin — what the inspector said about him. How surprised the member of the board had been, that time, to see everything so clean about the light. What the inspector had said about Fedderson's being stuck here in a second-class light — best keeper on the coast. And so on and so on, till either he or I had to go aloft and have a look at the wicks.

He'd been there twenty-three years, all told, and he'd got used to the feeling that he was kept down unfair — so used to it, I guess, that he fed on it and told himself how folks ashore would talk when he was dead and gone — best keeper on the coast — kept down unfair. Not that he said that to me. No, he was far too loyal and humble, and respectful, doing his duty without complaint, as anybody could see.

And all the time, night after night, hardly ever a word out of the woman. As I remember it, she seemed more like a piece of furniture than anything else — not even a very good cook, nor over and above tidy. One day, when he and I were trimming the lamp, he passed the remark that his *first* wife used to dust the lens and take a pride in it. Not that he said a word against Anna, though. He never said a word against any living mortal; he was too upright.

I don't know how it came about; or, rather, I *do* know, but it was so sudden, and so far away from my thoughts, that it shocked me, like the world turned over. It was at prayers. That night I remember Fedderson was uncommon long-winded. We'd had a batch of newspapers out by the tender, and at such times the old man always made a long watch of it, getting the world straightened out. For one thing, the United States minister to Turkey was dead. Well, from him and his soul, Fedderson got on to Turkey and the Presbyterian college there, and from that to heathen in general. He rambled on and on, like the surf on the ledge, *woom-woom-woom,* never coming to an end.

You know how you'll be at prayers sometimes. My mind strayed. I counted the canes in the chair seat where I was kneeling; I plaited a corner of the tablecloth between my fingers for a spell, and by and by my eyes went wandering up the back of the chair.

The woman, sir, was looking at me. Her chair was back to mine, close, and both our heads were down in the shadow under the edge of the table, with Fedderson clear over on the other side by the stove. And there was her two eyes hunting mine between the spindles in the shadow. You won't believe me, sir, but I tell you I felt like jumping to my feet and running out of the room — it was so queer.

I don't know what her husband was praying about after that. His voice didn't mean anything, no more than the seas on the ledge away down there. I went to work to count the canes in the seat again, but all my eyes were in the top of my head. It got so I couldn't stand it. We were at the Lord's Prayer, saying it singsong together, when I had to look up again. And there her two eyes were, between the spindles, hunting mine. Just then all of us were saying, "Forgive us our trespasses . . . " I thought of it afterward.

When we got up she was turned the other way, but I couldn't help seeing her cheeks were red. It was terrible. I wondered if Fedderson would notice, though I might have known he wouldn't — not him. He was in too much of a hurry to get at his Jacob's ladder, and then he had to tell me for the tenth time what the inspector'd said that day about getting him another light — Kingdom Come, maybe, he said.

I made some excuse or other and got away. Once in the storeroom, I sat down on my cot and stayed there a long time, feeling queerer than anything. I read a chapter in the Bible, I don't know why. After I'd got my boots off I sat with them in my hands for as much as an hour, I guess, staring at the oil tank and its lopsided shadow on the wall. I tell you, sir, I was shocked. I was only twenty-two, remember, and I was shocked and horrified.

And when I did turn in, finally, I didn't sleep at all well. Two or three times I came to, sitting straight up in bed. Once I got up and opened the outer door to have a look. The water was like glass, dim, without a breath of wind, and the moon was going down. Over on the black shore I made out two lights in a village, like a pair of eyes watching. Lonely? My, yes! Lonely and nervous. I had a horror of her, sir. The dinghy boat hung on its davits just there in front of the door, and for a minute I had an awful hankering to climb into it, lower away, and row off, no matter where. It sounds foolish.

Well, it seemed foolish next morning, with the sun shining and everything as usual — Fedderson sucking his pen and wagging his head over his eternal "log," and his wife down in the rocker with her head in the newspaper, and her breakfast work still waiting. I guess that jarred it out of me more than anything else — sight of her slouched down there, with her stringy, yellow hair and her dusty apron and the pale back of her neck, reading the society notes. *Society notes!* Think of it! For the first time since I came to Seven Brothers I wanted to laugh.

I guess I did laugh when I went aloft to clean the lamp and found everything so free and breezy, gulls flying high and little whitecaps making under a westerly. It was like feeling a big load dropped off your shoulders. Fedderson came up with his dust rag and cocked his head at me.

"What's the matter, Ray?" said he.

"Nothing," said I. And then I couldn't help it. "Seems kind of out of place for society notes," said I, "out here at Seven Brothers."

He was the other side of the lens, and when he looked at me he had a thousand eyes, all sober. For a minute I thought he was going on dusting, but then he came out and sat down on a sill.

"Sometimes," said he, "I get to thinking it may be a mite dull for her out here. She's pretty young, Ray. Not much more'n a girl, hardly."

"Not much more'n a *girl!*" It gave me a turn, sir, as though I'd seen my aunt in short dresses.

"It's a good home for her, though," he went on slow. "I've seen a lot worse ashore, Ray. Of course, if I could get a shore light — "

"Kingdom Come's a shore light."

He looked at me out of his deep-set eyes, and then he turned them around the lightroom, where he'd been so long.

"No," said he, wagging his head. "It ain't for such as me."

I never saw so humble a man.

"But look here," he went on, more cheerful. "As I was telling her just now, a month from yesterday's our fourth anniversary, and I'm going to take her ashore for the day and give her a holiday — new hat and everything. A girl wants a mite of excitement now and then, Ray."

There it was again, that "girl." It gave me the fidgets, sir. I had to do something about it. It's close quarters for last names in a light, and I'd taken to calling him Uncle Matt soon after I came. Now when I was at table that noon, I spoke over to where she was standing by the stove, getting him another help of chowder.

"I guess I'll have some, too, *Aunt* Anna," said I, matter-of-fact.

She never said a word nor gave a sign — just stood there kind of round-shouldered, dipping the chowder. And that night at prayers I hitched my chair around the table, with its back the other way.

You get awful lazy in a lighthouse, some ways. No matter how much tinkering you've got, there's still a lot of time and there's such a thing as too much reading. The changes in weather get monotonous, too, by and by; the light burns the same on a thick night as it does on a fair one. Of course there's the ships, northbound, southbound — windjammers, freighters, passenger boats full of people. In the watches at night you can see their lights go by and wonder what they are, how they're laden, where they'll fetch up, and all. I used to do that almost every evening when it was my first watch, sitting out on the walk-around up there with my legs hanging over the edge and my chin propped on the railing — lazy. The Boston boat was the prettiest to see, with her three tiers of portholes lit, like a string of pearls wrapped round and round a woman's neck — well away, too, for the ledge must have made a couple of hundred fathoms off the light, like a white dogtooth of a breaker, even on the darkest night.

Well, I was lolling there one night, as I say, watching the Boston boat go by, not thinking of anything special, when I heard the door on the other side of the tower open and footsteps coming around to me.

By and by I nodded toward the boat and passed the remark that she was fetching in uncommon close tonight. No answer. I made nothing of that, for oftentimes Fedderson wouldn't answer, and after I'd watched the lights crawling on through the dark a spell, just to make conversation I said I guessed there'd be a bit of weather before long.

"I've noticed," said I, "when there's weather coming on, and the wind in the northeast, you can hear the orchestra playing aboard of her just over there. I make it out now. Do you?"

"Yes. Oh — yes! *I hear it all right!*"

You can imagine I started. It wasn't him, but *her.* And there was something in the way she said that speech, sir — something — well — unnatural. Like a hungry animal snapping at a person's hand.

I turned and looked at her sidewise. She was standing by the railing, leaning a little outward, the top of her from the waist picked out bright by the lens behind her. I didn't know what in the world to say, and yet I had a feeling I ought not to sit there mum.

"I wonder," said I, "what that captain's thinking of, fetching in so handy tonight. It's no way. I tell you, if 'twasn't for this light, she'd go to work and pile up on the ledge some thick night — "

She turned at that and stared straight into the lens. I didn't like the look of her face. Somehow, with its edges cut hard all around, and its two eyes closed down to slits, like a cat's, it made a kind of mask.

"And then," I went on, uneasy enough, "— and then where'd all their music be of a sudden, and their goings on and their singing — "

"And dancing!" She clipped me off so quick it took my breath.

"D-d-dancing?" said I.

"That's dance music," said she. She was looking at the boat again.

"How do you know?" I felt I had to keep on talking.

Well, sir — she laughed. I looked at her. She had on a shawl of some stuff or other that shined in the light; she had it pulled tight around her with her two hands in front at her breast, and I saw her shoulders swaying in tune.

"How do I *know?*" she cried. Then she laughed again, the same kind of a laugh. It was queer, sir, to see her, and to hear her. She turned, as quick as that, and leaned toward me. "Don't you know how to dance, Ray?" said she.

"N-no," I managed, and I was going to say "Aunt Anna," but the thing choked in my throat. I tell you she was looking square at me all the time with her two eyes and moving with the music as if she didn't know it. By heavens, sir, it came over me of a sudden that she wasn't so bad-looking, after all. I guess I must have sounded like a fool.

"You — you see," said I, "she's cleared the rip there now, and the music's gone. You — you — hear?"

"Yes," said she, turning back slow. "That's where it stops every night — night after night — it stops just there — at the rip."

When she spoke again her voice was different. I never heard the like of it, thin and taut as a thread. It made me shiver, sir.

"I hate 'em!" That's what she said. "I hate 'em all. I'd like to see 'em dead. I'd love to see 'em torn apart on the rocks, night after night. I could bathe my hands in their blood, night after night."

And do you know, sir, I saw it with my own eyes, her hands moving in each other above the rail. But it was her voice, though. I didn't know what to do or what to say, so I poked my head through the railing and looked down at the water. I don't think I'm a coward, sir, but it was like a cold — ice-cold — hand, taking hold of my beating heart.

When I looked up finally, she was gone. By and by I went in and had a look at the lamp, hardly knowing what I was about. Then, seeing by my watch it was time for the old man to come on duty, I started to go below. In the Seven Brothers, you understand, the stair goes down in a spiral through a well against the south wall, and first there's the door to the keeper's room, and then you come to another, and that's the living room, and then down to the storeroom. And at night, if you don't carry a lantern, it's as black as the pit.

Well, down I went, sliding my hand along the rail, and as usual I stopped to give a rap on the keeper's door, in case he was taking a nap after supper. Sometimes he did.

I stood there, blind as a bat, with my mind still up on the walk-around. There was no answer to my knock. I hadn't expected any. Just from habit, and with my right foot already hanging down for the next step, I reached out to give the door one more tap for luck.

Do you know, sir, my hand didn't fetch up on anything. The door had been there a second before, and now the door wasn't there. My hand just went on going through the dark, on and on, and I didn't seem to have sense of power enough to stop it. There didn't seem any air in the well to breathe, and my ears were drumming to the surf — that's how scared I was. And then my hand touched the flesh of a face, and something in the dark said, "Oh!" no louder than a sigh.

Next thing I knew, sir, I was down in the living room, warm and yellow-lit, with Fedderson cocking his head at me across the table, where he was at that eternal Jacob's ladder of his.

"What's the matter, Ray?" said he. "Lord's sake, Ray!"

"Nothing," said I. Then I think I told him I was sick. That night I wrote a letter to A. L. Peters, the grain dealer in Duxbury, asking for a job — even though it wouldn't go ashore for a couple of weeks, just the writing of it made me feel better.

It's hard to tell you how those two weeks went by. I don't know why, but I felt like hiding in a corner all the time. I had to come to meals. Bu: I didn't look at her, though, not once, unless it was by accident. Fedders)n thought I was still ailing and nagged me to death with advice and so ( n. One thing I took care not to do, I can tell you, and that was to knock on nis door till I'd made certain he wasn't below in the living room — thou; n I was tempted to.

Yes, sir; that's a queer thing, and I wouldn't tell you if I hadn't set out to give you the truth. Night after night, stopping there on the landing in that black pit, the air gone out of my lungs and the surf drumming in my ears and sweat standing cold on my neck — and one hand lifting up in the air — God forgive me, sir! Maybe I did wrong not to look at her more, drooping about her work in her gingham apron, with her hair stringing.

When the inspector came off with the tender, that time, I told him I was through. That's when he took the dislike to me, I guess, for he looked at me kind of sneering and said, soft as I was, I'd have to put up with it till next relief. And then, said he, there'd be a whole house-cleaning at Seven Brothers, because he'd gotten Fedderson the berth at Kingdom Come. And with that he slapped the old man on the back.

I wish you could have seen Fedderson, sir. He sat down on my cot as if his knees had given way. Happy? You'd think he'd be happy, with all his dreams come true. Yes, he was happy, beaming all over — for a minute. Then, sir, he began to shrivel up. It was like seeing a man cut down in his prime before your eyes. He began to wag his head.

"No," said he. "No, no; it's not for such as me. I'm good enough for Seven Brothers, and that's all, Mr. Bayliss. That's all."

And for all the inspector could say, that's what he stuck to. He'd figured himself a martyr so many years, nursed that injustice like a mother with her first-born, sir; and now in his old age, so to speak, they weren't going to rob him of it. Fedderson was going to wear out his life in a second-class light, and folks would talk — that was his idea. I heard him hailing down as the tender was casting off:

"See you tomorrow, Mr. Bayliss. Yep. Coming ashore with the wife for a spree. Anniversary. Yep."

But he didn't sound much like a spree. They *had* robbed him, partly, after all. I wondered what *she* thought about it. I didn't know till night. She didn't show up to supper, which Fedderson and I got ourselves — had a headache, he said. It was my early watch. I went and lit up and came back to read a spell. He was just finishing off the Jacob's ladder, and thoughtful, like a man that's lost a treasure. Once or twice I caught him looking about the room on the sly. It was pathetic, sir.

Going up the second time, I stepped out on the walk-around to have a look at things. She was there on the seaward side, wrapped in that silky thing. A fair sea was running across the ledge, and it was coming on a little thick — not too thick. Off to the right the Boston boat was blowing, *whroom-whroom!* Creeping up on us, quarter-speed. There was another fellow behind her, and a fisherman's conch farther offshore.

I don't know why, but I stopped beside her and leaned on the rail. She didn't appear to notice me, one way or another. We stood and we stood, listening to the whistles, and the longer we stood the more it got on my nerves, her not noticing me. I suppose she'd been too much on my mind lately. I began to be put out. I scraped my feet. I coughed. By and by I said out loud:

"Look here, I guess I better get out the foghorn and give those fellows a toot."

"Why?" said she, without moving her head — calm as that.

"*Why?*" It gave me a turn, sir. For a minute I stared at her. "Why? Because if she don't pick up this light before very many minutes she'll be too close in to wear — tide'll have her on the rocks — that's why!"

I couldn't see her face, but I could see one of her silk shoulders lift a little, like a shrug. And there I kept on staring at her, a dumb one, sure enough. I know what brought me to was hearing the Boston boat's three sharp toots as she picked up the light — mad as anything — and swung her helm aport. I turned away from her, sweat dripping down my face, and walked around to the door. It was just as well, too, for the feed pipe was plugged in the lamp and the wicks were popping. She'd have been out in another five minutes, sir.

When I'd finished, I saw that woman standing in the doorway. Her eyes were bright. I had a horror of her, sir, a living horror.

"If only the light had been out," said she, low and sweet.

"God forgive you," said I. "You don't know what you're saying."

She went down the stair into the well, winding out of sight, and as long as I could see her, her eyes were watching mine. When I went myself, after a few minutes, she was waiting for me on that first landing, standing still in the dark. She took hold of my hand, though I tried to get it away.

"Good-by," said she in my ear.

"Good-by?" said I. I didn't understand.

"You heard what he said today — about Kingdom Come? Be it so — on his own head, I'll never come back here. Once I set foot ashore — I've got friends in the Brightonboro, Ray."

I got away from her and started on down. But I stopped. "Brightonboro?" I whispered back. "Why do you tell *me?*" My throat was raw to the words, like a sore.

"So you'd know," said she.

Well, sir, I saw them off next morning, down that new Jacob's ladder into the dinghy boat, her dress of blue velvet and him in his best cutaway and derby — rowing away, smaller and smaller, the two of them. And then I went back and sat on my cot, leaving the door open and the ladder still hanging down the wall, along with the boat falls.

I don't know whether it was relief, or what. I suppose I must have been worked up even more than I'd thought those past weeks, for now it was all over I was like a rag. I got down on my knees, sir, and prayed to God for the salvation of my soul, and when I got up and climbed to the living room it was half past twelve by the clock. There was rain on the windows and the sea was running blue-black under the sun. I'd sat there all that time not knowing there was a squall.

It was funny; the glass stood high, but those black squalls kept coming and going all afternoon, while I was at work up in the lightroom. And I worked hard, to keep myself busy. First thing I knew it was five, and no sign of the boat yet. It began to get dim and kind of purplish gray over the land. The sun was down. I lit up, made everything snug, and got out the night glasses to have another look for that boat. He'd said he intended to get back before five. No sign. And then, standing there, it came over me that of course he wouldn't be coming off — he'd be hunting *her*, poor old fool. It looked like I had to stand two men's watches that night.

Never mind. I felt like myself again, even if I hadn't had any dinner or supper. Pride came to me that night on the walk-around, watching the boats go by — little boats, big boats, the Boston boat with all her pearls and her dance music. They couldn't see me; they didn't know who I was; but to the last of them, they depended on *me*. They say a man must be born again. Well, I was born again. I breathed deep in the wind.

Dawn broke hard and red as a dying coal. I put out the light and started to go below. Born again; yes, sir. I felt so good I whistled in the well, and when I came to that first door on the stair I reached out in the dark to give it a rap for luck. And then, sir, the hair prickled all over my scalp, when I found my hand just going on and on through the air, the same as it had gone once before, and all of a sudden I wanted to yell, because I thought I was going to touch flesh. It's funny what their just forgetting to close their door did to me, isn't it?

Well, I reached for the latch and pulled it to with a bang and ran down as if a ghost was after me. I got up some coffee and bread and bacon for breakfast. I drank the coffee. But somehow I couldn't eat, all along of that open door. The light in the room was blood. I got to thinking. I thought how she'd talked about those men, women, and children on the rocks, and how she'd made to bathe her hands over the rail. I almost jumped out of my chair then; it seemed for a wink she was there beside the stove watching me with that queer half smile — really, I seemed to see her for a flash across the red tablecloth in the red light of dawn.

"Look here!" said I to myself, sharp enough; and then I gave myself a good laugh and went below. There I took a look out of the door, which was still open, with the ladder hanging down. I made sure to see the poor old fool come pulling around the point before very long now.

My boots were hurting a little, and, taking them off, I lay down on the cot to rest, and somehow I went to sleep. I had horrible dreams. I saw her again standing in that blood-red kitchen, and she seemed to be washing her hands, and the surf on the ledge was whining up the tower, louder and louder all the time, and what it whined was, "Night after night — night after night." What woke me was cold water in my face.

The storeroom was in gloom. That scared me at first I thought night had come, and remembered the light. But then I saw the gloom was of a storm. The floor was shining wet, and the water in my face was spray, flung up through the open door. When I ran to close it, it almost made me dizzy to see the gray-and-white breakers marching past. The land was gone; the sky shut down heavy overhead; there was a piece of wreckage on the back of a swell, and the Jacob's ladder was carried clean away. How that sea had picked up so quick I can't think. I looked at my watch, and it wasn't four in the afternoon yet.

When I closed the door, sir, it was almost dark in the storeroom. I'd never been in the light before in a gale of wind. I wondered why I was shivering so, till I found it was the floor below me shivering, and the walls and stair. Horrible crunchings and grindings ran away up the tower, and now and then there was a great thud somewhere, like a cannon shot in a cave. I tell you, sir, I was alone, and I was in a mortal fright for a minute or so. And yet I had to get myself together. There was the light up there not tended to, and an early dark coming on and a heavy night and all, and I had to go. And I had to pass that door.

You'll say it's foolish, sir, and maybe it *was* foolish. Maybe it was because I hadn't eaten. But I began thinking of that door up there the minute I set foot on the stair, and all the way up through that howling dark well I dreaded to pass it. It told myself I wouldn't stop. I didn't stop. I felt the landing underfoot and I went on, four steps, five — and then I couldn't. I turned and went back. I put out my hand and it went on into nothing. That door, sir, was open again.

I left it be; I went on up to the lightroom and set to work. It was bedlam there, sir, screeching bedlam, but I took no notice. I kept my eyes down. I trimmed those seven wicks, sir, as neat as ever they were trimmed; I polished the brass till it shone, and I dusted the lens. It wasn't till that was done that I let myself look back to see who it was standing there, half out of sight in the well. It was her, sir.

"Where'd you come from?" I asked. I remember my voice was sharp.

"Up Jacob's ladder," said she, and hers was like the sirup of flowers. I shook my head. I was savage, sir. "The ladder's carried away."

"I cast it off," said she, with a smile.

"Then," said I, "you must have come while I was asleep." Another thought came on me heavy as a ton of steel. "And where's *he?*" said I. "Where's the boat?"

"He's drowned," said she, as easy as that. "And I let the boat go adrift. You wouldn't hear me when I called."

"But look here," said I. "If you came through the storeroom, why didn't you wake me up? Tell me that!" It sounds foolish enough, me standing like a lawyer in court, trying to prove she *couldn't* be there.

She didn't answer for a moment. I guess she sighed, though I couldn't hear for the gale, and her eyes grew soft, sir, so soft.

"I couldn't," said she. "You looked so peaceful — dear one."

My cheeks and neck went hot, sir, as if a warm iron was laid on them. I didn't know what to say. I began to stammer: "What do you mean — " but she was going back down the stair, out of sight. My God, sir, and I used not to think she was good-looking!

I started to follow her. I wanted to know what she meant. Then I said to myself, "If I don't go — if I wait here — she'll come back." And I went to the weather side and stood looking out of the window. Not that there was much to see. It was growing dark, and the Seven Brothers looked like the mane of a running horse, a great, vast, white horse running into the wind. The air was awelter with it. I caught one peep of a fisherman, lying down flat trying to weather the ledge, and I said, "God help them all tonight," and then I went hot at the sound of that "God."

I was right about her, though. She was back again. I wanted her to speak first, before I turned, but she wouldn't. I didn't hear her go out; I didn't know what she was up to till I saw her coming outside on the walk-around, drenched wet already. I pounded on the glass for her to come in and not be a fool; if she heard she gave no sign of it.

There she stood, and there I stood watching her. Lord, sir — was it just that I'd never had eyes to see? Or are there women who bloom? Her clothes were shining on her, like a carving, and her hair was let down like a golden curtain tossing and streaming in the gale, and there she stood with her lips half open, drinking, and her eyes half closed, gazing straight away over the Seven Brothers, and her shoulders swaying, as if in tune with the wind and water and all the ruin. And when I looked at her hands over the rail, sir, they were moving in each other as if they bathed, and then I remembered, sir.

A cold horror took me. I knew now why she had come back again. She wasn't a woman — she was a devil. I turned my back on her. I said to myself: "It's time to light up. You've got to light up" — like that, over and over, out loud. My hand was shivering so I could hardly find a match; and when I scratched it, it only flared a second and then went out in the back draft from the open door. She was standing in the doorway, looking at me. It's queer, sir, but I felt like a child caught in mischief.

"I-I-was going to light up," I managed to say, finally.

"Why?" said she. No, I can't say it as she did.

"*Why?*" said I. "*My God!*"

She came nearer, laughing, as if with pity, low, you know. "Your God? And who is your God? What is God? What is anything on a night like this?"

I drew back from her. All I could say anything about was the light.

"Why not the dark?" said she. "Dark is softer than light — tenderer — dearer than light. From the dark up here, away up here in the wind and storm, we can watch the ships go by, you and I. And you love me so. You've loved me so long, Ray."

"I never have!" I struck out at her. "I don't. I don't."

Her voice was lower than ever, but there was the same laughing pity in it. "Oh yes, you have." And she was near me again.

"I have?" I yelled. "I'll show you! I'll show you if I have!"

I got another match, sir, and scratched it on the brass. I gave it to the first wick, the little wick that's inside all the others. It bloomed like a yellow flower. "I *have?*" I yelled, and gave it to the next.

Then there was a shadow, and I saw she was leaning beside me, her two elbows on the brass, her two arms stretched out above the wicks, her bare forearms and wrists and hands. I gave a gasp:

"Take care! You'll burn them! For God's sake — "

She didn't move or speak. The match burned my fingers and went out, and all I could do was stare at those arms of hers, helpless. I'd never noticed her arms before. They were rounded and graceful and covered with a soft down, like a breath of gold. Then I heard her speaking, close to my ear:

"Pretty arms!" she said. "Pretty arms!"

I turned. Her eyes were fixed on mine. They seemed heavy, as if with sleep, and yet between their lids they were two wells, deep and deep, and as if they held all the things I'd ever thought or dreamed in them. I looked away from them, at her lips. Her lips were red as poppies, heavy with redness. They moved, and I heard them speaking:

"Poor boy, you love me so, and you want to kiss me — don't you?"

"No," said I. But I couldn't turn around. I looked at her hair. I'd always thought it was stringy hair. Some hair curls naturally with damp, they say, and perhaps that was it, for there were pearls of wet on it, and it was thick and shimmering around her face, making soft shadows by the temples. There was green in it, queer strands of green like braids.

"What is it?" said I.

"Nothing but weed," said she, with that slow, sleepy smile.

Somehow or other I felt calmer than I had any time. "Look here," said I. "I'm going to light this lamp." I took out a match, scratched it, and touched the third wick. The flame ran around, bigger than the other two together. But still her arms hung there. I bit my lip. "By God, I will!" said I to myself, and I lit the fourth.

It was fierce, sir, fierce! And yet those arms never trembled. I had to look around at her. Her eyes were still looking into mine, so deep and deep, and her red lips were still smiling with that queer sleepy droop; the only thing was that tears were raining down her cheeks — big, showing, jewel tears. It wasn't human, sir. It was like a dream.

"Pretty arms!" she sighed, and then, as if those words had broken something in her heart, there came a great sob bursting from her lips. To hear it drove me mad. I reached to drag her away, but she was too quick, sir; she cringed from me and slipped out from between my hands. It was like she faded away, sir, and went down in a bundle, nursing her poor arms and mourning over them with those terrible, broken sobs.

The sound of them took the manhood out of me — you'd have been the same, sir. I knelt down beside her on the floor and covered my face.

"Please," I moaned. "Please! Please!" That's all I could say. I wanted her to forgive me. I reached out a hand, blind, for forgiveness, and I couldn't find her anywhere. I had hurt her so, and she was afraid of me, of *me,* sir, who loved her so deep it drove me crazy.

I could see her down the stair, though it was dim and my eyes were filled with tears. I stumbled after her, crying, "Please! Please!" The little wicks I'd lit were blowing in the wind from the door and smoking the glass beside them black. One went out. I pleaded with them, the same as I would plead with a human being. I said I'd be back in a second. I promised. And I went down the stair, crying like a baby because I'd hurt her, and she was afraid of me — of *me,* sir.

She had gone into her room. The door was closed against me and I could hear her sobbing beyond it, brokenhearted. My heart was broken too. I beat on the door with my palms. I begged her to forgive me. I told her I loved her. And all the answer was that sobbing in the dark.

And then I lifted the latch and went in, groping, pleading. "Dearest — please! Because I love you!"

I heard her speak down near the floor. There wasn't any anger in her voice; nothing but sadness and despair.

"No," said she. "You don't love me, Ray. You never have."

"I do! I have!"

"No, no," said she, as if she was tired out.

"Where are you?" I was groping for her. I thought, and lit a match. She had got to the door and was standing there as if ready to fly. I went toward her, and she made me stop. She took my breath away. "I hurt your arms," said I, in a dream.

"No," said she, hardly moving her lips. She held them out to the match's light for me to look, and there was never a scar on them — not even that soft, golden down was singed, sir. "You can't hurt my body," said she, sad as anything. "Only my heart, Ray; my poor heart."

I tell you again, she took my breath away. I lit another match. "How can you be so beautiful?" I wondered.

She answered in riddles — but oh, the sadness of her, sir.

"Because," said she, "I've always so wanted to be."

"How come your eyes so heavy?" said I.

"Because I've seen so many things I never dreamed of," said she.

"How come your hair so thick?"

"It's the seaweed makes it thick," said she, smiling queer, queer.

"How come seaweed there?"

"Out of the bottom of the sea."

She talked in riddles, but it was like poetry to hear her, or a song.

"How come your lips so red?" said I.

"Because they've wanted so long to be kissed."

Fire was on me, sir. I reached out to catch her, but she was gone, out of the door and down the stair. I followed, stumbling. I must have tripped on the turn, for I remember going through the air and fetching up with a crash, and I didn't know anything for a spell — how long I can't say. When I came to, she was there, somewhere, bending over me, crooning, "My love — my love —" under her breath like, a song.

But then, when I got up, she was not where my arms went; she was down the stair again, just ahead of me. I followed her. I was tottering and dizzy and full of pain. I tried to catch up with her in the dark of the storeroom, but she was too quick for me, sir, always a little too quick for me. Oh, she was cruel to me, sir. I kept bumping against things, hurting myself still worse, and it was cold and wet and a horrible noise all the while, sir; and then, sir, I found the door was open, and a sea had parted the hinges.

I don't know how it all went, sir. I'd tell you if I could, but it's all so blurred — sometimes it seems more like a dream. I couldn't find her any more; I couldn't hear her; I went all over, everywhere. Once, I remember, I found myself hanging out of that door between the davits, looking down into those big black seas and crying like a baby. It's all riddles and blur. I can't seem to tell you much, sir. It was all — all — I don't know."

I was talking to somebody else — not her. It was the inspector. I hardly knew it was the inspector. His face was as gray as a blanket, and his eyes were bloodshot, and his lips were twisted. His left wrist hung down, awkward. It was broken coming aboard the light in that sea. Yes, we were in the living room. Yes, sir, it was daylight — gray daylight. I tell you, sir, the man looked crazy to me. He was waving his good arm toward the weather windows, and what he was saying, over and over, was this:

*"Look what you done, damn you! Look what you done!"*

And what I was saying was this:

*"I've lost her!"*

I didn't pay any attention to him, nor him to me. By and by he did, though. He stopped his talking all of a sudden, and his eyes looked like the devil's eyes. He put them up close to mine. He grabbed my arm with his good hand, and I cried, I was so weak.

"Johnson," said he, "is that it? By the living God — if you got a woman out here, Johnson!"

"No," said I. "I've lost her."

"What do you mean — lost her?"

"It was dark," said I — and it's funny how my head was clearing up — "and the door was open — the storeroom door — and I was after her — and I guess she stumbled, maybe — and I lost her."

"Johnson," said he, "what do you mean? You sound crazy — downright crazy. Who?"

"Her," said I. "Fedderson's wife."

*"Who?"*

"Her," said I. And with that he gave my arm another jerk.

"Listen," said he, like a tiger. "Don't try that on me. It won't do any good — that kind of lies — not where *you're* going to. Fedderson and his wife, too — the both of 'em's drowned deader 'n a doornail."

"I know," said I, nodding my head. I was so calm it made him wild.

"You're crazy! Crazy as a loon, Johnson!" And he was chewing his lip red. "I know, because it was me that found the old man laying on Back Water Flats yesterday morning — *me!* And she'd been with him in the boat, too, because he had a piece of her jacket tore off, tangled in his arm."

"I know," said I, nodding again, like that.

"You know what, you *crazy, murdering fool?*" Those were his words to me, sir.

"I know," said I, "what I know."

"And I know," said he, "what *I* know."

And there you are, sir. He's inspector. I'm nobody.

*John W. Vandercook*

# THE CHALLENGE

OME IN! COME IN!" Since the strained, high-pitched voice must be assumed to be his host's, Professor Nadelman obeyed. Though the knob turned readily, the big, white-painted door seemed extraordinarily heavy. Professor Nadelman put down his rope-tied cardboard suitcase so that he could use both hands. It was, he thought calmly, as if he were pushing against something soft — like a great weight of feathers.

The small, alert-looking man in tweeds who stood some paces back in the hallway was staring into the angle behind the now half-opened door. Professor Nadelman looked. There was nothing there.

"Try it, please. Again!"

This time the door swung easily. Professor Nadelman opened it all the way, then closed it. The obstruction, whatever it was, had disappeared.

With a visible effort Mr. Pelerin recovered himself and put out his hand. The two men frankly surveyed each other.

Professor Nadelman, as he had expected, found this distinguished American art critic, to whom he was already so enormously indebted, entirely to his liking. Mr. Pelerin's gray eyes flashed intelligence. His closely trimmed dark hair was graying. His slender body radiated energy. An air of preoccupation, Professor Nadelman put down to nerves.

For his part Mr. Pelerin was shocked. He had expected to be shocked. But not like this. The world-famous authority on the Renaissance was a scarecrow. Even though Professor Nadelman was thinner than any human being he had ever seen, the suit of cheap black shoddy he wore was many sizes too small for him. The hawklike, learned face was literally gray. Since Mr. Pelerin had heard no car, Professor Nadelman must have carried his heavy suitcase from the depot. It was unbelievable. But — he had pushed back the door.

Nadelman saw the look of astonishment.

"You must not, my dear benefactor," he said in his gently accented English, "be concerned about me. I have great endurance. I learned it," he smiled faintly, "in an excellent school. Believe me, I am very well."

Mr. Pelerin took both his guest's bony hands in his.

"And you, I beg of you, must never think of me, much less call me, your 'benefactor.' When I heard — when all our own little world — heard that you were still alive — " Mr. Pelerin's smile was charming: " 'There was great rejoicing.' You will stay here as long as you choose. When you feel able we shall work. I am alone. It is a big house."

"It is," said Professor Nadelman politely, "a beautiful house."

"It was a hideous house," said Mr. Pelerin sharply. "Grotesquely, almost brutally, ugly. I bought it because the land was good and the village charming. The house was a challenge. A problem in practical esthetics. All my adult life I have taught what we so mincingly call 'good taste.' This was my chance to learn if I could apply my preaching."

"You have," inquired Professor Nadelman slowly, "won?"

Mr. Pelerin looked at him acutely. Nadelman's English, he knew, was faultless. His brilliant *Age of Alexander VI* had been written in it. Nadelman had not said "succeeded." He had said "won."

"I am not sure," said Mr. Pelerin. "I am not at all sure."

"Perhaps," suggested the emaciated scholar, "I can assist." His mouth, though gentle, had unexpected firmness. "I am not — " Apologetically Professor Nadelman stretched out his right arm so the sleeve of the scanty jacket slid up. On the underside of his forearm was tattooed, in blue, the number 53696. "I am not," he repeated, "without experience."

Mr. Pelerin's taste was exquisite. What he had brought to this house in a New Hampshire village represented the accumulation of years of discriminating travel. The rugs, pale Ispahans and robust Bokharas, were like old gardens. The small El Greco *View of Toledo* over the Adams' mantel, which Pelerin had discovered in a Cordoba junkshop, brought real tears of pleasure to Elias Nadelman's eyes. But the stench, the pain of

Buchenwald and the rat-like life he had led since then in the ruins of the land he had once thought his, had sharpened new perceptions. All that Pelerin had done was a thin glaze. For all his skill, he had disguised this house, he had not yet changed it. The spirit of the place still leered with sudden and unresting anger through the hand-blocked wallpapers and the triple coats of dove-gray paint. Nadelman could feel the weight of it.

Though Mr. Pelerin concealed the fact with the urbanity of the man of parts he was, his guest could see he was uneasy. In a lesser man, the word would have been fear. It was an emotion Elias Nadelman had known well. But that had been long ago . . .

AFTER dinner and a short hour of talk before the open fire — for the spring night was chill — Mr. Pelerin suggested they retire. Early bedtime, he explained, was a village custom into which he had readily fallen. With characteristic thoughtfulness he did not offer to escort the older man to his room. The host-and-guest relationship, he had resolved, must be abolished at once. The exile must be made to feel this house was his.

Professor Nadelman was glad that he had not been escorted. For he saw the weight the moment he switched on the light in his bedroom.

The center of the white candlewick spread on the spool bed was depressed, as if a dog were lying on it. Professor Nadelman strode forward and, leaning, seized the spread's four corners and brought them together. Though the weight — he had not expected it would be so great — made him stagger, he turned swiftly and swung the sacklike bundle with all his force against the edge of the half-open door.

There was no sound. But, as if water ran from it, the spread grew lighter. In a few seconds it was empty. Professor Nadelman shook it out, folded it neatly, and hung it over the back of a chair.

The bed was the softest in which he had slept since the hard and heavy men in black boots had come one summer night to his house just off the Ringsträsse, which he had never seen again, and taken him away. That had been twelve years ago. In those years he had learned much.

It was true, he was a little tired. The bony arm marked with the five blue numbers reached out and turned out the light.

. . . IT WAS curious, Mr. Pelerin reflected. It was very curious indeed. He should feel that he was Nadelman's protector. The guest was older. Whatever he might say, he looked inconceivably fragile. He was penniless. Instead, it was Nadelman who gave him assurance. Starved and horribly beaten scarecrow though he was, he exuded calm, confidence — yes, survival. It was good to have him. Mr. Pelerin said so.

He did not say why.

In the year he spent in Cloverly, New Hampshire, the only real friend Mr. Pelerin had made was a doctor who lived across the street.

Doctor George Gage, his graying-reddish hair and his tweeds both looking as if they had been deliberately mussed, and clutching his scarred old faggot of a bulldog pipe in his strong teeth, strolled over during the morning when they were walking in the yard.

Together the three men surveyed the house. The new owner had painted it a gleaming white. With his quick gestures and birdlike energy, Pelerin explained that once it had been red, the color of dried blood; that he had removed a veranda, two turrets, and rods of fretwork. Despite his efforts, he had not been able to make grass grow within twenty feet of the foundations. Perhaps it was because he had not yet brought himself to cut down the giant black spruces which surrounded it.

Unlike most householders, Mr. Pelerin did not seem to expect praise.

It was as well. The big box of a place was still too high, too square. Its windows were too narrow. They stared like slitted, baleful python's eyes.

IT WAS Mr. Pelerin's custom to spend a certain time each day at work in his study. Since it seemed, when the hour came, that Pelerin was hanging back, Professor Nadelman made an excuse to accompany him. The door opened. There was no obstruction nor any indication of an abnormal presence. Then Nadelman walked across the shaded street to call on Doctor Gage.

Gage greeted him in a cluttered surgery. "Come over for a check-up?"

The refugee, the tips of his long, thin fingers together, shook his head. "One of the best physicians in Europe assured me I am imperishable. So was he. We were fellow prisoners."

Doctor Gage chewed his empty pipe and nodded. "Our friend?"

"Not yet. The house itself. Who has lived in it?"

Reflectively, Gage tapped the pipe in the palm of his left hand. "Pelerin's the second buyer since the Mullens. The first was a retired farmer. It was too much for him. Too hard to take care of. He let it go back to the bank for a small mortgage. Before Pelerin came along the place had been empty for twelve years. A terrible eyesore. Pelerin's done wonders."

"There was," his visitor inquired, "no other suggestion?"

Gage peered at him under shaggy eyebrows. "Any fanciful suggestion, you mean?"

Professor Nadelman smiled. "I spent, my dear Doctor Gage, eight years in Nazi prison camps. It is an experience which does not encourage — fancy. These Mullens? Who were they?"

Gage teetered back in a battered chair supported by a coiled black spring. "They were dinosaurs. The old man came here back in the nineties and built that house. You've not been here long enough for it to have any implication when I tell you they built a factory. You can see what's left of it down by the depot. But this is an old town, a quiet town, in the middle of good farming country. It needed a factory about as much as it needed typhus." Gage paused and sucked at his cold pipe to sort and simplify his tale. Then he continued. "There was the old man and his son. Two-hundred-pounders, both of 'em. Black hair, big hands, and sharp little pig's eyes. They were partners. In business and under the skin. They hated each other's guts. It was in the days of free immigration. They got their labor from New York. Droves. As helpless and confused as cattle. They always took care to bring more than they wanted, so there'd be plenty without jobs. The town hated it. But the Mullens, I regret to say, waxed rich."

"And what," urged Professor Nadelman, "became of them?"

Doctor Gage studied the hawk-narrow but resolute face for a long moment.

"The old man," he said matter of factly, "went first. Crushed. The cable of an overhead crane gave way. A huge bucket of scrap iron."

"An accident?"

"Certainly! There was an inquest. Everything was perfectly clear. Since he and Frank — Frank was the son — were alone at the plant when it happened, there was gossip, of course. This is a small town, Nadelman. But it came to nothing." Doctor Gage snorted. "Then it really started. Frank had married. A slim blonde girl from one of those Boston banking families. No one could figure how he'd done it, but he did. He brought her back to that old red house to live. I liked her."

Gage looked down and meaninglessly whacked his pipe three times on the arm of his chair. "I almost loved her. Delicate. A lady. Yet all the courage in the world. Frank was ambitious. Nothing else. For I always thought he despised her. But it turned out old man Mullen had left her his share of the plant. Fifty-one percent. That made her Frank's boss."

Doctor Gage pointed. "You didn't see much through those trees. Or hear much. But you could guess plenty. Things at the factory began to change. Some of those poor devils got raises. They were on a 60-hour week. It was cut to 48. Frank looked like a black cloud."

With elaborate care Doctor Gage put his pipe down on the desk. Professor Nadelman's eyes had already detected that the hand which held it had begun to tremble.

"Then one morning early I got a hurry call to come over. Frank, in his bathrobe, met me at the door." Gage broke off. "Funny. Funny reaction, I mean, but he held the door for some seconds before he let me in. All he said was that Carrie — that was her name — wasn't breathing when he woke up." He grunted with old anger.

"Cyanosed, we call it. Possibly heart. Or, on the other hand, suffocation. That is to say, deliberate suffocation. Murder. I was supposed to sign the death certificate. I wouldn't."

Gage came to as complete a stop as if his narrative were ended. He filled his pipe from a brass-topped glass humidor on the desk and carefully lit it. Without taking the now belching briar from his mouth he said to his guest through the clouds of smoke:

"You must be very persuasive, Nadelman. I don't generally do this sort of thing. There's no good raking up the past. I want you to promise. Keep this between ourselves. Our friend over there is in a state of nerves. His control's first-rate, but I'm a good enough doctor to see through it. All this wouldn't do him any good. If he knows already — and I don't think he does — that's his business. But it's not mine. Or, if you'll forgive my saying so, yours."

Professor Nadelman inclined his head in agreement. He absently examined the palm of his right hand. It was as heavily calloused as a peasant's.

"Tell me, Doctor," he said quietly. "This courageous young lady, this Carrie — she fought back?"

Gage's astonishment made his pipe leap from between his teeth and land with a shower of sparks in his lap. He beat them out with unnecessary violence.

"What made you say that?"

Nadelman spread his hands. "The house was empty. The factory those strong men built is in ruins. Somewhere there was victory."

The doctor nodded. "There was. There was, indeed."

"Continue, please."

"Well, I didn't like it. Admittedly, I was only guessing, but I thought she had been suffocated. As if — well, as if by some big weight. Say, a body. I told Frank flatly I wasn't satisfied. I reported to the coroner and stepped out."

Gage, with his slow, bear-like movements, got up and stood by a window which looked at the dark trees and the gleam of the white house across the street.

"The morning of the hearing Frank Mullen sent for me. He was in bed, just his shock of black hair, his hard mouth, and those little pig's eyes of his showing. Even his arms were under the covers. In his bullying, snarling way, he ordered me to take his temperature. Nothing else. It was none of my business what ailed him and he'd get better quicker if I'd not meddle with him. All he wanted of me was my report he was too sick to go to court. You usually did what Frank Mullen told you. I did. I still remember. 105 point 2. He wasn't faking. The hearing was put off. It was two days before he sent for me again."

Gage came back to his chair. "A doctor gets tough. Has to. But Frank Mullen scared me. You could hardly recognize him. He was swollen. A kind of red-purple. What you could see of his eyes burned like red coals. He was losing. He had lost. So he hated the whole wide world . . . . Not until he was dead did I have a chance to examine him. I knew what it was, but not why. Blood poisoning. We had no antibiotics then."

Gage put his pipe down to free both hands. Leaning forward, he shaped them into claws, reached up, and with startling violence ripped them downward through the air.

"On each of his arms, from the shoulders to below the elbows, were four parallel scratches. They had cut deep into the flesh. They had infected. They'd killed. They were made by the fingernails of human hands."

Gage nodded. "Yes, she'd fought back."

IT WAS for Mr. Pelerin to choose, and obviously he had chosen. The guest would respect his host's decision. They would not speak of it.

After his first weeks in Cloverly, Professor Nadelman became convinced that Pelerin was being tormented by the weight more and more frequently. In spite of his considerable gifts of self-control, the younger man was eating badly. His habit of inattention became more marked. Mr. Pelerin had high courage, but the invisible, soundless, formless persecution was wearing it away.

Professor Nadelman, on the other hand, began to encounter it less often. He thought he knew why.

The weight had no fixed timetable or locale. The door of a closet or a bedroom might, on opening, encounter ponderous, yet soft resistance. At first Nadelman would simply force it open. That the terrible years had made him strong as tempered wire gave him wry amusement. Then he hit upon the trick of opening doors behind which crouched the unseen weight by a sharp, swinging motion, by a repeated hammering of the oaken panels. And that particular form of annoyance soon grew less.

Once, alone, he entered Mr. Pelerin's little-used formal drawing-room and switched on the light. The floor was covered by a Chinese rug of singularly deep pile. Over an area of indeterminate shape, perhaps a square yard in extent, the wool threads were flattened. As he watched, the area began slowly to increase. In the light from the crystal chandelier he could see the erect tufts of the carpet lie down one by one and, as it were, harden, until the jute fabric underneath began to show.

He darted into the hall and came back with a bamboo walking-stick. With all his strength, he began to flail, to whip, the place on which the weight rested. The cane met no resistance. Each blow was completed against the rug. But instantly the area affected began to shrink. The tufts stood upright. In a moment, when Professor Nadelman paused for breath, it occupied no more space than could be covered by two spread hands.

Pelerin had heard him and was standing in the door, his hands clenched, his eyes staring, his lips sucked in. Before the professor could resume his offensive, the weight, with startling rapidity, sped across the room — its progress revealed by the flattening of the rug — until it came to a blind wall and disappeared.

To Nadelman the demonstration seemed complete. Clearly, the weight felt pain. Under counterattack, it fled. Pelerin was a man of intelligence. Nadelman must assume the lesson was not lost on him.

The two men walked in silence to the library. When Mr. Pelerin poured brandy his hands shook so that the neck of the decanter rattled a thin and frightened tune on the goblets' rims. Neither spoke. But both, now, had seen it. It was real.

It was Nadelman's conviction that the weight was hostile — to the changes in the house, *its* house, which Pelerin had made. And to them. It was also his belief the weight was subject to certain laws. Proof soon came.

In the room with the Adams' mantel stood one of Mr. Pelerin's most prized possessions, a Louis XV occasional table whose carved legs tapered to the diameter of a fountain pen. Pelerin owned many things of more value, but nothing of greater delicacy. The whole perfect, useless thing could be lifted by two fingers.

The two men were at lunch when they heard the reverberation of the bass keys of a piano, as if a cat had jumped on them, then, seconds later, the crash of splintering wood.

The little table, an irreparable ruin, lay in fragments on the floor.

They were just in time to see the fringed corner of a rug twisted aside by the weight's passing, before it disappeared.

The table had been crushed from the top downward. It was plain how it had happened. Mrs. Humphries, the woman from the village who "did" for them, in cleaning that morning had left the table away from its accustomed position close to the rosewood piano. A small footstool had been moved near the piano bench.

The weight, then, was like a variable quantity of soft, invisible putty, but a putty of concentrated mass which — no word quite fitted — *poured* itself forward and even upward; but it was subject to the laws of gravity. It had forced itself onto the footstool, then onto the bench, then by way of the keyboard onto the piano, whence it had dropped down upon the table. The act was one of pure vandalism, vindictiveness.

Professor Nadelman had to speak. "My dear friend," he said gently, "are you very sure you are right? Not desertion. I would not propose it, but perhaps a short absence?"

Mr. Pelerin's voice, though it shook a little, was steely. "Elias, I am not a coward."

The elderly, emaciated refugee inclined his head.

But he was worried. His generous savior, now his friend, was showing strain. Slight in build at best, Pelerin was visibly losing weight. His skin was a bad color. With the coming of the still July days he began to complain fretfully of the heat. In words Pelerin revealed nothing, but fear was peering through his eyes. Though the weight now avoided Nadelman almost completely, its remorseless, secret war upon his host was fast reaching, the professor began to believe, a mortal stage.

Then he was certain.

Pelerin was in his study. Through the closed door Elias Nadelman heard a high and piercing scream that in a mere instant choked into terrifying silence.

Mr. Pelerin sat at his big, leather-topped Sheraton desk. He had fainted. He had been examining a Chinese painting by separating with both extended hands the two sticks on which it was tightly rolled. His head lolled forward but his hands, the fingers wide, were still pressed hard upon the antique painted silk. The two rolled ends of the painting were flat and crumpled. The weight lay on them.

An Elizabethan dagger which Pelerin used as a paper cutter lay on the desk. With a pounce Nadelman took it and with swift yet carefully controlled savagery stabbed and stabbed again through the air just above the desk. Instantly he saw the blood flow back into Pelerin's pale hands. Released, they slid back across the desktop and fell supinely in his lap.

Nadelman could not be sure. It might have come from Pelerin's unconscious lips. But he thought he heard a moan.

An hour later he rang Doctor Gage's bell.

Without preamble or emotion Nadelman described the incidents of the preceding weeks — from the formless, invisible mass which had tried, harmlessly, to oppose his first opening of Mr. Pelerin's door to the physical assault which had just taken place.

When he had finished, Gage smiled, but only with his mouth.

"I assume, Elias," he said, "you didn't come for my opinion?"

"No, George."

"As a physician," Gage persisted, "and for the record, I suppose you know what it is. You and Pelerin are suffering from a collective hallucination. Why you are, or why it's taken this form, the good Lord may know." He held up a grizzled, capable hand to ward off interruption. "I know that between the two of you, you've got four times my brains. In these things, though, intelligence isn't a safeguard. Understand me, now. Diagnosis, right or wrong, doesn't alter anything. A fact of the mind is no less a fact than an aneurism. Maybe I'm just a country doctor, but I do know that. Let's simply say a condition exists. The point is, how do we treat it? What do you want of me?"

"I want you to send him away. I'm afraid."

Gage looked at him appraisingly. "And you don't scare easy, do you, Elias?"

"I'm afraid," Nadelman amended, "for our friend. Not for myself."

THE LATE afternoon sunlight streamed in the tall upstairs windows. Mr. Pelerin was in bed. His eyes were closed, his clever face against the white pillows looked thin and drained of strength. His hands were outside the sheet that on this summer day was all the covering needed.

Doctor Gage stood looking down at him. It had been thirty years since he had come into this room. Then it had been all sombre darkness. Now it was all light. . . . Obscurely, he was not so sure that it had changed.

Suddenly his eyes sharpened. Leaning, he picked up Pelerin's hands and put his face close to them. Putting them gently down, he summoned Nadelman to a far corner of the room.

"His hands," Gage whispered hoarsely, "are bruised! One of the nails has begun to darken. It's as if they had been crushed."

The professor smiled. "By an hallucination, doctor."

Mr. Pelerin spoke from the bed. The voice was so much his own, still so full of nervous force, that both men started.

"George! Elias! I beg of you! Surely at your times of life you should both know there is nothing so intensely irritating to an invalid as a whispered consultation. Especially when the invalid isn't ill."

Rather tiredly, Mr. Pelerin pulled himself higher on his pillows and cautiously laced the two bruised hands behind his head. "Come closer, both of you, so I can talk to you." He studied their faces for a moment before he went on. "You are both interested in my ailment. I can tell you what it is. Though the form — " Mr. Pelerin drew his hands from behind his head and held them motionless in the air for an instant before he put them back, "— though the particular form," he repeated, "is unusual, the complaint, I fear, is common. It is called — failure."

Pelerin looked away from them, his eyes clouded with reflection. "I have attempted to replace ugliness with — though the word has grown shabby I must use it — with beauty. Force — with grace. Strength with — what shall I say? — intelligence. The undertaking is notoriously hard. I have not succeeded. So one day I shall die of it."

"Nonsense!" In Doctor Gage's own ears the exclamation sounded strangely loud. He hurried on in a more normal tone. "You're tired. You've used yourself up, that's all."

Mr. Pelerin smiled, as if from far away. "So what, George, do you prescribe?"

"Rest. Distraction. For a month or two anyway you've got to go away."

"Go?" said Mr. Pelerin. "You mean 'run.' It would not be practicable, George. One cannot flee one's own inadequacy. Elias, don't you agree?"

"Your only inadequacy, my dear friend," said Nadelman sharply, "is your — technique. You rely on courage. The antagonist despises courage. You are firm, patient. You put your trust in superior example. The error is common. If persisted in, not only you but all civilization may very well 'die of it.' The Brute fears only pain."

In a different tone, Nadelman persisted, "George is right. For a short time you must go away. Gain strength. Gather your resources. It will not be easy for you, but you must learn to fight back, to be as ruthless as the enemy. I think you should go quickly."

The tip of Mr. Pelerin's tongue crept out to wet his lips.

"Very well. Tomorrow."

DOCTOR GAGE showed no disposition to go home. Nor to talk. Nadelman heard him wandering through the house, peering into concealed places and softly opening and closing doors.

They dined sketchily on a table in Mr. Pelerin's room. Since for the first time among them conversation limped, Nadelman talked at length about his chosen field, the Renaissance.

Afterward, all that remained in Doctor Gage's memory was one phrase:

*"Beauty was honored in a time of violence because it was defended with sharp steel."*

While Gage sat with Mr. Pelerin, Nadelman made his preparations for the night.

In the cheap cardboard suitcase he had brought from Europe was a whip. The handle was short, the butt of lead, and the woven lash of discolored leather about six feet long. It was a curious souvenir for an elderly professor of esthetics to have kept. He had picked it up at Buchenwald where Block Leader Hansel had dropped it in the hurry of his departure at the news that the Americans were near. The black whip had cut so often into Nadelman's own skin, been stained with so much of his own blood, that he knew it intimately. Since then, he had learned to handle it.

Secretly, but with no shame, Professor Nadelman had always hoped for an opportunity to use it. There were debts it was unholy not to pay.

The distinguished author of *The Age of Alexander VI* rolled the whip tightly, hid it under his coat, and went to his host's room.

Mr. Pelerin was asleep. In a low voice Doctor Gage said he had injected a strong enough sedative to last through the night. Nadelman was not sure he approved but it was too late to object. After a little, saying he was to be called at any moment, Gage went home.

Professor Nadelman turned on the light in the ceiling and those by the mirror and the desk, so the room was a white glare. The chair he drew close to Mr. Pelerin's bedside was carefully selected. It was comfortable, yet not so luxurious as to tempt him into sleep. The manifestations of force were often cunning. He had taken care that every door in the cruel and sulking house was left ajar.

Elias Nadelman took the whip from under his coat. With a light shake he made it ready and laid it across his knees.

The hands of the tiny Limoges enamel clock on Pelerin's bedside table moved very slowly to midnight, to one, to two. At intervals Nadelman systematically moved his arms, his legs. He was not sleepy, but there was danger that without occupation his mind, his senses, might grow dull. The man in the bed slept without moving.

It was surprising that he noticed. It was a mark of the perfection of Pelerin's housekeeping that every hinge was oiled. The open door which gave onto the dark hall was slowly closing.

With a single leap the gaunt, prematurely aged man flung himself against it. The weight behind it made him grunt. Though his position was awkward he brought down the black lash of the whip into the emptiness outside with all the force he could summon. At the third stinging cut the door gave way so suddenly that Nadelman all but stumbled to his knees. At once he realized he had made an incomparable, grave mistake. Nowhere, except in Pelerin's own room, had he left on any lights. Precious seconds were lost while he found and snapped the switch. Nadelman sucked in his breath. Never had the weight been so great.

Just at the head of the stairs that led into the darkness of the floor below, the gray rug was pressed down hard over a loosely circular area nearly five feet in diameter. With a vicious whistle and a crack like a gunshot, the whip lashed down on the floor. Nadelman felt a sense of high and impure joy. Instantly the weight flung itself down the steps. Though nothing was to be seen, the steps creaked, the heavy oak banister shook.

Nadelman, the whip ready, was after it, his bony wrists thrusting from the short sleeves, his shoddy jacket flying. Once more time was lost while the lean pursuer groped in the air for the cord of the hanging lamp which lit the lower hall.

As he found it, the nearby door to the drawing-room, which opened inward, shut with a soft rush and a click of the brass latch. The weight tonight was moving more swiftly and with more appearance of intent than ever before. Twice in the next few moments Nadelman was sure he had stung it with his whip. The professor's lips were drawn back over his teeth, the skin of his face felt tight, and he was supremely happy.

In a silence unbroken but for the rasp of his own breathing and the whisk and crackle of the whip, the chase led on. Two more rooms were traversed. In each he lost time switching on the light.

In the high-ceilinged dining-room Nadelman stopped. He was panting. All trace of the antagonist had vanished. The pleasant room with its shining oval of mahogany was snug, at peace. Nadelman could hear no creak, or rustle.

Peering intently, he turned slowly around. A door into the cellar opened from an alcove at one end of the room. That, too, he had left open. He thought he saw it move. The fury — not just of the night, the house, but of the years — was hot in him. He was no longer thinking. With three long strides he reached the cellar door and stood staring down into the darkness. The door struck hard against the tensed calves of his legs, his back. He staggered, missed his footing, and plunged down. His head struck the jagged foundation wall, and Professor Nadelman lost consciousness.

It was impossible to tell. But when his senses struggled upward out of the black turmoil of insensibility, it seemed to him he had been unconscious only a few minutes. With a cry of fear he stumbled to his feet. His left arm hurt acutely. A groping hand encountered the feel of warm blood on his scalp. Moaning with terror, he scrambled up out of the sour darkness, ran with great pumping strides of his long legs through the hall, up the next flight, and into Mr. Pelerin's bedroom.

The sheets had been kicked into a tangle. One pillow was on the floor. Mr. Pelerin's hands were stiffly outspread, as if they had been arrested in the act of pushing. His face was purple.

For a moment the compound of despair, grief — above all, the knowledge of how he had been tricked — almost deprived Nadelman of sight. Seconds passed before his vision cleared. Pelerin was slightly built. The mattress and the rumpled pillow on which he lay were firm. Yet his light frame was pressed as deeply into them as if his body were a giant's. The weight still lay on him.

Nadelman had lost the whip. It must still be lying at the bottom of the cellar steps. He clawed his hands and with the energy of a madman began to scratch and rip and rake the empty air fractions of inches above Pelerin's face, chest, arms. He could feel nothing.

But he was winning. He was winning! Gradually his friend's contorted body *rose*. The inward slope of the spring mattress flattened. There was the faint sound of sucked-in breath. Pelerin was still alive. The weight had withdrawn.

There was a phone on the desk. Doctor Gage answered the first ring. In two minutes — clearly he had not undressed — he was in Pelerin's room. With hairy, clumsy hands suddenly turned skillful, he injected a stimulant; then pressed, relaxed, and pressed again on Pelerin's lower ribs. At last, satisfied, the doctor straightened the tangled sheets and made the still unconscious man comfortable. Not until he was done did he face the other man.

His eyes dark with hostility he took in the Jew's dust-smeared clothes, his panting breath, the blood upon his head.

"You knew, of course," Gage said harshly. "Last week Pelerin made a will. I witnessed it. He leaves you everything." He jerked his head. "You'd better go. I'm going to stay right here all night."

The import of the words made Nadelman physically reel. The fine head with the arched hawk-nose drew down between his lifted shoulders, his hands opened in a gesture of false obedience, of mocking submission as old and as little understood as time. Without a word Elias Nadelman turned and walked away.

In his own room, he did not turn on the light. Still dressed, the wound on his scalp forgotten, he lay down upon his bed . . . Was victory, real victory, impossible? He had thought Gage his friend. That look of hatred — what was worse, of unutterable distrust — when Gage had accused him of attempting the murder of his friend . . . it was as if he had seen it always. In Babylon. In Egypt. In Spain . . . In that moment the face of that good man had been the very face of force. The weight had many forms.

Of what use, then?

Of all use. The fight must never pause.


THE SCREAM sought him as if he were at the bottom of a well. Nadelman fought upward, as if through black waves of oil.

It was his name. "Elias! Nadelman! Elias! For God's sake, come!" It was Gage.

He was standing with his back against the wall, staring at the bed. Gage had left on only the night light on Pelerin's table. Yet even in half-shadow the doctor's ruddy face was gray, his lips loose with fear.

"Look!"

Even as he sprang to the bed Nadelman saw that this time he was too late. The weight had come again. And now it was going. Pelerin's body, slowly lifted by the released pressure of the springs on which he lay, was rising. In another second, with a queer limpness, it was free.

"Doctor!" said Nadelman.

With an effort, his movements made unsure by shock, Gage stumbled across the room. When he had listened to Mr. Pelerin's heart he shook his head.

As he put away his stethoscope his hands were shaking. "I fell asleep," said Doctor Gage humbly. "I am responsible."

During a perceptible pause Nadelman did not answer. "The weight, Doctor, made you its ally. The experience, alas, is not unknown. I, too, am guilty. Tonight I became not the defender but the aggressor. By that, I served its purpose and not mine. We must be most vigilant."

---

Not until the doctor, in the lighted safety of the living-room, had gulped down a copious drink of brandy did he raise his eyes.

"There are some things," he said quietly, "for which you can't say 'I'm sorry.' I thought this hocus-pocus . . . I can't think what got into me." He looked around him at the lovely room. "It's this house, Elias. Now that it's yours, in the name of Heaven, tear it down. Burn it!"

Professor Nadelman shook his head. "No, I shall stay. I shall — " he hesitated for a word: " — contend. And I think that I shall win."

"I do not pretend to understand," the professor went on calmly. "Here there was some focus. A concentration. A distilled and stubborn residue. But cruel force, the will to crush and kill, are as old as man. The forms are infinite. Sometimes open. Far more often, secret. Pelerin was gentle. He would not fight back. One must. *One must!*"

The thin old man smiled sadly, but his mouth was firm.

"I learned that, you see, long before I came here."

*Richard Frede*

# MR. MURDOCH'S GHOST

A T THE AGE OF thirty-eight Mr. Murdoch inherited, after taxes, nearly four million dollars. He had not planned on the inheritance — it came to him from a relative he had neither seen nor thought about since childhood.

Mr. Murdoch was unmarried and did not intend ever to marry. This was not a sexual disinclination — he always had a woman friend somewhere in his life. It was merely that he disliked encumbrances.

He was, at the time of his inheritance, working in an architect's office in Manhattan. He himself was an architect, but his workday was more that of a draftsman than that of a designer. Like his professional training, his background had prepared him for a better sort of life, but such were his abilities and luck that, until the inheritance, the better sort of life had eluded him.

Though he had made no formal plans for wealth, Mr. Murdoch had, since his eleventh year, entertained a fantasy which served him every bit as well as logical preparation. The fantasy had become, over the years, quite detailed. As detailed as a bookkeeper's books or, say, a draftsman's drawings.

When Mr. Murdoch was just between childhood and adolescence, he had once spent a night in what he came to think of as the most comfortable house he had ever been in. A classmate, not a real friend, had impulsively invited him home from their boarding school one cold Saturday afternoon when Murdoch had kicked the winning goal just before time was called in a soccer game against their school's traditional rival. Young Murdoch, whose first year this was in boarding school, had been unsuccessful at making friends, and he accepted the invitation happily.

The classmate's parents had driven them, in a paneled station wagon, to a country home about an hour away from the school. A jovial pair, the parents laughed and joked all the way home, but soon thereafter went out for the evening and slept late the next day. Young Murdoch hardly saw them at all until it was time for the father to drive the boys back to their school late the next afternoon.

A live-in cook-and-maid gave the boys a good dinner, and then they listened to radio in a book-lined den which had a real fireplace with a real fire going in it. Bread was being baked in the kitchen. But it was the house — the totality of it — which Murdoch loved. A white wooden house in black winter woods when they had come upon it in the station wagon, he learned that it predated the Revolution. There was a working fireplace in almost every room. Above him were the warm dark lines of exposed beams. There were the smells of burning wood and of baking bread. The old chairs and couches suggested rich conversation, good friendship, and the safety of times which have already passed.

But it was not these circumstances alone which finally determined Mr. Murdoch's lifelong fantasy. It was a threat. The threat came from young Murdoch's classmate, who, apparently grown bored with and perhaps a little antagonistic toward his afternoon's hero, instructed young Murdoch upon the dangers of the house. This was just before bedtime. They were standing in the spare room which young Murdoch was to occupy.

The classmate said, "You know, Murdoch, this house has a ghost and you had better understand that it is a real ghost. It hasn't struck often, but three people have died in this house in the last hundred years, two of them in this room, and there has never been any explanation. Save for laughter some people claim to have heard about the times of death. There was a man who lived here. He was wealthy, I guess. Then he lost everything. And the sheriff, I guess, came and told him he had to get out of this house. The man brooded, they say, and just before he had to get out of the house, he committed suicide. He left a note saying that no one would ever occupy this house or sleep in it without his approval. He said he was going to come back as a ghost and kill anyone he didn't like who slept here. As I say, it hasn't happened often, but it has happened three times since the man committed suicide. The ghost is like a snake, a viper really, who lives somewhere in the walls and strikes when he fancies. Well, Murdoch, good night. And sleep well."

Murdoch did not sleep at all. At least not until first light. But it was the most comfortable night of his life. Settling under the covers, the lights out, warm in the great, soft bed with the cold winter night about him, young Murdoch realized, after a few minutes, that he wasn't afraid of the ghost at all. In fact, the presence of the ghost, which he discovered he truly believed in, comforted him. He felt some liaison with the ghost and concluded that it was because both of them were friendless and lonely. He was sure the ghost understood him and liked him. Beyond that, he had the wonderfully comfortable and comforting feeling that the ghost, far from endangering him, was looking after him. It was the best feeling he ever had.

Young Murdoch was never invited back to that most comfortable of houses, though he tried often enough, in both fervor and embarrassment, to persuade his classmate to do so.

Young Murdoch had spent most of his life in the city, and though he knew little enough about the country that first year in boarding school, he realized that he detested the city. Not only the city in general, but the small apartment with his quarreling parents in particular. He had decided then, though he didn't realize it at the time, that as soon as he was able, when he was grown up and through with college, he would never again live with another person. And, if he were able, he would live in the country. In a white wooden house with exposed beams. There would be old furniture and a working fireplace in every room. One of the rooms would be a book-lined den. Another of the rooms would be a kitchen which could provide whatever food he desired. The kitchen would be attended by a woman who baked bread regularly. The house itself would be attended by a ghost.

As he grew older and had more experiences and knowledge of the world, the dream, the desire, the fantasy became exquisitely detailed. Plaid blankets for the beds. Slippery, silver-silked comforters. His own bed would be canopied. In the den, which he had come to think of as the library, some old books of the period of the house. On the walls, antique prints and engravings dealing with themes martial, naval, equestrian, and sporting. He would have a good wine cellar. In the dining room there would be a crystal chandelier overhanging a polished and shining, dark wood table. When he entertained there would be gleaming silver next to bright white linen. He would entertain carefully and well, never more than six at table. Sometimes he would prepare the meal himself, sometimes his cook would. In any circumstances, she would not live in. He would ride, but he would not keep a horse, at least not keep a horse he had to attend to himself. He would indulge in a modicum of blood sport. Shoot bird, but not deer. He would live where there was skiing nearby, and his friends would visit him in the snowtime. There would be fires in the fireplaces, and his friends would see him standing before the fireplace in the living room, smiling, beckoning them to enjoy his beneficence. A gracious lady would take his arm as they all went in to dinner. He would give them a good bottle of wine and food worthy of comment. They would go back to the city reporting their amazing host and his house. At night, when he was there by himself, he would go to bed with feelings of sureness and safety, for the ghost would be overseeing his principality and giving him protection.

Mr. Murdoch had hoped it would happen but never really expected that it would.

The first thing Mr. Murdoch did after coming into the inheritance and quitting his job was to go looking for a paneled station wagon. He finally settled on a green one. The brown paneling was actually plastic, but it was the best he could do. He bought a new wardrobe in the best stores and handsome luggage in which to carry it, and he departed Manhattan in the station wagon and drove north to New England in search of his house. It was a fine, golden summer, and Mr. Murdoch enjoyed the driving, but a search through Connecticut and then western Massachusetts and then the length of Vermont failed to discover a single house suitable to the details of Mr. Murdoch's fantasy. He became disheartened. Then he became anxious, quite as if his life depended upon finding that special vehicle for turning his fantasy into reality. He lay awake at night in country inns and he was not comfortable at all.

One chilly, wet day, when the wind blew the rain in sheets across the road in front of him, Mr. Murdoch crossed over into southern New Hampshire intending to drive to Boston for some refreshment. He had, he had decided, been working much too hard. Using a map, he attempted a series of shortcuts on minor roads and got lost. This brought him to the village of Glenhaven, a gem of a village, Mr. Murdoch immediately appreciated. A few white houses, a white church, a white general store, and hills and meadows all about. In the store he inquired of a real-estate agent, and an hour later a Mr. Franklin came over from a nearby town. Franklin affected a country style but was as rich as anybody about and just as knowledgeable. He listened to Mr. Murdoch and then said, "Haven't got anythin' that's pre-Revolutionary, but I got one that's pretty close."

In Mr. Franklin's car they took a road about a mile into the woods. Abruptly they came out into a small meadow. Up against the woods was a white wooden house. It was somewhat similar to the one which Mr. Murdoch had experienced in his youth, and after the disappointments of his search so far, he was willing to ignore, temporarily, the obvious dissimilarities.

Mr. Franklin said, "This house was built in 1797."

Mr. Murdoch said, "Colonial?"

Mr. Franklin said, "Not Colonial. Federal. On the other hand, nobody knows what Federal is."

Mr. Franklin started to get out of the car. "If you don't mind," Mr. Murdoch said, "I'd rather go in alone. I'd like to see what it feels like by myself."

"I quite understand," Mr. Franklin said, though Mr. Murdoch doubted that he did. Mr. Franklin handed Mr. Murdoch a key.

Mr. Murdoch went to the door of the house. The door would require a brass knocker. The house would need to be repainted, not because it was peeling, but because it could be still whiter. Mr. Murdoch went in.

He went about from room to room. What first concerned him was that the rooms seemed to be rather too quiet for even an unoccupied house — there was no other presence. But there was a living room with a huge fireplace and a sitting room with a smaller one. The fireplace in the smaller room had been covered over, but the mantel was still there. It was a room which might serve a gentleman for his library. The kitchen was a large shedlike attachment to the house itself. A perfectly proportioned dining room for a table of six also seemed to have a fireplace hiding in one of its walls. Steep narrow stairs took him to the second story. A master bedroom with yet another closed-over fireplace. A private bath to the master bedroom. There were three other smaller bedrooms and another bath. There was evidence of still another closed-over fireplace in one of the lesser bedrooms. Nowhere did Mr. Murdoch find any signs of insect or rodent damage, and the roof and walls, he noted, had kept the weather out nicely. He went down to the basement. The cellar floor was dirt and it was dry. A huge chimney arch rose from the middle of the floor into the center of the upstairs, suggesting several fireplaces above it. Mr. Murdoch went back to the first floor. The boards there were narrow and thus disappointing to him. The beams were hidden by plaster ceilings. All in all, Mr. Murdoch decided he didn't mind that. It seemed more elegant to him.

But there were two basic problems to the house, one soluble and the other — if indeed it existed — not so. One of the problems was that the house had been subject to "updatings" by its various tenants. Each generation of occupants had done things to the house to make it look more in style with whatever architectural vogue had currently been fancied. Outcroppings, like architectural weeds, sprang at Mr. Murdoch's offended eye everywhere, both inside and out. There were touches of neo-Roman and of neo-Greek. *Art nouveau* contested for attention with Gothic Revival. A misguided intrusion of Third Empire France was surrounded by Bauhaus innuendo. All that could be seen to.

The other problem could not be seen to. There was the unbecoming silence, the *absence,* Mr. Murdoch thought. There was no ghost. He was sure of it.

A knocking on the front door and Mr. Murdoch opened it. Mr. Franklin said, "Been through it?"

"Yes."

"Then you've seen that it's fit, Mr. Murdoch. A man could move himself and his family in here tonight, if he got the water turned on and the electricity goin'. Old as it is, this house is fit."

"Does it have a ghost?" Mr. Murdoch asked.

"Definitely not," said Mr. Franklin, but then, noting a reaction in Mr. Murdoch which was, perhaps, a signal of dissatisfaction, he said, "Leastways not that I ever hear tell of. But, then, I don't hear tell of everythin'. And it *is* an old house."

"How much are you asking?"

"Twenty-two," said Mr. Franklin.

"Eighteen," said Mr. Murdoch.

"Well, I could go twenty-one five," said Mr. Franklin. "If you're prepared to conclude the transaction this week."

"I am," said Mr. Murdoch. "Eighteen five."

"There's a stable you haven't seen," said Mr. Franklin. "It'd make a nifty carpentry shop."

"Eighteen five."

"Then there's a brook where I've taken trout myself."

"But no ghost," said Mr. Murdoch. "Eighteen five."

"There's an apple orchard comes with it over to the next — "

"But no ghost," said Mr. Murdoch. "Eighteen five."

"This house is fit. It don't need no fixin'."

"It doesn't have a ghost," said Mr. Murdoch. "Twenty thousand.

That is my top offer. If it is inadequate, there is no need for further discussion."

During the next few days the title was searched, payment was made, and papers were passed. The house became the property of Mr. Murdoch.

Mr. Murdoch then returned to New York City and disposed of the physical accumulations of his former life while at the same time acquiring yet other goods which befitted his concept of what his new life would be. He bought a fine shotgun. He had two tweed suits and three tweed jackets made. He bought a pair of skis for normal conditions and another pair for icy conditions and then, because he happened to see it, cross-country ski equipment. In the same store he came upon snowshoes and bought two pairs — one pair for a guest. He bought perfumes for the guest bath — a grace note which had impressed him in yet another house he had enjoyed. He bought delicacies for his larder and wines for his cellar and batteries of utensils for his kitchen. He determined the sort of china and silver which would be appropriate to his new home, for — when he was not shopping and buying and shipping to the new home — he was in a library studying the details of domestic architecture and furnishings in the Federal period. He ordered copies of the pertinent books to take back with him for his own library, and when they proved to be unavailable, he had his bookstore advertise for them.

On his way back to Glenhaven, the station wagon bearing a share of his new acquisitions (including a copy of *The Federalist Papers*), Mr. Murdoch drove into a new season. Exposed to bright colors and chill air, Mr. Murdoch found his senses newly awakened, not having known that they were asleep or dozing. The smell of woodsmoke itself was new and welcome and invigorating. Mr. Murdoch began his new life by returning his old house to its past.

He took up temporary residence in a motel several miles away and went about interviewing contractors, carpenters, particular craftsmen, and others. He had much of the wiring and plumbing in the house re-placed and amplified to his specifications. The kitchen was modernized — Mr. Murdoch's major concession to the present. He had a search begun for a copper tub for his personal bath. The pineboard floors throughout the house had been painted. So he had them stripped and stained dark. He had the wainscoting stripped. He had the ceilings replastered. He had the outside of the house given a new coat of white paint so that it glistened in the sun during the day and seemed to illuminate its own exterior at night. Where color was used in the interior, the colors were first justified by the books. Pine shelves were secured from other old houses and built into the sitting room to make it his library. He had the fireplaces uncovered and the chimneys and flues opened and swept. He ordered cords of wood. He found dealers who had plundered houses similar to his own, and he acquired from them old square bricks for a hearth and old small bricks to repair the fireplaces. He had the fanlight over the door reconstructed. He found the small windowpanes — the nuisance panes — required and had them put back all through the house. He searched out proper wooden shingles and had the slate ones on the roof replaced. Someone had begun (irresponsibly, to Mr. Murdoch's mind) to convert the stable into a carpentry shop. Mr. Murdoch had the offending adaptations ripped out and the stable restored to its original purpose. He purchased a canopied bed and some brass-appointed campaign chests, and in the midst of winter, the rougher and dirtier work of the refurbishment completed, he moved in. The house smelt of paint. At a greenhouse some two hours' drive away, he was able to purchase traditional herbs and other growing things to make the air in his house smell worthily. At night there was a fire in the fireplace in his bedroom as he read before sleeping. He awoke to the fire's embers in the morning. The master bedroom, including a copper tub, was in spanking order. He found and retained a Mrs. Trowbridge, who then came in to clean and to cook. She baked bread and rolls three times a week.

By catalogue, correspondence, and agent, Mr. Murdoch scoured the auction houses, galleries, and antique stores of London for the sort of table or place setting he had decided upon. In this fashion he acquired, from a London auction and for $8000, a crystal chandelier for over the dining room table — though he did not yet have a dining room table. A man had to be brought up from New York to sort the pieces and then assemble and hang the chandelier. It took him several days. Mr. Murdoch himself spent several days a month in Boston and New York nosing out the needs of his house. Galleries and auctioneers began inviting him to private previews. Sometimes his fancy enlarged upon itself as when, in Boston, while looking for maritime prints of the Federal period, he came upon an oil portrait of a gentleman of that time and decided that suitably venerable oils which were to his liking might also abide upon the walls of his house.

Secretly, Mr. Murdoch hung a picture of young Murdoch in a closet in his bedroom. Young, friendless, yearning Murdoch of the preparatory school days. When Mr. Murdoch opened the closet, he saw young Murdoch's unhappiness, and he felt compassion for the boy and pride in the man he had become and the man's accomplishment — this house.

At night he prayed for sounds. But there were none, save those which were so mundane that reason could account for them.

By spring, the house — very nearly bare that first winter save for the canopied bed, the campaign chests, the copper tub, and the crystal chandelier — began to fill out with the details of which Mr. Murdoch had put it in want. Crystal goblets and a dining table arrived from London. Silver was found in Boston and brought home in the plastic-paneled station wagon. A set of six prints depicting the various dress uniforms of officers in Napoleon's armies was found in New York. Two chairs of the period for the library were found in Boston as well as a stuffed couch which, though not of the period, Mr. Murdoch had caused to be covered in material appropriate to the period.

Also in the spring Mr. Murdoch acquired two fine horses. He named them After Midnight and Post Noon and rode each only at its own time of day. He hired a high-school student to tend the stable and groom the horses. He discovered that the apple orchard on his property had gone very nearly to ruin. He spent several thousand dollars having it revived and brought to health. In the fall he could always send baskets of apples to friends. He liked the idea very much.

He began to entertain. Local nobility — of which there was a surprising plenty in the nearby woods. A present congressman. A former governor. A movie actress and her baseball-player husband. Some writers and artists. Local professionals. Some well-known Harvard professors who were retired or who came over from Cambridge for weekends and summers. A famous pianist. A respected physicist. A man who owned one of the biggest private companies in the country. A man who was chief pilot of an airline. A woman who owned an advertising agency. A countess. Others. Mr. Murdoch enjoyed entertaining them and showing them about his house. As the years went by and the furnishings became more complete, the tours took longer, protracted by the anecdotal biography attending each of Mr. Murdoch's many acquisitions.

In the spring and summer and fall, Mr. Murdoch, who took good care of himself, played golf and tennis. He tried to do these things as a gentleman — that is, with no thought of winning. But winning was always on his mind. In the summer he kept a boat on a nearby lake and sailed. Also, in the summer, he fished trout from the brook behind his house. These he served cooked in butter or cooked in wine, sometimes with almonds. A light white wine, well-chilled, always accompanied the trout. Usually, cold asparagus with his own mayonnaise or vinaigrette. For dessert, fresh strawberries and cream, sometimes preceded by cheese. Dinner was never served until after dark, thus occasioning candles. Mrs. Trowbridge waited table. In the fall Mr. Murdoch shot birds at a private club, had Mrs.

Trowbridge pluck, blood, eviscerate, and clean them; and then he himself prepared them for his table. His guests were invariably complimentary to his skill in the kitchen and impressed by the manner in which he had provided the birds.

But always at night Mr. Murdoch lay awake and listened for sounds, for sounds of something present. But what he heard was absence and he was not at all comfortable.

The second winter he bought a basset hound to lie at his feet in front of the fire. The second spring he began a most ambitious rock garden. The third summer he found a barn full of wide pine boards such as must have originally floored his house. He purchased the barn for its boards and moved to the motel for a few weeks while the old narrow-board floors were torn out of his house and the wide boards put in. The house was repainted yearly, and Mr. Murdoch never ceased in carefully and deliberately acquiring and installing the real details of what had been a fantasy.

A visitor from New York asked Mrs. Trowbridge, "What will Mr. Murdoch do with himself when he finishes it?"

Mrs. Trowbridge, who was astute, replied simply, "He will never finish it. It's his life."

And so he did not finish it for some years. But, so scrupulous had Mr. Murdoch been, after ten years there was nothing else to be done or even to be redone. Mr. Murdoch looked outside. But the rock garden needed nothing more than tending. The apple orchard flourished. There was nothing left to be landscaped, and what was landscaped was cared for by a gardener. Mr. Murdoch inspected the rooms of his house over and over and found nothing but perfection. To modify or add to what he had done would be like purposely tarnishing the brass at his door or the silver at his table. He would not do it.

There was, of course, no ghost. And so, thought Mr. Murdoch, after all, after *all,* he did not have perfection. Though there was no way in which he could improve upon what he already had.

He had always enjoyed cooking, and so he sought to relieve his sense of failure, bleak and irrevocable failure, by creating perfection in his kitchen where he had been unable to do so in his house. Days were spent on the details of a meal, a part of a meal. Days were spent traveling to get even a single bottle of wine which Mr. Murdoch thought the meal demanded. He shopped in the ethnic neighborhoods of several different cities to find what he required, sometimes flying from one city to another to get individual items for the same dinner. Still rarer items were sought out through catalogues and in international telephone conversations and were then shipped to him from all over the world.

One winter's weekend, just before Christmas, it happened that Mr. Murdoch was visited by two couples from New York of whom he was most particularly fond. It was in their esteem especially that he enjoyed a reflection on himself. The two couples had suggested that they bring along a mystery guest — about whom Mr. Murdoch was told only that she was a young woman whose name he would know. He agreed to the additional guest. If his friends thought so well of her, he wanted strongly that she think well of him.

The dinner Mr. Murdoch chose to do for them all took six weeks to prepare. Two weeks of reading and studying, two weeks of traveling and searching to find some of the ingredients, and finally, two weeks of work in the kitchen. He constructed the menu so that everything could be prepared ahead of time and, indeed, had to be prepared ahead of time in order that peaks of flavor and maturity be reached and could then, at a suitable hour, be heated by Mrs. Trowbridge. Mr. Murdoch's intention was to ski all day with his friends and then come home and be his own guest. A bit of sherry while he bathed in the copper tub and got the chill out and relaxed. Good conversation while his friends had their martinis and whiskeys and he had a second sherry and then his remarkable dinner together with an extraordinary wine, which, unfortunately, no one there other than himself would be knowledgeable enough to fully appreciate.

That is more or less how the evening progressed, from fireplace in the living room to fireplace and candlelight in the dining room. The unknown guest was attractive and pleasant and no older than twenty-five. She had written (to Mr. Murdoch's mind) a rather nasty little novel, which, nonetheless, had had both critical and financial success and was to be made into a movie. Her novel was set in the Federal period. No one in the period had had her admiration, and Mr. Murdoch had wondered why she'd been intent on writing of that time. However, to Mr. Murdoch's pleasure, she took pleasure in Mr. Murdoch's house. She was the first person to come to his house who readily understood what he had created, or re-created. She recognized the nuances. She understood the careful compromises with the present. Mr. Murdoch was delighted with her.

Mr. Murdoch decided that he and his guests would take brandy and liqueur in the library. Its size and seating arrangements were more intimate than those of the living room, and its mannerly fire was, just then, its only illumination. Mr. Murdoch decided not to change the situation.

When his guests — a lawyer and his wife, a doctor and his wife, and the novelist — were seated and served and Mr. Murdoch returned with a liqueur for himself, he found that they were talking about ghosts, about haunted houses. "You see," said the lawyer, "I was talking about visiting a house when I was a child and an incident which happened there which I just can't explain. Unless I admitted to ghosts, which I don't."

"When we were on our honeymoon," the doctor's wife said and then told a rather lewd, but chilling story of something that had happened to them one night they had spent in a castle.

The doctor said, "I wouldn't want my patients to know this, but there is no doubt in my mind that something supernatural happened to us that night."

"Did you ever notice," said the novelist, "that people who have had weird experiences, sometimes even *horrible* experiences with ghosts, or whatever you want to call the phenomena — have you ever noticed how people have an affection, a positive *affection,* for the places where they had the experiences? They may not be fond of the experience itself, but they're fond of the place where they had the experience, and they talk about it whenever anyone will listen. Sometimes they're even fond of the experience." She then told the story of having been raped one night, while still an adolescent virgin, in her own bed, in the present century, by a man whom she later, accidentally and in a book, discovered to be General Alexander Farnsworth, a Federalist in time, if not in persuasion. She'd woken in the morning bleeding. "It turned out," she said, "that General Farnsworth had spent his latter years in that same house where I grew up. If you've read my book, you know he was a very bitter man there toward the end. May I have a bit more brandy?"

When Mr. Murdoch came back with her brandy, he heard her voice before he entered the library. He paused outside the doorway and out of sight and heard her saying to the others: "Yes, he's done a super job, an *immaculate* job, but that's just it, it's immaculate, there's just no sense of the past here. Not in the sense of what *occupies* the house. Do you notice there's a silence here sometimes as if *nothing* is here?"

The rest of the evening was spent, in Mr. Murdoch's silence, listening to his guests describe, at first tentatively and later enthusiastically, the strange and wonderful places where they had been haunted, where there was a ghost, where they had been, however briefly, terrified by a *presence.*

That was the phrase the novelist used. "There was a *presence.*"

In the presence of such fervent commemorations of other houses, Mr. Murdoch felt his own house, and himself with it, become as nothing. He felt that his old friends were being wantonly and flagrantly and deliberately rude to him. In particular he despised the novelist. Pleading fatigue, he went to his room. The eighteenth-century equestrian engravings which faced him there from over the mantel in his bedroom were, to his eye, pieces of paper, and paper only now. The house itself might have been part of a Long Island development. He lay awake, most uncomfortable, lonely and friendless, and winter all about. There was no secret sound to comfort him, no *presence*.

In the morning he sent word by Mrs. Trowbridge that he was ill and would rather not see anyone, not even to say good-by. His guests left immediately after being served brunch.

Christmas week came, and though he had been invited to a number of parties, Mr. Murdoch kept to himself. No matter what time of day or night, he felt chilly. He checked the thermostat for both setting and reading. It always assured him that he should be feeling warm and comfortable. He listened to the heat in the ducts and spouting from the registers, but felt none of it. Fires in all the fireplaces had no effect upon him. He thought, "I am a man of substance, a substantial man with a substantial house, why should I be this way?"

New Year's Day was but forty-eight hours away, and Mr. Murdoch told himself sternly, "I cannot go through another week this way, much less an entire year."

On the eve of New Year's Eve, as he lay awake, chilly and lonely and friendless, listening for sounds, waiting for that feeling of presence he had known briefly as a boy, he came suddenly and joyfully to a conclusion, a solution, almost as if that long-ago ghost had come to him for an instant to instruct him. Mr. Murdoch decided to commit suicide and take up ghostly residence in his own house. Nothing could be more logical or esthetically pleasing than that he himself be the culmination and completion of his dream, his work of art, the perfect house presided over and protected by a ghost. He felt flushed with warmth.

Mr. Murdoch hugged himself. He would have his house and he would have his ghost and he would have himself. "World without end," Mr. Murdoch thought joyfully. He spent the remainder of the night — long hours which passed as so many quick minutes — determining the details of maintaining his residence in the future and deciding upon what he came to think of as "the engine" of his demise. Leave-taking of his body had to be brief and as painless as possible, and the means by which it was accomplished had to be immediately available. He thought of the fine shotgun. But that would be messy, and he did not want to do anything which would physically blemish his house, even its cellar. And were he to commit suicide *outside* the house, he wasn't sure but that he might have to haunt the place of death. So the fine shotgun, suitable as it appeared to be, was not suitable at all. An overdose of something, while physically clean, might be painful, or it might not work. Carbon monoxide poisoning from his faithful old station wagon would be painless, but that would require death in the garage, a separate building, and Mr. Murdoch had no intention of haunting a garage . . . except that . . .

At eight thirty the following morning he was at his lawyer's, and such was Mr. Murdoch's custom with the man that he was able to claim all of the man's time in spite of other appointments. By noon a trust had been drawn up which guaranteed and funded, in the event of Mr. Murdoch's death, the preservation of the house and its effects in their present condition. Certain people — rather a long list of them — would have guest privileges which they might exercise one night a year. Mr. Murdoch particularly looked forward to a visit by the young novelist. He could see her going back to New York amazed at the presence she had felt, talking about and perhaps even writing about the Murdoch house and the Murdoch ghost. Mrs. Trowbridge, or a trust-appointed successor, would tend the house daily. Mr. Murdoch left Mrs. Trowbridge five thousand dollars, but otherwise everything else went into the trust once it was converted to cash. By one o'clock the trustees had been chosen and had accepted their office. Mr. Murdoch drove over to a builders' supply store in a nearby town and purchased a great length of two-inch hose. He was back in Glenhaven at four o'clock. The trust had been typed up and the appropriate signatures were put to it. On his way home Mr. Murdoch stopped for the few odd gallons of gasoline needed to top off the station wagon's tank. Back in his garage Mr. Murdoch bound one end of the hose tightly about the exhaust pipe of the station wagon. He introduced the other end of the hose into the library through a window. He taped heavy cardboard inside and outside the window to close off the open area not occupied by the hose. He wrote a note and placed it in an envelope and placed the envelope on the table beside the chair he had chosen to sit in. The note set forth his intention and his motivations. He cautioned such friends and acquaintances as might be inclined to do so not to grieve for him, for, as he wrote, *I die a happy man.* Mr. Murdoch went to his wine cellar and brought up the very best bottle he had. He wondered whether carbon monoxide would affect its taste or bouquet. Nonsense, he thought, carbon monoxide is odorless. Then — Even so, he thought — but dismissed the detail as insignificant. He placed the open bottle and a glass on the table beside the chair in the library. He closed the fireplace flue and closed both doors to the library. He went out to the station wagon and started the engine. He went back to the library, closing the door behind him, and sat in the chosen chair and prepared to enjoy his bottle of wine, or part of it, as he looked at the open mouth of the hose and heard the distant engine. Carbon monoxide may be odorless, Mr. Murdoch thought, but really, the other exhaust fumes are a nuisance.

Mrs. Trowbridge found him. She was most upset and had to be given a sedative. A relative of his, of whom Mr. Murdoch had been unaware, contested the will and broke the trust and acquired Mr. Murdoch's worldly goods. The relative put the house on the market and hired a representative who advertised the furnishings.

One spring day, just before the active house-buying season usually began, Mr. Franklin, with whom it was listed, stopped in at Mr. Murdoch's house and found Mrs. Trowbridge there.

Mr. Franklin said, "It sure is a corker of a house now. But I'm going to have a hard time selling it. Maybe more trouble than any house I got. Could take years. People just don't want a house where there was a suicide. They won't admit it, but most people believe in ghosts and they're scared silly of them."

"There isn't one," Mrs. Trowbridge said. "There's no ghost here."

"Well, now, *I'm* not real serious personally," said Mr. Franklin. "*I* don't believe in ghosts."

"I do," said Mrs. Trowbridge. "I can say flatly there is no ghost in this house. Furthermore, I can prove it."

"You can?" said Mr. Franklin. "That would be interesting. I mean, Mrs. Trowbridge, how do you prove the nonexistence of something which is nonexistent?"

"Well, I don't know about all that philosophical stuff, Mr. Franklin. But I do know this. Ghosts are the spirits of people who died real unhappy. Now Mr. Murdoch, he died happy. His note says so. 'I die a happy man.' He was completing his life and his house and providing his house with a ghost. But a man who dies happy can't become a ghost. No ghost of Mr. Murdoch."

Dealers came from Boston, New York, and even London, and soon the house was bare again, with no sign of Mr. Murdoch, save its architectural restoration, which, anyway, was not attributed to him but to local contractors, carpenters, and other craftsmen.

Mr. Franklin sold the house sooner than he had expected. The new occupants reported nothing untoward.

Even so, Mrs. Trowbridge had been wrong, and the house was indeed haunted, though not by Mr. Murdoch. The house was haunted — inescapably so — by the lost and voiceless boy, young Murdoch, who had disappeared those many years before and who could effect nothing, and so was never seen nor heard nor felt in the house, just as had been his lot in life, save for one long-ago and now-forgotten soccer goal on a winter weekend's afternoon.

*Leroy Yerxa*

# CARRION CRYPT

I T ISN'T A pleasant task to record the story of Jason Ford. Ford was one of those strange men who spend their lives snooping into the strange corners of the world.

Jason Ford was a member of the Explorers' Club, and that's the one thing we had in common. We were, if I'm allowed to stretch the point a bit, both explorers. However, I confine my wandering to the safer places of the world. I like Mexico, and the deep valleys of Alaska. Jason Ford didn't fit into the "local" class.

I recall expressing admiration for Ford's courage in making several trips into the forbidden territory of Tibet.

"To my way of thinking," I said one night as we sat in the lounge, "Tibet is a part of the world that I wouldn't mind flying over, but it would be like poison to get dropped into."

Jason Ford downed his shot of scotch, which I had learned he could drink in vast quantities without any visible effect. His face, very tanned from a recent trip to Africa, suddenly showed tired, worried lines. He leaned back in the well worn leather chair and sighed.

"Tibet once held a great attraction for me," he confessed. "There are times when I feel that I'd like to go back. I'm afraid all the doors are locked and barred against my return."

I was amazed.

"But the Barnes-Ferris caravan came out only two months ago. Surely . . . ?"

He nodded.

"I said that *I* was forbidden to enter Tibet. There are others who come and go with no trouble."

I was on the scent of a good story. I ordered another bottle of scotch from the bar, and bit by bit, I got the story from Ford. He didn't enjoy telling it, but I knew it was one of those things that *had* to be told. It had been gnawing away inside of him until it had become a raw sore.

"I WAS AT Tashi-Lunpo that year," Jason Ford said. "I had been invited to witness the Tibetan New Year, and would gain a personal interview with the highest of all high, the Grand Lama."

I nodded.

"The man who is God in human body. The supreme being."

Jason Ford's eyes were suddenly alive with fire. It was as though in these magic moments, he had been bodily transported back to Tibet.

"Heavenly Buddha of Measureless Light," he almost whispered. "Although I *did* witness the celebration of the New Year, and spoke to the Grand Lama many times, these incidents do not have any direct bearing upon my story.

"The Grand Lama and I became fast friends. I believe that everyone who saw him, worshipped him for his wonderful goodness."

I was amazed at his sincerity. I had always imagined Jason Ford as a hard-headed, hard-hitting realist.

"You weren't converted to the faith?"

As I spoke, I knew that I was making a mistake. It was none of my business. I know that my own faith has certain dogmas which it cannot escape. Who was I to judge what was right and wrong?

"Every man to his faith," Jason admitted. "One must live in Tibet to understand. The vastness of it. The cold, icy grandeur of it. One must renounce the world and learn the ageless secrets of Tibet. One must forget all else."

I didn't interrupt him, and he went on speaking in a dreamy voice.

"I decided to stay in Tibet. I adopted the cloak and peaked cap of the monks. I resigned myself to the lonely life of the monastery."

He smiled bitterly. I swear that he was reliving those days in wind-swept Tibet. Jason Ford had returned in spirit to the roof of the world, and could once more hear the temple drums and the steady clicking of the prayer wheels.

"I was sure of myself. I was very sure. *Om-mani-padme-hum.*"

The last phrase was a soft sign. He smiled at me.

*"Salvation is found only in true faith,"* he said.

His hands were clenched.

"Once I went to the Temple of Linga. I should never have gone there. I entered the long, dark hall, and still new at the monastery, I was frightened and awed by the place. Sacrificial gifts of corn and brass bowls of water were placed on the altar. Rats scurried about, interrupted from their meal."

His facial muscles grew rigid.

"Deep under the spell of the place, I fully expected to see the horrible features of Yama, god of the infernal regions, leaning over me. I watched the sacred dog, a mongrel of the filthiest sort, as he paced back and forth outside the grotto of Sande-puk.

"It was a place of the dead, and I was about to leave it hurriedly when a procession of monks came slowly up the hill from the monastery. I wasn't supposed to be here alone. Frightened, I hid in the darkness and they entered the temple.

"They went directly to the grotto and two of them entered and placed a threadbare rug on the stone floor. One of their members entered the grotto and kneeled there alone. It was then that I received the shock. I'll never quite forget it. They all set to work calmly to seal the grotto. They closed every crack through which light might seep. They left only a small, dirty gutter at the bottom. When the task was finished, they prayed, clicked their little prayer wheels and left that monk alone, sealed in a crypt, without light or warmth."

HE PASSED his hand over his eyes. Ford was stirred deeply, even in re-living the scene.

"Long after — I think three months, I learned the story. The Old Lama of the monastery told me that the Nameless Monk had chosen to enter the grotto and end his life there in prayer and meditation. He would be fed daily through the gutter. He would be without light, and when the winter came, only his tattered robe would warm his body. He would wait, perhaps a year, perhaps fifty years, until at last he would stretch out his skinny arms and greet death in the form of a splendid, brilliant rainbow of light. Then and only then would his soul be cleansed and ready for its reward."

Ford stared at me intently.

"Do you realize what effect that secret can have on a man? Do you know the hell it opened up for me?"

I shook my head. I didn't trust my voice.

"I couldn't stand it," he said, and gulped half a glass of scotch. "Every day for twelve long months, I watched a single monk climb the hill to the temple. For a long year, I watched him with the bowl of food which he would push along the slimy sides of the gutter to the *thing* that lived beyond the wall."

His voice was shaking.

"Do you think I could go on living, and knowing that a *man*, a breathing, suffering mortal was sealed beyond that wall? Every night I dreamed of him. I saw him sitting there, eyes glazed over, arms hanging at his sides, waiting — for death. Death that might be kind and overtake him soon. Death that might wait fifty long years before it greeted him with cold arms. I lay awake, listening to that sacred dog howling out his lungs in the freezing stillness of the Tibetan night. I was going crazy. One night I had had enough.

"I left the monastery quietly and studied the hillside, naked under the moon. There was no one abroad for it was late. I hurried to the temple and listened, bending with my ear close to the gutter. There was no sound, and yet I knew that he was alive, for each day the bowl that carried food to him, returned empty.

"I found a slab of stone, and ripped it from the altar. The sacred dog was highly agitated by the whole thing. He sat on his haunches, growling and snarling, but never daring to come near. I was a madman by then, thinking only that I must save a mortal from slow death. I started hacking away at the wall.

"It was back-breaking work, but at last, every muscle in my body aching, perspiration pouring down my face, I managed to break open a small hole. It seemed hours before I had an opening large enough to crawl through. On my hands and knees, I found my way into the crypt. He was there all right, and he was alive.

"His eyes were sightless. He was hardly more than a skeleton, covered by pale, unhealthy skin, and clothed in the filthy remnants of his robe. He had no power to protest and I forced him through the hole and he tottered and fell flat on the cold stone floor of the temple."

JASON FORD trembled from head to foot. His arms, suddenly relaxed, dropped to the leather arms of the chair. He sighed.

"The cold night air hit his body, and he shivered — and died. The shock had been too great. The man had lived for a year in his tomb, and now, finding life once more, had been unable to face it. They found us there, for I had pressed myself close to his poor, freezing body, trying to force some of my own heat into it — trying to save something that could not be saved. They left the frame of him there in the temple and it was devoured, as is the custom, by the sacred dog."

Ford was utterly exhausted by his story. Now his voice became stronger and a touch of irony entered it.

"They did not punish me. They said I was no longer fit to be one of them. I was at liberty to leave Tibet, but should I ever come that way again, I would be beheaded.

"All hope for the Nameless Monk, they said, was gone. I had taken away his only chance to enter a heavenly place, and his soul would be consigned to purgatory. They told me that, and prayed for *me,* that the Nameless Monk would not return and wreak his vengeance upon me for what I had done."

THE STORY might have ended there. It didn't. Jason Ford left Washington a week later. I spent several months in South America, and had what I imagine were some rather tame experiences compared with Ford's trip into the Dark Continent. Some time later, while resting a week at my Arizona home, I received this note from Vermont.

Dear Mark Billings:
   I have settled for the summer in the town of Mayerville, Vermont. Come, when you have time, and we'll spend a week consuming a case of scotch which I brought with me from London. By the way, Mark, the sacred dog of the Temple of Linga is howling again. I'm afraid he means business.
                         Your Good Friend and Drinking Companion,
                                             Jason Ford

I hadn't planned a vacation. I didn't relish that trip east. I wanted to sit alone on my own front porch, absorbing good whiskey and admiring the barren beauty of the desert.

*The sacred dog of the Temple of Linga . . .*

I caught a plane from Tucson and arrived in New York the following morning. A fast train dropped me off at Mayerville, Vermont, just two days after I left home. It was a sleepy little farmer's town, hidden under the brow of a vast, evergreen clad mountain. I had some trouble finding a man who knew where Jason Ford had settled, but at last the clerk at the local grocery store gave me the necessary instructions for finding him.

There was no taxi at Mayerville, so I walked the entire five miles to the lonely little shingled cottage built well back from the equally lonely road.

I wish I had never found it.

THE HOUSE was neat appearing from the outside, and hidden among the pines about fifty yards from the rutted road. It was very old, with two windows and a single door that stared down at me like a weather-beaten face, and not at all friendly in its leering intentness. The shingles were brown and aged, and the white trim was chipping off.

There was a lean-to kitchen attached to the rear of the place, and the whole thing seemed to be supported by the steep hill at the rear, against which the lean-to was built. I had often seen the arrangement, built in a manner to allow a tunnel into the hillside, where food was preserved from the warmth of summer weather.

My knock brought only the sudden response of a barking dog. I don't know why the sound chilled my blood, but I remembered at once the sacred dog and the fact that Ford had mentioned the beast in his letter. I knocked several times, and finally, in desperation, I tried the door. It was open.

Until now, I had cursed myself for coming so far, only to find that Jason Ford had never so much as entered this place. I knew at once that he was here, or had been, for about the dusty front room was stacked trunk upon trunk, and pieces of his equipment were in evidence immediately. My eyes noted the elephant tusk tossed into a corner, and the African witch-doctor's headpiece hanging on its tip. Across one of the trunks lay the brilliant red robe and peaked cap of a Tibetan monk.

"Jason," I called. "It's Mark Billings, and I'm damned well thirsty."

No reply. The dog sneaked into the room, his tail curled tightly between his legs, and stood by the door with his teeth bared. I called again, but I didn't *expect* an answer. The dog, a mangy, filthy creature, growled at me.

I went toward him slowly, and tried to quiet him with my voice. I knew that I must pet him if possible and assure him that I was a friend. He would have nothing to do with me, but turned and slunk into the kitchen.

I had decided to search the entire house, then leave a note for Jason and return, for the night, to Mayerville. Jason would probably show up by tomorrow. I could hardly blame him for not being at home, for I hadn't notified him that I was coming.

I entered the kitchen. I had been right about the lean-to. Evidently the wall had been cut through to the hill, and a tunnel constructed into the rock. These tunnels made excellent storage places for all manner of foods.

One thing troubled me deeply. *The place where the wall of the house had been cut through, was sealed up tightly with huge, well worn slabs of rock.*

The dog howled at that moment, crossed the floor and stretched his lean frame out against the pine flooring. He pressed himself tightly to the rock wall, as though he was guarding whatever lay beyond.

I stared about the dark kitchen, and a feeling of indescribable horror came over me. The kitchen range, a wood burner, was rusted and in terrible condition. On its top were two brass bowls. One was filled with dried, shelled corn. The other was half full of dirty water. A little row of god images stared at me from the semi-darkness. At this moment, I knew that the wall was more than the sealed entrance to a cold-cellar. It was a reproduction of the Sande-puk grotto of the doomed monk.

Jason Ford was sealed behind that wall, and he was not sealed there by his own hand. I can't attempt to explain my reasoning, for I did not try to explain it logically. The stones were all in place, smooth and thick, and sealed from the outside.

*I knew that I would never open the crypt.*

I should. I should tear those stones down as fast as I could, and attempt to rescue what lay behind that wall. Jason Ford had not chosen this place for his home. He had been lured here, and had been sealed into that tunnel.

THERE WAS a sickening fear inside me. Once a monk had been sealed within a grotto. He had gone there of his own accord, and a white man had delivered him from a fate that he had been willing to face. The monk had had his revenge.

Jason Ford was alive, I thought. He would remain alive for a time, and I was, in reality, standing in the Temple of Linga, staring at the grotto and at the altar. I was alone here, with the sacred dog, and . . . ?

The dog howled at that moment, and I tried to thrust from my mind the image of the sniveling, groveling creature behind the wall. I tried to pray for strength, but prayer failed me in the presence of those Tibetan gods. I saw monks parading before me as shadows. Their weird peaked caps hid their faces, so that I was aware only of coal-black accusing eyes.

*I knew that I wasn't capable of saving Jason Ford's life.*

Most of all, I was incapable of facing the torture that was sure to come to me if I chose to tear down that wall. A coward? Yes! Of course I'm a coward. I think you might have been a coward also, if you had to dream of being sealed into the cold, dark grotto of Sande-puk.

I think you would have fled as I did, with the howl of the sacred dog echoing in your ears. I think you would have shivered in wretchedness until you were safely aboard your train, and then, in the privacy of your compartment, buried your head in your arms and sobbed like a child.

I can't be sure that all men are as cowardly as I.

PERHAPS they found Jason Ford's body. If they did, the storekeeper no doubt remembered that I had asked him where I could find Ford. I was never seen in or about Mayerville after that night. I suppose they called it murder and blamed the whole incident upon me, the "mysterious visitor." It's just as well.

I wonder if, locked behind that wall, alone with his thoughts, Jason Ford finally found the true salvation? I know that I am too much of a coward to interfere with the affairs of ghostly Tibetan monks. Perhaps if you had been there, events would have turned out otherwise. Perhaps you would have torn down the wall and found him alive.

If you had, perhaps *you* would have been sealed in such a place. Perhaps you would have been taught the words that Jason Ford must have found ample time to repeat over and over, desperately, behind the wall of his carrion crypt.

*Om-mani-padme-hum* — Salvation is found only in the true faith.

*Hortense Calisher*

# THE SUMMER REBELLION

T HE SINISTER thing about Hillsborough, since I come back, is that the soda parlors are gone. You have to know the place why. Since I *came* back — O.K. I could talk that way even before I left for the Agricultural; why else did my Aunt Mary bring me up to read every old book in the shop, and hang my junior excellence medal in the parlor — though she never hung the one for sharpshooting — and sell off, to the summer people to build a house of, that last old cypress-colored barn we had at the edge of where the acreage once was? They were going to use it to build a house. But if I like to talk that way at my convenience, it's like putting on jeans again after Sunday dinner and church — or it used to be. The whole trouble must have begun, I think, when the summer people started wearing our jeans. But that was way back; I don't go that far back personally. Our family goes eight generations in Hillsborough, but I only go as far back as when it began for us, when those two come to buy the barn. That's as far back as I like to go.

"Cedar," says the man, and the woman whispers *Did you ever see such weathering!* and I'm standing by, about fourteen years old, and I start to say, "Why, that ain't cedar, it's bir — ," when my aunt's fingers, steel-hard from sanding old trestle tables to the pine again and emerying off the chipped places on flint glass, grabs me at the neck. "Don't say 'ain't,'

Johnny One — you know how to talk right!" So I do; isn't she always jabbing at me "Talk like the summer people — you don't have to pay any attention to what they *say!*"

She's still holding me. "This boy has got hisself a medal," she says. She can say "himself" just as well, too. But this way, the pair will think the old shack — which isn't birch but isn't cedar either — is just what they want for front trim.

"Why do you call him Johnny One?" the woman says, curious.

This is the first time I date to that my aunt speaks the way she then does — vague — even for all that energy she's putting out, getting rid of all our junk first and then all she can find in the neighborhood. And how she looks; I notice that too. Faded. "Why do I call him Johnny One?" she says, the way people do, bidding for time, and when they've never noticed themselves before. "Why, my sister — what was her name? — she only left one." She smartened then — why she used to be so smart, smarter than me! "Why, I guess I call him Johnny One cause I haven't got two!" And then she and I, my neck free now, looked back triumphantly; from our ways lately, that explanation seemed clear enough.

They bought the barn — which wasn't a barn. But on their way off, I snaked through the woods alongside of the path they took back to their car — I used to like to watch summer people the way any boy, all of us children liked to watch the doings of ghosts who never intended or did anything mean to us except bring gifts and then in the fall fade away again — and I heard them talking, different than they talk to us, the way they talk to each other. " 'My sister, what was her name?' " said the woman. "Can you imagine!" When I went off to the A., I found out of course what she meant. Our town sure had been dragging its feet — though it wasn't the only hill town in New Hampshire to do it, not by a longshot, I found.

But at the moment I was more interested in what the man said. "You pipe the boy?" They don't always talk so fine themselves.

"Did I!" she said. "Whew."

"Quite an Apollo, wasn't he."

"If there were two," she said giggling, "who could bear it?" She sighed. "What a waste. Such a beautiful kid."

"Think that barn *is* birch?" said the man.

"Of course not. Let her think she's putting something over on us, poor thing, if she wants. But you and I know what it would cost at a lumberman's, aside from the *color*. To buy all that oak."

That was the way it always turned out between Hillsborough and the summer people, from the very first, when we sold off the land by the lakeshore that was no good for farmland if they only knew, and woods that didn't have nothing in them, anything in them but birch. Until I came home this June, I didn't know who was to blame. I found that out at the college. Let me tell you about Hillsborough, first.

When you come north by the state road, on your way to the White Mountains, the road goes straight for a while, past a few houses; then all of a sudden it humps up very sharp, through a few stores at the hilltop, with a side road going east over the hill and down out of sight. If you continue on, there's a garage and some empty stores at the bottom again, then whoosh, the town is gone. If you park your car at the top and stay a while — that's us. Or if you've been there forever.

In the summertime, with the summer people all here, used to be such a big bottleneck in that ring of stores, on a Friday shopping especially, that the town board had the hump all divided in those slanted, white-painted parking lines. Still is a bottleneck, but if you look hard and knowing enough, it's mostly all tourists, of a bright summer afternoon. As they drive up the hill, on their left side, first comes a few old mashed-together buildings every town here has, nobody knows much what they were, then comes the closed-up church, then the store where the number one soda parlor always was, and then the supermarket, once the barbershop and the corner shoe. It came the last few years ago, for the summer people, but it may be too late for them. Has a coke machine out front. Next to it is The Service Shop, still there. That's for sewing wools and stuffs, the kind of thing women call "notions," and seems to last, no matter what. Or old Mrs. Hupper who keeps it does. "Shut up shop, or hang herself," she says, before she'll go to selling junk as antiques. Still has a few customer ladies from the lakeshore, so old and pinkfaded they still look to us like all the lakeside houses and inhabitants used to, just a summer vision that would soon fade.

On the other side of the crest of our hill, hung over the steep road that goes off it down and east, is a numb little grocery, just the sort you'd think we'd shop in ourselves — washed-out cardboard signs in windows under the old house eaves, and packaged bread. But in the fall, you'd be surprised how bright it is, when the fishing talk is over and the gun talk begins. Fellow who owns it, used to have his gun collection hung on the wall right over the milk-and-cheese counter, until he sold it, all but one deer rifle, last year. And nowadays he stocks frozen food and all that, like for the summer people, and we eat it, hoping for health. But it may be too late for that too.

Next to him, just before you get to the crest, used to be the second soda place, just a home restaurant but where we kids could go for ice cream; now it sells sandwiches in booths meant for tourists, but it has no beer and looks like it would have the crummy coffee we do have, so they don't go in. And neither do we. And back down the hill, next to that, used to be a stationery and male notions sort of place; he had a malted-milk machine we could hang around too — but he was no Hupper, he's gone too, though not far. Most any afternoon until dusk, you can see him sitting there on his front lawn behind the tables with anything from hubcaps to kitchenware to framed saints' pictures on them; often he's there with a light, after dark. Or in the morning, if he's not, the tables are, and anybody takes the trouble to knock, he's out in a jiffy. "Just shavin'. What vase? Be one dollar, that vase." Anybody takes the trouble to go down any of our side roads, will find any of us with our things all set out, sitting back of the tables, or in a rocking chair if we're old, or inside. We're a town on a hill, so we can't stretch the business out straight like some can, and catch it all in one trough. And we haven't got the knowhow like Fitzwilliam, where the professionals are. Or the houses and granges and live churches to look at, like Hancock. Houses and hardware both, we run closer to junk than antiques. But you'll find us. Behind that hillside everywhere, is us. We're still there.

On the grocery's eave, pointing down the east road, there's a marker says Aunt Marietta's Antiques. That's us in particular, I and Aunt Mary, and her husband, my uncle Andy — in our family there's only one of each of us. Before you come to our house, there's the mill — the standard, red brick, New England, New Hampshire knitting mill, with its sluices and iron gone to rust, and what seems like a hundred gross of spidered windowpanes, not half enough of them knocked in. Those Victorian windowpanes stay orderly looking until the end, and good red brick don't ever seem to fall, or get haunted. Those greenery things, sumac and ailanthus, that always take over, look feathery nice around it. It could start up again in a minute, you think, passing by. Opposite it though, is what, after the church of course, used to be our real pride.

It's a chocolate-and-tan frame structure of some seven stories high, built in the seventies, with balconies and fretwork running even and complete around every story; if it leaned just a little, or was skinny and not square, it would look like a monument. As it is, it is supposed to be one of the last specimens of that architecture, and when we first had Aunt Mary's shop, she used to take picture postcards of it, which sold very well. I don't know why she hasn't the get-up to, anymore. Or I'm beginning to think I do. Anyway, the Geracis, who now own it, you sometimes hear one of them tell a tourist it was a hotel, but it never was; it was a kind of high-class rabbit warren for the mill workers to live in, with enough railing and banisters to match those factory windows across the way. To give the Geracis credit, they keep it painted. They're Italians, Hillsborough's only, and they still have the energy for a place like that, and the relatives; Italians can always take in each other's washing from all the other onlies in the towns roundabout, and keep separate that way; in the basement they even have a store none of us sets foot in, unless ours runs out of something and we haven't got the gall to sneak in opposite to the supermarket, which is what we would like best. The Geraci children still have separate names, too — saints' names, but separate.

And after Geraci's, down the road that leads straight to the lake shore and to all the summer people, that's us in particular. Our house is one of the larger old white ones, an old Apollo of a house, you might say, and we are accustomed to hearing, in summer, how beautiful it — could become. In winter we are inclined to think how comfortable it could be — to keep. But we still have it, and we're the only house out that way, with our back garden — or that once was — on a little rise too, and pointed straight toward the lake that is really a huge, circular "pond" as we call it — Willard Pond — and toward them. We're the only family on the way to them, and that is our peculiar distinction — though we have another. Between them and us, is our woods, or what used to be ours, where, last year, I used to make out with one of their Barbaras. From our back windows we can see them, in all their homes they've made out of our houses and our barns — stretching on and on in a half-circle, but even bright with upkeep though they are, a mirage.

In summer, what with boats and docks and waterskiers this year and all that gradual growth of plastic, they tend to seem brighter, and it's true every year they seem healthier, staying on longer each year. They like to keep up what they call their relationship with us; that helps to keep them healthy too. "That's *their* upkeep," my aunt once said tartly. Truth was, she thought some of their ladies liked to keep it up with my uncle, who at thirty-nine years old is blonder and taller than I am, a retired Marine with muscles that last year he used to maintain, too, with a set of barbells my aunt swapped somewhere.

The swap shop was no distinction, only what my aunt got into years ago out of sheer energy and not liking to embroider, starting it out as a gift shop with a line of dollclothes, and those new gilt memento cups — none stamped for Hillsborough, we were too small for that, but Portsmouth and so forth — when the new people came. If they started her on the antiques, always being so wistful after our chipped buttercrocks and old end-of-day vases, who was to blame? Meanwhile, it didn't say we weren't just as healthy as ever, only rightfully lazier — if now and then we swapped a bit of land. Or woods that were mostly only birch. White birch is good sure enough for those new-style kitchen cabinets. But the sawmill over at Nubanusit is all ailanthus too.

And meanwhile, there they were, only the summer people, that mirage across Willard Pond. We took care of their houses, shut off their waterpipes and promised to turn them on again come "the season," and to mow their first lawn. Come Labor Day, they began to go. Come October, they were gone. With their extra keys jingled away in our dresser drawer, we forgot them, or sometimes, just to check up of course, in the performance of duty, we toured their houses and habits from top to bottom, fingered their linen and the quilts they'd bought from us, laughed at that other junk, the cobalt glass bottles and a Stafford pitcher in the window and somebody from Antrim's greatgranny on the wall — and remembered to remind ourselves how faded, like the new owners, all this was. Come November, when gun talk was all over the grocery, bright as apples and the huntsmen's china teeth, we had forgotten them altogether. Mrs. Hupper took the needlepoint wool out of her window and hung there a glorious pink-and-purple afghan, with a sign saying it was to be raffled for the church, and chances could be bought right there. The church itself came open, with a visiting preacher every third Sunday. And then at last, our real mirages took over again all the way, from the woman in white you could see on one of the balconies at Geraci's on a moonlit evening, to the sea monster that was supposed to be in the Pond.

This was all the change I noticed until I went away and came home from college, but that's supposed to be natural, isn't it? — even though college wasn't the real state university I like to say. It was a state-run one, sure enough, but the old two-year Agricultural and Manual-training unit, switched off now from Guernseys, and onto economics and business courses — gone to that kind of grass. There were a lot of dopes there who would do well at these, plus a few hopelessly smart ones, still on the agriculture, like me. We quickly discovered who we were — there was usually about one of us from a particular town.

We were the aristocrats of the upkeepers, all of us, and many of us were the Apollos, too, who some summer person had stuck the idea of a scholarship in the mind of, or had even written away for to help him, all the way back from "Ooo, Aunt Mary, what a beautiful little boy you have, and so smart." And keep him away from my Barbara. We knew who we were, and began pooling our information right away. We were the elite.

And we were the ones (though we learned to hide it except among one another) who came from the towns where people's names had gone back to grass too. The way we found out about each other was — there were so many Johnnies. There are always a lot of people named John anywhere, I understand that. But were there ever so many boys who answered — unless they were quick enough — to the names of Johnny One, Johnny Two, Johnny Three and so on? We even had one Johnny Ten, but he was unusual. Our families weren't so big anymore.

"Sometimes even the summer people do better," said the boy in whose room we were, a skinny Johnny One from over to Contoocook, but still with a lot of tawny gumption in his cheek — he didn't eat their frozen, and his folk had a pig littered every spring; wouldn't let them eat *her,* wouldn't let them sell her either.

"Over our way," another said proudly, "we've still got Buddy names as well; my best friend is a Buddy Four" — but he wasn't much. And there were a few other reports of the old original names, the tombstone ones — Lukes and Patiences and so forth — though there would still be only two names to a family, for the girls and for the boys. But mostly, the families were running to Mary One, Two and Three and so forth for the girls, and Johnnies of the same.

"Why is it do you suppose it's happening?" said Johnny Ten, not the brightest of us, only there because if a Ten wasn't eligible, who was?

Nobody liked to say, even among us though there wasn't a boy didn't have an inkling.

"But I can tell you why we've still got our different last names," said the boy from Contoocook. "Otherwise, it would be too confusing to them — even though they don't much use those. And too noticeable. This way, we can just fade quietly. And they can keep tally on us, like they like to do of the oldest stones in the graveyard."

Well, we didn't do much but form the club, that year. Freshmen do that. Then we came home, and I suspect that ordinarily the same thing would have happened to the boys from those other towns as to me; clubs fade too, like winter seasons. But now it was summer again. And I was shocked to the gills when I saw my uncle and aunt. People not forty years old yet don't just all of a sudden look like that, not when they've both always been lively as a barn dance — not unless they have a mortal disease. And it wasn't as if they just suddenly looked older in any healthy way, or even downright old, the way some people's hair turns gray overnight. He was still blond as could be; she was still brown. Morning early, and evening late, that is. In the strongest noon light, you couldn't quite tell.

What's sucking them? — I thought, but we are a reserved family and I knew even if I could bring myself to ask, they wouldn't say. They moved lightly these days, and vaguely — my uncle, with tattoos half the length of his burly forearm, and his machinist's shoes and his heavy fingernails powerful as old yellow horn! — and their thoughts seemed to come from a long way back.

"Look at *him!*" cried my aunt when she saw me, "Oh, Johnny One." Her face puckered up, not much, just faintly, and then she stepped back, and put her hand to her hair in an absentminded way, and said in a thin voice, almost cold, and to my uncle, "Maybe he shouldn't of come back at all!" She hadn't the energy you see, to feel more.

But I was just inside the door and I hadn't tipped to any of it yet; I was waiting as usual for her to fall all over me and my growth like when I'd been to scout camp — in the winters, I'd used to hear her whispering at him in bed, "We've got to manage it for him another year, Andy, we've got to — we can't let him stay here all summer long." I was waiting for my uncle to thump me and kid around, and even for my aunt to say with a toss of her head that over at Willard Pond, they'd better look after their Barbaras, whereupon I would have to look both wise and innocent — for it was already too late to prevent that, too.

Instead my aunt came up to me and timidly touched me on the sleeve. And passed her finger like a dandelion-fluff over my cheek. "You're so red," she said. "And your eyes, so blue. Don't tell me they feed *you* packaged stuff." And I said, bewildered, "No, the college has got its own farm — part of the program is we have to work it." And before I could say any more, she burst out, "Oh Johnny One, Johnny One, maybe you should go away for good *now.*"

"What are you talking about?" I said. "This is our place." And it is too, though it's only free and clear because they won't give *us* a mortgage on it, and there isn't much to it except the windows and walls, still thick and healthy, and the bit of furniture we swapped to keep. We were lucky in some ways, some said. Some have waited until the place is so slatted to the roof, there's nothing of it to sell at all.

"You're not going to *sell,*" I said. "Why, I could paint it up here in no time — if you could get the paint. And the roof too — I see where the water's come through."

My aunt looked crafty — I'd never seen her look like that before. Even when she was cheating them a little, not with any outright lie; she'd look merry. "Not on your tintype," she said — when you haven't the energy, you sound hard and mean when you only intend to sound strong.

"Catch me doing up what they'd only tear away. This place won't tumble, not in our time. But I'll make them pay the higher for every fence hole, inside and out. They like it better that way — don't I know from the shop? They like to start from *scratch*."

Brrr. How that word sounded when she said it, half snake, half claw. I looked around me more carefully. The shop was gone of course — that went last year, no great decision, just weaseled away with the last load of goods. They could start up again, any time they had the gumption, and could fix the car. In the old farmland, it used to be when the cow died; now the cow is the car. But they still had their jobs surely.

"How're the Blazers?" I said. The Blazers are *our* summer people.

My uncle clicked a thumbnail. "Mr. Blazer is thinking of doing his own garden. He was telling me only the other day how healthy it makes him, not only to eat. 'The old customs, Andy; we should all go back to them.' He's learning to do it all quicker than me. Got a lot of energy, that man. He showed me. Only thing he don't do good yet is all that boxwood he just put in, front of the house. He's no hand with the clipping shears yet. But he learns fast."

I looked over at my aunt. She hung her head, then looked at me sideways and through her hair, like those moron-children in our local family of the same. O my darling chubby, freckle-tan aunt, where had she got to?

"Aunt Marietta!" I said. That was her full name, sunk away somehow. And do you know, she straightened a little, and the color came back to one cheek.

"That's it!" said my uncle. Usually he didn't do the thinking for the family. He took a step forward, stamping as hard as if it was a resolution all in itself. But he was all excited. "*We'll* go back to the old customs. I'll be Andrew again." Not Mr. Blazer's Andy, is what he meant. "And he'll be our John, or our Johnny. But not Johnny One. That way it won't touch him, he'll stay healthy. That way, he can stay."

"And I'll make a garden!" I said. "I could do it out on the — " And then I looked outside, and remembered. What wasn't all dock and burr, and those good New Hampshire boulders which take block-and-tackle to move where it doesn't take eight generations of wall-building — was gone to wood. We'd let our old woods, sold to them, creep up on us. They hadn't seemed to mind. But there was worse than that. The trouble really didn't begin when they started wearing our jeans. When the old tools began to go, that was the beginning — from when we couldn't tell, even ourselves, was a tool to stay in the barn or go to be sold in the shop?

My aunt hung her head down again. But my uncle's idea, poor Andy muscleman, had really bolstered him. "Marietta, our John is home," he said, all dignity. "I'm going to shave."

I watched him while he did it. His great weightlifter's arm, molded in biceps, always did look funny handling that delicate razor, but now it looked foreshortened too, like all the rest of him, as if something underneath the muscles was shrunk. He looked all shrunk and contorted, like those woodenheaded character dolls we used to find in a bunch of goods now and then, old shepherds and bent-over wives marked Nuremberg and Tyrol. That's the way it took him, not like my aunt; it doesn't take everybody the same. Funny thing too, I saw that though his beard and hair were still as blond as mine, the leavings in the bowl were different. I walked over to see for sure. He'd had a week's beard on him. Yes, the scrapings in the bowl were gray. Or you could call it a dim green.

All this time, my aunt, still peering at me now and then from under her hair, was fixing supper. And as the dusk came on, and before the lamps were lit, they began to look better to me. Maybe the green from outside, pressing in at the back window, rosied them a little; as we were told in art course, the complementary color to green is red. Oh I hadn't gone without learning that year; as well as the grammar and the art and the regular animal husbandry, we'd had a course in plant ecology too.

"What about that boxwood, what's that for?" I said idly, only wanting to make conversation. Soon's I got home, that's all I seemed to want to do, and not too much of it. I just wanted to sit, really. I felt tired, down to the hair on my limbs.

"Blazer wants to keep his privacy," said my uncle Andrew. "Oh, not from us." He gave a little snort — a weak one. "Not on the Pond and wood side. Round on the front side of the house. Seems the kids on their road are puttin' up a neighborhood affair to keep them out of mischief, center of that common lawn they have, used to be the old green. Oh he approves of it, helped to do that. Just don't want to see it, that's all, from the house. Band stand, or suthin'."

"Bandstand? They don't have any band," I said. Neither do we, anymore. We younger ones used to, mellaphone and xylophone. But all that beating and blowing takes it out of you. And over there, why should they bother with that stuff, summers?

"Close the window," said my aunt. "Don't look out." She went and closed the shutters, moving slow, like her own shawl. I'd never known her to wear a shawl before. And there was a line of dark on her upper lip. I never did like dark on the upper lips of ladies. Then she came and sat down again.

But I'd already seen the outside green, pressing in on us. Funny thing. Our own woods never seemed to close us in before — or out. But that was when they were our own.

"Think I'll go up the hill after supper," I said. "See what's doing at the soda parlor." It didn't have a name anymore, but they knew where I meant, the place next to the supermarket — where we young ones all make tracks for first. The number one Soda Parlor. Not such a bad dump that the Barbaras from over Willard Pond can't come looking for us.

"But it's gone," said my aunt.

I'd come in at night, hitching with a couple of salesmen kept me yapping and dropped me over the hill. But I'm quick to rally, at least in winter weather, or fresh from the Agricultural.

"Well, then, guess I'll have to go to the greasy spoon." The coffee-and-sandwich tourist place. No ice cream, but soda parlor number two, in a pinch. That's where they'd all be, if they couldn't the other.

"Closes at six, when it's open. Not open during the week."

Something in her tone put me wise. I hadn't been back all year.

"And Schlock's malted?"

"He's been junking since spring." My aunt began a kind of sing-song. "Kelley One, Kelley Two, up the Niansit Road, they're junking, doing the best of any, they've got Irish blood keeps them going, and they never even knew what was in that barn of theirs from thirty years ago when they bought the place, many's the time I tried to tell them. And Anderson, the real estate, of course they've been at it always, near far back as me, and they only do to dealers, but now the mother-in-law too. And Cargill at the Souhegan crossroads, and back of the Monadnock Road, and Pack Monadnock — " That's a mountain. "When they're not at the tables, they're digging for bottles. Bottles are very good this year. There's tables out everywhere. Up and down the Pack."

"Bottles" meant old "hand-blown" medicine bottles, from bitters to what can be only bromo-seltzers, or old commemoration bottles and so forth — I've dug those often, at the town dump, to sell back to *them*.

"But where do we hang out now?" I said.

My uncle meanwhile was rocking. Takes practice in our old Boston — he was going at it like a master. "I know what those kids — must be a grange. Saw all these colored lampshades going in, like we once had, the dining-room table. Kelleys sold them two. That's what it is. A grange."

Wasn't any reason my aunt should snap at him, more than at me. But she went for him, almost with her old spunk. "No it isn't," she said. "You know right well what it is and must be. It'll be like the woods, not to hunt in — for you. And not to swim in — for him. Like the Pond." Then she turned to me. "It's to be what they call a teenage hangout," she said.

So then I was so tired. I didn't say anything, didn't say nothing. Either way — I didn't. Supper was fixed; you'd never believe what. I ate it, but I won't talk about it, even now.

And the next morning, I was up early to go up over the hill and see for myself, about the town. At least I meant to, but somehow I slept until noon. When I got there, it looked lively enough, cramjam with tourists. They didn't stay on the hilltop long; just parked their cars in the white lines — and everywhere else — and spread out by foot. They have some idea that coming up to a table, if you don't see their license, you won't know they're not local and soak 'em for it. But they look so healthy, you can always tell. They're not a mirage, summer *or* winter. They're just passing through, so you can say it. They're real.

And I thought, not seeing anybody who was anybody — my age that is — that maybe the Agricultural gets out earlier than their schools would, from the old days when the farm boys had to get home. But there was none of our town kids around either; few as there are left, there wasn't a Johnny or Mary of any denomination, in sight. Later on, I knew where they were; if they weren't digging bottles, they were rocking in their junior-size rockers, to guard the tables, or just hanging on the front steps, looking sideways through their hair. But just then I had to walk up and down the whole street a dozen times, to convince myself. There wasn't a one of us kids, either from Willard Pond or our side, in town.

I hung around until after suppertime, not being over anxious for it, and at the grocery steps — ours of course. After supper would be the time, if any. Not much custom came by — two. One was a great strapping beauty of a girl we older boys had been warned away from ever since she went to live by herself, even before the school shut down for good. Other was her sister. Beautiful as sin they still were, even yet. Fading had even helped them; their hair was a cooler color, and it rippled, rippled down their backs. Going in and coming out, they made a sign of interest in me, but they couldn't maintain it. I could see they didn't know who I was anymore, but I wasn't only glad, as I watched them away, I was scared, past any connection with them alone. We always had some moustached old ladies in the town, and some of the Geracis have like a pencil smear, but this, on these girls' upper lips, above the pretty pucker, was different — a green mold. And I knew it didn't have anything to do with their sinfulness — on account of my aunt.

When they were gone, I got up and went inside the shop. The owner was sitting there, just like an album leftover of last year. Only thing shining was his china teeth; I never knew why the old hunting men around there always either had them, or else none. Maybe because only the old ones still knew how to hunt. I could see he didn't know me either, or try, though he was once the one first let me have a shot at the target. But they always have a big calendar, and there it was, hung right under the big long-barreled gun they never used but said was for deer.

"I just want to see the date," I said. "The day of the month. I just want to see for sure what day it is in June." For though I was sure I'd been home long enough for any school to be out by now, I couldn't remember.

He didn't move any more than a wooden Indian. He let me lean right over him. I saw that the calendar page was still at October. Had an Audubon picture above the empty days, a mother woodcock with her brood nice and quiet and ready, in a field. I started to lift the page.

"Leave that be." He didn't move. His eyes were pink, from staring ahead.

"I just wanted to — "

He raised his hand to the gun. The hand was shaking, but kind of an old brown-pink too, almost healthy. And by God, the gun barrel was shining too, more than anything else in sight in Hillsborough. I had to admire his energy.

"It's always October here," he said as I left the shop.

But being the age I am, the soda parlors seemed to me the most sinister. "Sinister" is a word our plant-and-forestry instructor begins the hour with almost every morning; it's his first year too, and he comes from one of the fancy places, Cornell. He's only teacher-in-training to us, before he goes off to the job he's going to get after the summer, in research. "Be seated, gentlemen," he always says, "and let me impart to you another sinister fact about the ecology of our world." Then he flashes a grin at us, to show us we can be at our ease, but if he gave the command, he could keep some of us straight in our chairs for double the time. Talk about D.D.T., that's only the beginning; he can tell you a hundred different ways, from detergents to depth-bombs, how the natural balance of the world is being upset. And another hundred brave ways of how nature plans to keep it. About the rise and fall of all plants, and how certain plants, even trees, have to have other trees near by them, little numbly ones you would never look at for themselves, in order to survive. "Survive" is another word he's always at, when he isn't at the other. Boy, has he ever given it to us. Even Johnny Ten knows what Ecology is. It's our favorite course. "Even about the Dutch elm, boys, don't be so quick to blame it all on that beetle, or even that aphid they're blaming now. Look for some tree, maybe the commonest genus in the world, that isn't standing by any more, and once used to be."

It was about eight o'clock or less when I left the grocery, still to be light for an hour or so, and I decided to go to the woods and think about making out. How else was I going to meet her, otherwise? I could go through our old wood and up to the rim of Willard Pond, just one open place on it, but I couldn't go round the rim to their side, that's all theirs, and we younger ones never do — did. They always used to come here. And that's how it happened between her and me last year. I just went and sat at the edge of our woods, in the high, flat, mossy place I'd known forever, where you could lie and be seen or not seen, as you chose. I used to sit there regularly, day and evening, always at the same times, so that anybody saw me from over there, they'd begin to know. I used to just sit there, and think about making out with girls. And one day, parting the birches, from where she'd come around the rim, there she was. Of course we'd seen each other at the soda parlor before.

Usually they come in twos, if they come at all. But she came alone; that's what interested me. I like things interesting in that style. And she felt the same. We found that out quick enough about each other. But in fact, what with her family owning her place for four years now and our summer staring at each other across the soda parlor for two of those, we already knew. There are sides to a soda parlor too of course, or were — ours and theirs. But sometimes, like a wood, it can be crossed.

"Why don't you ever come and swim," she said, sitting down as graceful on my moss as if it were her own — which it partly was. She knew why of course. The Pond is private. But they like to ask. To hear us answer. Especially if we're handsome.

But I wasn't going to give her that satisfaction.

"Because of the leeches," I said.

The leeches in the pond — we'd never told any of them, when we sold off a patch of shoreline, that these were in the pond thick as seeds at the edge, or how to avoid them — by flat-diving and swimming out quick — or how to get one off if it fastened on you. Let them find out for themselves. But wouldn't you know, just as with the land and the shack that wasn't any good to us, after a while the leeches went away — the summer people's blood wasn't rich enough yet. "All goes into their money," my aunt said. We did used to swim some of course, sneaking it in early or after they'd gone. But I hadn't seen a leech in years.

"Why, I've never seen one, what do they look like?" she said.

Well, no use going over all of it. It wasn't a large conversation. She never did like to hear me talk much, and all this last year through we didn't write, didn't either of us plan any mention of that. And we'd each made out with other persons before.

But she did say that one thing.

"I'd never make out with any other one of you," she said. "Only you."

And I thought the same, or even better. It's like when the one tree knows that the other tree is in the forest, standing by. And I thought to myself that there ought to be a better word for it, than — making out.

So that evening, I went back through the woods, to our joint-owned mossy place, that evening and many more, and daytimes, too. All through what must have been the rest of June, and then July and part of August, I sat there; I hunted up a calendar at home, and counted it out. Except to creep into a store for my aunt — and then I'd sneak into Geraci's when I could on credit, for it was healthier — I never went up the hill to town at all.

And as I sat there, high in my open eyrie, I could see well enough what they were building. My, it was sharp and bright, as shining as anything on the state highway, with a baby-sized turret, orange-sherbet colored with a rod waiting for the weathercock to be fixed on it, and a plateglass entrance you could see in through, just like the state liquor store. I have excellent sight. I could see it all, like an anthill milling, at all hours of the day and late on into the evening, when they kept worklamps burning. That's why it went on for so long; they were doing it themselves, as they had learned more and more to do. I could see the boys and girls bending to their jobs, but could not always tell one girl from the other, because of that long hair style falling over their faces, and their same halters and jeans. Sometimes I could. My, how bright and particular and blooming it had gotten to be over there on the lakeshore, and not all with plastic either! Browning that way in their gardens, putting up their preserves in our old Mason jars, even hoisting lumber as if they saw a block-and-tackle every day in the week — they're getting healthier. I could see well enough what they were up to. I clenched my hands in the moss, and thought about it. It wasn't so far to across there; it only had always seemed to be.

Then, one day just at the end of summer, she came. It had taken a long devotion of my sitting there, but I had always known she would. And if it had taken longer than last year, this was because back then I'd just been dreaming on it generally, on making out with any girl. I hadn't been thinking of it with Barbara Blazer.

That's who it was of course. After all, even after another summer, if it is known where to look, the tree can see the tree.

When she parted the birches and came in, I wondered how I could ever have confused her with the others, even at a distance. Her hair was the longest, long and straight as any sin. A gold hoop hung in the ear I could see. The lobe was red, where the hoop of light pinched it. Her mouth matched the ear. Above, the sun was just going down, ahead of the dusk. My, I said to myself — she looks strange for a member of that mirage. So rosy and separate.

She came and sat down beside me, graceful as ever, on the moss. I dug my fingers in it, but I couldn't make it just mine any more. It's too late for it.

"Late this year," I said. "Aren't you."

She tossed back her hair. The other ear had a hoop in it too, and a pulse of red. "Oh, we're *very* late — we meant to have it ready by midsummer." She flicked a look at me, and away, and sighed. "Like father says, you have to work hard to know how hard work *is*."

For a minute I didn't answer. Then I said, "Well, you'll have long enough to use it. If you're going to stay on longer this year."

Or all year round. That's what I'd been telling myself. That's what my aunt had been telling me. When able.

While the sun went down, she didn't answer. Then she said low — I will say she speaks low, not screech-owl like some of them — "It was you, wasn't it, put that pine-pillow heart under my bed pillow, up at the house? After the house was closed?" We were neither looking at the other, but she felt my nod. "You dope," she said, "wouldn't you know my mother'd find it before I did. But we were lucky. 'How sentimental of her,' my mother said. 'Guess she wants to show us how much she likes us, to stay on.' She thought it was your aunt."

"It was sentimental," I said. But the thing had been around our family a long time. I thought they liked that. I'd even had to mend it. "I thought you'd like it." And it was all I had.

"A Pillow of Pine for a Sweetheart of Mine," she said. "You dope." But she smiled. "It was pretty grundgy by the time I got it. You must have put it there way last fall."

"I've been away since then."

"I know." We still weren't looking at each other. "But we know you all go through the house when we're not there and look us over. We've always known. We can tell." And then, maybe even not conscious of it, just as I looked at her, she wrinkled her nose.

Anger makes for strength. "I was at *college,* all year."

"I heard. We're very proud of you — the only one in town. And that's why I came over." Her hair hid her face. She spoke through it. "I thought maybe you could do something with your aunt and uncle. Mainly with your aunt. Before my mother has to tell her. She's gotten so — careless with herself — not even worth her pay, my mother says. The house was a sight, when we walked in. All spidery. And your uncle remembered to turn the water back on, but left the sump-pump going. Oh that's all right, we're sentimental too, my father says — to a point. But — "

I thought she would never be done, and the funny thing was it almost didn't seem to matter. When it's too late altogether, what can it matter — once you know that?

"But we've had a new baby," she said. "And around a new baby, you simply can't have somebody like that. Could you somehow — jack her up?"

It's all in the balance of it. They don't intend to be mean.

Laughing helps too. I rolled back against one of the birches, laughing as hard as I could, and then sat up again. "Why she must be forty years old. Your mother." She's forty-two; we know everything about them. And how dare she, with her skinny little bikini figure and dyed red curls? When there hadn't been a baby in our family since me — and my mother'd died of it.

She giggled. "Oh, the country's great for us. Even the doctor said it. Or maybe it's the moons."

"Going to be one tonight," I said.

Say a thing like that, and it shakes you with it. My hand walked across the ground and took hers.

"Oh golly, don't say it," she said. "We've got to open the place by the full moon, we've promised ourselves. Lanterns and all." But her voice was false; she wasn't listening to it half as much as to her hand. She let me keep it. And then at last, she looked up.

It was dusk by now, but I tried to see myself in her eyes like in a mirror; we don't have a good one at home any more.

"What's the baby?" I said. "Boy or girl?"

"Girl." Her hand was still in mine. "You're so pale," she said. "Whatever makes you look so pale?"

Must be the hair on my head, I thought; with no barbershop on the hill, I hadn't had a trim all summer; how do their heads support all that hair?

"How many Barbaras does that make in your family?" For I knew she had at least one sister; couldn't remember if more. "Will that make her Barbara Three or Four?"

"Her name's *Anne*," she said. "What do you mean?" But she knew. Her hand had come away from mine. "That's moron stuff," she said. "That's that awful family with the whiteheaded, pink-eyed children. Down back of the factory. They say that." Her lip shivered, and she held it with her teeth. They aren't china. "You were always just Johnny."

My hand felt lonely. I made like sweeping a cap off my head to my knee. I was standing up by now, braced against the birch. "Let me introduce you. To Johnny One."

Her hand went to her mouth. She was still on the ground, at my feet. "You were still so handsome," she said. "Just a little while ago, when you first came back." She looked about to cry. "What's the matter with you people?"

"You were watching," I said. "All the time?"

"Yes — I was watching." It sounded as if she hated it.

"Can you really see us that well, over there? I always wondered." I leaned against the birch, which helped. Some of the full grown birches have one high fork, like a giraffe face up there on its long, scribbled bark neck. But this one is just a sapling, with the crotch still low enough to rest an elbow in.

"Not really. But I can always see you."

It was like our last year's promise. I dropped back to the ground. That was a relief. I was about to kiss her. Two can suck strength together. Then I saw the black spot on her leg.

"What's that! Barbara Blazer — you've got a leech there."

"Oh golly, have I? They're in the lake in droves this year."

It was on the calf of her right leg. Both of us stared down. I for one never saw anything like it, on us. The little black thing wasn't deep in yet. But it was already fat and red too. Rich.

"You wait right here," I said. "I'll go back for matches. You know what we have to do." If it's not too far in, it'll shrivel. "Or you could come back with me —" I hadn't meant to say that. But maybe if she saw us at home, with everything still there that couldn't be sold — the fanlight, and the banister like a turned ribbon, and the floors — maybe they'd see us better. "If it's in too deep, my aunt has a special knife." Or did once. "She's very good at it."

"Don't be sil — " Though we had our arms round each other, her voice had turned silvery again. "Don't be ar*chai*-ic. We've had them all summer. Daddy's got a compound you just touch them with — they drop right off. And I wouldn't want your aunt — " In spite of herself, she shivered. I saw the nostril again. But she didn't mean to. It's their strength.

"Won't it suck your strength?" I said. "Hadn't you better — ?" But I knew she could wait. I touched the hoop in her ear — the thinnest wire.

"I'll go home in a minute," she said, snuggling deep into my shoulder. "Then I'll come back." The voice was last year's voice. And my mouth was already on her mouth, taking strength.

How did she spring away? They're like electric, these people. Their feet these days must scarcely touch the ground. There she was, arms spread out against another young birch, yards away. "What's that awful thing on your lip?"

The moon was up. We could see each other clearly. But I knew she wouldn't let me move back close, to see myself in her eye-mirror. And I knew what it was. My hand went to my upper lip, rubbing. At first I couldn't feel anything; then it was there, cool as down under my forefinger. "It's — my moustache." But I knew I was looking at her sideways.

"Green?" She whispered it. "Green?"

"It's the moon. It must be." I whispered back. Funny though, how you fade all the faster. Once you know.

For she made a sound in her throat like a squirrel. "Johnny. Look at your *hands*."

It was the nails, really. There was a line of green around each of them. I suppose it takes each person according to his substance. "It's only our moss," I said.

But I could only stand there, hands hanging, glad even that I could stand. Even if at first it takes you according to your own nature, in the end, won't it be all the same? I could feel the down on my lip now without touching it. Growing slow, like a shawl. Like the two girls at the grocery, like my aunt and uncle — I was going back to the green, to the grass, to the ground.

It was then she shrieked; I've never heard screech-owl worse. "You've got a disease! A mortal disease!" She bent over to the thing on her leg, and brushed at it as if it were me. Her head down low and forward, like a dog covering me, she breathed deep and growling, all the voices of the Blazers, hardened into one. "Keep away. Keep away. Don't you ever come near us again, any of you." She shrank back behind the birch tree. "Don't you ever even let us *remember* you." And then she ran off, low to the ground and bawling, her hand clapped to her leg.

But she had a long way to go, around *our* pond or *their* lake — anyway you look at it, and I could hear her for a considerable time, crashing her way — the sound of the mirage, going back where it belonged.

And the moon through the trees helped me find my echo. The moon was riding higher now, like a sign of how much time I had.

I called after her. "Why am I Johnny One?" I called, "Johnnnnny Onn-ne? Because there aren't two." And I knew she heard me. All her way back, my echo would carry it.

Then I went home, to see how much time I and the other boys would have to gather, home to look it up on my aunt's calendar, which is a large one, turned regularly to the last days of summer, and with many almanac directions, including moons. The strength her kiss hadn't given me, her scream had.

ON THE night of the full moon to be, we were ready for them. For almost a week past, never in our house had there been such lights and noises and creepings, such a stamping and a brawling and a *blazing* — not in my time. I'd gathered them in by every marathon way I could think of, by bikes stole at evening and then passed on, by notes sent on by the diesel gas trucks — their drivers were the decentest, by tokens jammed in the pay telephone and then a message to the firehouse, where a town had one, by everything but drumbeat — and a little of that too it almost seemed, as the call got nosed about stronger — and always by our best chariot, shank's mare. It was always hard to believe that something so modern as the Agricultural was only thirty miles away and most of the boys in near the same radius, but now that fact was gold to us. And I had done it, I and my best deputy, the skinny Johnny from Contoocook, who I'd remembered was a Johnny One too. If we had more get-up-and-go than the rest of them, it was because the onlies, like with some plants, fade slower than the rest. And we'd done it. We'd gathered in the club. Once I'd got them collected, I wondered why I hadn't saved my strength by just staring at the sky and calling them in by mental telepathy. For funny thing, I didn't hardly have to open my mouth, to tell them what they were here for.

And now here they were, lolling knees up, or on elbow and stomach, draped around like any boys you might see around a roaring fireplace, though the golden flames made them seem a mite rosier than they were. Gold of any other sort, we didn't have much of. And now, though it was only five o'clock in the afternoon and the moon not to be up for several hours yet, we could tell by our blood that it was going to be one of those Hampshire early in September nights with scarcely a nip in it. The last of the locust-nights; that's what it was. This was the way men in the wilderness used to tell the hours for fires and club-gatherings — by the blood.

And lolling with them, staring to the flames, I was almost happy, in thinking of the gathering business itself, and knowing they were too. I hadn't yet told them everything. They didn't know we were to gather at our side of Willard Pond earlier than they thought; but I'd about decided we weren't to wait for the moon. But they knew all the rest of it, learning it as they brought in the wood from here and there — because for a long time at home there hadn't been axe or arm for it — and bringing in the food by raid, like a cat with a chipmunk, or from some overlooked last pocket of rightful ownership. Bringing in the tools — that gathers people, like proudflesh to a wound. And even bringing in money if you happen to have any; it was Johnny Ten who brought in a sack, that first night we were up to score — a full dozen of us — and showed us old pennies like beans in it, and took one out, an Indian head, and then another, and said, "What's it say? Read it out." It was an old one too. "E Pluribus," I said. Anyone knew that — if you've had my aunt.

Even she and my uncle had helped me as they could, bringing out things from the attic like ideas we hadn't known we had. The old pine-needle mattresses came from the spare rooms we never went into. Like pine pillows they were, though without any inscription. My uncle'd brought out a sackful of bottles to sell, dug from the quarry once, and in ten minutes and four different directions we'd sold them, to buy the steakmeat I'd gone bold as a bear into the supermarket to buy for our strength — and we'd just now eaten, for the early supper I'd insisted on. Even my aunt said every morning "I'll make you a flag" — though she didn't quite know what for, and by evening had forgotten it. I lay there thinking of all this, from that first minute of the week, when John of Contoocook came up the heaved stones of the front walk, just as I was thinking on him, thinking on him — and I said to him, grinning. "How's that pig of yours?" And laying down the sack he was carrying, he answered me, grinning. "Here."

Gathering is the gold. They knew that now as well as I. But I lay there wondering, as any leader must, whether it wasn't all the gold we needed, whether the gathering itself mightn't be enough. But there wouldn't be time to go back to school, to find out.

"We'll train in that barn," I'd said, that first morning we were all here. Plus a peewee little Johnny from the morons; we didn't know what was his count and neither did he. He kept running in and out of our ranks, more trouble to shoo him than to let him stay. And we had to conserve our energy.

"As soon as we get the tools," I said, "we'll train. Go round to all the woodpiles and tight barns, there still are some on our side — and get the axes. Drag 'em, if you can't heft. Go round to all the antique tables after dark — hook anything sharp, or that looks like a tool. There's a thing called a sausage-grinder down in Kelley Two's barn, you'll surely have to drag that." I hadn't made definite plans yet, but that would come. "Scythes," I said.

"Will crocks be useful?" said Johnny from Contoocook. I could tell he was puzzled for a plan of action too.

"No, I don't think . . . pitchforks . . . no, there's no time for *torture* . . . it's too serious for that." I found I'd decided. "Permanent useful tools only." That way, whatever we made use of for training purposes would come in handy later also, if there was to be a later time. Would that depend on the training? And then the thought came to me, though I hadn't since told any of them, even my deputy — guns. Or at least one gun. I knew who had a sharpshooter's medal — before it was sold. Guns would be best.

You have to understand about the training. Wasn't anything we could plan to do with any weapon — tool, that is — before we could lift. That's what our training was. Over-the-summer had come to be like a hibernation time for our kind, and if we let ourselves get any weaker, this summer would likely be our last. When we could lift again, and swing and grind and mow and reap, each man alone, and not staggering onto the next one or cooling his temple against any wall that was left him to do it on, then maybe we could start to talk about action — or more of it than just a gathering on the night of the moon when their building was to be done, to make a great clatter to scare them with, over there on the opposite shore.

"Or going all the way round to their side to get our message across," said Johnny from Contoocook. "If we are able."

"Carrying the tools, of course," I said.

He looked at me over the others, stern and thoughtful as always. "Oh yes," he said, nudging me to note a Johnny Three from Nelson, who could almost lift a log singlehanded now, and a Four from West Wilton, who could handle the smallest axe. We had a couple of those Buddy names too, the one kids back at school had been so proud of — and what do you know, they turned out to be the weakest of all. "Oh yes. Carrying the tools."

And here we were, on the very night, and almost able, if that steakmeat could be trusted — and I still had no plan of action. But I had the gun.

I'd hooked it from the store maybe easier than I could handle it. Couldn't even call it a steal. He never even moved a shoulder, when I reached up above him and took it from the wall, up above the calendar. Had all I could do not to drop it; I don't know what kind of game he and his china-teeth friends ever thought they'd need a gun like that for, this part of the country. It's a high-powered rifle all right — a thirty-ought-six. With a telescopic lens. I was halfway out the screendoor dragging it in the gunnysack I'd brought, when he opened his mouth and said one word.

"Cartridges."

They were in a tin box on the counter in front of him. So I had to go back in.

And so I practiced in secret with the gun, the way they all were doing with their implements, their tools. I didn't worry about marksmanship. Once I could heft the gun, steadying my arm maybe in the crotch of a convenient tree, I knew I could fire it. And they all watched me, my army, and never said any more to me about our plan of action, just left it to me. But one thing more, I said to them. I was the leader. "We've got numbers to our names, can't help that, it's too late for it." I happened to glance over at Johnny Ten, the highest of us in number and in brain the lowest; his big round face with the silly smile on it looked just like the hubcaps he'd chosen to carry but I wouldn't let him. "But we won't say Johnny any more; that's how they weaken us too." I took a look at my uncle, snoring there in the rocker. "We'll at least say 'John.' " And my dear deputy, who worried me so, he was getting thinner every day — John of Contoocook — grinned at that too. So that's the way that was. Only one we couldn't get to understand it was the little peewee, the moron, and he didn't count; he'd be a Johnny until the end.

Otherwise, it worked fine. We'd had some trouble at first making Johnny Ten understand that our plan of action couldn't be motorcycles. "Get those snazzy foreign ones!" he'd say every day, at training-time. "Wear those black-and-white crash helmets! Then — *zoom.*" And he'd raise the pick-axe with a hubcap on it, almost high. No use telling him that we had as much chance of motorcycles as of getting boats to cross the lake with, like from England to France. There's never been any boats *between* them and us, only the boats on their side.

"What would that do for us, Ten?" my deputy would answer. His fingers were so dreamy-thin, looked as if they went round the scythe-handle twice. "No, it would just mean that we'd be the ones to move away."

Watching us try to shoulder arms — nobody would exactly see twelve high-class buck-privates. Sometimes I wondered if, even with the training, anybody could see us at all — we were so faded. My own eyesight is still so damn good. But I consoled myself with seeing how at least getting into some action must have helped our circulation. And thinking forward to being Johns again seemed to satisfy everybody, and to improve our complexion too. For the mold that had spotted everyone of us, sometimes in places you wouldn't like to think it — was gone.

One thing we talked out loud about, in those last evenings as we fed the fire before sleeping — was our ecology. We talked a lot about that, and what our summer rebellion could mean to the world. I wished I could ask the instructor. Sometimes we talked about him too, laughing at our secret nickname for him — Mr. Wilderness. For the funniest thing about him, what with all his talk about going to do research work or get him a job as a government forester in one of those high, wild tower overlooks where you can't even have a wife — was that right out in front of the classroom, where we could all see it, he had the brightest, fastest, hottest little bug of a new red two-seater sport car.

And while we talked, I sometimes watched my aunt and uncle, him barefoot now in his rocker, her in her shawl. Soon he would be only ten yellow fingernails and ten toenails — he was going back to the horn. She was dozing, my tawny aunt, with her mouth open; soon she would be only a lost freckle on the air. Was this only the way it always should be, for the other generation? But then, what about us young? I wished I could ask the instructor — even *him*. I hadn't ever told for sure whether his eyes, always so blind with teaching, hadn't seen more about us than we thought he knew. Maybe he could be our control-group, I decided; he'd taught us that in any experiment where you're matching one group of specimens against the other, in the best testing there ought to be still a third. One group, something gets done to it to produce *its* condition; to the second group, you do the opposite. The control doesn't get anything done to it at all to narrow down its condition; that's what it already is. He could be that.

So two nights ago, I had written him a letter. He could listen to what we had in mind, I thought. Better still, I thought, as I was writing, he could come to be a witness; it was nothing to that red car, only thirty miles. So I wrote giving him directions where to come and when, and what to look for, and mailed it myself and according to what I knew the distribution time for the mail was out there — so he'd get it just in time to decide to come along for the show or not to; after all that effort I didn't want us prevented. "We're having a summer rebellion," I wrote. "It's to be a test. Not a battle." For I knew it couldn't be that. "It can't be that," I said, "even with the gun. Will you be our witness?" I wrote in the best grammar I had, deciding to use that from now on too, for the other only made me weaker. And I signed it "John," without any number at all. What I'd wanted to do was to put my full last name after it, like one of their signatures — but I didn't feel up to that, yet. Besides, he'd know by the postmark and the handwriting. And he always took the trouble to talk to me specially. He'd know.

So here we were, me and my deputy and all twelve of us, not counting that little thirteenth peewee with his white albino head and pink eyes held away from the firelight. Here we are, I said to myself, in our house that hasn't caved in yet, in our flesh that isn't mold yet, and with our tools we've rescued. And over there, on the other side of Willard Pond, their work is done. Turret on the outside — waiting for the weathercock, but that they'll hang at the ceremony — and on the inside, hammered brass and hanging lanterns, and tables and chairs like a soda parlor's, and a milk bar like a counter — and a fireplace, for winter. They couldn't have an outside sign, not with their zoning rules, but just for today they had a great poster up on a tripod, with one of our iron kettles hanging on a chain beneath it. "Dedication ceremony. Everybody come and see us hang the weathercock. Six o'clock." But inside, through the glass door, I'd seen that they had a sign saying The Pancake Palace. So that's where our soda parlor number one, the old sign once on it, had gone. So there they are. Hadn't I seen it all in the storekeeper's binoculars, which on the way out his screen door the second time, he'd let me hock too? They had finished their job in time.

I went outside though, to look again for sure. Yes. It was now only a little past five o'clock, but small as the woods were, I'd better give us three quarters of an hour to get through it, even with the steak. A leader has got to plan. And I hoped I'd thought of everything, except what would have to be left to the last minute — my gun and its target. I'd half wanted to ask him that in the letter, but finally had let it be. For if I have a gun, but don't know my own target — what do I have a gun for at all?

Outside, there was even a kind of double omen. The sun was still shining in that fool's gold way it has at five o'clock. But on the other side of the world, not in any fair balance yet but trying, there was the palest full moon I'd ever seen in a sky. Even my keen sight could barely see it. Couldn't see how it would ever have the energy to rise, except that moons do.

I went back inside, slamming the house door so that it shuddered back, wide-open. That was to be our signal. We don't waste our energy. "Here we are," I said. "And it's time."

One by one, we got each other up from the pine mattresses, and began helping the others fit themselves to their tools. Yes, we still had to do that — we'd only had a week. We were still twelve in number and made an honorable display. We'd kept the pitchforks after all, they handle so easy, and even if you aren't going to use them in any other way, still their outline is so plain. I'd turned the house out, looking for my uncle's clipping-shears, then found out he'd been using Blazer's. So, after two of the forks, and counting my deputy's scythe, we had four axes, large and small according to which could best carry the weight of them, two long butcher knives, one queer-angled iron earthtiller so antique we didn't know what it was for but judged we ought to have it for that reason alone — and a hoe. Ten had let the little peewee have his hubcaps to clash.

I myself helped John of Contoocook with his scythe. We had to strap it on him; this was the only way he could manage it, and I'd have been doubtful of that except for his grin, which was still there. "Know you'll do it," I whispered to him. "After all, we don't have to do anything after we get there but stand. But stand *by!*" It was the first time I'd used that expression out loud, and his eyes flickered at it. And you have the gun, he could have said to me, but didn't. He's like me in a way, with the difference that I'd hung on to more energy. Matter of fact, he was worse off than any of us. I couldn't forbear asking him why. "Why do you suppose it is?" I whispered as I buckled the strap. His grin was like the moon, just barely there, and like the sun, getting ready to set. "It was the pig," he answered. "She was my ecology." He's hopelessly smart.

At the door then, I addressed my men at large as they went by me, both of us in a manner not to waste breath — in silence. My eyes keen upon them, I called their ghostly roll. "Johns of Four and Five — pitch-forks. Johns Two and Three, Buddy Two — axes. A John Two and a Buddy One — knives." Him with the tiller. Him with the hoe. And the rear guard. "John of Contoocook. Scythe."

To make sure that none would fall by the wayside unless all did, I roped us all together. At the last minute, one of the knives broke down and couldn't make it — one of the Buddies, wouldn't you know? So to fill up the dozen, we had to count the peewee in anyway. Then they were all ready, weaponed and gathered at the door in the formation I'd decided on

— a half circle which could at need fall into line. "You of Hillsborough," I said to them. "Of Jaffrey and Hancock, of Dublin and Antrim, of Rindge and of Nelson, and even of Keene. You of the Monadnock Region. And of the winter time. Get ready. Get Set. G — "

And then my uncle got up from his rocking chair.

He faltered over to me, clickety-click. He was even able to dig his sharp fingers into my chest; he's been a strong man in his day. "The old customs," he said, in his wooden-doll voice. "We'll go back to them. But first, we ought to know who we are, son, oughtn't we." He drew himself up straight as he could. "I'm Andrew. And that is Marietta, my wife." Hearing that name, my aunt woke, looked around bewildered, at this battalion in her old sitting room, and then smiled straight at me, too, from her shawl. "And I know you're John," said my uncle. "I *know* you're John. But son — " I felt his nails through my sweatshirt. "Son, remind me. What's our last name? Our *sur*name, as people used to say. I rock and I rock, but I can't remember it."

I smiled back at them, for love and for leaving, both. For who could know what would be, when and if we came back? And I had an awful temptation to say — "It's Wilderness." That little red bug-on-wheels maybe even now skipping toward us — he would like that. But that is not my style of interest. I know who we are. We're not that faded, not to me. And I know who I am. I've always known. It's our *other* distinction.

"It's Willard," I said. "For the Pond."

And then we filed out the door, and made up our formation again, outside it. I hadn't even had to say Go. But as we closed ranks, shouldering each as we could, with one hand, and ready to help his neighbor with the other, I heard my aunt's voice. "I'm going to make you a flag."

Then we were on the march. Marching is useful too; some say that all by itself it's as useful to the spirit as gathering is, but in our state it wasn't gold to us; it was simply what we had to do. Funny thing though, the woods, pine to maple to birch, were in perfect order for it. Even the underbrush lay quiet, as if somebody had swept. Yet I knew that although they across there had got as far as browning in the gardens and on the water, they hadn't been much to the woods yet, for health. And they hadn't paid to clear here; who would they pay that was left? Sometimes, toward autumn but before the leaves start twirling down, woods look like that, in perfect order for — something one can't say. From tree to tree, these ragged woods of my forefathers let us by now, not putting out a root to trip us, passing us on, tree to tree. They stood by us. And we walked.

And we walked. Some might have called our pace a stumble. Or only a dragging, with a rope. But it was our pace. And we did it in silence. We had no extra breath for songs. Even the peewee's hubcaps, heavy enough in his tiny hands scaled with skin rash like a lizard's, were still.

Only my gun talked, braced on my shoulder. And only I heard it; it had such a soft voice. "Blazer, Blazer, go away," it said. "Come again some other day." But that was for rain, not people. I knew that, though my own head seemed now and then about to twirl and fall. Then it said, "Hickory, dickory, your son John, took our Barbara with his britches on." Only a nursery rhyme, and wrong at that, but marching was not my true rhythm, and the air at this hour of the day was hot and cold by turns, shiver and blister both. I prayed to the steak in my stomach. I thought I could see the others were too; behind the iron and steel, their lips were moving. But for me, there was worse to come. That gun tried everything. And by the last yard of it — the whole woods isn't half a mile — that gun and I had fallen in rhythm together. "Bar-bar-a Blazer," it said, "is beautiful." And my feet answered, "Beautiful" — treading on moss now, for we were there.

We were on the shoreline of my forefathers' pond. We were on the peculiarly mossy and stony patch of it that I could call at least jointly mine, and I turned round to look at my men. They had formed their half-circle again, almost without command from me — my army, my posse, my eleven other Johns and one Buddy. And one whiteheaded peewee. But this was all they could manage. Everything had stopped, but my anger. Above our heads, the sun and moon had stopped too. Or were in perfect balance.

"At ease, men," I said. In silence, their weapons slid to the ground. One voice slid after them. "Hadn't ought to do that, John One. We'll never be able to get them up again."

"Don't worry," I said. "Anger is slow, eight generations slow. But it never stops." And trusting I was right, I inspected my ranks, as must be done before battle — or before testing, to the specimen.

Under that sky of double omen, my friends seemed to me only a step mistier than myself. Their heads were bowl-cut or longhaired like mine, but not in the new style, and their jeans and shirts were ragged, but not ragged new. They were ragged in the old style. They were a strange, weak sight, my winter Apollos, and when their arsenal was raised against that sky, they would be odder still. But maybe the people over there would see them the better for it. That's what specimens are. And they were standing by. In spite of all suffered or lazed or blamed away, they had not utterly gone down yet — into the grass, the ground.

I addressed them.

"We're a little late," I said. "It's past six o'clock." We'd taken a little longer than estimated, to go that half mile. "But I see that over across there, they are late too." I raised the binoculars, to hearten the men behind me, though I could see perfectly well without. And faithfully, my men looked heartened, though as they stared sideways under their weedy fringes of hair, I could tell that they saw across the water just as well as me. "We and they are late together," I said. "Maybe that's an omen, too."

None of my men had been with me to the shoreline before, only me and my deputy, to scout. And now, in their faces I saw all the sight before us across the water — its glass doors open to the shining games inside, and all the tanned people streaming in, or sitting without caution on the green itself. In the face of my Johnny Three, John Three — I saw a pair over there, going in through the door in their waterskis and goggles. Inside the new soda parlor, its hanging lamps were already lit to pale taffy against all that fresh white; I saw their sign, Pancake Palace, in the face of a John Two. One of our Buddies, the one left to us, was seeing that there were even red paper flames in the cookpot under the poster — the Buddy with the knife. Every man and his implement was seeing a detail of it, of that milling, laughing group of sports and silk-headed grandmothers bobbing like cotton — the whole foolish, rosy, expensive Blazer-crowd. On a bench out in front, sat a fat man, no not fat, burly, in bow tie and a flower in his jacket buttonhole — Blazer himself. There were babies scattered like plants all over the place, all with the round, superior look of babies whose mothers were not going to die. I could see it all in my men's faces. Wasn't it the way we had always seen the summer people, in the pale, expensive orange-light of the health-money they were always making? In the dream-face next to one's own, isn't that the way one always sees the mirage?

No, said the gun. This time you are seeing by yourself.

Against that joyous little turret, flipped up in paint-glow to the sun, they were now raising a black, lacy ladder. A band began to play; they had the breath for it. And to each ladder of the song, a golden-legged couple was climbing a step gracefully, hand over hand to the platform at the top. He had on cut-off jeans only, carefully sawtoothed off at the knees, the way they do, and his water-streaked hair had been cut with a scissors. The female of a genus, we had been taught, often has more protective coloration. She had on an orange and white swimsuit, sunset-colored as her limbs, and her hair floated, leafing out along the wind. When the two reached the platform, they stepped up on it, then turned and waved — two shadows, two golden statues, waving to one side and then to another, but not to over here. And I saw that the place for the weathercock was still bare. What were they going to raise there — the sun and moon both?

Down below them, Blazer was speaking. On that side of the water, the whole world was orange with the healthy glow of them. Blazer had a nasturtium in his buttonhole.

"Get ready," I said. "Get set."

All the better for their light, I told myself. We will make better shadow.

"The test is — will they see us?" I said. "That is the battle."

I had never revealed this to my men before, and I turned to them now, to see how they would take it. I saw that they already knew.

"When I give the command," I said, "raise your weapons. They cannot fail to see us — four axes, a scythe, a knife and a tiller, two pitchforks, and a hoe."

My deputy spoke softly. "And a gun."

I turned my back on him.

Across the way, they had raised the weathercock. It was in place. In the old days the style was often a flying horse or a golden rooster; we had sold them in the shop many a time, whenever we could find an old weathercock to sell. I'd expected it would be one of those; they wouldn't buy new. There are other shapes, of course, including our own from the house, gone so long ago that I'd forgotten what it was. The shape of this one was new to me, or so at first I thought. It was a double pennant, flying to the breeze from where it was fixed on its rod, fixed there by a heartshape over on its side, pierced by an arrow. Then I recognized it. It was exactly the same in shape as the one high on the Meetinghouse at Hancock, hard by Norway Pond. Had they dared to lift it from there? They were so powerful. And the shoreline at Norway Pond is off-limits for some of us, too. Even if nobody but a country is named after it.

The shape of that weathercock troubled me. In the flame of the wind, it looked like a man on his side, blowing in the wind, blowing, his head a heart on its side, and an arrow in his head. Maybe they got it from a closed-up church.

Behind me, I heard a murmur. My men were troubled too. And I had brought them here, over a week and a wood, to this shoreline. What else could I do?

"Shoulder arms," I said.

I turned to watch them, proud. They were tall, all except the Buddy knife and the peewee, and they helped one another until all their artillery was up, shining its broadside against the evening clouds and the woods behind. I went from one to the other, straightening them. The scythe was the highest. And the hill we were on was higher than any rise of theirs, and the couple on the platform was still turning and waving, waving and turning. They couldn't help but see us, I thought. We stood there, a thin rank of us, but sightable surely, black and separate, but gathered too. Even the Pond, rising to the last sun, sent off a sheet of light like a thunderflash, to encourage us.

"Steady," I said. "Stand like the trees."

We waited. *Stand by,* I said to myself. I was the only one of us without a weapon to his shoulder. I don't want to be a John One either, I prayed to them across the water. I only want to be John Willard. See us, standing by.

And then the peewee was the one to say it, in his scratchy, dead-white voice. "They don't see us."

Then the Buddy. Then all of them. "They don't see us. We are nothing to them." They murmured it like the leaves. This was all the breath they had.

All except John, my deputy, who swung his weapon high. How could they not see him, even if, all bone as he now was, they only saw the scythe? "If I had a good New Hampshire boulder to ring it on, instead of these old slates!" he cried, and buried the tip in the ground. It made no sound. The others did the same, but a tiller is not made to speak loud against slate, or even granite. The peewee's hubcaps, clashed together, made a faint cry. We had chosen our place too well, or had they chosen it for us? We were moss to the ankles, like the stones in the graveyard those across the water love so well.

"All right," I said. "Stand back." And I bent to the gun. "You can talk," I said. And without any help, bracing myself against a birch tree that presented itself like an aide-de-camp, I shouldered the thirty-ought-six.

Across the water, the couple on the platform each held up a little flag, while the crowd applauded. I could hear them, see them, clear as clear, as pond water. Did the men from Valley Forge, crossing the Delaware, have a flag? They had a boat.

Through the telescopic lens, on the crosshair, I could see the weathercock; slowly it turned in the evening wind, a double pennant, a man on his side, blowing in the wind. I shifted the gun past the boy in his sawed-off jeans. He was a Blazer too, but only her brother. Shaking under the weight of the gun like a body on my shoulder, I brought her slowly to center, on the crosshairs. And there she was, my summer Venus, shining to the wind like the weathercock of a country I had never seen to the full before, her arms spread to its birches. Would she be the rosier without us, without me?

"Shall I shoot our weathercock?" I whispered to my deputy. "Or the weathercock girl." But nobody answered behind me, nobody at all. And the gun bore down. But the birch bore up, lifting me like a brother. This was why it took so long to decide.

Caught on the crosshair with her, was all her new countryside. I could see it well. The horses were returning to fill the barns again. In time, as the summer people lingered, there might even be cows. I couldn't see Blazer in the old grocery store for all the teeth in China, but if I studied it with care I could see the son; I could see it well. And what of us? Would we go to the city in our turn, hoping to be seen again by someone? Or back to the freckle on the air, the horn. And is all this just the balance again, blowing like the wind?

They don't need to see you, Johnny One. Or not much. No more than a mirage of upkeepers, holding up the summertime. All that's needed now, is what already is. *You see them.*

So spoke the gun.

How gray your skies will be without them. They were what drew you through the woods — the biggest mirage of all; you couldn't have done it without them.

So spoke the birch.

My eyes were burning with the choice, and I couldn't last the weight much longer — what did they ever plan to kill with a gun like this, the old-timers?

I centered the gun, holding aim. They would see me across there this time. I shoot to kill.

Was it the birch, holding me? Stand by, John Willard, all of you. It's not just a summer rebellion. Stand by.

Or the last minute, did my foot twitch, saying — "beautiful?"

No. I aimed higher than either, high between the sun and the moon. To shoot a mirage, you have to shoot that high. And I aimed to kill us both.

I fired.

They saw me then.

Everything stopped over there, too. And I could see they saw me, milling and talking among themselves. Some had already scattered, on their way around the rim of the Pond, to this side. One took a boat — still carrying her flag. Others got into it. As they all scattered toward me, I could even see what they had in their mind's-eye. Now that I had put down the gun, or fired it high, I could be a hero if I wanted — for a day. I have excellent sight.

I turned to my companions behind me. Their final effort had been too much for them. They could gather for a week, to help a friend with his summer. They could stumble through his wood, behind him on a string — he was their control. But now they were done for. Except for their implements, they were now so faded that nobody but me would see them at all.

Just then the bushes parted, back where the woods begin — and what do you know? I never expected him to come, even though I wrote. But here he was — nobody could miss him! — in a jumping red shirt that matched the car. He was panting. "Don't shoot!" he called. "Don't shoot." And he panted up to me.

"I couldn't lift it again," I said, "if I tried."

"I had to leave the car at the edge of the woods, that's why I'm late. I had to *walk*."

"We're all a little late," I said. And I could see he was still walking round me in his mind.

"How are your researches?" I said.

"Fine, just fine." He was looking at the people just beginning to straggle up the rim of the hill from below on this side — they would have to climb a bit to get here. "And how are you, Johnny — you see I got your letter."

"Oh, everything's stopped," I said. "For the moment." Down below, a boat was pulling into shore. There wasn't much time. "There's something I want to ask you though," I said. "You're the instructor." Then I looked over at my army, so quiet there without any acknowledgment, almost like the trees. "But first — let me introduce my — assistants," I said. "Axe, Hoe, Tiller, Pitchfork, Knife. One Buddy. The rest — Johns. Too late to do anything about that. They all look as dead as stones in a graveyard, I know, but they'll revive shortly, once they remember their last names. All except him, my deputy, there under the scythe." I was watching my new arrival sharply.

He was watching me too, but he strolled nonchalantly to the edge of that mossy precipice. "So this is Willard Pond," he said, staring over the water. "What a great natural oval. I wouldn't mind being buried here myself."

"It belongs to us," I said. Who can sell a grave?

He nodded. "All yours?"

"All ours," I said. "All mine." But I faltered. The boat had docked.

"And those?" he said, half-smiling, pointing to my weapons, which were standing up bravely to the evening, planted one to a mound.

"Those are my forefathers," I said, half-smiling.

"Both?" he said, looking at each mound with its implement.

"Both."

I drew him to the mound under the scythe. "John of Contoocook is his name." I like to say it; it brings back the rivers and the towns, the woods and the ponds. "He was earlier than any of the others. He needed animals, it's said, the way we others only need the winter weather. He'd have been all right if we could have got a pig to him in time."

He stood there, looking down. "We had a boy from Contoocook in class too, didn't we."

"Don't confuse me." I put my hand on the scythe — so thin. "He was the earliest." And could not survive.

He stood there thinking. "Johnny —" he said. "You were my smartest boy." Then why did he look so miserable?

What can you answer, when you know your own condition exactly?

"Is there — a question you wanted to ask me?" he said.

I looked over the rim. They were out of the boat now and on the land on this side — her and her brother, and even her mother with the curls, and burly Blazer too. And on either side of us I could hear the crowd which had gone round by way of the shore, crashing through the underbrush. They don't know how to walk in a wood yet. And the woods are not yet on their side. They were closing in, from all directions except the woods in back of me.

I nodded at him. "About them — and us. I wanted to ask you. Is it just the balance again, like the elms, like the aphids? Will they ever see us for more than a minute? Can you answer me that? You're the instructor. Can't you teach us which tree is which to the other? Is a rifle across the water the only way? Can't we *both* stand by?"

It was some dose of a question, of course. Though I waited politely, I'd already seen by his shirt he couldn't answer it; he was only Mr. Wilderness.

And when I looked away from him, I saw them all now in their half-circle around me. They thought they had me closed in.

"I see you," I said. Mildly, for after all the gun was still at my feet. "And you see me. Don't you." Even though I could tell from their eye-mirrors how they saw me, it was a satisfaction. And their misery wouldn't last.

But I don't intend meanness either. It's my weakness does it.

"Oh, don't you take all the blame," I said. I cast back a farewell glance at my fallen ones, behind me. "Who can sell a grave? *Us.*"

And then, what do you know, there was a great, windy sob from the middle of them. "Ohhhh Johnny, Johnny One!" It was Barbara the weathercock, with sentiment streaming down her face.

"Don't be so proud," I said. "I didn't dip the gun for you. I raised it. I did it for the birch."

"Oh Johnny."

She crept nearer me.

"How's your leg?" I said.

She showed me a patch on it I hadn't seen from across the water. She reached out to touch me. "Let me — "

"Let you what?"

"Take you — home with us. To rest."

"Don't come any nearer," I said. "Don't even — remember me. The way you look at me, so proud, I might have shot *myself.*" And what would I do with a flag?

Just then, down at the edge of it all, I felt a tugging at my elbow. It was the peewee. I had forgotten him. "Interduce *me,*" he said. He's a moron, but he can't help it.

I took his scaly hand. "This is one of my friends also," I said. "He's the one you can see."

But he wasn't satisfied. Still tugging, he sent up a scratch of a question, like the voice of the moss itself. "Did we do it, Johnny? Did we do it? Is it over?"

He was only a moron, but I had to tell someone. "Yes — we did it," I said. "But it's over. The summer people are real."

*J. A. Pollard*

# OLD WOMAN

F OR A MOMENT Old Woman lay quietly in the snow where she had
fallen.

"Kitchtan!" she jabbered. "Great God! Spirit!"

She tried to raise herself, but pain was in her legs. And hands.

She thought for a moment she would pull her mittens off and scream,
but didn't. Because her fingers wouldn't move.

"If only I could rub my toes," she thought. "Just rub my toes!"

Visions of firelight and soup flickered through her mind.

"I know where they've gone," she mumbled. And tears ran down both
cheeks, freezing.

Her head felt very heavy, but she lifted it and saw she was on the side
of a little ridge. Afternoon light was fading, but the snow was thicker.

"If I don't find their tracks soon . . ." she worried. And then remembered she wasn't going to.

Her face grimaced, then grinned slyly, cracking the lips over nearly
empty gums.

"If I can prove I'm strong . . . Empty-headed dunce!" she chattered.

Was it warming? It always did with snow.

She looked around.

Perhaps her feet were responding to the rest a bit.

But it was growing dark. Lying in the deep snow with the night coming wasn't good.

To the right was a little birch. Old Woman tasted snow and pushed up on her elbows. Her feet felt like seals dragging. And the pain . . . the cold. But they were warming. Weren't they? Soon she would be up and running.

"And I'll catch you, Toonas!"

He had sat on the sledge beside her when the flakes started . . . to the west. Behind her. The dogs were in the lee of them and she knew Oomla and the children had gone ahead, hurrying toward the fort where they wintered with the Narragansetts. She was folded in the deer skins like a birch leaf.

"Wind is rising," he told her.

"Yes," she snapped. "I can read the weather."

"You taught me," he agreed.

For a moment they looked deeply at one another. Old Woman began thrusting aside skins. Matoonas put a hand out, stopping her. Then dropped his gaze. He was a short Nipmuc, strong and square. Old Woman pushed the last skin back and swung her legs slowly over the sled. It took a long time. And all the while he sat there silently, eyes downcast. Finally she stood.

"You always were a plodder!"

She couldn't keep herself from spitting.

He accepted quietly, head bowed.

"Mother . . . "

"You were always slow!"

"I know. Mother . . . "

"Never like me! So quick! So . . . "

"Mother . . . "

They had come to it.

He sat on the sledge holding nothing in his mittens, smelling the things in the wind, calculating. She knew he would take them wherever they needed with a sure, steady hand. Tears glistened on her withered cheeks.

"Slow!" she said proudly, rather than "Sure!"

But there was this understanding between them so that he knew what she meant and that her bitterness kept her from it.

Bitterness at what? At the winter? Darkness? Something in her had railed at life all through it. Something strong and proud and undefeated. She was so tiny now he could hold her in one hand, nearly. So frail the wind made her tremble. At night Oomla fed her soup because she could not chew.

He looked into the darkening day and said the thing then: "You cannot chew, Mother."

"What of it?"

"You cannot keep up with the moving."

"I can!"

"Game is scarce. There are the little ones."

She knew, of course. And it was winter. Much better than swimming out into the bay and drowning. Ah! She could almost hear the ice breaking. The spring surging. Ah!

The birch stood whiter against the sky: a frost-flower etching on a world turning darker gray. But her feet and hands . . .

Old Woman stopped her fuming and considered seriously. The cold had been a swordsman attacking from every point: up her fingers, through her toes, into both sides. She had put her arms across her thin chest. But now her extremities were losing all feeling.

I must be warming, she thought dreamily. And realized suddenly she had dozed.

"I mustn't sleep!"

But the relief of numbing feet and arms was such that she relaxed further into the snow.

"I shall get up in another minute."

She had forgotten that numbed feet wouldn't walk, and when she tried to rise again she seemed to have lost control of something.

She remembered Toonas had wept.

When he stood up and started after the others she saw that tears were trickling in rivers down both cheeks. He glanced at her. She knew he wanted to rush to her, embrace her, and she protected him.

"I shall go this way," she had said waspishly. "You never did understand direction!"

Thus dismissed, he went heavily to the sled. She thought for a moment she would not watch him leave, but turned as if her heartbeats were in his throat, her longing so intense, imperious . . . She had sat down quickly to hide the vision of his short, thick figure floundering in the snowdrifts crying. Then she walked slowly to the east, but at a southerly angle.

"They will have gone there!" she chuckled angrily. "I shall meet them in the camp!"

Snow swirled a bit.

Deliberately she headed for the snow ridge she could see.

"Men!" she thought suddenly. "Ungrateful men!" She snorted and her breath was like smoke. "Ungrateful brutes. Who imagine all their lives that women love them! Sons and lovers! Ah!"

Matoonas had been an easy birth as births went. He was her last. She could still smell the birthing blood. She could see the fire in the oil lamps and the women around her watching. She could hear herself groaning. For a moment she pushed again, chuckling grimly. "Never too old for that!" she mumbled. And in the pushing, in the strain, in the suffocating, grinding shove that brought new life out of old, she remembered his tiny wrinkled face, his body, his features covered with the mucus, the pale gray mucus that gave his purpling body a look of being lichen-wrapped. She remembered how she had put her fingers into it and pushed it out of his eyes, his nose. How she had shoved a finger into his mouth and pushed the mucus out . . . and heard his gasping life-cry. Matoonas! Little one! My son! My son!

Old Woman drew her breath in and spat it out. Looking after Toonas she saw that he had disappeared. Wind was talking. Something far away joined in. She was alone with white sky, white earth, white water falling on her face. She clasped her arms about her chest near the snow ridge and fell forward crying loudly.

"The birch!" she thought. "I shall sit a while under the birch bush. I am feeling . . . too much!"

She couldn't seem to stop the crying. It went on and on, and she kept imagining she would walk to the birch to sit beneath it, resting. But she lay instead in the snow which came billowing up around her so that her legs were covered and the lower part of her arms.

"He crossed his little arms over his chest and slept," she murmured. Smiling.

She opened her eyes.

"White world!" she fumed. "White white white!"

Out of the silentness came a long, thin sound like a musical instrument.

Old Woman stiffened.

It was not answered.

"Strange," she thought. For several moments she listened calmly, thinking about the life style of wolves.

"It was to the east," she thought. Matoonas would have noted, and the children. Oomla, who ignored the wolves, would pay no attention.

"Except perhaps tonight," Old Woman thought smugly. As if she had finally scored a point.

"Ah, he is clever, yes!" she thought. He would survive a long, long time. "And maybe someday his son, his son would lead them out . . . "

She could almost see him staggering through the snowdrifts, weeping.

"It must be done properly," she said stiffly to herself. "And with respect!"

He had struggled through the wild tern nesting grounds, she remembered. That small thing called her son. Short, bandy-legged, man-child. He had snuffled under stones and into nests collecting. He had plodded slowly, methodically, collecting until his pile was largest . . . while his brothers had joked and wrestled and sometimes dropped the eggs. To the others Old Woman remonstrated, but to Matoonas she had said, "So! You get them all!"

And he had studied her gravely, even then, even at four studying so seriously; so that you didn't know what went on behind the black eyes and the impassive stare.

But Old Woman knew. She always knew.

She had smiled then, ruffling his hair. She had squatted before him, saying, "The others do out of stupidity what you must learn to do carefully, for unless some eggs are left, the birds will not return."

He had studied her, and then methodically replaced some eggs as bidden.

"You will go into camp now!" Old Woman cried at the birch bush. "Into camp, my pet, my darling . . . "

A shadow came down the snow ridge and hovered.

Old Woman stopped chattering and looked at the snow carefully for a while, her eyes straining in the fading light.

"Late afternoon!" she complained. "Night and snow and cold . . . "

But her arms were gone.

She drew a quick breath when the shadow seemed to come closer, and coughed painfully. It hurt to breathe sometimes when the temperature was low.

"If it clears, the snow will squeak," she thought. "The crystals rubbing against each other with the falling temperature . . . "

Was it a shadow coming down the snow ridge towards the birch bush?

Old Woman pulled herself onto her knees and tried to stand. No use. She struggled several times before falling, panting, slightly frightened. Then she thought, "I shall rest a bit longer. Then I shall go around by the birch bush and turn north and get to them."

For a moment her resolve, which she hadn't known about, wavered. She thought "north" wistfully; then, muttering angrily, imagined she flung herself by hands and knees towards the birch, going eastward. She could still see Toonas floundering in the drifts.

"Ah! Children!" she thought. "All my life — children. Carrying, nursing, birthing, teaching." She remembered food and skin preparation. And Spanum, husband, dead on the bay, falling out of the canoe into the ice-blue depths.

"Men!" thought Old Woman. "Always managing! Always killing themselves!"

The old wolf was watching from where he sat under the birch bush. He was hungry. But he had been hungry before. This time it was a total hunger, as if no matter what he ate it would not be enough.

He had come silently over the snow ridge and seen the old woman in the snowbank. She was talking to herself, and he knew her to be crazy. Humans who sat alone in the snow and talked were crazy. Or very young.

He was strangely tired. The snow bothered. He felt blinded.

He couldn't make out what she was doing. He was aware of angriness. He could taste it in his nostrils.

"Toonas!" said Old Woman, who had spied him sitting there.

"You always were a blunderer! Nothing you could manage was ever graceful!"

Her tone gentled.

"But it was nice of you to come back to me . . ."

She squinted, trying to make the form come clear.

"You might be warm . . . "

Her legs and arms were thoroughly numb now. It was great relief. She tipped over onto one arm, and tried to drag her body closer to the birch again.

"No good, Matoonas!" said Old Woman crossly. "Whining gets you nowhere. Not with me! You tried it often enough, to be sure. Little Toonas always whining. With the mucus running down your lips, always looking for a thing to chew on. If not me and my body, then the meat. Or the strawberries in summer. Ah . . . "

Here she leaned nearly to the snow.

"The strawberries in summer."

With an arm like a stick she gestured heavily at the birch bush.

"Come here and keep me warm!"

The old wolf whined again. He couldn't seem to concentrate. He lay down, putting his head onto his huge paws, raised it, stood nervously but slowly.

What did the mad human thing want?

He ought to mark the bush so the young ones would understand.

Instead he took a slow step forward toward Old Woman.

"That's my Toonas!"

And then another.

Steadily she watched the gray shadow approach out of the birch bush. With the pain gone in her feet and hands she felt nearly rested. But the anger was working.

"Don't be so slow!" she scolded, and didn't know it was a whisper.

"Always slowly. Slowly. Into the berries even. Even in the summertime, slowly. Always considering. Careful. That's my Toonas!"

Now the old wolf stood an arm's length from her, his head dropped, the huge yellow eyes watching. A gush of dizziness took him, and he staggered slightly, shook his muzzle.

Old Woman laughed.

"Awkward still. Little awkward Toonas!"

The stick hand came out again. Old Wolf had his eyes closed trying to concentrate, and her fingers, cold as ice in the fur mittens, brushed his chest.

He growled.

Old Woman listened gravely.

"Yes. Oh yes," she agreed. "You always did complain. 'Wait for me, Mama. Help me, Mama. Feed me, Mama.' Always complaining."

The stiff hand brushed his chest again.

It had been a long time since the old wolf had enjoyed a mate. The faint hand-brush woke something dimly in him, some memory of touching and of joy, of pups in the tunnel he had helped dig, of mice squealing in the underbrush where he trapped them.

He put his head slowly onto Old Woman's hand where it was dropping.

And Old Woman couldn't draw herself back now, for she was falling into the snow deeply towards him.

"Toonas," she whimpered. "Matoonas!"

Day was going. Old Wolf suddenly felt very tired.

"Keep me warm," said Old Woman.

He touched her hand again.

Cold was seeping into the pads of his feet, those tough pads which had carried him so many miles, on so many hunts, so many matings. It was odd to feel them cold as if he were a candle guttering.

For a moment the world capsized.

The Old Wolf blinked his eyes and looked at Old Woman lying in the snow.

She was no longer talking.

If they no longer talk, he decided, are they no longer mad?

But she was whimpering.

He leaned closer. It was necessary to take some steps. He really must go back and mark the birch. But one of his legs appeared to be dragging. He felt his hind-quarters begin to slip, and whimpered.

Old Woman comforted.

So he dragged himself to her, stretching out his muzzle. She was slightly warm and the cold was sinking into him.

If only we were under the birch bush, they thought together.

Old Woman's eyes were still open. They saw the shadow coming towards her, and for a moment she thought, "Wolf!" and fear tried to enter, but then she thought, "Toonas!" and the fear dissolved into love, annoyance, superiority.

"Ah, Toonas," she thought, "you always needed mother's warmth!"

The wolf found his body dropping beside her, his back against her back. He whined again. And put his head onto his crossed paws as he had done when a young wolf, sunning on his den's mound, waiting for the female, listening to the pups down in the tunnel wrestling, joking, driving their mother frantic. He would wait for the bachelor who would come shortly to take them away, tire them out with playing. And then he and the she-wolf would speed away, going out to hunt the mice, the hare, whatever. For a moment he was speeding, and his body twitched with dreaming. He opened his eyes, and the snow was falling quickly in the gray daylight. The birch bush stood up whiter. There would be no moon. Night was being swallowed in the white surge, and they would both be covered before morning.

There was pain in his lungs, and he whined again, but his hind-quarters had gone numb already. He tried to lick his paws.

Again his eyes closed and he was running, and thought he heard distinctly a long message being sent, something about the snow falling. He tried to rise, but couldn't. And settled more firmly into Old Woman's back.

The feel of his warm, furred body had brought into Old Woman's dreaming the memory of Matoonas' father. And with it a great, choking rage of loving and remembering impossible to bear. She gave a shudder, nearly choking . . . and stepped out of herself into the greyness.

There was an ease, a lightness about it that impressed her. Like swimming without clothes in summer. She stood up quickly, thinking, "These old limbs still are working. Won't Toonas be surprised at that?"

Not that it mattered. Not that anything mattered. Not the cold or the snow blowing or the birch tree or the wolf . . .

She looked behind her, thinking for the first time that it had been a wolf after all who had come to meet her, not her husband, not her children . . . and he was lying in the snow beside a whitening mound that looked like a woman with its hand stretched out. The wolf had shuddered close against the woman's body, pressing against it back-to-back, as if it had fallen there. The great head lay on the two crossed paws . . . a huge wolf, surely. Huge.

The wolf looked slowly up. For just a moment the two yellow eyes gleaming through the gray snowfall saw her standing there.

"Old Wolf," she said considerately. "Ah, you are dying!"

She looked at the body in the snow beside it.

"Ah yes," she said.

The wolf raised its head slightly, nearly whined.

Old Woman beckoned.

"Don't stay there," she whispered. "Come!"

He whimpered.

She beckoned, going lightly backwards.

He gave a shudder, closed his eyes . . . the snow swirled faster . . . then she saw him getting up to follow. Gaily he trotted up to her. They stopped. She put her hand upon the thick, gray skull. They gazed at one another. Old Woman smiled. Then they turned and looked together at the bodies in the snow behind them.

*Dana Burnet*

# FOG

I HAD COME OUT of the city, where story-telling is a manufactured science, to the country where story-telling is a by-product of life. Mr. Siles had arrived to paint my piazza, as per a roundabout agreement between my cook, my cook's cousin, my cook's cousin's wife, who had been a Miss Siles, and finally — Mr. Siles himself. If that sentence is somewhat involved, so was my contract with Mr. Siles. In the country, a semicircle is the shortest line between two points.

I came at the strange story of Wessel's Andy in something of the same circuitous manner. Mr. Siles, as I have said, had arrived to paint my piazza; but after a long look at the heavens and the heaving sea, he opined that it would be a wet day and that the painting had best be left till to-morrow. I demurred. I was acquainted with the to-morrows of this drowsy Maine village. But while we were arguing the point, a white ghost began to roll in from the deep.

"Fog," said Mr. Siles.

"Yes," I admitted grudgingly.

He stared into the thickening mists with an expression that puzzled me. I have seen the same look upon the face of a child compelled to face the dark alone.

"I mistrust it," said Mr. Siles, simply.

"Mistrust the fog?"

He nodded, his iron-gray beard quivering with the intensity of the assent.

"Take it in a gale of wind," he said, "that's honest weather, though it blows a man's soul to Kingdom Come. But fog — "

"I suppose strange things do happen in it," I replied. It was a chance shot, but it struck home.

"Strange!" cried Mr. Siles. "You may well say strange! There was somethin' happened right here in this village — "

I settled myself comfortably against the naked piazza railing, and Mr. Siles told me this story.

He was born a thousand miles from deep water. His folks were small farmers in a middle western grain state, and he was due to inherit the farm. But almost before he could talk they knew he was a queer one. They knew he was no more farmer than he was college professor. He was a land hater from the beginnin'. He hated the look and the feel and the smell of it. He told me afterward that turnin' a furrow with a plow set his teeth on edge like when you scrape your finger nail along a piece of silk. His name was Andy.

When he was about thirteen year' old he found a picture of a ship in a newspaper. It was like a glimpse of another world. He cut it out and pasted it on the attic wall over his bed. He used to look at it a hundred times a day. He used to get up in the middle of the night, and light a match and look at it. Got so, Andy's father came up early one mornin' with a can o' whitewash and blotted the whole thing out against the wall. The boy didn't say a word until the ship was gone. Then he laughed, a crazy sort o' laugh.

"That's the way they go," he says, "right into the fog," he says, "and never come out again!"

He was sick after that. Some sort of a fever. I guess it made him a little delirious. He told me he was afraid they were goin' to blot him out, same as the picture. Used to dream he was smotherin' to death, and pleasant things like that. Queer, too. . . .

When the fever finally burned out of him, he was nothin' but skin and bones. His people saw he was too sickly to work, so they let him mope around by himself. He used to spend most of his time in the woodshed, whittlin' pine models o' that whitewashed schooner. He was known all through those parts as Wessel's Andy, Wessel bein' his fam'ly name. See for yourself what Wessel's Andy meant. It didn't mean Andrew Wessel, by the grace o' God free, white and twenty-one. It meant "that good-for-nothin', brain-cracked boy over to Wessel's." That's what it amounted to in plain words.

But the strange thing about that name was how it followed him. It came east a thousand miles, and there wasn't a town but it crawled into, on its belly, like a snake into long grass. And it poisoned each place for him, so that he kept movin' on, movin' on, always toward deep water. It used to puzzle him how strangers knew to call his name hindside foremost. 'Twan't any puzzle to me. He hadn't been in my place two minutes askin' for a job, but I say "What's your name?" And he says, starin' hard at the model of the *Lucky Star* schooner that hung over my counter, "I'm Wessel's Andy," he says, never takin' his eyes off the schooner. Likely he'd done the same absent-minded trick all along the road, though not for just that reason.

I rec'llect the evenin' he came into my place. I was keepin' a ship's supply store in those days — fittin's and supplies, down by the Old Wharf. He shuffled in toward sundown, his belongin's done up in a handkerchief, his clothes covered half an inch thick with dust.

"I want a job," says he.

"What kind of a job?" says I.

"Oh, anything," says he.

"All right," I told him, "you can start in here to-morrow. I been lookin' for somebody to help around the store." Then I asked him his name and he answered "Wessel's Andy." Some of the boys was standin' 'round and heard him say it. He was never called anything but Wessel's Andy from that time on.

Quietest young fellow ever I saw — plenty willin' to work, but not very strong. I paid him four dollars a week and let him bunk in with me at the back o' the store. He could have made more money some'ers else, but he wouldn't go. Naturally there were a good many seafarin' men in and out o' the shop, and some evenin's they used to sit around yarnin' to one another. Often I've seen Wessel's Andy hunched up on a soap box behind the counter, his eyes burnin' and blinkin' at the model of the *Lucky Star* on the opposite wall, his head bent to catch the boys' stories. Seemed as if he couldn't get enough o' ships and the sea.

And yet he was afraid to go, himself. I found that out one night when we were lockin' up after the boys had gone.

"Have you ever felt yourself to be a coward, Mr. Siles?" he says, in one of his queer fits o' talkin'.

"Why as for that," I says, "I guess I been pretty good and scared, a time or two."

"Oh, I don't mean that," he says. "I don't mean scared. I mean afraid — day and night, sleepin' and wakin'."

"No," I says, "and nobody else with good sense would be. Ain't nothin' in this world to frighten a man steady like that, unless it's his own sin."

Wessel's Andy shook his head, smilin' a little.

"Maybe not in this world," says he, white and quiet, "but how about — other worlds?"

"What you drivin' at?" says I. "You mean ghosts?"

"Not ghosts," he says, lowerin' his voice and lookin' out the side window to where the surf was pawin' the sand. "Just the feelin' o' ghosts."

"Come to bed," I says. "You've worked too hard to-day."

"No. Please let me tell you. Please sit up awhile. This is one of the times when I can talk."

He grabbed my hand and pulled me down to a chair. His fingers were as cold as ice. Then he dragged his soap box out from the counter and sat opposite me, a few feet away.

"I'll tell you how I know I'm a coward," he says. And he told me everything up to the time of his leavin' home.

"You see," he says, "I had to come. It was in me to come East. I've been four years workin' my way to open water, and I've had a hell of a time . . . a hell of a time. But it was in me to come. There has been a ship behind my eyes ever since I can remember. Wakin' or sleepin' I see that ship. It's a schooner, like the *Lucky Star* there, with all her tops'ls set and she's disappearin' in a fog. I know," he says, lookin' at me so strange and sad it sent the shivers down my back, "I know I belong aboard o' that ship."

"All right," I says, as though I didn't think anything of his queer talk, "all right, then go aboard of her. You'll find a hundred vessels up and down the coast that look like the *Lucky Star*. Not to a seafarin' man, maybe. But you're a farmer. You couldn't tell one from t'other. Take your pick o' the lot," I says, "and go aboard of her like a man."

But he just smiled at me, a sickly sort o' smile.

"There's only one," he says, "there's only one, Mr. Siles. When she comes I'll go aboard of her, but I — won't — go — like — a — man!"

Then all at once he jumped up with a kind o' moanin' noise and stood shakin' like a leaf, starin' out the window to the sea.

"There," he says, kind o' chokin'. "There, I saw it then! Oh, God, I saw it then!"

I grabbed him by the shoulders and shook him.

"You saw what?" I says. "Tell me!"

His fingers dug into my arm like so many steel hooks.

"At the end of the Old Wharf. A sail! Look, don't you see it?"

I forced him down onto the soap box.

"Sit there," I says, "and don't be a fool. It's low tide," I says, "and there ain't enough water off the Old Wharf to float a dory."

"I saw it," he says, draggin' the words out slow as death, "I saw it, just as I always knew I would. That's what I came East for. . . a thousand miles. And I'm afraid to go aboard of her. I'm afraid, because I don't know what it's for."

He was rockin' himself back and forth like a crazy man, so I ran and got a drop o' whiskey from the back room.

"Here," I says. "Drink this."

He swallowed it straight, like so much water. In a few minutes he quieted. "Now then," I says, "you come to bed. This night's entertainment is over."

But it wasn't. About midnight I woke up with the feelin' that somethin' was wrong. First thing I saw was the lamp burnin' high and bright. Next thing was Wessel's Andy, sittin' in his underclothes on the edge o' the bunk, my whiskey flask in his hands.

"Mr. Siles," says he, as straight and polite as a dancin' master, though his eyes burned, "I have made free with your whiskey. I have drunk it all, I think."

"Great Jehosophat," I says, "there was pretty nigh a quart in that flask!"

"I hope you don't begrudge it," says he, still smooth as wax, "because it has made me feel like a man, Mr. Siles, like a man. I could talk — and even laugh a little, I think. Usually I can only feel. Usually I am afraid. Afraid of what, Mr. Siles? Afraid of goin' aboard without knowin' what for. That's the fear to eat your heart out, Mr. Siles. That's the fear to freeze your blood. *The not knowin' what for!*"

I was wide awake by this time and wonderin' how I could get him back to bed. I didn't want to lay hands on him any more than you'd want to lay hands on a person with nightmare. So I started to argy with him, like one friend to another. We were a queer lookin' pair, I'll warrant, sittin' there in our underclothes, facin' each other.

"Look here," I says, calm as a judge, "if it's your fate to ship aboard of a vessel, why don't you go peaceable and leave the reasons for it to God Almighty? Ain't anything holdin' you, is there?"

"There is somethin' holdin' me," he says; and then, very low: "What is it, Mr. Siles, that holds a man back from the sea?"

"Saints and skittles!" I says, jolted out o' my play-actin', "you ain't gone and fallen in love, have you?"

He didn't answer. Just sat there starin' at me, his face whiter than I ever saw a livin' man's face. Then all at once he turned his head, exactly as he would have done if a third person had walked into the room. He was gazin' straight at the lamp now. His eyes had a sort o' dazzled look.

"No," he says. "No, I won't tell that. It's — too — beautiful."

And before I could jump to catch him he pitched in a dead faint onto the floor.

It was two or three days before he was well enough to go to work again. Durin' that time he hardly spoke a word. But one afternoon he came to me.

"Mr. Siles," he said. "I'm queer, but I'm not crazy. You've been kind to me, and I wanted you to know it wasn't that. There are people in this world," he said, "whose lives aren't laid down accordin' to the general rule. I'm one o' them."

And that's all he ever said about his actions the night he drank the whiskey.

It was a week or so later that Wessel's Andy heard the story o' Cap'n Salsbury and the *Lucky Star*. I suppose he was bound to hear it sooner or later, it bein' a fav'rite yarn with the boys. But the way of his hearin' it was an accident, at that.

One afternoon, late, a fisherman from Gloucester put into the harbor. He had carried away some runnin' gear on his way to the Newf'n'land Banks and was stoppin' in port to refit. After supper the skipper came into the shop, where the boys was sittin' round as usual. First thing he saw was that model o' the *Lucky Star* on the wall.

"What has become o' Dan Salsbury?" says he, squintin' aloft. "What has become o' Dan Salsbury that used to go mackrelin' with the fleet?"

So they told him what had become o' Dan Salsbury, three or four o' them pitchin' in together. But finally it was left to old Jem Haskins to tell the story. In the first place, Jem had the longest wind and in the second place his cousin Allie used to keep house for Cap'n Dan. So Jem knew the ins and outs o' the story better than any o' the rest. As he began to talk, I saw Wessel's Andy pick up his soap box and creep closer. . . . And this is the story that he heard:

Cap'n Dan Salsbury was a deep-sea fisherman, owner and master o' the schooner *Lucky Star*. He had been born and raised in the village and was one of its fav'rite citizens. He was a fine, big man to look at, quiet and unassumin' in his ways and fair in his dealin', aship and ashore. If ever a man deserved to be happy, Dan Salsbury deserved it. But somehow happiness didn't come to him.

First his wife died. He laid her in a little plot o' ground on the hill back of his house, took his year-old girl baby aboard the *Lucky Star* and sailed for God knows where. He was gone ten months. Then he came back, opened his cottage on Salsbury Hill and set out to make little Hope Salsbury the richest girl in the village. He pretty nigh did it, too. His luck was supernat'ral. His catches were talked about up and down the coast. He became a rich man, accordin' to village standards.

Hope Salsbury grew up to be the prettiest girl in town. She was never very strong, takin' after her mother that way, and there was an air about her that kept folks at a distance. It wasn't uppish or mean. She was as kind as an angel, and just about as far-away as one. There wasn't a youngster in the village but would have died to have her, but she scared 'em speechless with her strange, quiet talk and her big misty eyes. Folks said Hope Salsbury wouldn't look at a man, and they were right. She looked straight *through* him.

It worried Cap'n Dan. He didn't want to get rid of Hope, by a long shot, but he knew he was failin' and he wanted to see her settled with a nice, dependable boy who could take care of her after he had gone. There was a man for every woman, said Cap'n Dan. But Hope didn't seem to find her man. She got quieter and quieter, and lonelier and lonelier, till the Cap'n decided somethin' was wrong somewhere. So he asked her straight out if there was anyone she wanted, anyone she cared enough about to marry. She said no, there wasn't. But she said it so queer that the Cap'n began to suspect it was a case of the poor child lovin' somebody who didn't love her. It took him a long time to find the courage to ask that question. But when he did, she only smiled and shook her head.

"Hope," says the Cap'n, "there's only one thing in the world that makes a young girl wilt like you're wiltin', and that's love. Tell me what it is you want, and we'll go searchin' the seven seas till we find it."

"I don't know what it is myself," the girl answered. "It's as though I was in love with someone I had met long ago, and then lost."

"Lost can be found," says the Cap'n. "We'll go 'round the world in the *Lucky Star*."

Within a month's time the old schooner was overhauled and refitted and made ready for sea. It was June when she sailed out o' the harbor, but she hadn't gone far enough to clear the Cape when a fog shut down and hid her from sight. Most of the village was standin' on the wharf to wave goodbye. But they never saw the *Lucky Star* again. The fog lasted all day and all night and by mornin' o' the second day Cap'n Dan Salsbury and his daughter were a part o' the blue myst'ry across the horizon. They never came back. The *Lucky Star* was lost with all hands in the big blow off Hatteras two years ago this summer. . . . So little Hope Salsbury never found her man, and that branch o' the Salsbury family died, root, stock, and branch.

As old Jem broke off, I glanced at Wessel's Andy. The boy was crouched forward on his soap box, his eyes burnin' like two coals in the shadow. When he saw me lookin' at him, he shrank back like a clam into its shell. That night, as we were undressin' in the back room, he turned to me all of a sudden.

"Mr. Siles," says he, "is there a picture o' Miss Hope Salsbury in this village?"

"Why," I answered, "I don't know as there is — and I don't know as there isn't. Come to think, I guess Cap'n Dan's cousin Ed Salsbury might have a likeness. He inherited most of the Cap'n's prop'ty. Probably find one in the fam'bly album."

"Which house is Ed Salsbury's?"

"Third to the right after you climb the Hill. You aren't thinkin' o' goin' up there tonight, are you?"

Wessel's Andy was kind o' smilin' to himself. He didn't answer my question. But he got into bed all right and proper, turned his face to the wall and was soon breathin' quiet and regular. I never suspected for a minute that he was shammin'.

It was just four o'clock in the mornin' when the telephone in the store began to ring — I looked at the clock as I jumped up to answer the call. I was on a party wire and my call was 13 — one long and three shorts. I had never thought about it bein' unlucky till that minute. But it struck me cold to hear that old bell borin' through the early mornin' silence . . .

"Hello," I says, takin' down the receiver.

"This is Ed Salsbury," says the other party. "Come up to my house right away and take your crazy clerk off my hands. I found him sittin' in the parlor when I came down to start the fires. Asked him what he was doin' and he said he had come to steal things. If you ain't up here in fifteen minutes I'll call the deputy sheriff."

I was up there in less than fifteen minutes. I cursed that fool boy every step of the way, but I went. I don't know why I took such trouble about him. Maybe I was a part o' that fate o' his.

Ed met me at the door of his cottage.

"Siles," says he, "there's somethin' queer about this. It's against nature. That boy — I've been talkin' to him — swears he came up here last night to steal. He pried open one o' the front windows and got into the parlor. That's enough to send him to jail for a good long bit, but I'm blessed if I want to send him. I've got a suspicion that the lad is lyin', though why any human should lie himself *into* the penitentiary instead of *out* of it, blamed if I know. You got any ideas on the subject?"

"What was he doin' when you found him?" says I.

"That was funny, too. He was sittin' at the table, with the lamp lit, as home-like as you please. And — "

"And what?"

"Lookin' at that old fam'ly album of ours."

"Ed," I says, "I'll go bond for that boy. Don't say anything about this down at the village. Some day I'll tell you why he came up here at dead o' night to peek into that old album of yours. It ain't quite clear in my own mind yet, but it's gettin' clearer."

"Queer how he looked at me when I came in the door," says Ed. "Just as though he was the one belonged here and I was the trespasser. His eyes — "

"I know," I said. "Where is the boy, Ed? I'll take him home now."

"He's in the kitchen," Ed answered, kind o' sheepish, "eatin' breakfast."

The Salsburys always were the biggest-hearted folk in the village.

So I took Wessel's Andy back to the store, but instead o' talkin' to him like I meant to, I never so much as opened my mouth the whole way home. I couldn't. He looked too *happy*. It was the first time I'd seen him look anything but glum and peaked. Now, he was a changed man. There was a light on his face, and when I say light I mean *light*. Once he burst out laughin' — and it wasn't the sort o' laugh that comes from thinkin' o' somethin' funny. It was just as though he'd seen some great trouble turned inside out and found it lined with joy. He made me think of *a bridegroom*, somehow, stridin' along there in the early dawn. . . .

I believe he would have gone straight on past the store, but for my hand on his arm. He followed me into the back room like a blind man, and there for the first time he spoke.

"I shan't work to-day," he says, drawin' a deep breath. Again I thought of a *bridegroom.*

"No," I says, "you'll go to bed and get some sleep."

"Yes," he says, "I must sleep." He began to peel off his clothes, and when I came back an hour later he was sleepin' like a baby, and smilin' . . .

He slept well into the afternoon. Then he got up, shaved, washed and put on the best clothes he owned. He didn't have only the one suit, but he brushed it till it looked like new. Instead o' the blue shirt that he wore around the shop he had on a white one with a standin' collar and a *white tie*. I found him standin' by the window in the back room, lookin' out to sea.

"Mr. Siles," he says, not turnin' round, "I am goin' to leave you."

"Leave?" I says.

"Yes."

"When you goin'?"

"Soon," he says. And then he faced me.

"That ship," he says, "that ship I told you about" — he was speakin' slow and quiet — "it's comin' for me very soon. I shan't have to wait much longer now. I feel that it is near. And I am glad."

"I thought you didn't want to go?" I says, tryin' to get at the real meanin' of his words. I felt like a man in a dark room that's reachin' for somethin' he knows is there but can't quite locate.

"That was yesterday," he says, smilin' like he had smiled in his sleep. "To-day I'm glad. To-day I want to go. It's the natural thing to do, now. It's so natural — and good — that I don't mind talkin' about it any more. Sit down," he says, "and I'll tell you. You've been my friend, and you ought to know."

I sat down, feelin' kind o' weak in the knees. By this time it was beginning to grow dark. A slight mist was formin' on the water.

"I've already told you," he says, "about the ship that was always behind my eyes. There was somethin' else, Mr. Siles, somethin' I've never told a livin' soul. Ever since I was a little boy I've been seein' a face. It was a child's face to begin with, but it grew as I grew. It was like a beautiful flower, that changes but is always the same. At first I only dreamed it, but as I grew older I used to see it quite clearly, both day and night. I saw it more and more frequently, until lately" — he put his hand to his eyes — "it has become a livin' part o' me. It is a woman's face, Mr. Siles, and it calls me.

"Until last night I had never connected this face in any way with the ship in the fog. You see, one was the most beautiful thing in the world — the *only* beautiful thing in my world — and the other was horrible. But it called me, too, and I was afraid; afraid that I would have to go before I found *her*."

He leaned forward and put his hand on my knee.

"Mr. Siles," says he, in the voice of a man speakin' of his Bride, "I saw that face last night in Mr. Salsbury's old album. It was the face of Hope Salsbury."

I jumped up and away from him. My brain had been warnin' me all along that something like this was comin', but it was a shock, just the same.

"She's dead," I says. "She's dead!"

It was the only thing I could think to say. My mouth was dry as a bone. Words wouldn't come to me.

"Oh, no," he cried, and his voice rang. "Oh, no, Mr. Siles. There's no such thing as bein' dead. There are more worlds than one," he says. "As many more as a man needs," he says. "This is only a poor breath of a world. There are others, others! I know," he says — and laughed — "I know how it is with men. They think because their eyes close and their mouths are still and their hearts stop beatin' that it's the end o' happiness. And maybe it is with some. I can't say. Maybe if folks are entirely happy in this world they don't need the others. But it's every man's right to be happy, Mr. Siles, and the Lord God knows His business. Trust Him, Mr. Siles, trust Him. Don't I know? I used to be afraid, but now I see how it is."

"Lord help me," I says. "What am I to do?"

"Why, nothin'," he says pattin' my knee. "It's all right, Mr. Siles. You go ahead with your life," he says, "the same as though I had never come into it. Take all the happiness you can get, Mr. Siles, for that's as God intended. But never think it ends here."

I couldn't look at him. There was a blur before my eyes. I got up and went out o' the store, headin' down the beach. I wanted to be alone, to sit down quietly and *think*. My brain was spinnin' like a weathercock in a gale.

I must have blundered up the beach a good two miles before I noticed that the mist was thickenin'. I stopped dead still and watched it creep in, blottin' the blue water as it came. It was like the white sheet that a stage magician drops between him and the audience just before he does his great trick. I wondered what was goin' on behind it.

The sun was settin' behind Salsbury Hill. There was a sort o' glow to the fog. It began to shine like a piece of old silver that has been rubbed with a rag. All at once I heard Wessel's Andy say, clear as a bell: "Mr. Siles, I am goin' to leave you!"

I turned toward home, walkin' fast. But somethin' kept pesterin' me to hurry, hurry! I began to run, but I couldn't get ahead of the black fear that was drivin' me. I saw Wessel's Andy standin' at the window and lookin' out to sea. I heard him say: "It's comin' for me very soon." I ran till my heart pounded in my side . . .

The beach curved before me like the blade of a scythe, with the Old Wharf for the handle. The edge of it was glistenin' in the afterglow and the surf broke against it like grain against the knife. I was still half a mile from home when I saw a single figure walk out on that shinin' blade and stand with his arms folded, starin' into the fog. It was Wessel's Andy.

I tried to run faster, but the sand caught my feet. It was like tryin' to run in a dream. I called and shouted to him, but he didn't hear. All the shoutin' in the world wouldn't have stopped him then. Suddenly he threw out his arms and walked down into the water. I was so near by that time that I could see his face. It was like a lamp in the mist.

I called again, but he was in the surf now, and there were other voices in his ears. A wave broke over his shoulders. He struggled on, his hands kind o' gropin' ahead of him. I caught another glimpse of his face. He was smilin' . . .

I gathered myself to jump. I remember the foam on the sand and the water swirlin' underfoot and the new wave makin' and the fog over all. I remember thinkin' o' the strong tide, and how little a man looked in the sea . . .

And then I saw the *Lucky Star*.

I would have known her anywhere. She was just haulin' out o' the mist, on the starboard tack, with all her canvas set. As I looked she melted in the fog — she that should have been lyin' fathoms deep — and after that I only saw her by glances. But I saw her plain. She was no color at all, and there wasn't the sign of a light to mark her, but she came bow on through water that wouldn't have floated a dory, closer and closer until I could make out the people on her decks. They were like statues carved out o' haze. There was a great figure at the wheel, and others up for'ard, in smoky oilskins. And at the lee rail I saw a young girl leanin' against the shrouds, one hand to her heart, the other held out as though to tear aside the mist. . . .

I was in the water then, and it was cold. A wave picked me up and carried me forward. I saw Wessel's Andy flounderin' in the trough ahead o' me. I swam for him. My hand touched his shoulder. He twisted half about and looked at me. His hair was like matted seaweed over his eyes and his face was as pale as the dead. But again, in all that wildness, I thought of *a bridegroom* . . .

A great wave, with a cruel curved edge, lifted above us. I made ready to dive, but he flung his arms out and waited . . . I saw white bows ridin' on the crest of it, and the silver belly of a drawin' jib, and it seemed to me I heard a laugh! Then the wave hit me . . .

When I came to, I was lyin' on the beach with some o' the boys bendin' over me. They had heard me shoutin' and arrived just in time to pull me away from the tide. They never found *him*. They said it was because of the strong undertow. But I knew better. I knew that Wessel's Andy had gone aboard of his vessel at last, and that all was well with him.

MR. SILES stopped abruptly and drew his hand across his eyes. I found myself staring at the gray wall of fog as though it had been the final curtain of a play. I longed for it to lift — if only for an instant — that I might see the actors out of their parts. But the veil was not drawn aside.

Then I heard some one speaking monotonously of a piazza that would be painted on the morrow, and turning a moment later saw Mr. Siles just vanishing in the mist, a smoky figure solely inhabiting an intangible world.

I went into my house and closed the door.

*Thomas A. Easton*

# ROLL THEM BONES

I finally gave Bonny the ring the week before Christmas. I did it over drinks at the Foxfire, the new restaurant in Dick Witham's Oak Lane Shopping Center.

Bonny wasn't surprised. After all, we had been living together, more or less engaged, for over a year by then. She knew me, and she had to know the time was ripe. Still, she raised her eyebrows when I fished the gift-wrapped package from my jacket pocket, said, "Oh, Harry!" when she'd opened it, and leaned across the table to kiss me.

Ignoring the smiles of the other diners, I took the ring and fitted it onto her finger. She held it up to admire it. The stone wasn't big — maybe a quarter carat — but it caught the candlelight and sparkled just the way a diamond should.

I sipped my scotch and said, "Want to set a date?"

Her drink was a Manhattan. She didn't touch it as she answered. "I've always thought New Year's Day would be nice. Is it possible?"

"We'll have to see."

Our table was near the Foxfire's big picture window. We had a good view of the slope twenty feet below, of the trees silhouetted against the snowy ground, of the stream beyond, rocks crusted with frozen spray. The glass gleamed with reflections of the candles on the restaurant's tables, dim images of diners and their silverware. I glanced at Bonny in the glass, the soft green of her dress, the curves of neck and arm and bust. I had loved to watch her since the day I hired her, a secretary for a small-town Mayor. I thought I always would, even if, like now, I couldn't always meet her eyes. Her attention was for the room's interior.

She spoke softly. "This is an eerie place, Harry."

I followed her gaze. "I suppose it is." The walls glowed with phosphorescent skeletons and skulls and gravestones. Bats were painted on the ceiling. The tablecloths were black. The waiters and waitresses wore loose tunics meant to suggest shrouds. I pointed with a breadstick. "Those stones would have been real, not plaster, if it hadn't been for Howie. Or this place wouldn't have been built. Take your pick."

This time she sipped her drink and I left mine alone. "I heard about that," she said. "The strike and all. But I was away that month. I didn't get back till it was all over."

True, I thought. I had forgotten for a moment. Though I shouldn't have. God knows I had missed her enough while she was settling her mother's estate.

"But I didn't hear Howie was mixed up in it. Tell me."

"Let's order first."


THE STORY had really begun just over a year ago, when Dick Witham had looked me up in the office of my oil business. I was at my desk, working over the piles of paper, bills to pay, bills to send out. It was a one-man operation, except for the drivers, but that was enough for our town, with its six thousand souls.

Dick hadn't made an appointment, but that didn't matter. If I'd been with someone else, he'd have waited or come back later. As it was, he waltzed in, unzipped his jacket, pulled the other office chair up to the corner of my desk, and said, "Hi, Harry."

Dick was a little less than average height, fortyish, and thick-bodied. His thinning hair was brushed straight back, and the rims of his glasses were almost invisible. He looked more like a desk-bound clerk than a successful realtor and insurance agent.

I took a second to finish adding up a column of figures on the calculator, wrote the answer down, and used a burner nozzle for a paperweight. "Hello yourself," I said. I gestured at my desktop. "Autumn leaves, I call 'em. They blow in here every year about this time. Haven't seen you for a few days, Dick. What's up?"

He waved a hand and grinned without showing his teeth. "Up to Boston," he said by way of explanation. "Bankers, lawyers, architects."

"The shopping center?" I knew he was working on one, collecting permits, buying land, lining up occupants.

"Yup." His voice softened, became a shade huskier. It seemed to emphasize the cologne he wore. "We're almost ready to break ground now. But we do need one more bit of land."

Ah, I thought. If he had wanted to see me as Mayor, he'd have gone to the Town Hall. But he was here. And I did own a few acres around and about.

"The old Cross property. You willing to sell?"

I shrugged. "If the price is right."

"It is. Enough to cover what your father paid for it, plus inflation, plus a profit."

It sounded good. It sounded even better when he named the price he had in mind. Enough cash to make even a profiteer happy. Perhaps, I told myself, there were advantages to dealing with old friends. But though I was willing to sell, I wasn't sure he would really want this particular piece of land when he knew more about it. I said as much, and he laughed. "It's just what we need," he assured me. "Gives us a parcel that just fits the architect's ideas. Good spot for the restaurant, too."

"But there's an old cemetery there, Dick. And an odd story, too."

He looked skeptical. I suggested we have a look at the property before we did anything else.

TWENTY minutes later, we were driving down the rutted dirt lane that led past the graveyard. We came to a sign that read, "Posted Bridge — Limit 5 Tons." We stopped beside the mossy pillars that marked what had once been the cemetery's entrance. The picket fence and gate had long since rotted into the soil, one with the guests it had protected from intrusion. What path there was, overgrown with brambles and low shrubs, flanked by heavy-trunked trees, had been trodden out by deer and hunters, fishermen and berry-pickers. This burying ground had been left to nature more than a century before. I told Dick, "I poked around in here once. Latest stone I found was marked eighteen twenty-three."

He didn't bother to hush his voice. The atmosphere, despite all the bare branches, blowing leaves, and ancient stones, didn't really seem to call for it. The dead were too long gone. "What was the oldest?" he asked.

"Hiram Cross's. That's the one I want to show you."

We left the path to push our way among the oaks and maples and occasional wild cherries. We scuffed leaves, picked an apple, and bore to the left, down the slope toward the stream. We passed graves, few of them with upright stones. They had been heaved by years of roots and frost. Many were flat and broken, their inscriptions unreadable. A few leaned like drunks clutching for nonexistent lamp posts. There were none of the elaborate monuments of less rural cemeteries, no obelisks or mausoleums. All the stones were simple slate or limestone slabs, headstones the size of chairbacks, footstones more like loaves of petrified bread.

We paused where one of the stones had tumbled into the path. It had broken into three pieces, and the breaks were as encrusted with lichen as the original surfaces. We could make out the blurred outline of a cross on one of them. "It has been awhile, hasn't it?" said Dick. He kicked at the ground. "Hah!" I looked. There was a yellow gleam in the forest mould, and in a moment he held a gold ring.

"Better put it back."

He shook his head and slipped the ring onto a finger. "A luck piece. An antique, too."

The sound of the breeze rattling among the boughs and the chuckling of the stream down the hill reminded me, at least, that the dead, deprived of the respect they deserved, could be vengeful. But I said nothing, and in a moment we were at our goal.

Hiram Cross's marker was the largest we had seen, and it was nearly upright, thanks to a trunk that had stopped its lean. The name upon it was clear. The dates below were barely legible.

Dick looked at it for a moment before he spoke. Then he said, "Did you know there's Crosses in my family? My grandmother was one."

I hadn't known. I didn't know what difference it might make, either. I said, "Sixteen sixty-six to seventeen fifty. And an epitaph."

"Ayuh," said Dick. "But you can't read it."

"Not now, maybe." You could count the lines — six — but you couldn't quite make out the words. A letter here and there was clear. The rest was obliterated by lichen and decay. "But you could when I was a kid. At least, you could puzzle it out."

"You remember how it went?"

"I think so." I had been searching my memory ever since he had asked about the property. I could have given him the gist of it without any trouble. But I wanted to give him the whole of it, and he wanted the same thing. After a suitably dramatic pause, I recited:

> "For all his days
> He grew no moss
> At last at rest

construction site. It was about then that we got the phone call about Bonny's mother and she had to leave me for awhile.

Dick brought in three bulldozers, but before they got to the graveyard, he had the stones gathered up and set aside. He was already thinking of how he might use them in the restaurant.

When they did get to the graveyard, all went well at first. All might have stayed well, too, if the ground hadn't been so full of stumps and roots and, as usual in this state of Maine, rocks. But to smooth the ground at all, the dozers had to bite deep. They had to break into the graves and scatter bones and bits of rotten coffins throughout the site.

That was when it happened. All three dozers broke down, and within an hour of each other at that. "How" was no problem — one had a clot of grave mould jammed in its air intake; another had a corroded brass coffin nail through its radiator; the third had a thigh bone caught between the drive wheel and the tread. Nothing disastrous, nothing irreparable, but annoying, time-consuming, and ominous. The "why" was the mystery.

It took the rest of that day and half the next to get the machines fixed and back to work. But it didn't last, and this time the delay was worse. A worker, idle on his lunch hour, was scraping lichen off the stacked gravestones when he discovered Hiram's and read the epitaph. He told his mates, and they unanimously refused to go back to work "till the curse was off."

I heard about the strike when Dick dropped into my office, the one in the Town Hall. With Bonny gone, there wasn't any secretary to show him in, so the first I knew he was there was when he cleared his throat and said, "Mayor Bowen."

I looked up from the grant application I was examining. He was disheveled, his hands were dirty, his suit smudged. "Hello, Dick," I said. "What's up?"

He told me. The breakdowns. The strike. That impossible curse! He still didn't believe in it, but what was he to do?

"It sounds," I suggested, "like you've at least got to go through the motions of taking the hex off. If you want to get the job done, that is." My pipe was lying beside the ashtray. I picked it up, tapped the ashes down, and lit it. I blew a cloud of smoke at the desktop. It fanned out like dust behind an unloading dump truck.

He thought about it. He realized I wasn't telling him the curse was real, and he accepted that. Going through motions was something he knew how to do. He nodded. He said, "But what do I do?"

"For openers, we go look for Howie Wyman."

HOWIE was an old friend of mine, an unambitious, odd-jobbing country boy who liked nothing better than fishing and hunting. He usually wore a green felt hat whose brim flapped in the breeze, dirty overalls, faded checked shirts, and well-aged leather boots. Today was no exception, except that the hat was off — his wife, Emma, saw to that when he was in the house — and his shaggy gray head was open for inspection. Not that anyone would want to get too close.

We found him at home, a brick ranch full of aging furnishings Emma kept spotless and shining. She showed us into the living room, where Howie was watching a soap opera, his feet up on a hassock and a beer in his hand. She turned the sound down on the TV, and we all found seats. Dick took the couch, Emma a straight-backed chair. I chose a platform rocker that might have been new when my father was a boy.

When we'd finished saying hello, I said, "Dick's got a problem, Howie. Maybe you can help."

"Ayuh." He drained his beer and fished a plug of linty tobacco from his hip pocket. As he tore a chunk free, Emma got up, crossed the room, and pulled an empty lard can from behind the couch. Her lips were pursed as she set it down beside her husband's chair. She set it down hard.

Dick began to explain the background, but he was hardly through with his description of the project when Emma interrupted. "We *don't* need another shopping center," she said. "Downtown should be good enough without taking some poor farmer's fields and . . ."

We heard her out, and when she ran down, Howie said, "Want to go outside? There's a bench or two by the orchard."

We went, leaving the soap opera to Emma, and Dick picked up his story again. When he was done, Howie spat a dark brown stream toward one of his apple trees. I looked at the tree. Its bark bore a large stain, the mark of Howie's constant target practice, but the tobacco juice didn't seem to have hurt it. It was covered with the tiny green nubbins that, every year, replace the blossoms. I thought of how they would swell, turn red, and touch the air with wine, and my mouth watered.

Howie said, "You're a Cross yourself, ain't you?" Dick nodded and looked interested. Howie added, "Well, old Hiram was a family man, even if he weren't home much. Might count for somethin'."

"What do you mean?" asked Dick. I could see he wasn't too happy. Howie seemed to be taking the curse seriously.

"Can't undo anythin'. But you might mollify him. Put him back to bed and build you a house right over him."

"You mean, give him a family life again?" I put in.

"Ayuh."

"It is a good spot for a house," I added. "The brook and all."

"Impossible!" said Dick. "That's going to be the restaurant. It's in the blueprints." Going through the motions was clearly one thing, but this! This just wouldn't do! Live with a graveyard in the basement? No way! Watching the feelings fly across his face, I almost laughed.

Howie just shrugged. He spat again. "Ayuh. Won't help, but you might replant him in another graveyard."

"*That* I'll try," said Dick.

AND HE did. He talked the workers into gathering up all the bones they could find, tossing them helter-skelter into packing cases, and moving them across town to another old cemetery. He hired a minister to say a few words. Then he covered the old bones up and tried to forget them.

I was on hand for the brief ceremony. So was Howie, and it was clear that my friend did not find Dick's optimism very realistic. When Dick left to get work going again on his shopping center, Howie shook his head and muttered, "Won't work." I don't think anyone heard him but me.

For the next few days, Dick seemed more right than Howie. All went well. The dozers finished preparing the site. The workers knocked forms together and began to pour the footings and walls. But when they got to pouring the walls for the restaurant, walls that would enclose what had been the graveyard . . .

Dick burst into my office, dressed in overalls and speckled with bits of dry, gray concrete. His eyes were wide and his face was ambiguously blotched, simultaneously flushed and pale. His hands shook. At first, I thought he was angry. Then I said to myself, "He's scared."

He was both. That was quickly clear, as he stumbled into a chair and gasped, "I was right there. And it happened. Just like that. What'll I tell his mother?"

I calmed him down with a drink from the office bottle. Then I got the story out of him. He had been supervising the pouring of the concrete, helping out as necessary. "I was standing right on top of the form," he told me. "And it gave way. I grabbed the mixer's chute, but Sam . . ." Sam was one of the younger workers on the crew. He had been standing on the ground when the still-liquid concrete burst its restraints, knocked him down, and covered him. Before they could get him out, he had suffocated.

"There was no warning. It didn't creak or groan or anything," said Dick. He held out his glass. I filled it again. And then he gave me the punch line: When they had cleaned up the mess, they had found a jawbone, still caught on the edge of a form plate. The men swore it hadn't been there when they put the forms together, and now they were on strike again.

Somehow, I wasn't surprised. I called Howie, gave him the tale, and he wasn't either. He did, however, say he wanted to see what had happened. Would we meet him there?

THERE wasn't a worker in sight when we arrived. There was just Howie, pacing the tops of what walls were standing, surveying the layout. We headed across the piles of dirt and rubble toward him. As we passed the construction company's office trailer, the door opened and a small man came out. Dick stopped to wait for him, saying, "That's the architect. Saul Nemmers."

I studied the approaching figure. Nemmers was clad in suntans, with black curls escaping from beneath a visored cap. His face was square, and he wore a toothbrush mustache under a blunt nose. He was younger than I might have expected, still in his twenties.

He didn't say a word when he joined us. He just fell in as we started walking again. When we reached Howie, my friend was staring at the site of the graveyard. He turned to look down at Dick from his vantage atop the wall. "Happened here?"

"You can see the gap in the forms."

"Ayuh." Howie shook his head. He spat into the dust and jumped off the wall to land beside us. "So I was right the first time."

Only then did Nemmers say anything. "What do you mean?"

I explained. Howie thought old Hiram might forgive the shaking up Dick had given his bones if only Dick, a descendant, would give him a family life again. Put Hiram back where he belonged, build a house over his grave, and live in it.

Nemmers opened his mouth. He shut it. He looked thoughtful. Finally he said, "Would an apartment do?"

We all looked at him. I laughed, but wasn't that what architects were for? To solve the problems that plagued any construction project?

Howie must have guessed my thought, for he smiled as he said, "Might."

Dick said, "But the restaurant!"

Nemmers said, "Put it on a second floor. You'd get a better view that way anyway."

AND THAT'S the way it worked out. The very next day, while Nemmers revised his blueprints, Dick had the crates full of bones retrieved. Howie solved the problem of sorting Hiram's remains from all the rest by spilling all the bones out in a line, bending two brass rods into L shapes, and walking down the line holding the short legs of the L's in his fists. When the long legs dipped, he had another piece of Hiram.

When Howie was done with his dowsing, Hiram got a new coffin. His neighbors were simply parcelled out into as many piles as there were headstones, one skull to a pile, and packed into cardboard boxes for their third burial. I was sure we made some odd bedfellows that way, but I didn't think they were in any state to mind. Then we laid the stones flat, about where they'd been in the first place, and poured a slab of concrete over the whole shebang. That would be the apartment floor.

Howie spoke to the workers, too, and they came back. Most of them, anyway. There were a few who had been scared enough to look for other jobs. Those who did come back had no more problems. The rest of the work went without a hitch, and the revised design, leaning toward the stream the way it does, was even better than the original. It actually won Nemmers an award.

BY THE time I'd finished, Bonny and I were both full of white wine and scallops. We were on the cheesecake and coffee, and she was shaking her head. Her lips were pursed as if in disgust, though there was a twitch to the corner of her mouth. "That story doesn't help the atmosphere at all," she said. "Imagine! Eating dinner over a graveyard!"

I nodded and sipped my coffee. "It's a busy place, though. That story doesn't keep folks away."

At that moment, I felt a hand on my shoulder. "Everything all right, Bonny? Harry?"

We both looked up. It was Dick. The owner, circulating among his guests, greeting friends and regulars. His hand, which still wore the gold ring he had kicked out of the dirt, held a glass half full of clear liquid. "Just fine," I said. "Couldn't be better."

"Where did you find your chef?" asked Bonny.

"Dug him up in Portland. I have nightmares they'll want him back." He patted my shoulder, nodded to Bonny, and left to visit another table.

Bonny and I looked at each other. The bags under Dick's eyes were the size and color of used teabags, and his breath smelled of gin. She shook her head, her dark hair bouncing, and said, "I don't think he sleeps enough to have nightmares."

I followed Dick with my eyes. He wasn't married, and bachelors didn't have much of a family life to offer anyone, much less a ghost. I nodded, once. "Hiram was a mite active, you know. Maybe he still is."

*H. P. Lovecraft*

# THE SHUNNED HOUSE

ROM EVEN THE greatest of horrors irony is seldom absent. Sometimes it enters directly into the composition of the events, while sometimes it relates only to their fortuitous position among persons and places. The latter sort is splendidly exemplified by a case in the ancient city of Providence, where in the late forties Edgar Allan Poe used to sojourn often during his unsuccessful wooing of the gifted poetess, Mrs. Whitman. Poe generally stopped at the Mansion House in Benefit Street — the renamed Golden Ball Inn whose roof has sheltered Washington, Jefferson, and Lafayette — and his favourite walk led northward along the same street to Mrs. Whitman's home and the neighbouring hillside churchyard of St. John's whose hidden expanse of eighteenth-century gravestones had for him a peculiar fascination.

Now the irony is this. In this walk, so many times repeated, the world's greatest master of the terrible and the bizarre was obliged to pass a particular house on the eastern side of the street; a dingy, antiquated structure perched on the abruptly rising side hill, with a great unkept yard dating from a time when the region was partly open country. It does not appear that he ever wrote or spoke of it, nor is there any evidence that he even noticed it. And yet that house, to the two persons in possession of certain information, equals or outranks in horror the wildest phantasy of the genius who so often passed it unknowingly, and stands starkly leering as a symbol of all that is unutterably hideous.

The house was — and for that matter still is — of a kind to attract the attention of the curious. Originally a farm or semi-farm building, it followed the average New England colonial lines of the middle eighteenth century — the prosperous peaked-roof sort, with two stories and dormerless attic, and with the Georgian doorway and interior panelling dictated by the progress of taste at that time. It faced south, with one gable end buried to the lower windows in the eastward rising hill, and the other exposed to the foundations toward the street. Its construction, over a century and a half ago, had followed the grading and straightening of the road in that especial vicinity; for Benefit Street — at first called Back Street — was laid out as a lane winding amongst the graveyards of the first settlers, and straightened only when the removal of the bodies to the North Burial Ground made it decently possible to cut through the old family plots.

At the start, the western wall had lain some twenty feet up a precipitous lawn from the roadway; but a widening of the street at about the time of the Revolution sheared off most of the intervening space, exposing the foundations so that a brick basement wall had to be made, giving the deep cellar a street frontage with the door and two windows above ground, close to the new line of public travel. When the sidewalk was laid out a century ago the last of the intervening space was removed; and Poe in his walks must have seen only a sheer ascent of dull grey brick flush with the sidewalk and surmounted at a height of ten feet by the antique shingled bulk of the house proper.

The farmlike grounds extended back very deeply up the hill, almost to Wheaton Street. The space south of the house, abutting on Benefit Street, was of course greatly above the existing sidewalk level, forming a terrace bounded by a high bank wall of damp, mossy stone pierced by a steep flight of narrow steps which led inward between canyon-like surfaces to the upper region of mangy lawn, rheumy brick walls, and neglected gardens whose dismantled cement urns, rusted kettles fallen from tripods of knotty sticks, and similar paraphernalia set off the weatherbeaten front door with its broken fanlight, rotting Ionic pilasters, and wormy triangular pediment.

What I heard in my youth about the shunned house was merely that people died there in alarmingly great numbers. That, I was told, was why the original owners had moved out some twenty years after building the place. It was plainly unhealthy, perhaps because of the dampness and fungous growth in the cellar, the general sickish smell, the draughts of the hallways, or the quality of the well and pump water. These things were bad enough, and these were all that gained belief among the persons whom I knew. Only the notebooks of my antiquarian uncle, Dr. Elihu Whipple, revealed to me at length the darker, vaguer surmises which formed an undercurrent of folklore among old-time servants and humble folk, surmises which never travelled far, and which were largely forgotten when Providence grew to be a metropolis with a shifting modern population.

The general fact is, that the house was never regarded by the solid part of the community as in any real sense "haunted." There were no widespread tales of rattling chains, cold currents of air, extinguished lights, or faces at the window. Extremists sometimes said the house was "unlucky," but that is as far as even they went. What was really beyond dispute is that a frightful proportion of persons died there; or more accurately, *had* died there, since after some peculiar happenings over sixty years ago the building had become deserted through the sheer impossibility of renting it. These persons were not all cut off suddenly by any one cause; rather did it seem that their vitality was insidiously sapped, so that each one died the sooner from whatever tendency to weakness he may have naturally had. And those who did not die displayed in varying degree a type of anaemia or consumption, and sometimes a decline of the mental faculties, which spoke ill for the salubriousness of the building. Neighbouring houses, it must be added, seemed entirely free from the noxious quality.

This much I knew before my insistent questioning led my uncle to show me the notes which finally embarked us both on our hideous investigation. In my childhood the shunned house was vacant, with barren, gnarled and terrible old trees, long, queerly pale grass and nightmarishly misshapen weeds in the high terraced yard where birds never lingered. We boys used to overrun the place, and I can still recall my youthful terror not only at the morbid strangeness of this sinister vegetation, but at the eldritch atmosphere and odour of the dilapidated house, whose unlocked front door was often entered in quest of shudders. The small-paned windows were largely broken, and a nameless air of desolation hung round the precarious panelling, shaky interior shutters, peeling wallpaper, falling plaster, rickety staircases, and such fragments of battered furniture as still remained. The dust and cobwebs added their touch of the fearful; and brave indeed was the boy who would voluntarily ascend the ladder to the attic, a vast raftered length lighted only by small blinking windows in the gable ends, and filled with a massed wreckage of chests, chairs, and spinning-wheels which infinite years of deposit had shrouded and fes-tooned into monstrous and hellish shapes.

But after all, the attic was not the most terrible part of the house. It was the dank, humid cellar which somehow exerted the strongest repul-sion on us, even though it was wholly above ground on the street side, with only a thin door and window-pierced brick wall to separate it from the busy sidewalk. We scarcely knew whether to haunt it in spectral fascina-tion, or to shun it for the sake of our souls and our sanity. For one thing, the bad odour of the house was strongest there; and for another thing, we did not like the white fungous growths which occasionally sprang up in rainy summer weather from the hard earth floor. Those fungi, grotesquely like the vegetation in the yard outside, were truly horrible in their outlines; detestable parodies of toadstools and Indian pipes, whose like we had never seen in any other situation. They rotted quickly, and at one stage became slightly phosphorescent; so that nocturnal passers-by sometimes spoke of witch-fires glowing behind the broken panes of the foetor-spread-ing windows.

We never — even in our wildest Hallowe'en moods — visited this cellar by night, but in some of our daytime visits could detect the phospho-rescence, especially when the day was dark and wet. There was also a subtler thing we often thought we detected — a very strange thing which was, however, merely suggestive at most. I refer to a sort of cloudy whitish pattern on the dirt floor — a vague, shifting deposit of mould or nitre which we sometimes thought we could trace amidst the sparse fungous growths near the huge fireplace of the basement kitchen. Once in a while it struck us that this patch bore an uncanny resemblance to a doubled-up human figure, though generally no such kinship existed, and often there was no whitish deposit whatever. On a certain rainy afternoon when this illusion seemed phenomenally strong, and when, in addition, I had fancied I glimpsed a kind of thin, yellowish, shimmering exhalation rising from the nitrous pattern toward the yawning fireplace, I spoke to my uncle about the matter. He smiled at this odd conceit, but it seemed that his smile was tinged with reminiscence. Later I heard that a similar notion entered into some of the wild ancient tales of the common folk — a notion likewise alluding to ghoulish, wolfish shapes taken by smoke from the great chimney, and queer contours assumed by certain of the sinuous tree-roots that thrust their way into the cellar through the loose foundation-stones.

NOT TILL my adult years did my uncle set before me the notes and data which he had collected concerning the shunned house. Dr. Whipple was a sane, conservative physician of the old school, and for all his interest in the place was not eager to encourage young thoughts toward the abnormal. His own view, postulating simply a building and location of markedly unsanitary qualities, had nothing to do with abnormality; but he realized that the very picturesqueness which aroused his own interest would in a boy's fanciful mind take on all manner of gruesome imaginative associations.

The doctor was a bachelor; a white-haired, clean-shaven, old-fashioned gentleman, and a local historian of note, who had often broken a lance with such controversial guardians of tradition as Sidney S. Rider and Thomas W. Bicknell. He lived with one manservant in a Georgian homestead with knocker and iron-railed steps, balanced eerily on the steep ascent of North Court Street beside the ancient brick court and colony house where his grandfather — a cousin of that celebrated privateersman, Capt. Whipple, who burnt His Majesty's armed schooner *Gaspee* in 1772 — had voted in the legislature on May 4, 1776, for the independence of the Rhode Island Colony. Around him in the damp, low-ceiled library with the musty white panelling, heavy carved overmantel and small-paned, vine-shaded windows, were the relics and records of his ancient family, among which were many dubious allusions to the shunned house in Benefit Street. That pest spot lies not far distant — for Benefit runs ledgewise just above the court house along the precipitous hill up which the first settlement climbed.

When, in the end, my insistent pestering and maturing years evoked from my uncle the hoarded lore I sought, there lay before me a strange enough chronicle. Long-winded, statistical, and drearily genealogical as some of the matter was, there ran through it a continuous thread of brooding, tenacious horror and preternatural malevolence which impressed me even more than it had impressed the good doctor. Separate events fitted together uncannily, and seemingly irrelevant details held mines of hideous possibilities. A new and burning curiosity grew in me, compared to which my boyish curiosity was feeble and inchoate. The first revelation led to an exhaustive research, and finally to that shuddering quest which proved so disastrous to myself and mine. For at last my uncle insisted on joining the search I had commenced, and after a certain night in that house he did not come away with me. I am lonely without that gentle soul whose long years were filled only with honour, virtue, good taste, benevolence, and learning. I have reared a marble urn to his memory in St. John's churchyard — the place that Poe loved — the hidden grove of giant willows on the hill, where tombs and headstones huddle quietly between the hoary bulk of the church and the houses and bank walls of Benefit Street.

The history of the house, opening amidst a maze of dates, revealed no trace of the sinister either about its construction or about the prosperous and honourable family who built it. Yet from the first a taint of calamity, soon increased to boding significance, was apparent. My uncle's carefully compiled record began with the building of the structure in 1763, and followed the theme with an unusual amount of detail. The shunned house, it seems, was first inhabited by William Harris and his wife Rhoby Dexter, with their children, Elkanah, born in 1755, Abigail, born in 1757, William, Jr., born in 1759, and Ruth, born in 1761. Harris was a substantial merchant and seaman in the West India trade, connected with the firm of Obadiah Brown and his nephews. After Brown's death in 1761, the new firm of Nicholas Brown & Co. made him master of the brig *Prudence,* Providence-built, of 120 tons, thus enabling him to erect the new homestead he had desired ever since his marriage.

The site he had chosen — a recently straightened part of the new and fashionable Back Street, which ran along the side of the hill above crowded Cheapside — was all that could be wished, and the building did justice to the location. It was the best that moderate means could afford, and Harris hastened to move in before the birth of a fifth child which the family expected. That child, a boy, came in December; but was still-born. Nor was any child to be born alive in that house for a century and a half.

The next April sickness occurred among the children, and Abigail and Ruth died before the month was over. Dr. Job Ives diagnosed the trouble as some infantile fever, though others declared it was more of a mere wasting-away or decline. It seemed, in any event, to be contagious; for Hannah Bowen, one of the two servants, died of it in the following June. Eli Lideason, the other servant, constantly complained of weakness; and would have returned to his father's farm in Rehoboth but for a sudden attachment for Mehitabel Pierce, who was hired to succeed Hannah. He died the next year — a sad year indeed, since it marked the death of William Harris himself, enfeebled as he was by the climate of Martinique, where his occupation had kept him for considerable periods during the preceding decade.

The widowed Rhoby Harris never recovered from the shock of her husband's death, and the passing of her firstborn Elkanah two years later was the final blow to her reason. In 1768 she fell victim to a mild form of insanity, and was thereafter confined to the upper part of the house; her elder maiden sister, Mercy Dexter, having moved in to take charge of the family. Mercy was a plain, raw-boned woman of great strength; but her health visibly declined from the time of her advent. She was greatly devoted to her unfortunate sister, and had an especial affection for her only surviving nephew William, who from a sturdy infant had become a sickly, spindling lad. In this year the servant Mehitabel died, and the other servant, Preserved Smith, left without coherent explanation — or at least, with only some wild tales and a complaint that he disliked the smell of the place. For a time Mercy could secure no more help since the seven deaths and case of madness, all occurring within five years' space, had begun to set in motion the body of fireside rumour which later became so bizarre. Ultimately, however, she obtained new servants from out of town; Ann White, a morose woman from that part of North Kingstown now set off as the township of Exeter, and a capable Boston man named Zenas Low.

It was Ann White who first gave definite shape to the sinister idle talk. Mercy should have known better than to hire anyone from the Nooseneck Hill country, for that remote bit of backwoods was then, as now, a seat of the most uncomfortable superstitions. As lately as 1892 an Exeter community exhumed a body and ceremoniously burnt its heart in order to prevent certain alleged visitations injurious to the public health and peace, and one may imagine the point of view of the same section in 1768. Ann's tongue was perniciously active, and within a few months Mercy discharged her, filling her place with a faithful and amiable Amazon from Newport, Maria Robbins.

Meanwhile poor Rhoby Harris, in her madness, gave voice to dreams and imaginings of the most hideous sort. At times her screams became insupportable, and for long periods she would utter shrieking horrors which necessitated her son's temporary residence with his cousin, Peleg Harris, in Presbyterian Lane near the new college building. The boy would seem to improve after these visits, and had Mercy been as wise as she was well-meaning, she would have let him live permanently with Peleg. Just what Mrs. Harris cried out in her fits of violence, tradition hesitates to say; or rather, presents such extravagant accounts that they nullify themselves through sheer absurdity. Certainly it sounds absurd to hear that a woman educated only in the rudiments of French often shouted for hours in a coarse and idiomatic form of that language, or that the same person, alone and guarded, complained wildly of a staring thing which bit and chewed at her. In 1772 the servant Zenas died, and when Mrs. Harris heard of it she laughed with a shocking delight utterly foreign to her. The next year she herself died, and was laid to rest in the North Burial Ground beside her husband.

Upon the outbreak of trouble with Great Britain in 1775, William Harris, despite his scant sixteen years and feeble constitution, managed to enlist in the Army of Observation under General Greene; and from that time on enjoyed a steady rise in health and prestige. In 1780, as a Captain in Rhode Island forces in New Jersey under Colonel Angell, he met and married Phebe Hetfield of Elizabethtown, whom he brought to Providence upon his honourable discharge in the following year.

The young soldier's return was not a thing of unmitigated happiness. The house, it is true, was still in good condition; and the street had been widened and changed in name from Back Street to Benefit Street. But Mercy Dexter's once robust frame had undergone a sad and curious decay, so that she was now a stooped and pathetic figure with hollow voice and disconcerting pallor — qualities shared to a singular degree by the one remaining servant Maria. In the autumn of 1782 Phebe Harris gave birth to a still-born daughter and on the fifteenth of the next May Mercy Dexter took leave of a useful, austere, and virtuous life.

William Harris, at last thoroughly convinced of the radically unhealthful nature of his abode, now took steps toward quitting it and closing it forever. Securing temporary quarters for himself and wife at the newly opened Golden Ball Inn, he arranged for the building of a new and finer house in Westminster Street, in the growing part of the town across the Great Bridge. There, in 1785, his son Dutee was born; and there the family dwelt till the encroachments of commerce drove them back across the river and over the hill to Angell Street, in the newer East Side residence district, where the late Archer Harris built his sumptuous but hideous French-roofed mansion in 1876. William and Phebe both succumbed to the yellow fever epidemic of 1797, but Dutee was brought up by his cousin Rathbone Harris, Peleg's son.

Rathbone was a practical man, and rented the Benefit Street house despite William's wish to keep it vacant. He considered it an obligation to his ward to make the most of all the boy's property, nor did he concern himself with the deaths and illnesses which caused so many changes of tenants, or the steadily growing aversion with which the house was generally regarded. It is likely that he felt only vexation when, in 1804, the town council ordered him to fumigate the place with sulphur, tar and gum camphor on account of the much-discussed deaths of four persons, presumably caused by the then diminishing fever epidemic. They said the place had a febrile smell.

Dutee himself thought little of the house, for he grew up to be a privateersman, and served with distinction on the *Vigilant* under Capt. Cahoone in the War of 1812. He returned unharmed, married in 1814, and became a father on that memorable night of September 23, 1815, when a great gale drove the waters of the bay over half the town, and floated a tall sloop well up Westminster Street so that its masts almost tapped the Harris windows in symbolic affirmation that the new boy, Welcome, was a seaman's son.

Welcome did not survive his father, but lived to perish gloriously at Fredericksburg in 1862. Neither he nor his son Archer knew of the shunned house as other than a nuisance almost impossible to rent — perhaps on account of the mustiness and sickly odour of unkempt old age. Indeed, it never was rented after a series of deaths culminating in 1861, which the excitement of the war tended to throw into obscurity. Carrington Harris, last of the male line, knew it only as a deserted and somewhat picturesque center of legend until I told him my experience. He had meant to tear it down and build an apartment house on the site, but after my account decided to let it stand, install plumbing, and rent it. Nor has he yet had any difficulty in obtaining tenants. The horror has gone.

## III

IT MAY well be imagined how powerfully I was affected by the annals of the Harrises. In this continuous record there seemed to me to brood a persistent evil beyond anything in nature as I had known it; an evil clearly connected with the house and not with the family. This impression was confirmed by my uncle's less systematic array of miscellaneous data — legends transcribed from servant gossip, cuttings from the papers, copies of death certificates by fellow-physicians, and the like. All of this material I cannot hope to give, for my uncle was a tireless antiquarian and very deeply interested in the shunned house; but I may refer to several dominant points which earn notice by their recurrence through many reports from diverse sources. For example, the servant gossip was practically unanimous in attributing to the fungous and malodorous *cellar* of the house a vast supremacy in evil influence. There had been servants — Ann White especially — who would not use the cellar kitchen, and at least three well-defined legends bore upon the queer quasi-human or diabolic outlines assumed by tree-roots and patches of mould in that region. These latter narratives interested me profoundly, on account of what I had seen in my boyhood, but I felt that most of the significance had in each case been largely obscured by additions from the common stock of local ghost lore.

Ann White, with her Exeter superstition, had promulgated the most extravagant and at the same time most consistent tale; alleging that there must lie buried beneath the house one of those vampires — the dead who retain their bodily form and live on the blood or breath of the living — whose hideous legions send their preying shapes or spirits abroad by night. To destroy a vampire one must, the grandmothers say, exhume it and burn its heart, or at least drive a stake through that organ; and Ann's dogged insistence on a search under the cellar had been prominent in bringing about her discharge.

Her tales, however, commanded a wide audience, and were the more readily accepted because the house indeed stood on land once used for burial purposes. To me their interest depended less on this circumstance than on the peculiarly appropriate way in which they dove-tailed with certain other things — the complaint of the departing servant Preserved Smith, who had preceded Ann and never heard of her, that something "sucked his breath" at night; the death-certificates of fever victims of 1804, issued by Dr. Chad Hopkins, and showing the four deceased persons all unaccountably lacking in blood; and the obscure passages of poor Rhoby Harris's ravings, where she complained of the sharp teeth of a glassy-eyed, half-visible presence.

Free from unwarranted superstition though I am, these things produced in me an odd sensation, which was intensified by a pair of widely separated newspaper cuttings relating to deaths in the shunned house — one from the *Providence Gazette and Country-Journal* of April 12, 1815, and the other from the *Daily Transcript and Chronicle* of October 27, 1845 — each of which detailed an appallingly grisly circumstance whose duplication was remarkable. It seems that in both instances the dying person, in 1815 a gentle old lady named Stafford and in 1845 a school-teacher of middle age named Eleazar Durfee, became transfigured in a horrible way; glaring glassily and attempting to bite the throat of the attending physician. Even more puzzling, though, was the final case which put an end to the renting of the house — a series of anaemia deaths preceded by progressive madnesses wherein the patient would craftily attempt the lives of his relatives by incisions in the neck or wrists.

This was in 1860 and 1861, when my uncle had just begun his medical practice; and before leaving for the front he heard much of it from his elder professional colleagues. The really inexplicable thing was the way in which the victims — ignorant people, for the ill-smelling and widely shunned house could now be rented to no others — would babble maledictions in French, a language they could not possibly have studied to any extent. It made one think of poor Rhoby Harris nearly a century before, and so moved my uncle that he commenced collecting historical data on the house after listening, some time subsequent to his return from the war, to the first-hand account of Drs. Chase and Whitmarsh. Indeed, I could see that my uncle had thought deeply on the subject, and that he was glad of my own interest — an open-minded and sympathetic interest which enabled him to discuss with me matters at which others would merely have laughed. His fancy had not gone so far as mine, but he felt that the place was rare in its imaginative potentialities, and worthy of note as an inspiration in the field of the grotesque and macabre.

For my part, I was disposed to take the whole subject with profound seriousness, and began at once not only to review the evidence, but to accumulate as much as I could. I talked with the elderly Archer Harris, then owner of the house, many times before his death in 1916; and obtained from him and his still surviving maiden sister Alice an authentic corroboration of all the family data my uncle had collected. When, however, I asked them what connection with France or its language the house could have, they confessed themselves as frankly baffled and ignorant as I. Archer knew nothing, and all that Miss Harris could say was that an old allusion her grandfather, Dutee Harris, had heard of might have shed a little light. The old seaman, who had survived his son Welcome's death in battle by two years, had not himself known the legend; but recalled that his earliest nurse, the ancient Maria Robbins, seemed darkly aware of something that might have lent a weird significance to the French ravings of Rhoby Harris, which she had so often heard during the last days of that hapless woman. Maria had been at the shunned house from 1769 till the removal of the family in 1783, and had seen Mercy Dexter die. Once she hinted to the child Dutee of a somewhat peculiar circumstance in Mercy's last moments, but he had soon forgotten all about it save that it was something peculiar. The grand-daughter, moreover, recalled even this much with difficulty. She and her brother were not so much interested in the house as was Archer's son Carrington, the present owner, with whom I talked after my experience.

Having exhausted the Harris family of all the information it could furnish, I turned my attention to early town records and deeds with a zeal more penetrating than that which my uncle had occasionally shown in the same work. What I wished was a comprehensive history of the site from its very settlement in 1636 — or even before, if any Narragansett Indian legend could be unearthed to supply the data. I found, at the start, that the land had been part of the long strip of the lot granted originally to John Throckmorton; one of many similar strips beginning at the Town Street beside the river and extending up over the hill to a line roughly corresponding with the modern Hope Street. The Throckmorton lot had later, of course, been much subdivided; and I became very assiduous in tracing that section through which Back or Benefit Street was later run. It had, a rumour indeed said, been the Throckmorton graveyard; but as I examined the records more carefully, I found that the graves had all been transferred at an early date to the North Burial Ground on the Pawtucket West Road.

Then suddenly I came — by a rare piece of chance, since it was not in the main body of records and might easily have been missed — upon something which aroused my keenest eagerness, fitting in as it did with several of the queerest phases of the affair. It was the record of a lease in 1697, of a small tract of ground to an Etienne Roulet and wife. At last the French element had appeared — that, and another deeper element of horror which the name conjured up from the darkest recesses of my weird and heterogeneous reading — and I feverishly studied the platting of the locality as it had been before the cutting through and partial straightening of Back Street between 1747 and 1758. I found what I had half expected, that where the shunned house now stood the Roulets had laid out their graveyard behind a one-story and attic cottage, and that no record of any transfer of graves existed. The document, indeed, ended in much confusion; and I was forced to ransack both the Rhode Island Historical Society and Shepley Library before I could find a local door which the name of Etienne Roulet would unlock. In the end I did find something; something of such vague but monstrous import that I set about at once to examine the cellar of the shunned house itself with a new and excited minuteness.

The Roulets, it seemed, had come in 1696 from East Greenwich, down the west shore of Narragansett Bay. They were Huguenots from Caude, and had encountered much opposition before the Providence selectmen allowed them to settle in the town. Unpopularity had dogged them in East Greenwich, whither they had come in 1686, after the revocation of the Edict of Nantes, and rumour said that the cause of dislike extended beyond mere racial and national prejudice, or the land disputes which involved other French settlers with the English in rivalries which not even Governor Andros could quell. But their ardent Protestantism —

too ardent, some whispered — and their evident distress when virtually driven from the village down the bay, had moved the sympathy of the town fathers. Here the strangers had been granted a haven; and the swarthy Etienne Roulet, less apt at agriculture than at reading queer books and drawing queer diagrams, was given a clerical post in the warehouse at Pardon Tillinghast's wharf, far south in Town Street. There had, however, been a riot of some sort later on — perhaps forty years later, after old Roulet's death — and no one seemed to hear of the family after that.

For a century and more, it appeared, the Roulets had been well remembered and frequently discussed as vivid incidents in the quiet life of a New England seaport. Etienne's son Paul, a surly fellow whose erratic conduct had probably provoked the riot which had wiped out the family, was particularly a source of speculation; and though Providence never shared the witchcraft panics of her Puritan neighbours, it was freely intimated by old wives that his prayers were neither uttered at the proper time nor directed toward the proper object. All this had undoubtedly formed the basis of the legend known by old Maria Robbins. What relation it had to the French ravings of Rhoby Harris and other inhabitants of the shunned house, imagination or future discovery alone could determine. I wondered how many of those who had known the legends realized that additional link with the terrible which my wider reading had given me; that ominous item in the annals of morbid horror which tells of the creature *Jacques Roulet, of Caude,* who in 1598 was condemned to death as a daemoniac but afterward saved from the stake by the Paris parliament and shut in a madhouse. He had been found covered with blood and shreds of flesh in a wood, shortly after the killing and rending of a boy by a pair of wolves. One wolf was seen to lope away unhurt. Surely a pretty hearthside tale, with a queer significance as to name and place; but I decided that the Providence gossips could not have generally known of it. Had they known, the coincidence of names would have brought some drastic and frightened action — indeed, might not its limited whispering have precipitated the final riot which erased the Roulets from the town?

I now visited the accursed place with increased frequency; studying the unwholesome vegetation of the garden, examining all the walls of the building, and poring over every inch of the earthen cellar floor. Finally, with Carrington Harris's permission, I fitted a key to the disused door opening from the cellar directly upon Benefit Street, preferring to have a more immediate access to the outside world than the dark stairs, ground floor hall, and front door could give. There, where morbidity lurked most thickly, I searched and poked during long afternoons when the sunlight filtered in through the cobwebbed above-ground door which placed me only a few feet from the placid sidewalk outside. Nothing new rewarded my efforts — only the same depressing mustiness and faint suggestions of noxious odours and nitrous outlines on the floor — and I fancy that many pedestrians must have watched me curiously through the broken panes.

At length, upon a suggestion of my uncle's, I decided to try the spot nocturnally; and one stormy midnight ran the beams of an electric torch over the mouldy floor with its uncanny shapes and distorted, half-phosphorescent fungi. The place had dispirited me curiously that evening, and I was almost prepared when I saw — or thought I saw — amidst the whitish deposits a particularly sharp definition of the "huddled form" I had suspected from boyhood. Its clearness was astonishing and unprecedented — and as I watched I seemed to see again the thin, yellowish, shimmering exhalation which had startled me on that rainy afternoon so many years before.

Above the anthropomorphic patch of mould by the fireplace it rose; a subtle, sickish, almost luminous vapour which as it hung trembling in the dampness seemed to develop vague and shocking suggestions of form, gradually trailing off into nebulous decay and passing up into the blackness of the great chimney with a foetor in its wake. It was truly horrible, and the more so to me because of what I knew of the spot. Refusing to flee, I watched it fade — and as I watched I felt that it was in turn watching me greedily with eyes more imaginable than visible. When I told my uncle about it he was greatly aroused; and after a tense hour of reflection, arrived at a definite and drastic decision. Weighing in his mind the importance of the matter, and the significance of our relation to it, he insisted that we both test — and if possible destroy — the horror of the house by a joint night or nights of aggressive vigil in that musty and fungus-cursed cellar.

IV

ON WEDNESDAY, June 25, 1919, after a proper notification of Carrington Harris which did not include surmises as to what we expected to find, my uncle and I conveyed to the shunned house two camp chairs and a folding camp cot, together with some scientific mechanism of greater weight and intricacy. These we placed in the cellar during the day, screening the windows with paper and planning to return in the evening for our first vigil. We had locked the door from the cellar to the ground floor; and having a key to the outside cellar door, we were prepared to leave our expensive and delicate apparatus — which we had obtained secretly and at great cost — as many days as our vigils might need to be protracted. It was our design to sit up together till very late, and then watch singly till dawn in two-hour stretches, myself first and then my companion; the inactive member resting on the cot.

The natural leadership with which my uncle procured the instruments from the laboratories of Brown University and the Cranston Street Armory, and instinctively assumed direction of our venture, was a marvellous commentary on the potential vitality and resilience of a man of eighty-one. Elihu Whipple had lived according to the hygienic laws he had preached as a physician, and but for what happened later would be here in full vigour today. Only two persons suspect what did happen — Carrington Harris and myself. I had to tell Harris because he owned the house and deserved to know what had gone out of it. Then too, we had spoken to him in advance of our quest; and I felt after my uncle's going that he would understand and assist me in some vitally necessary public explanations. He turned very pale, but agreed to help me, and decided that it would now be safe to rent the house.

To declare that we were not nervous on that rainy night of watching would be an exaggeration both gross and ridiculous. We were not, as I have said, in any sense childishly superstitious, but scientific study and reflection had taught us that the known universe of three dimensions embraces the merest fraction of the whole cosmos of substance and energy. In this case an overwhelming preponderance of evidence from numerous authentic sources pointed to the tenacious existence of certain forces of great power and, so far as the human point of view is concerned, exceptional malignancy. To say that we actually believed in vampires or werewolves would be a carelessly inclusive statement. Rather must it be said that we were not prepared to deny the possibility of certain unfamiliar and unclassified modifications of vital force and attenuated matter; existing very infrequently in three-dimensional space because of its more intimate connection with other spatial units, yet close enough to the boundary of our own to furnish us occasional manifestations which we, for lack of a proper vantage-point, may never hope to understand.

In short, it seemed to my uncle and me that an incontrovertible array of facts pointed to some lingering influence in the shunned house; traceable to one or another of the ill-favoured French settlers of two centuries before, and still operative through rare and unknown laws of atomic and electronic motion. That the family of Roulet had possessed an abnormal affinity for outer circles of entity — dark spheres which for normal folk hold only repulsion and terror — their recorded history seemed to prove.

Had not, then, the riots of those bygone seventeen-thirties set moving certain kinetic patterns in the morbid brain of one or more of them — notably the sinister Paul Roulet — which obscurely survived the bodies murdered and continued to function in some multiple-dimensioned space along the original lines of force determined by a frantic hatred of the encroaching community?

Such a thing was surely not a physical or biochemical impossibility in the light of a newer science which includes the theories of relativity and intra-atomic action. One might easily imagine an alien nucleus of substance or energy, formless or otherwise, kept alive by imperceptible or immaterial subtractions from the life-force or bodily tissue and fluids of other and more palpably living things into which it penetrates and with whose fabric it sometimes completely merges itself. It might be actively hostile, or it might be dictated merely by blind motives of self-preservation. In any case such a monster must of necessity be in our scheme of things an anomaly and an intruder, whose extirpation forms a primary duty with every man not an enemy to the world's life, health, and sanity.

What baffled us was our utter ignorance of the aspect in which we might encounter the thing. No sane person had even seen it, and few had ever felt it definitely. It might be pure energy — a form ethereal and outside the realm of substance — or it might be partly material; some unknown and equivocal mass of plasticity, capable of changing at will to nebulous approximations of the solid, liquid, gaseous, or tenuously unparticled states. The anthropomorphic patch of mould on the floor, the form of the yellowish vapour, and the curvature of the tree-roots in some of the old tales, all argued at least a remote and reminiscent connection with the human shape; but how representative or permanent that similarity might be, none could say with any kind of certainty.

We had devised two weapons to fight it; a large and specially fitted Crookes tube operated by powerful storage batteries and provided with peculiar screens and reflectors, in case it proved intangible and opposable only by vigorously destructive ether radiations, and a pair of military flamethrowers of the sort used in the World War, in case it proved partly material and susceptible of mechanical destruction — for like the superstitious Exeter rustics, we were prepared to burn the thing's heart out if heart existed to burn. All this aggressive mechanism we set in the cellar in positions carefully arranged with reference to the cot and chairs, and to the spot before the fireplace where the mould had taken strange shapes. That suggestive patch, by the way, was only faintly visible when we placed our furniture and instruments, and when we returned that evening for the actual vigil. For a moment I half-doubted that I had ever seen it in the more definitely limned form — but then I thought of the legends.

Our cellar vigil began at 10 P.M., daylight saving time, and as it continued we found no promise of pertinent developments. A weak, filtered glow from the rain-harassed street-lamps outside, and a feeble phosphorescence from the detestable fungi within, showed the dripping stone of the walls, from which all traces of whitewash had vanished; the dank, foetid and mildew-tainted hard earth floor with its obscene fungi; the rotting remains of what had been stools, chairs and tables, and other more shapeless furniture; the heavy planks and massive beams of the ground floor overhead; the decrepit plank door leading to bins and chambers beneath other parts of the house; the crumbling stone staircase with ruined wooden hand-rail; and the crude and cavernous fireplace of blackened brick where rusted iron fragments revealed the past presence of hooks, andirons, spit, crane, and a door to the Dutch oven — these things, and our austere cot and camp chairs, and the heavy and intricate destructive machinery we had brought.

We had, as in my own former explorations, left the door to the street unlocked; so that a direct and practical path of escape might lie open in case of manifestations beyond our power to deal with. It was our idea that our continued nocturnal presence would call forth whatever malign entity lurked there; and that being prepared, we could dispose of the thing with one or the other of our provided means as soon as we had recognised and observed it sufficiently. How long it might require to evoke and extinguish the thing, we had no notion. It occurred to us, too, that our venture was far from safe; for in what strength the thing might appear no one could tell. But we deemed the game worth the hazard, and embarked on it alone and unhesitatingly; conscious that the seeking of outside aid would only expose us to ridicule and perhaps defeat our entire purpose. Such was our frame of mind as we talked — far into the night, till my uncle's growing drowsiness made me remind him to lie down for his two-hour sleep.

Something like fear chilled me as I sat there in the small hours alone — I say alone, for one who sits by a sleeper is indeed alone; perhaps more alone than he can realise. My uncle breathed heavily, his deep inhalations and exhalations accompanied by the rain outside, and punctuated by another nerve-racking sound of distant dripping water within — for the house was repulsively damp even in dry weather, and in this storm positively swamp-like. I studied the loose, antique-masonry of the walls in the fungus-light and the feeble rays which stole in from the street through the screened windows; and once, when the noisome atmosphere of the place seemed about to sicken me, I opened the door and looked up and down the street, feasting my eyes on familiar sights and my nostrils on wholesome air. Still nothing occurred to reward my watching; and I yawned repeatedly, fatigue getting the better of apprehension.

Then the stirring of my uncle in his sleep attracted my notice. He had turned restlessly on the cot several times during the latter half of the first hour, but now he was breathing with unusual irregularity, occasionally heaving a sigh which held more than a few of the qualities of a choking moan. I turned my electric flashlight on him and found his face averted, so rising and crossing to the other side of the cot, I again flashed the light to see if he seemed in any pain. What I saw unnerved me most surprisingly, considering its relative triviality. It must have been merely the association of an odd circumstance with the sinister nature of our location and mission, for surely the circumstance was not in itself frightful or unnatural. It was merely that my uncle's facial expression, disturbed no doubt by strange dreams which our situation prompted, betrayed considerable agitation, and seemed not at all characteristic of him. His habitual expression was one of kindly and well-bred calm, whereas now a variety of emotions seemed struggling within him. I think, on the whole, that it was this *variety* which chiefly disturbed me. My uncle, as he gasped and tossed in increasing perturbation and with eyes that had now started open, seemed not one but many men, and suggested a curious quality of alienage from himself.

All at once he commenced to mutter, and I did not like the look of his mouth and teeth as he spoke. The words were at first indistinguishable, and then — with a tremendous start — I recognised something about them which filled me with icy fear till I recalled the breadth of my uncle's education and the interminable translations he had made from anthropological and antiquarian articles in the *Revue des Deux Mondes.* For the venerable Elihu Whipple was muttering in French, and the few phrases I could distinguish seemed connected with the darkest myths he had ever adapted from the famous Paris magazine.

Suddenly a perspiration broke out on the sleeper's forehead, and he leaped abruptly up, half awake. The jumble of French changed to a cry in English, and the hoarse voice shouted excitedly, "My breath, my breath!" Then the awakening became complete, and with a subsidence of facial expression to the normal state my uncle seized my hand and began to relate a dream whose nucleus of significance I could only surmise with a kind of awe.

He had, he said, floated off from a very ordinary series of dream-pictures into a scene whose strangeness was related to nothing he had ever read. It was of this world, and yet not of it — a shadowy geometrical confusion in which could be seen elements of familiar things in most unfamiliar and perturbing combinations. There was a suggestion of queerly disordered pictures superimposed one upon another; an arrangement in which the essentials of time as well as of space seemed dissolved and mixed in the most illogical fashion. In this kaleidoscopic vortex of phantasmal images were occasional snap-shots, if one might use the term, of singular clearness but unaccountable heterogeneity.

Once my uncle thought he lay in a carelessly dug open pit, with a crowd of angry faces framed by straggling locks and three-cornered hats frowning down on him. Again he seemed to be in the interior of a house — an old house, apparently — but the details and inhabitants were constantly changing, and he could never be certain of the faces or the furniture, or even of the room itself, since doors and windows seemed in just as great a state of flux as the more presumably mobile objects. It was queer — damnably queer — and my uncle spoke almost sheepishly, as if half expecting not to be believed, when he declared that of the strange faces many had unmistakably borne the features of the Harris family. And all the while there was a personal sensation of choking, as if some pervasive presence had spread itself through his body and sought to possess itself of his vital processes. I shuddered at the thought of those vital processes, worn as they were by eighty-one years of continuous functioning, in conflict with unknown forces of which the youngest and strongest system might well be afraid; but in another moment reflected that dreams are only dreams, and that these uncomfortable visions could be, at most, no more than my uncle's reaction to the investigations and expectations which had lately filled our minds to the exclusion of all else.

Conversation, also, soon tended to dispel my sense of strangeness; and in time I yielded to my yawns and took my turn at slumber. My uncle seemed now very wakeful, and welcomed his period of watching even though the nightmare had aroused him far ahead of his allotted two hours. Sleep seized me quickly, and I was at once haunted with dreams of the most disturbing kind. I felt, in my visions, a cosmic and abysmal loneness; with hostility surging from all sides upon some prison where I lay confined. I seemed bound and gagged, and taunted by the echoing yells of distant multitudes who thirsted for my blood. My uncle's face came to me with less pleasant associations than in waking hours, and I recall many futile struggles and attempts to scream. It was not a pleasant sleep, and for a second I was not sorry for the echoing shriek which clove through the barriers of dream and flung me to a sharp and startled awakeness in which every actual object before my eyes stood out with more than natural clearness and reality.

## V

I HAD BEEN lying with my face away from my uncle's chair, so that in this sudden flash of awakening I saw only the door to the street, the more northerly window, and the wall and floor and ceiling toward the north of the room, all photographed with morbid vividness on my brain in a light brighter than the glow of the fungi or the rays from the street outside. It was not a strong or even a fairly strong light; certainly not nearly strong enough to read an average book by. But it cast a shadow of myself and the cot on the floor, and had a yellowish, penetrating force that hinted at things more potent than luminosity. This I perceived with unhealthy sharpness despite the fact that two of my other senses were violently assailed. For on my ears rang the reverberations of that shocking scream, while my nostrils revolted at the stench which filled the place. My mind, as alert as my senses, recognised the gravely unusual; and almost automatically I leaped up and turned about to grasp the destructive instruments which we had left trained on the mouldy spot before the fireplace. As I turned, I dreaded what I was to see; for the scream had been in my uncle's voice, and I knew not against what menace I should have to defend him and myself.

Yet after all, the sight was worse than I had dreaded. There are horrors beyond horrors, and this was one of those nuclei of all dreamable hideousness which the cosmos saves to blast an accursed and unhappy few. Out of the fungus-ridden earth steamed up a vaporous corpse-light, yellow and diseased, which bubbled and lapped to a gigantic height in vague outlines half human and half monstrous, through which I could see the chimney and fireplace beyond. It was all eyes — wolfish and mocking — and the rugose insect-like head dissolved at the top to a thin stream of mist which curled putridly about and finally vanished up the chimney. I say that I saw this thing, but it is only in conscious retrospection that I ever definitely traced its damnable approach to form. At the time it was to me only a seething dimly phosphorescent cloud of fungous loathsomeness, enveloping and dissolving to an abhorrent plasticity the one object to which all my attention was focused. That object was my uncle — the venerable Elihu Whipple — who with blackening and decaying features leered and gibbered at me, and reached out dripping claws to rend me in the fury which this horror had brought.

It was a sense of routine which kept me from going mad. I had drilled myself in preparation for the crucial moment, and blind training saved me. Recognising the bubbling evil as no substance reachable by matter or material chemistry, and therefore ignoring the flame-thrower which loomed on my left, I threw on the current of the Crookes tube apparatus, and focussed toward that scene of immortal blasphemousness the strongest ether radiations which men's art can arouse from the spaces and fluids of nature. There was a bluish haze and a frenzied sputtering, and the yellowish phosphorescence grew dimmer to my eyes. But I saw the dimness was only that of contrast, and that the waves from the machine had no effect whatever.

Then, in the midst of that daemoniac spectacle, I saw a fresh horror which brought cries to my lips and sent me fumbling and staggering towards that unlocked door to the quiet street, careless of what abnormal terrors I loosed upon the world, or what thoughts or judgments of men I brought down upon my head. In that dim blend of blue and yellow the form of my uncle had commenced a nauseous liquefaction whose essence eludes all description, and in which there played across his vanishing face such changes of identity as only madness can conceive. He was at once a devil and a multitude, a charnel-house and a pageant. Lit by the mixed and uncertain beams, that gelatinous face assumed a dozen — a score — a hundred — aspects; grinning, as it sank to the ground on a body that melted like tallow, in the caricatured likeness of legions strange and yet not strange.

I saw the features of the Harris line, masculine and feminine, adult and infantile, and other features old and young, coarse and refined, familiar and unfamiliar. For a second there flashed a degraded counterfeit of a miniature of poor Rhoby Harris that I had seen in the School of Design Museum, and another time I thought I caught the rawboned image of Mercy Dexter as I recalled her from a painting in Carrington Harris's house. It was frightful beyond conception; toward the last, when a curious blend of servant and baby visages flickered close to the fungous floor where a pool of greenish grease was spreading, it seemed as though the shifting features fought against themselves, and strove to form contours like those of my uncle's kindly face. I like to think that he existed at that moment, and that he tried to bid me farewell. It seems to me I hiccoughed a farewell from my own parched throat as I lurched out into the street; a thin stream of grease following me through the door to the rain-drenched sidewalk.

The rest is shadowy and monstrous. There was no one in the soaking street, and in all the world there was no one I dared tell. I walked aimlessly south past College Hill and the Athenaeum, down Hopkins Street, and over the bridge to the business section where tall buildings seemed to guard me as modern material things guard the world from ancient and unwholesome wonder. Then the grey dawn unfolded wetly from the east, silhouetting the archaic hill and its venerable steeples, and beckoning me to the place where my terrible work was still unfinished. And in the end I went, wet, hatless, and dazed in the morning light, and entered that awful door in Benefit Street which I had left ajar, and which still swung cryptically in full sight of the early householders to whom I dared not speak.

The grease was gone, for the mouldy floor was porous. And in front of the fireplace was no vestige of the giant doubled-up form in nitre. I looked at the cot, the chairs, the instruments, my neglected hat, and the yellowed straw hat of my uncle. Dazedness was uppermost, and I could scarcely recall what was dream and what was reality. Then thought trickled back, and I knew that I had witnessed things more horrible than I had dreamed. Sitting down, I tried to conjecture as nearly as sanity would let me just what had happened, and how I might end the horror, if indeed it had been real. Matter it seemed not to be, nor ether, nor anything else conceivable by mortal mind. What, then, but some exotic emanation; some vampirish vapour such as Exeter rustics tell of as lurking over certain churchyards? This I felt was the clue, and again I looked at the floor before the fireplace where the mould and nitre had taken strange forms. In ten minutes my mind was made up, and taking my hat I set out for home, where I bathed, ate, and gave by telephone an order for a pickaxe, a spade, a military gas-mask, and six carboys of sulphuric acid, all to be delivered the next morning at the cellar door of the shunned house in Benefit Street. After that I tried to sleep; and failing, passed the hours in reading and in the composition of inane verses to counteract my mood.

At 11 A.M. the next day I commenced digging. It was sunny weather, and I was glad of that. I was still alone, for as much as I feared the unknown horror I sought, there was more fear in the thought of telling anybody. Later I told Harris only through sheer necessity, and because he had heard odd tales from old people which disposed him ever so little toward belief. As I turned up the stinking black earth in front of the fireplace, my spade causing a viscous yellow ichor to ooze from the white fungi which it severed, I trembled at the dubious thoughts of what I might uncover. Some secrets of inner earth are not good for mankind, and this seemed to me one of them.

My hand shook perceptibly, but still I delved; after a while standing in the large hole I had made. With the deepening of the hole, which was about six feet square, the evil smell increased; and I lost all doubt of my imminent contact with the hellish thing whose emanations had cursed the house for over a century and a half. I wondered what it would look like — what its form and substance would be, and how big it might have waxed through long ages of life-sucking. At length I climbed out of the hole and dispersed the heaped-up dirt, then arranging the great carboys of acid around and near two sides, so that when necessary I might empty them all down the aperture in quick succession. After that I dumped earth only along the other two sides; working more slowly and donning my gas-mask as the smell grew. I was nearly unnerved at my proximity to a nameless thing at the bottom of a pit.

Suddenly my spade struck something softer than earth. I shuddered and made a motion as if to climb out of the hole, which was now as deep as my neck. Then courage returned, and I scraped away more dirt in the light of the electric torch I had provided. The surface I uncovered was fishy and glassy — a kind of semi-putrid congealed jelly with suggestions of translucency. I scraped further, and saw that it had form. There was a rift where a part of the substance was folded over. The exposed area was huge and roughly cylindrical; like a mammoth soft blue-white stovepipe doubled in two, its largest part some two feet in diameter. Still more I scraped, and then abruptly I leaped out of the hole and away from the filthy thing; frantically unstopping and tilting the heavy carboys, and precipitating their corrosive contents one after another down that charnel gulf and upon this unthinkable abnormality whose titan *elbow* I had seen.

The blinding maelstrom of greenish-yellow vapour which surged tempestuously up from that hole as the floods of acid descended, will never leave my memory. All along the hill people tell of the yellow day, when virulent and horrible fumes arose from the factory waste dumped in the Providence River, but I know how mistaken they are as to the source. They tell, too, of the hideous roar which at the same time came from some disordered water-pipe or gas main underground — but again I could correct them if I dared. It was unspeakably shocking, and I do not see how I lived through it. I did faint after emptying the fourth carboy, which I had to handle after the fumes had begun to penetrate my mask; but when I recovered I saw that the hole was emitting no fresh vapours.

The two remaining carboys I emptied down without particular result, and after a time I felt it safe to shovel the earth back into the pit. It was twilight before I was done, but fear had gone out of the place. The dampness was less foetid, and all the strange fungi had withered to a kind of harmless greyish powder which blew ashlike along the floor. One of earth's nethermost terrors had perished forever; and if there be a hell, it had received at last the daemon soul of an unhallowed thing. And as I patted down the last spadeful of mould, I shed the first of many tears with which I have paid unaffected tribute to my beloved uncle's memory.

The next spring no more pale grass and strange weeds came up in the shunned house's terraced garden, and shortly afterward Carrington Harris rented the place. It is still spectral, but its strangeness fascinates me, and I shall find mixed with my relief a queer regret when it is torn down to make way for a tawdry shop or vulgar apartment building. The barren old trees in the yard have begun to bear small, sweet apples, and last year the birds nested in their gnarled boughs.

*Robert M. Coates*

# THE HOUR AFTER WESTERLY

DAVIS HARWELL was a district salesman working out of New Haven for the firm of Haight & Brownell, dealers in wholesale hardware. He was also a methodical man, and when he left Providence that late July afternoon, starting back to New Haven and home, it was only natural that he should check the time. It was four-eighteen precisely — by his own watch, that is; it was four-twenty-two by the clock in front of a jeweller's shop, a few steps down the street from where he had parked his car.

But his watch was one that he knew could be depended on, and anyway the difference was so slight that it hardly mattered. New Haven was roughly a hundred miles from Providence, or so it was supposed to be, though it always turned out to be a little more than that on the road. Add four miles for West Haven, where his home was, and you had maybe a hundred and ten, all told, or slightly more than three hours, average driving.

He would be home in time for dinner, he thought, or at least not so late that there need be much complaining. His wife, Edna, always liked him to be home for his meals — "for the family's sake," as she put it — and she also liked him to be home in good time, "for the children's," and it was sometimes difficult to combine her demands with those of business necessity. But today, having hurried his afternoon calls a little, he was pretty sure he'd be able to make out all right. He'd be home at seven-thirty, he thought, at the latest, and, of course, if he was delayed on the way, he could phone.

He thought of all this as he was angling out from the curb into the stream of traffic on Westminster Street, where he had parked the car, and yet in a way he wasn't really thinking. He knew his wife and her little peculiarities, he knew the route and the distance, having travelled it many times, and he was merely checking over the obvious and the familiar — settling into it, really — as a way of relaxing after the tensions and sudden, unpredictable demands of the business day.

It was all clear sailing now. He pulled out behind a truck and turned left on Winter Street; in a minute or two more he was rolling out Broad toward Elmwood and the junction of Route 3 and the Boston Post Road. He didn't think of time again — or if he did, he wasn't conscious of it — until he had passed New London.

He was going down a stretch of black asphalt then, with a sort of wooded knoll on the one side and what looked like a stretch of salt marsh on the other, and at first he didn't know where he was; for a moment or two he had that feeling of blank unbelongingness that sometimes comes with a sudden awakening, and the road might have been any road in the world and he anywhere upon it, for all the sense of familiarity it brought to him. Then he passed a crossroad with a sign pointing down it that said, "Niantic 2M," and that oriented him. He was on the Post Road, right enough, about halfway between New London and Saybrook, with a good hour or more of driving ahead of him before he reached New Haven. But the sky seemed darker than he had somehow expected it to be, and when he glanced at his watch, he saw that it was seven-thirty, almost exactly.

This was the beginning of a curious episode in Davis Harwell's life, but at the moment he saw nothing in his lateness to surprise him. There was an odd sense of dullness, or pressure, upon him — he thought afterward that it was as if a weight had been bearing on his mind and had as yet only partly lifted — and the one clear idea that presented itself to his mind was that if it was that late, and if he was *that* tired (he felt suddenly very tired), it was time he was having some dinner. It wasn't till he had stopped at a roadside restaurant a little farther on — it wasn't, really, until he'd finished a plate of clams and was waiting for the dish of fried scallops he'd ordered — that the weight finally lifted and all the incongruities of the situation rushed in upon him.

He was looking at a clock on the restaurant wall at the moment, and the clock said six minutes past eight. It was eight-six by his own watch, too, by that time, but the clock on the wall seemed somehow more impartial and authoritative. It was eight-six, and suddenly, surprisingly, in Davis Harwell's mind it *was* eight-six, and on the instant a whole series of questions that had existed before only as a dull disturbance in his consciousness came immediately into focus.

It was eight-six, and here he was, not yet past Saybrook. Why wasn't he in New Haven? He had left Providence at a little past four — four-eighteen, wasn't it? yes, he remembered clearly — and he remembered thinking even then that he'd be home by seven-thirty, if not earlier. And he hadn't stopped anywhere, except once to buy gas, and that had taken — well, maybe five minutes at the most. And yet here he was, only just past Niantic, and if that clock didn't lie . . .

The waitress slid a platter with the scallops, some cole slaw, and French-fried potatoes onto the table before him and then stood looking down at him. "Want anything with it?" she said.

"With what?" said Davis. He was still staring at the clock.

"With the scallops."

"Oh," said Davis. He remembered the stop for gas distinctly — the yellow-stuccoed little peaked-roofed building with the two pumps before it, and the rather awkward-looking, loose-jowled, elderly man who took care of his needs. He had taken seven gallons, he remembered, and it pleased him to recall the transaction so exactly. He felt lost here, somehow. He should be in New Haven.

"I mean," the waitress said patiently, "you want some beer or something? Do you want your coffee?"

"No, no coffee," Davis said. "Or I mean I'll have the coffee later. Is that clock up there right?"

"Always has been," said the waitress. Then she turned and called to a man standing talking to the girl behind the cashier's desk. "Mr. Osgood, is that clock right, do you suppose?"

The man pulled an old-fashioned hunting-case watch from his pocket, snapped it open, and glanced at it. "On the dot," he called back, and smiled briefly at Davis Harwell.

"On the dot," said the waitress. "I was pretty sure."

He could remember the gas station. He found, when he put his mind to it, that he could remember a good deal about the journey; though he had made the same trip so many times before that it tended to fall into a pattern, there were still little individual incidents that came back to him — a woman's hand dangling languidly from a car window as he passed the car (that had been about an hour out of Providence), the big truck on the hill that delayed him farther on, the yellow roadster that whizzed past, and the hay wagon with the kids on top, the picnickers — little things in themselves, but things that still distinguished this trip from any other and made it possible for him to say with assurance that he had passed by that way, and remembered.

The trouble was that there were other things he *didn't* remember. He ate his scallops and the waitress brought him his coffee. He hardly noticed. The whole thing, he was beginning to realize, was an unusual experience. Somewhere, somehow, he had lost an hour, but that wasn't all; he had lost memory as well, and there was a whole section of the trip, from — well from about where he'd seen those picnickers (and that had been back on the other side of New London, while he was still in Rhode Island) to the moment of his awakening near Niantic, that had simply dropped out of his mind completely. There were towns that he must have passed through, or he wouldn't be here; turns and stretches of road that he must have taken, cars and people he must have passed. . . . He found now that he couldn't remember them at all.

It was as if he had been driving in a fog, and the one thing he did remember was an image as precise and as unrelated as something one might see through a sudden parting of a fog — a group of small white houses grouped at an intersection, and a clock (was it on a steeple?) with the clock's hands pointing to ten minutes to six. There was a faint suggestion of a dirt road, too, but even as he tried to consider it, it floated off into nothingness.

Or the fog, or whatever it was, covered it. There was a blank there, that was it, and he couldn't help wondering what had happened. He wasn't worried, exactly. Davis Harwell was a methodical man, and his impulse was to find a logical explanation for the phenomenon that confronted him. Once before, he had had a similar experience — when he had gone to his brother-in-law's wedding and, not being a drinking man, usually, had taken more than he should have before he knew it, and had found himself home next morning, with the car in the garage and him and Edna in bed, without having any idea at all of how he had got there. But he had got through safely then, though he had had some bad moments afterward, and this time, too, he must have managed all right, or he wouldn't be here.

He had been working too hard — that was probably it. Or he had made the trip back and forth so much that it had become mere routine and he had fallen into a daydream at the wheel — and then, naturally, he had slowed up his driving, which would account for the lost time. He was here, anyway, and the main thing to do now was to get on. It's perhaps significant though, in view of what happened later, that he had paid his bill and left the restaurant, was about to get into his car, before he remembered that he hadn't yet telephoned Edna, who would of course be wondering.

"I was held up," he said when he had gone back and called her over the pay phone, and as soon as he heard her reply — *"Held up!"* she almost screamed — he realized that she had got the wrong meaning.

"No, not that, dear," he told her patiently. It occurred to him that she was always getting wrong meanings. "I mean held up in a business way. I was delayed. Things came up that upset my schedule. I was late getting started." He hung up, and when he got back in the car again, he sat awhile in the dark interior before turning on the headlights and stepping on the starter.

He felt, in a queer way, lonely. In his methodical way, he had decided to disregard the incident, and yet he couldn't help thinking about it, and as he thought about it, an odd sort of detachment took hold of him; he could see himself *there,* leaving Providence, driving out in his car among all the other men at the wheels of their cars in the afternoon traffic — and then *here,* late, alone, in a dark car, lonely. . . . For a moment, he had an odd, frightened feeling, in itself quite illogical: Was he even the same person now that he had been, leaving Providence? And if not, what had changed him?

Davis thought about the whole thing a good deal in the days and weeks that followed, but he didn't allow it to become an obsession. It was an incident, and an odd one, certainly, but in Davis' mind its very oddness tended to drive it out of his consciousness. He sought logic and not illogic, and the very fact that this strange lapse of his had no apparent explanation was enough to make him give up looking for an explanation.

Yet it stuck in his mind, and when he next drove back from Providence (he made the trip, on an average, twice a month), he found himself, at the beginning of the trip, checking off the places that he remembered — the long hill where the truck had delayed him (it was just before a town called Hope Valley, he discovered); the sharp curves that the yellow roadster had taken so recklessly, and the wooded country where, suddenly, he had come upon the hay wagon; the little knoll where the picnickers had been sitting (it was vacant when he passed this time, but he could still see the old black sedan parked beside the road, the two women and the children, and the man in his shirtsleeves, just unscrewing the top of the thermos as he passed) — and approaching, with trepidation, the invisible point where his memory ended and the unknown began.

He found he couldn't locate the dividing line exactly. To remember is one thing, but to define what you *don't* remember is another, and that, in a way, was what Davis was trying to do. About all he could tell was that somewhere around the state line between Rhode Island and Connecticut a sort of assurance left him; he knew the road from then on, of course, and he followed it, but it seemed, in an odd way, strange to him, and when he reached the Niantic crossroad ("Niantic 2M," the sign still said) and found himself again on ground that was completely familiar, a sort of sadness overcame him, as if he had lost something that now might never be regained.

All the way, too, he had been looking for the group of white houses, and the clock, and the steeple. He had looked for them without quite admitting to himself that he was looking, because, in keeping with his common-sense view of things, he had decided that that little scene must be an entirely extraneous impression — a dream, maybe; anyway, something really unconnected with the trip. But he didn't find it, and that, too, added to the strange sense of loss, and of sadness because of loss, that he felt as he drove on through Saybrook and Clinton and Guilford and — the darkness now falling — the other towns leading into New Haven.

He didn't find the white houses until nearly six weeks later, and then it was largely by accident. There are two main ways of going from Providence to New Haven — one by the old Boston Post Road, which follows the shore line and the towns along it, windingly, and the other by a newer road, which cuts across the bulging headlands of western Rhode Island in a straight line from Providence to New London, where it joins the old Post Road again. This, being shorter, was the road Davis usually followed, but this time he turned off it. He had heard that there was a new hardware store being opened at Westerly, Rhode Island, and on the chance of getting their account he decided to drive down and look the place over.

Westerly is a coastal town, so it's on the Post Road, and a good deal of the route that Davis followed, getting down to it, was unfamiliar. Yet it had, in an odd way, a feeling of familiarity, too. It was like something that he had seen once and had half forgotten but that recalled itself to him, landmark by landmark, as he went along; it was in that sense, just the opposite of his previous experience, when he had forgotten what he had gone through, and although he had decided to put that out of his mind — and by this time had almost succeeded in doing so; after all, he had had his own regular daily life to occupy him meanwhile — he could not help a feeling of rising excitement as he drove into the town of Westerly.

Once again, though, it wasn't *the* town. There were houses that white (after all, almost all New England houses are white), and they were grouped around an intersection. But they weren't the right houses, in the right arrangement, and the hardware store, too, turned out to be a disappointment. Two young men were running it, neither of them with any experience to amount to much, and their plans were, if anything, too grandiose. They had taken over an old shop front and were in the midst of having it remodelled. But the scale of things on which they had planned the venture was far above what their chances of profit would warrant, and, after sizing things up, Davis — he thought wisely — decided to go cautiously about establishing relations with them. He asked directions for getting on to New London, followed them through the center of town, lost them somewhere on the outskirts, and then — just as he was deciding that in spite of the stubborn feeling of rightness about the way he was going, he would have to turn back and start over — ran smack into the group of white houses, and the clock, and the steeple.

It was an odd sensation. The whole business was something that he had decided by now to forget about; common sense had demanded it. And yet here it was — or, rather, here they were — three houses, two on one side and the other across from them, with a dirt road in between, and with a number of details about them — the picket fence and the elm tree in the yard of one, the dormer windows and the tarred hip roof of another, the lilac bushes — that, though he couldn't have described them before, now fell instantly into a remembered pattern. Beyond, and set back a little from the road, on the left, was the church, and the steeple. The clock, he noticed, said twenty-seven minutes to six.

Davis stopped the car and sat for a while. Then he did what was for him an unusual thing. He was off the right road by now, and he knew it, and he knew further, that to go on in the way he was headed (unless, just possibly, there was a short cut somewhere — and had he had that thought before?) would take him even more out of the way. Yet he put the car in gear and drove on down the dirt road between the white houses.

It was odd, but as soon as he started, he felt a strange sort of freedom. It was mid-September by then and the country was beginning to take on its autumn coloration; there was red in the sumacs and the climbing ivy along the roadside, and, in the fields beyond, the high grasses were beginning to turn brown at the tips and the stalks were yellowish. There were few houses. The road had dipped a little at the start. Then it rose, and when he came to the top of the rise, the land levelled off again. He was on a sort of tableland now, with that look of limitlessness about it which meant that the sea was its boundary. He was heading out, probably, toward a point of some sort, and that meant, almost certainly, that he'd have to turn back in the end, and yet he couldn't now, even if he'd wanted to, keep from going on.

For that matter, though, he didn't want to. He had started with the idea of retracing the way that he must have followed that other time, and if he had come down this road before — and the white houses seemed to indicate it — he had thought it would bring back remembrances. It didn't. He remembered nothing; instead, the road gave him a feeling of newness that was in itself surprising. It and everything about it — the ruts, deep in spots and shallower in others, the wiry strip of brown grass that ran between them, the earth's look with the sunlight on it — all seemed new in a way that no similar things had ever looked to him before. Farther out, on what seemed to be the ultimate point of the headland, there was a scattering of summer cottages, with the sun flashing here and there on a roof when its angle was right. They looked brand-new, too, and with much the same feeling that a sailor might have setting his boat's prow for a new shore ahead, Davis set the car's course for the cottages and drove on.

It was when he passed the first of them that the strange thing occurred. It was a small house, red-roofed and gray-shingled; it had a screened-in porch facing toward the sea and awnings over the windows, a garage and a tiny plot of lawn and a hedge around it, and since the soil, here far out on the headland, was undoubtedly sandy, both the hedge and the lawn looked a little scraggly.

It was a typical summer cottage, and there was a woman on the lawn before it who looked typically summer-resident, too. About all he could tell as he approached was that she was a woman of middle age. She had hair that was either very light or that was graying, but she had a slim, attractive figure, and her legs and her arms were long and brown and fit-looking. She was wearing gray shorts and a snug blue jersey, and when Davis first noticed her, she was kneeling on the lawn, doing something to a row of flowers. She glanced up as the car came past, and saw him; he saw her face, and — without even faintly recognizing her; he was sure he had never seen the woman before in his life — he found himself suddenly occupied with a curious impulse, almost a compulsion, to head the car in toward the hedge at the roadside and stop there.

He didn't, of course, though there had been a weird moment when it had seemed, for some reason, that he *must* stop, when even the car seemed to want it and he'd almost had to wrestle with it to keep going. But that had probably been simply his imagining; after all, a man's car didn't just take things in its hands like that, not sensibly. There had been, too, a moment when it seemed to him that she recognized him, that she'd raised her hand sharply, as if just starting to wave to him, and then dropped it again as the car went past. But that was a thought that came to him later, when he was a little way down the road, so he couldn't be sure of the details that prompted it, and he put that down, too, to his imagining. And most likely, if she had raised her hand at all, it had been merely to brush back her hair.

About all he knew for certain was that once he had passed the cottage, all the sense of adventurousness left him. Coming down the road, he had had a feeling of newness, as if something unexpected were bound to happen, but he had lost that now; he was simply a man who had taken a wrong turning somewhere on a journey and was getting a little anxious about reaching his destination on time.

He drove on. There were a dozen or so more cottages, growing closer together as he approached the center of the tiny settlement. There was a crossroads there, and a bar in a box-like building on one corner, and since there were no signposts anywhere, Davis stopped and went into the bar to ask directions.

It was a typical summer-settlement bar. There was a neon-lighted sign, advertising someone's beer, in the window, and visible in reverse from inside. At the rear, there was a sort of trellis, opening on a large rather cavernous room, dim now and dreary-looking, with a small, polished dance floor and a number of tables neatly arranged around it, all silently awaiting Saturday night's festivities. The barroom was dim, too, or it seemed so after the sunlight outside, and Davis was just getting his bearings when he heard a voice say, "Well, hel-*lo!*" and saw the bartender, or the proprietor, coming down from the farther end of the bar.

He was a short, stocky man in an Army shirt, with an air that was at once tough and cheery, and he spoke in such an obviously welcoming tone that Davis, who had merely intended to inquire the nearest way to New London, was taken aback for a moment. By that time, the man was opposite the beer taps. "Beer?" he said, still smiling.

"Yes," said Davis, and the man picked up a glass and started to fill it. As he did so, he glanced up once at Davis, quickly, and then looked down at the glass, slowly filling. When it was filled, he put it on the drain strip before him, knifed off the foam, and then carried it down and set it before Davis. "You know, it's funny," he said. "For a minute there, I thought you was someone I knew. Or — you know — a guy that come into the bar one time. I remember faces. I got a mind for it." He looked at Davis again. "You never been here before?"

"I — " said Davis, and hesitated. For an instant, he felt himself poised on the edge of something perilous, and his instinct, quite naturally, was to get away from it. "No," he said. He didn't look at the man, and he gulped half the beer down hastily. He was wondering why he had ever come down that road at all. "What I wanted to know was, really, could you tell me the nearest way to New London?"

Then the man did a strange thing, too. He put his arms down, folded, on the bar and stared silently at Davis for a moment. "You aren't kidding?" he demanded, almost menacingly, and then, perhaps because he had seen Davis' look — surprised, puzzled, half fearful — he seemed to change his mind. "O.K., we'll play it your way," he said. And slowly, carefully, he gave Davis his road directions.

Davis went back to the headland once more, however, and drove past the house and, this time, turned the car and drove back again. That last time had been in mid-September. Now it was nearly three weeks later, and at the seaside those few weeks can mark a critical change of seasons. The fields, the grass, the road itself were hardly altered; they looked perhaps a little browner, a little more withered, and that was all. But the thing was that the whole region looked lonelier. It was in the atmosphere — a kind of emptiness, a kind of barrenness. And when he came to the cottage, he was not surprised to find that it looked lonelier, too.

There was no one on the lawn, but then, of course, you couldn't expect her to be always there, waiting for him. But the awnings were down, and the screens, and the wide, seaward-facing porch had a curiously bare, wintry look without them. He drove past, though, cautiously. That first time (or had it been the second?), he had tried as he went on down the road to catch a glimpse of her through the rear-view mirror to see if she were really waving. But the angle had been wrong and he hadn't seen her, and the mere fact that he'd tried, and *hadn't* seen her, gave him, oddly, a greater sense of spying than if he had.

This time, too, he had something of the same feeling. He drove past and she wasn't there, and he turned and drove back again, and then turned once more and went back before he dared stop the car and get out. There was no one there. He was late this time; the steeple clock had said eight minutes to six when he'd started down the road, and the lateness of the season made it seem later still; it was now almost dark, and if there had been anyone there, there would have been lights on somewhere, and he would have seen them, even behind the shutters. But there was no one, no one.

He walked about the lawn, still cautiously (for some reason, he didn't go up to the house), and the main thing he remembered afterward was the

His bones ne'er toss
Who stirs his dust
Will count his loss."

Dick laughed. "A traveler, then. And happy to be home at last."

"You don't find it ominous?"

"Not hardly. I'm not superstitious. But what's the story you mentioned?"

We found a log from which we could see old Hiram's stone and sat down. I stuffed and lit my pipe. Dick lit a cigarette. "It was before my time, you understand. Back in the twenties, I believe. Some archaeologist down from Boston started digging here. Opened the coffins, collected what trinkets he could, took out the skulls to measure them."

"So?"

I pointed down the hill toward the stream with my pipe. "The day he got to Hiram, that night his car ran off the bridge there. Nearly drowned."

"But what could Hiram have had to do with it?"

I shrugged. "Who knows? But they did find a tooth caught in the steering mechanism, I hear. They put it back in Hiram's jaw, put the skull back in the box, and filled the hole in again. The archaeologist went home to Boston."

Dick was silent for a moment. Then he stood up, turned his back on the stone, and said, "It had to be coincidence. A freak accident. Besides, I've lived here most of my life, and I never heard such a thing. You've gotta be making it up."

"Not a bit of it."

"But if you don't want to sell. . . ."

I gestured him back onto the log. "That's not it, Dick, and you know it. I just want you to know what you're up against. Informed consent, they call it."

"Hah!" He must have thought me as hagridden as any Appalachian hillbilly. He should have known better. I had laughed at such things myself, once, but since then I'd learned enough to make me keep an open mind. I'd even learned some of it in the course of my public duties, and he should have remembered that. It would have saved him trouble.


WE CLOSED the deal the next week, and that gave Dick all the land he needed for his shopping center. Over the winter, he had a crew in to clear the site, sell off the wood, and burn the slash. Come April, once the mud had firmed up a bit, he brought in another crew to start preparing the usualness of everything. He had expected a sign of some sort, but there was none. The grass was just grass underfoot and the gravelled path just gravel; the wind, coming in lightly from the sea (there was a hint of rain in it, he noticed), was the same wind that was blowing in over Providence, New Haven and elsewhere, and he had walked about the place for only a few minutes before he recognized the aimlessness of what he was doing. Though he stopped for a while when he returned to the car, and looked back at the house, he soon realized that that was mere aimlessness, too, and he got back in the car and started the motor.

Almost all the other cottages that he passed were closed for the winter, too, but the bar at the corner was still open, and in the growing darkness, the neon-lighted sign in the window shone out boldly — "Narragansett Beer," it said. For a moment, he was tempted to stop there. But then he thought there was no need to, really. The man had given him good enough directions the last time: a left turn at the first traffic light, then a right and another left, and then under the railroad and onto the Post Road. And besides, it was far too late.

*Edith Wharton*

# THE TRIUMPH OF NIGHT

IT WAS CLEAR that the sleigh from Weymore had not come; and the shivering young traveler from Boston, who had counted on jumping into it when he left the train at Northridge Junction, found himself standing alone on the open platform, exposed to the full assault of nightfall and winter.

The blast that swept him came off New Hampshire snowfields and ice-hung forests. It seemed to have traversed interminable leagues of frozen silence, filling them with the same cold roar and sharpening its edge against the same bitter black-and-white landscape. Dark, searching and swordlike, it alternately muffled and harried its victim, like a bullfighter now whirling his cloak and now planting his darts. This analogy brought home to the young man the fact that he himself had no cloak, and that the overcoat in which he had faced the relatively temperate air of Boston seemed no thicker than a sheet of paper on the bleak heights of Northridge. George Faxon said to himself that the place was uncommonly well-named. It clung to an exposed ledge over the valley from which the train had lifted him, and the wind combed it with teeth of steel that he seemed actually to hear scraping against the wooden sides of the station. Other building there was none: the village lay far down the road, and thither —

since the Weymore sleigh had not come — Faxon saw himself under the necessity of plodding through several feet of snow.

He understood well enough what had happened: his hostess had forgotten that he was coming. Young as Faxon was, this sad lucidity of soul had been acquired as the result of long experience, and he knew that the visitors who can least afford to hire a carriage are almost always those whom their hosts forget to send for. Yet to say that Mrs. Culme had forgotten him was too crude a way of putting it. Similar incidents led him to think that she had probably told her maid to tell the butler to telephone the coachman to tell one of the grooms (if no one else needed him) to drive over to Northridge to fetch the new secretary; but on a night like this, what groom who respected his rights would fail to forget the order?

Faxon's obvious course was to struggle through the drifts to the village, and there rout out a sleigh to convey him to Weymore; but what if, on his arrival at Mrs. Culme's, no one remembered to ask him what this devotion to duty had cost? That, again, was one of the contingencies he had expensively learned to look out for, and the perspicacity so acquired told him it would be cheaper to spend the night at the Northridge inn, and advise Mrs. Culme of his presence there by telephone. He had reached this decision, and was about to entrust his luggage to a vague man with a lantern, when his hopes were raised by the sound of bells.

Two sleighs were just dashing up to the station, and from the foremost there sprang a young man muffled in furs.

"Weymore? No, these are not the Weymore sleighs."

The voice was that of the youth who had jumped to the platform — a voice so agreeable that, in spite of the words, it fell consolingly on Faxon's ears. At the same moment the wandering station lantern, casting a transient light on the speaker, showed his features to be in the pleasantest harmony with his voice. He was very fair and very young — hardly in the twenties, Faxon thought — but this face, though full of a morning freshness, was a trifle too thin and fine-drawn, as though a vivid spirit contended in him with a strain of physical weakness. Faxon was perhaps the quicker to notice such delicacies of balance because his own temperament hung on lightly quivering nerves, which yet, as he believed, would never quite swing him beyond a normal sensibility.

"You expected a sleigh from Weymore?" the newcomer continued, standing beside Faxon like a slender column of fur.

Mrs. Culme's secretary explained his difficulty, and the other brushed it aside with a contemptuous "Oh, *Mrs. Culme!*" that carried both speakers a long way toward reciprocal understanding.

"But then you must be — " The youth broke off with a smile of interrogation.

"The new secretary? Yes. But apparently there are no notes to be answered this evening." Faxon's laugh deepened the sense of solidarity which had so promptly established itself between the two.

His friend laughed also. "Mrs. Culme," he explained, "was lunching at my uncle's today, and she said you were due this evening. But seven hours is a long time for Mrs. Culme to remember anything."

"Well," said Faxon philosophically, "I suppose that's one of the reasons why she needs a secretary. And I've always the inn at Northridge," he concluded.

"Oh, but you haven't, though! It burned down last week."

"The deuce it did!" said Faxon; but the humor of the situation struck him before its inconvenience. His life, for years past, had been mainly a succession of resigned adaptations, and he had learned, before dealing practically with his embarrassments, to extract from most of them a small tribute of amusement.

"Oh, well, there's sure to be somebody in the place who can put me up."

"No one *you* could put up with. Besides, Northridge is three miles off, and our place — in the opposite direction — is a little nearer." Through the darkness, Faxon saw his friend sketch a gesture of self-introduction. "My name's Frank Rainer, and I'm staying with my uncle at Overdale. I've driven over to meet two friends of his, who are due in a few minutes from New York. If you don't mind waiting till they arrive I'm sure Overdale can do you better than Northridge. We're only down from town for a few days, but the house is always ready for a lot of people."

"But your uncle — ?" Faxon could only object, with the odd sense, through his embarrassment, that it would be magically dispelled by his invisible friend's next words.

"Oh, my uncle — you'll see! I answer for *him!* I dare say you've heard of him — John Lavington?"

John Lavington! There was a certain irony in asking if one had heard of John Lavington! Even from a post of observation as obscure as that of Mrs. Culme's secretary the rumor of John Lavington's money, of his pictures, his politics, his charities and his hospitality, was as difficult to escape as the roar of a cataract in a mountain solitude. It might almost have been said that the one place in which one would not have expected to come upon him was in just such a solitude as now surrounded the speakers

— at least in this deepest hour of its desertedness. But it was just like Lavington's brilliant ubiquity to put one in the wrong even there.

"Oh, yes, I've heard of your uncle."

"Then you *will* come, won't you? We've only five minutes to wait," young Rainer urged, in the tone that dispels scruples by ignoring them; and Faxon found himself accepting the invitation as simply as it was offered.

A delay in the arrival of the New York train lengthened their five minutes to fifteen; and as they paced the icy platform Faxon began to see why it had seemed the most natural thing in the world to accede to his new acquaintance's suggestion. It was because Frank Rainer was one of the privileged beings who simplify human intercourse by the atmosphere of confidence and good humor they diffuse. He produced this effect, Faxon noted, by the exercise of no gift but his youth, and of no art but his sincerity; and these qualities were revealed in a smile of such sweetness that Faxon felt, as never before, what Nature can achieve when she deigns to match the face with the mind.

He learned that the young man was the ward, and the only nephew of John Lavington, with whom he had made his home since the death of his mother, the great man's sister. Mr. Lavington, Rainer said, had been "a regular brick" to him — "But then he is to everyone, you know" — and the young fellow's situation seemed in fact to be perfectly in keeping with his person. Apparently the only shade that had ever rested on him was cast by the physical weakness which Faxon had already detected. Young Rainer had been threatened with tuberculosis, and the disease was so far advanced that, according to the highest authorities, banishment to Arizona or New Mexico was inevitable. "But luckily my uncle didn't pack me off, as most people would have done, without getting another opinion. Whose? Oh, an awfully clever chap, a young doctor with a lot of new ideas, who simply laughed at my being sent away, and said I'd do perfectly well in New York if I didn't dine out too much, and if I dashed off occasionally to Northridge for a little fresh air. So it's really my uncle's doing that I'm not in exile — and I feel no end better since the new chap told me I needn't bother." Young Rainer went on to confess that he was extremely fond of dining out, dancing and similar distractions; and Faxon, listening to him, was inclined to think that the physician who had refused to cut him off altogether from these pleasures was probably a better psychologist than his seniors.

"All the same you ought to be careful, you know." The sense of elder-brotherly concern that forced the words from Faxon made him, as he spoke, slip his arm through Frank Rainer's.

The latter met the movement with a responsive pressure. "Oh, I *am:* awfully, awfully. And then my uncle has such an eye on me!"

"But if your uncle has such an eye on you, what does he say to your swallowing knives out here in this Siberian wild?"

Rainer raised his fur collar with a careless gesture. "It's not that that does it — the cold's good for me."

"And it's not the dinners and dances? What is it, then?" Faxon good-humoredly insisted; to which his companion answered with a laugh: "Well, my uncle says it's being bored; and I rather think he's right."

His laugh ended in a spasm of coughing and a struggle for breath that made Faxon, still holding his arm, guide him hastily into the shelter of the fireless waiting room.

Young Rainer had dropped down on the bench against the wall and pulled off one of his fur gloves to grope for a handkerchief. He tossed aside his cap and drew the handkerchief across his forehead, which was intensely white, and beaded with moisture, though his face retained a healthy glow. But Faxon's gaze remained fastened to the hand he had uncovered: it was so long, so colorless, so wasted, so much older than the brow he passed it over.

"It's queer — a healthy face but dying hands," the secretary mused: he somehow wished young Rainer had kept on his glove.

The whistle of the express drew the young men to their feet, and the next moment two heavily-furred gentlemen had descended to the platform and were breasting the rigor of the night. Frank Rainer introduced them as Mr. Grisben and Mr. Balch, and Faxon, while their luggage was being lifted into the second sleigh, discerned them, by the roving lantern gleam, to be an elderly grey-headed pair, of the average prosperous business cut.

They saluted their host's nephew with friendly familiarity, and Mr. Grisben, who seemed the spokesman of the two, ended his greeting with a genial — "and many many more of them, dear boy!" which suggested to Faxon that their arrival coincided with an anniversary. But he could not press the inquiry, for the seat allotted him was at the coachman's side, while Frank Rainer joined his uncle's guests inside the sleigh.

A swift flight (behind such horses as one could be sure of John Lavington's having) brought them to tall gateposts, an illuminated lodge, and an avenue on which the snow had been leveled to the smoothness of marble. At the end of the avenue the long house loomed up, its principal bulk dark, but one wing sending out a ray of welcome; and the next moment Faxon was receiving a violent impression of warmth and light, of hothouse plants, hurrying servants, a vast spectacular oak hall like a stage setting, and, in its unreal middle distance, a small figure, correctly dressed, conventionally featured, and utterly unlike his rather florid conception of the great John Lavington.

The surprise of the contrast remained with him through his hurried dressing in the large luxurious bedroom to which he had been shown. "I don't see where he comes in," was the only way he could put it, so difficult was it to fit the exuberance of Lavington's public personality into his host's contracted frame and manner. Mr. Lavington, to whom Faxon's case had been rapidly explained by young Rainer, had welcomed him with a sort of dry and stilted cordiality that exactly matched his narrow face, his stiff hand, and the whiff of scent on his evening handkerchief. "Make yourself at home — at home!" he had repeated, in a tone that suggested, on his own part, a complete inability to perform the feat he urged on his visitor. "Any friend of Frank's . . . delighted . . . make yourself thoroughly at home!"

## II

IN SPITE of the balmy temperature and complicated conveniences of Faxon's bedroom, the injunction was not easy to obey. It was wonderful luck to have found a night's shelter under the opulent roof of Overdale, and he tasted the physical satisfaction to the full. But the place, for all its ingenuities of comfort, was oddly cold and unwelcoming. He couldn't have said why, and could only suppose that Mr. Lavington's intense personality — intensely negative, but intense all the same — must, in some occult way, have penetrated every corner of his dwelling. Perhaps, though, it was merely that Faxon himself was tired and hungry, more deeply chilled than he had known till he came in from the cold, and unutterably sick of all strange houses, and of the prospect of perpetually treading other people's stairs.

"I hope you're not famished?" Rainer's slim figure was in the doorway. "My uncle has a little business to attend to with Mr. Grisben, and we don't dine for half an hour. Shall I fetch you, or can you find your way down? Come straight to the dining room — the second door on the left of the long gallery."

He disappeared, leaving a ray of warmth behind him, and Faxon, relieved, lit a cigarette and sat down by the fire.

Looking about with less haste, he was struck by a detail that had escaped him. The room was full of flowers — a mere "bachelor's room," in the wing of a house opened only for a few days, in the dead middle of a New Hampshire winter! Flowers were everywhere, not in senseless profusion, but placed with the same conscious art that he had remarked in the grouping of the blossoming shrubs in the hall. A vase of arums stood on the writing table, a cluster of strange-hued carnations on the stand at his elbow, and from bowls of glass and porcelain clumps of freesia bulbs diffused their melting fragrance. The fact implied acres of glass — but that was the least interesting part of it. The flowers themselves, their quality, selection and arrangement, attested on someone's part — and on whose but John Lavington's? — a solicitous and sensitive passion for that particular form of beauty. Well, it simply made the man, as he had appeared to Faxon, all the harder to understand!

The half hour elapsed, and Faxon, rejoicing at the prospect of food, set out to make his way to the dining room. He had not noticed the direction he had followed in going to his room, and was puzzled, when he left it, to find that two staircases, of apparently equal importance, invited him. He chose the one to his right, and reached, at its foot, a long gallery such as Rainer had described. The gallery was empty, the doors down its length were closed; but Rainer had said: "The second to the left," and Faxon, after pausing for some chance enlightenment which did not come, laid his hand on the second knob to the left.

The room he entered was square, with dusky picture-hung walls. In its center, about a table lit by veiled lamps, he fancied Mr. Lavington and his guests to be already seated at dinner; then he perceived that the table was covered not with viands but with papers, and that he had blundered into what seemed to be his host's study. As he paused Frank Rainer looked up.

"Oh, here's Mr. Faxon. Why not ask him — ?"

Mr. Lavington, from the end of the table, reflected his nephew's smile in a glance of impartial benevolence.

"Certainly. Come in, Mr. Faxon. If you won't think it a liberty — "

Mr. Grisben, who sat opposite his host, turned his head toward the door. "Of course Mr. Faxon's an American citizen?"

Frank Rainer laughed. "That's all right! . . . Oh, no, not one of your pin-pointed pens, Uncle Jack! Haven't you got a quill somewhere?"

Mr. Balch, who spoke slowly and as if reluctantly, in a muffled voice of which there seemed to be very little left, raised his hand to say: "One moment: you acknowledge this to be — ?"

"My last will and testament?" Rainer's laugh redoubled. "Well, I won't answer for the 'last.' It's the first, anyway."

"It's a mere formula," Mr. Balch explained.

"Well, here goes." Rainer dipped his quill in the inkstand his uncle had pushed in his direction, and dashed a gallant signature across the document.

Faxon, understanding what was expected of him, and conjecturing that the young man was signing his will on the attainment of his majority, had placed himself behind Mr. Grisben, and stood awaiting his turn to affix his name to the instrument. Rainer, having signed, was about to push the paper across the table to Mr. Balch; but the latter, again raising his hand, said in his sad imprisoned voice: "The seal — ?"

"Oh, does there have to be a seal?"

Faxon, looking over Mr. Grisben at John Lavington, saw a faint frown between his impassive eyes. "Really, Frank!" He seemed, Faxon thought, slightly irritated by his nephew's frivolity.

"Who's got a seal?" Frank Rainer continued, glancing about the table. "There doesn't seem to be one here."

Mr. Grisben interposed. "A wafer will do. Lavington, you have a wafer?"

Mr. Lavington had recovered his serenity. "There must be some in one of the drawers. But I'm ashamed to say I don't know where my secretary keeps these things. He ought to have seen to it that a wafer was sent with the document."

"Oh, hang it — " Frank Rainer pushed the paper aside: "It's the hand of God — and I'm as hungry as a wolf. Let's dine first, Uncle Jack."

"I think I've a seal upstairs," said Faxon.

Mr. Lavington sent him a barely perceptible smile. "So sorry to give you the trouble — "

"Oh, I say, don't send him after it now. Let's wait till after dinner!"

Mr. Lavington continued to smile on his guest, and the latter, as if under the faint coercion of the smile, turned from the room and ran upstairs. Having taken the seal from his writing case he came down again, and once more opened the door of the study. No one was speaking when he entered — they were evidently awaiting his return with the mute impatience of hunger, and he put the seal in Rainer's reach, and stood watching while Mr. Grisben struck a match and held it to one of the candles flanking the inkstand. As the wax descended on the paper Faxon remarked again the strange emaciation, the premature physical weariness, of the hand that held it: he wondered if Mr. Lavington had ever noticed his nephew's hand, and if it were not poignantly visible to him now.

With this thought in mind, Faxon raised his eyes to look at Mr. Lavington. The great man's gaze rested on Frank Rainer with an expression of untroubled benevolence; and at the same instant Faxon's attention was attracted by the presence in the room of another person, who must have joined the group while he was upstairs searching for the seal. The newcomer was a man of about Mr. Lavington's age and figure, who stood just behind his chair, and who, at the moment when Faxon first saw him, was gazing at young Rainer with an equal intensity of attention. The likeness between the two men — perhaps increased by the fact that the hooded lamps on the table left the figure behind the chair in shadow — struck Faxon the more because of the contrast in their expression. John Lavington, during his nephew's clumsy attempt to drop the wax and apply the seal, continued to fasten on him a look of half-amused affection; while the man behind the chair, so oddly reduplicating the lines of his features and figure, turned on the boy a face of pale hostility.

The impression was so startling that Faxon forgot what was going on about him. He was just dimly aware of young Rainer's exclaiming: "Your turn, Mr. Grisben!" of Mr. Grisben's protesting: "No — no; Mr. Faxon first," and of the pen's being thereupon transferred to his own hand. He received it with a deadly sense of being unable to move, or even to understand what was expected of him, till he became conscious of Mr. Grisben's paternally pointing out the precise spot on which he was to leave his autograph. The effort to fix his attention and steady his hand prolonged the process of signing, and when he stood up — a strange weight of fatigue on all his limbs — the figure behind Mr. Lavington's chair was gone.

Faxon felt an immediate sense of relief. It was puzzling that the man's exit should have been so rapid and noiseless, but the door behind Mr. Lavington was screened by a tapestry hanging, and Faxon concluded that the unknown looker-on had merely had to raise it to pass out. At any rate he was gone, and with his withdrawal the strange weight was lifted. Young Rainer was lighting a cigarette, Mr. Balch inscribing his name at the foot of the document, Mr. Lavington — his eyes no longer on his nephew — examining a strange white-winged orchid in the vase at his elbow. Everything suddenly seemed to have grown natural and simple again, and Faxon found himself responding with a smile to the affable gesture with which his host declared: "And now, Mr. Faxon, we'll dine."

## III

"I WONDER how I blundered into the wrong room just now; I thought you told me to take the second door to the left," Faxon said to Frank Rainer as they followed the older men down the gallery.

"So I did; but I probably forgot to tell you which staircase to take. Coming from your bedroom, I ought to have said the fourth door to the right. It's a puzzling house, because my uncle keeps adding to it from year to year. He built this room last summer for his modern pictures."

Young Rainer, pausing to open another door, touched an electric button which sent a circle of light about the walls of a long room hung with canvases of the French Impressionist school.

Faxon advanced, attracted by a shimmering Monet, but Rainer laid a hand on his arm.

"He bought that last week. But come along — I'll show you all this after dinner. Or *he* will, rather — he loves it."

"Does he really love things?"

Rainer stared, clearly perplexed at the question. "Rather! Flowers and pictures especially! Haven't you noticed the flowers? I suppose you think his manner's cold; it seems so at first; but he's really awfully keen about things."

Faxon looked quickly at the speaker. "Has your uncle a brother?"

"Brother? No — never had. He and my mother were the only ones."

"Or any relation who — who looks like him? Who might be mistaken for him?"

"Not that I ever heard of. Does he remind you of someone?"

"Yes."

"That's queer. We'll ask him if he's got a double. Come on!"

But another picture had arrested Faxon, and some minutes elapsed before he and his young host reached the dining room. It was a large room, with the same conventionally handsome furniture and delicately grouped flowers; and Faxon's first glance showed him that only three men were seated about the dining table. The man who had stood behind Mr. Lavington's chair was not present, and no seat awaited him.

When the young men entered, Mr. Grisben was speaking, and his host, who faced the door, sat looking down at his untouched soup plate and turning the spoon about in his small dry hand.

"It's pretty late to call them rumors — they were devilish close to facts when we left town this morning," Mr. Grisben was saying, with an unexpected incisiveness of tone.

Mr. Lavington laid down his spoon and smiled interrogatively. "Oh, facts — what *are* facts? Just the way a thing happens to look at a given minute. . . . "

"You haven't heard anything from town?" Mr. Grisben persisted.

"Not a syllable. So you see. . . . Balch, a little more of that *petite marmite*. Mr. Faxon . . . between Frank and Mr. Grisben, please."

The dinner progressed through a series of complicated courses, ceremoniously dispensed by a prelatical butler attended by three tall footmen, and it was evident that Mr. Lavington took a certain satisfaction in the pageant. That, Faxon reflected, was probably the joint in his armor — that and the flowers. He had changed the subject — not abruptly but firmly — when the young men entered, but Faxon perceived that it still possessed the thoughts of the two elderly visitors, and Mr. Balch presently observed, in a voice that seemed to come from the last survivor down a mine shaft: "If it *does* come, it will be the biggest crash since '93."

Mr. Lavington looked bored but polite. "Wall Street can stand crashes better than it could then. It's got a robuster constitution."

"Yes; but — "

"Speaking of constitutions," Mr. Grisben intervened: "Frank, are you taking care of yourself?"

A flush rose to young Rainer's cheeks.

"Why, of course! Isn't that what I'm here for?"

"You're here about three days in the month, aren't you? And the rest of the time it's crowded restaurants and hot ballrooms in town. I thought you were to be shipped off to New Mexico?"

"Oh, I've got a new man who says that's rot."

"Well, you don't look as if your new man were right," said Mr. Grisben bluntly.

Faxon saw the lad's color fade, and the rings of shadow deepen under his gay eyes. At the same moment his uncle turned to him with a renewed intensity of attention. There was such solicitude in Mr. Lavington's gaze that it seemed almost to fling a shield between his nephew and Mr. Grisben's tactless scrutiny.

"We think Frank's a good deal better," he began; "this new doctor —"

The butler, coming up, bent to whisper a word in his ear, and the communication caused a sudden change in Mr. Lavington's expression. His face was naturally so colorless that it seemed not so much to pale as to fade, to dwindle and recede into something blurred and blotted out. He half rose, sat down again and sent a rigid smile about the table.

"Will you excuse me? The telephone. Peters, go on with the dinner."

---

With small precise steps he walked out of the door which one of the footmen had thrown open.

A momentary silence fell on the group; then Mr. Grisben once more addressed himself to Rainer. "You ought to have gone, my boy; you ought to have gone."

The anxious look returned to the youth's eyes. "My uncle doesn't think so, really."

"You're not a baby, to be always governed by your uncle's opinion. You came of age today, didn't you? Your uncle spoils you . . . that's what's the matter. . . ."

The thrust evidently went home, for Rainer laughed and looked down with a slight accession of color.

"But the doctor — "

"Use your common sense, Frank! You had to try twenty doctors to find one to tell you what you wanted to be told."

A look of apprehension overshadowed Rainer's gaiety. "Oh, come — I say! . . . What would *you* do?" he stammered.

"Pack up and jump on the first train." Mr. Grisben leaned forward and laid his hand kindly on the young man's arm. "Look here: my nephew Jim Grisben is out there ranching on a big scale. He'll take you in and be glad to have you. You say your new doctor thinks it won't do you any good; but he doesn't pretend to say it will do you harm, does he? Well, then — give it a trial. It'll take you out of hot theaters and night restaurants, anyhow. . . . And all the rest of it. . . . Eh, Balch?"

"Go!" said Mr. Balch hollowly. "Go *at once,*" he added, as if a closer look at the youth's face had impressed on him the need of backing up his friend.

Young Rainer had turned ashy pale. He tried to stiffen his mouth into a smile. "Do I look as bad as all that?"

Mr. Grisben was helping himself to terrapin. "You look like the day after an earthquake," he said.

The terrapin had encircled the table, and been deliberately enjoyed by Mr. Lavington's three visitors (Rainer, Faxon noticed, left his plate untouched) before the door was thrown open to readmit their host.

Mr. Lavington advanced with an air of recovered composure. He seated himself, picked up his napkin and consulted the gold-monogrammed menu. "No, don't bring back the filet. . . . Some terrapin; yes. . . ." He looked affably about the table. "Sorry to have deserted you, but the storm has played the deuce with the wires, and I had to wait a long time before I could get a good connection. It must be blowing up a blizzard."

"Uncle Jack," young Rainer broke out, "Mr. Grisben's been lecturing me."

Mr. Lavington was helping himself to terrapin. "Ah — what about?"

"He thinks I ought to have given New Mexico a show."

"I want him to go straight out to my nephew at Santa Paz and stay there till his next birthday." Mr. Lavington signed to the butler to hand the terrapin to Mr. Grisben, who, as he took a second helping, addressed himself again to Rainer. "Jim's in New York now, and going back the day after tomorrow in Olyphant's private car. I'll ask Olyphant to squeeze you in if you'll go. And when you've been out there a week or two, in the saddle all day and sleeping nine hours a night, I suspect you won't think much of the doctor who prescribed New York."

Faxon spoke up, he knew not why. "I was out there once: it's a splendid life. I saw a fellow — oh, a really *bad* case — who'd been simply made over by it."

"It *does* sound jolly," Rainer laughed, a sudden eagerness in his tone.

His uncle looked at him gently. "Perhaps Grisben's right. It's an opportunity — "

Faxon glanced up with a start: the figure dimly perceived in the study was now more visibly and tangibly planted behind Mr. Lavington's chair.

"That's right, Frank: you see your uncle approves. And the trip out there with Olyphant isn't a thing to be missed. So drop a few dozen dinners and be at the Grand Central the day after tomorrow at five."

Mr. Grisben's pleasant grey eye sought corroboration of his host, and Faxon, in a cold anguish of suspense, continued to watch him as he turned his glance on Mr. Lavington. One could not look at Lavington without seeing the presence at his back, and it was clear that, the next minute, some change in Mr. Grisben's expression must give his watcher a clue.

But Mr. Grisben's expression did not change; the gaze he fixed on his host remained unperturbed, and the clue he gave was the startling one of not seeming to see the other figure.

Faxon's first impulse was to look away, to look anywhere else, to resort again to the champagne glass the watchful butler had already brimmed; but some fatal attraction, at war in him with an overwhelming physical resistance, held his eyes upon the spot they feared.

The figure was still standing, more distinctly, and therefore more resemblingly, at Mr. Lavington's back; and while the latter continued to gaze affectionately at his nephew, his counterpart, as before, fixed young Rainer with eyes of deadly menace.

Faxon, with what felt like an actual wrench of the muscles, dragged his own eyes from the sight to scan the other countenances about the table; but not one revealed the least consciousness of what he saw, and a sense of mortal isolation sank upon him.

"It's worth considering, certainly —" he heard Mr. Lavington continue; and as Rainer's face lit up, the face behind his uncle's chair seemed to gather into its look all the fierce weariness of old unsatisfied hates. That was the thing that, as the minutes labored by, Faxon was becoming most conscious of. The watcher behind the chair was no longer merely malevolent: he had grown suddenly, unutterably tired. His hatred seemed to well up out of the very depths of balked effort and thwarted hopes, and the fact made him more pitiable, and yet more dire.

Faxon's look reverted to Mr. Lavington, as if to surprise in him a corresponding change. At first none was visible: his pinched smile was screwed to his blank face like a gaslight to a whitewashed wall. Then the fixity of the smile became ominous: Faxon saw that its wearer was afraid to let it go. It was evident that Mr. Lavington was unutterably tired too, and the discovery sent a colder current through Faxon's veins. Looking down at his untouched plate, he caught the soliciting twinkle of the champagne glass; but the sight of the wine turned him sick.

"Well, we'll go into the details presently," he heard Mr. Lavington say, still on the question of his nephew's future. "Let's have a cigar first. No — not here, Peters." He turned his smile on Faxon. "When we've had coffee I want to show you my pictures."

"Oh, by the way, Uncle Jack — Mr. Faxon wants to know if you've got a double?"

"A double?" Mr. Lavington, still smiling, continued to address himself to his guest. "Not that I know of. Have you seen one, Mr. Faxon?"

Faxon thought: "My God, if I look up now they'll *both* be looking at me!" To avoid raising his eyes he made as though to lift the glass to his lips; but his hand sank inert, and he looked up. Mr. Lavington's glance was politely bent on him, but with a loosening of the strain about his heart he saw that the figure behind the chair still kept its gaze on Rainer.

"Do you think you've seen my double, Mr. Faxon?"

Would the other face turn if he said yes? Faxon felt a dryness in his throat. "No," he answered.

"Ah? It's possible I've a dozen. I believe I'm extremely usual-looking," Mr. Lavington went on conversationally; and still the other face watched Rainer.

"It was . . . a mistake . . . a confusion of memory. . . ." Faxon heard himself stammer. Mr. Lavington pushed back his chair, and as he did so Mr. Grisben suddenly leaned forward.

"Lavington! What have we been thinking of? We haven't drunk Frank's health!"

Mr. Lavington reseated himself. "My dear boy! . . . Peters, another bottle. . . ." He turned to his nephew. "After such a sin of omission I don't presume to propose the toast myself . . . but Frank knows. . . . Go ahead, Grisben!"

The boy shone on his uncle. "No, no. Uncle Jack! Mr. Grisben won't mind. Nobody but *you* — today!"

The butler was replenishing the glasses. He filled Mr. Lavington's last, and Mr. Lavington put out his small hand to raise it. . . . As he did so, Faxon looked away.

"Well, then — All the good I've wished you in all the past years. . . . I put it into the prayer that the coming ones may be healthy and happy and many . . . and *many,* dear boy!"

Faxon saw the hands about him reach out for their glasses. Automatically, he reached for his. His eyes were still on the table, and he repeated to himself with a trembling vehemence: "I won't look up! I won't. . . . I won't. . . ."

His fingers clasped the glass and raised it to the level of his lips. He saw the other hands making the same motion. He heard Mr. Grisben's genial "Hear! Hear!" and Mr. Balch's hollow echo. He said to himself, as the rim of the glass touched his lips: "I won't look up! I swear I won't! —" and he looked.

The glass was so full that it required an extraordinary effort to hold it there, brimming and suspended, during the awful interval before he could trust his hand to lower it again, untouched, to the table. It was this merciful preoccupation which saved him, kept him from crying out, from losing his hold, from slipping down into the bottomless blackness that gaped for him. As long as the problem of the glass engaged him he felt able to keep his seat, manage his muscles, fit unnoticeably into the group; but as the glass touched the table his last link with safety snapped. He stood up and dashed out of the room.

IV

IN THE gallery, the instinct of self-preservation helped him to turn back and sign to young Rainer not to follow. He stammered out something about a touch of dizziness, and joining them presently; and the boy nodded sympathetically and drew back.

At the foot of the stairs Faxon ran against a servant. "I should like to telephone to Weymore," he said with dry lips.

"Sorry, sir; wires all down. We've been trying the last hour to get New York again for Mr. Lavington."

Faxon shot on to his room, burst into it, and bolted the door. The lamplight lay on furniture, flowers, books; in the ashes a log still glimmered. He dropped down on the sofa and hid his face. The room was profoundly silent, the whole house was still: nothing about him gave a hint of what was going on, darkly and dumbly, in the room he had flown from, and with the covering of his eyes oblivion and reassurance seemed to fall on him. But they fell for a moment only; then his lids opened again to the monstrous vision. There it was, stamped on his pupils, a part of him forever, an indelible horror burnt into his body and brain. But why into his — just his? Why had he alone been chosen to see what he had seen? What business was it of *his,* in God's name? Any one of the others, thus enlightened, might have exposed the horror and defeated it; but *he,* the one weaponless and defenceless spectator, the one whom none of the others would believe or understand if he attempted to reveal what he knew — *he* alone had been singled out as the victim of this dreadful initiation!

Suddenly he sat up, listening: he had heard a step on the stairs. Someone, no doubt, was coming to see how he was — to urge him, if he felt better, to go down and join the smokers. Cautiously he opened his door; yes, it was young Rainer's step. Faxon looked down the passage, remembered the other stairway and darted to it. All he wanted was to get out of the house. Not another instant would he breathe its abominable air! What business was it of *his,* in God's name?

The darkness was deep, and the cold so intense that for an instant it stopped his breathing. Then he perceived that only a thin snow was falling, and resolutely he set his face for flight. The trees along the avenue marked his way as he hastened with long strides over the beaten snow. Gradually, while he walked, the tumult in his brain subsided. The impulse to fly still drove him forward, but he began to feel that he was flying from a terror of his own creating, and that the most urgent reason for escape was the need of hiding his state, of shunning other eyes till he should regain his balance.

He had spent the long hours in the train in fruitless broodings on a discouraging situation, and he remembered how his bitterness had turned to exasperation when he found that the Weymore sleigh was not awaiting him. It was absurd, of course; but, though he had joked with Rainer over

Mrs. Culme's forgetfulness, to confess it had cost a pang. That was what his rootless life had brought him to: for lack of a personal stake in things his sensibility was at the mercy of such trifles. . . . Yes; that, and the cold and fatigue, the absence of hope and the haunting sense of starved aptitudes, all these had brought him to the perilous verge over which, once or twice before, his terrified brain had hung.

Why else, in the name of any imaginable logic, human or devilish, should he, a stranger, be singled out for this experience? What could it mean to him, how was he related to it, what bearing had it on his case? . . . Unless, indeed, it was just because he was a stranger — a stranger everywhere — because he had no personal life, no warm screen of private egotisms to shield him from exposure, that he had developed this abnormal sensitiveness to the vicissitudes of others. The thought pulled him up with a shudder. No! Such a fate was too abominable; all that was strong and sound in him rejected it. A thousand times better regard himself as ill, disorganized, deluded, than as the predestined victim of such warnings!

He reached the gates and paused before the darkened lodge. The wind had risen and was sweeping the snow into his face. The cold had him in its grasp again, and he stood uncertain. Should he put his sanity to the test and go back? He turned and looked down the dark drive to the house. A single ray shone through the trees, evoking a picture of the lights, the flowers, the faces grouped about that fatal room. He turned and plunged out into the road. . . .

He remembered that, about a mile from Overdale, the coachman had pointed out the road to Northridge; and he began to walk in that direction. Once in the road he had the gale in his face, and the wet snow on his moustache and eyelashes instantly hardened to ice. The same ice seemed to be driving a million blades into his throat and lungs, but he pushed on, the vision of the warm room pursuing him.

The snow in the road was deep and uneven. He stumbled across ruts and sank into drifts, and the wind drove against him like a granite cliff. Now and then he stopped, gasping, as if an invisible hand had tightened an iron band about his body; then he started again, stiffening himself against the stealthy penetration of the cold. The snow continued to descend out of a pall of inscrutable darkness, and once or twice he paused, fearing he had missed the road to Northridge; but, seeing no sign of a turn, he ploughed on.

At last, feeling sure that he had walked for more than a mile, he halted and looked back. The act of turning brought immediate relief, first because it put his back to the wind, and then because, far down the road, it showed him the gleam of a lantern. A sleigh was coming — a sleigh that might perhaps give him a lift to the village! Fortified by the hope, he began to walk back toward the light. It came forward very slowly, with unaccountable zigzags and waverings; and even when he was within a few yards of it he could catch no sound of sleigh bells. Then it paused and became stationary by the roadside, as though carried by a pedestrian who had stopped, exhausted by the cold. The thought made Faxon hasten on, and a moment later he was stooping over a motionless figure huddled against the snowbank. The lantern had dropped from its bearer's hand, and Faxon, fearfully raising it, threw its light into the face of Frank Rainer.

"Rainer! What on earth are you doing here?"

The boy smiled back through his pallor. "What are *you*, I'd like to know?" he retorted; and, scrambling to his feet with a clutch on Faxon's arm, he added gaily: "Well, I've run you down!"

Faxon stood confounded, his heart sinking. The lad's face was grey.

"What madness —" he began.

"Yes, it *is*. What on earth did you do it for?"

"I? Do what? . . . Why I. . . . I was just taking a walk. . . . I often walk at night. . . ."

Frank Rainer burst into a laugh. "On such nights? Then you hadn't bolted?"

"Bolted?"

"Because I'd done something to offend you? My uncle thought you had."

Faxon grasped his arm. "Did your uncle send you after me?"

"Well, he gave me an awful rowing for not going up to your room with you when you said you were ill. And when we found you'd gone we were frightened — and he was awfully upset — so I said I'd catch you. . . . You're *not* ill, are you?"

"Ill? No. Never better." Faxon picked up the lantern. "Come; let's go back. It was awfully hot in that dining room."

"Yes; I hoped it was only that."

They trudged on in silence for a few minutes; then Faxon questioned: "You're not too done up?"

"Oh, no. It's a lot easier with the wind behind us."

"All right. Don't talk any more."

They pushed ahead, walking, in spite of the light that guided them, more slowly than Faxon had walked alone into the gale. The fact of his companion's stumbling against a drift gave Faxon a pretext for saying: "Take hold of my arm," and Rainer obeying, gasped out: "I'm blown!"

"So am I. Who wouldn't be?"

"What a dance you led me! If it hadn't been for one of the servants happening to see you — "

"Yes; all right. And now, won't you kindly shut up?"

Rainer laughed and hung on him. "Oh, the cold doesn't hurt me. . . ."

For the first few minutes after Rainer had overtaken him, anxiety for the lad had been Faxon's only thought. But as each laboring step carried them nearer to the spot he had been fleeing, the reasons for his flight grew more ominous and more insistent. No, he was not ill, he was not distraught and deluded — he was the instrument singled out to warn and save; and here he was, irresistibly driven, dragging the victim back to his doom!

The intensity of the conviction had almost checked his steps. But what could he do or say? At all costs he must get Rainer out of the cold, into the house and into his bed. After that he would act.

The snowfall was thickening, and as they reached a stretch of the road between open fields the wind took them at an angle, lashing their faces with barbed thongs. Rainer stopped to take breath, and Faxon felt the heavier pressure of his arm.

"When we get to the lodge, can't we telephone to the stable for a sleigh?"

"If they're not all asleep at the lodge."

"Oh, I'll manage. Don't talk!" Faxon ordered; and they plodded on. . . .

At length the lantern ray showed ruts that curved away from the road under tree darkness.

Faxon's spirits rose. "There's the gate! We'll be there in five minutes."

As he spoke he caught, above the boundary hedge, the gleam of a light at the farther end of the dark avenue. It was the same light that had shone on the scene of which every detail was burnt into his brain; and he felt again its overpowering reality. No — he couldn't let the boy go back!

They were at the lodge at last, and Faxon was hammering on the door. He said to himself: "I'll get him inside first, and make them give him a hot drink. Then I'll see — I'll find an argument. . . ."

There was no answer to his knocking, and after an interval Rainer said: "Look here — we'd better go on."

"No!"

"I can, perfectly — "

"You shan't go to the house, I say!" Faxon redoubled his blows, and at length steps sounded on the stairs. Rainer was leaning against the lintel, and as the door opened the light from the hall flashed on his pale face and fixed eyes. Faxon caught him by the arm and drew him in.

"It *was* cold out there," he sighed; and then, abruptly, as if invisible shears at a single stroke had cut every muscle in his body, he swerved, drooped on Faxon's arm, and seemed to sink into nothing at his feet.

The lodgekeeper and Faxon bent over him, and somehow, between them, lifted him into the kitchen and laid him on a sofa by the stove.

The lodgekeeper, stammering: "I'll ring up the house," dashed out of the room. But Faxon heard the words without heeding them: omens mattered nothing now, beside this woe fulfilled. He knelt down to undo the fur collar about Rainer's throat, and as he did so he felt a warm moisture on his hands. He held them up, and they were red. . . .

<h2 style="text-align:center">V</h2>

THE PALMS threaded their endless line along the yellow river. The little steamer lay at the wharf, and George Faxon, sitting in the verandah of the wooden hotel, idly watched the coolies carrying the freight across the gangplank.

He had been looking at such scenes for two months. Nearly five had elapsed since he had descended from the train at Northridge and strained his eyes for the sleigh that was to take him to Weymore: Weymore, which he was never to behold! . . . Part of the interval — the first part — was still a great grey blur. Even now he could not be quite sure how he had got back to Boston, reached the house of a cousin, and been thence transferred to a quiet room looking out on snow under bare trees. He looked out a long time at the same scene, and finally one day a man he had known at Harvard came to see him and invited him to go out on a business trip to the Malay Peninsula.

"You've had a bad shake-up, and it'll do you no end of good to get away from things."

When the doctor came the next day it turned out that he knew of the plan and approved it. "You ought to be quiet for a year. Just loaf and look at the landscape," he advised.

Faxon felt the first faint stirrings of curiosity.

"What's been the matter with me, anyway?"

"Well, overwork, I suppose. You must have been bottling up for a bad breakdown before you started for New Hampshire last December. And the shock of that poor boy's death did the rest."

Ah, yes — Rainer had died. He remembered. . . .

He started for the East, and gradually, by imperceptible degrees, life crept back into his weary bones and leaden brain. His friend was patient and considerate, and they traveled slowly and talked little. At first Faxon had felt a great shrinking from whatever touched on familiar things. He seldom looked at a newspaper and he never opened a letter without a contraction of the heart. It was not that he had any special cause for apprehension, but merely that a great trail of darkness lay on everything. He had looked too deep down into the abyss. . . . But little by little health and energy returned to him, and with them the common promptings of curiosity. He was beginning to wonder how the world was going, and when, presently, the hotelkeeper told him there were no letters for him in the steamer's mailbag, he felt a distinct sense of disappointment. His friend had gone into the jungle on a long excursion, and he was lonely, unoccupied and wholesomely bored. He got up and strolled into the stuffy reading room.

There he found a game of dominoes, a mutilated picture puzzle, some copies of *Zion's Herald* and a pile of New York and London newspapers.

He began to glance through the papers, and was disappointed to find that they were less recent than he had hoped. Evidently the last numbers had been carried off by luckier travelers. He continued to turn them over, picking out the American ones first. These, as it happened, were the oldest: they dated back to December and January. To Faxon, however, they had all the flavor of novelty, since they covered the precise period during which he had virtually ceased to exist. It had never before occurred to him to wonder what had happened in the world during that interval of obliteration; but now he felt a sudden desire to know.

To prolong the pleasure, he began by sorting the papers chronologically, and as he found and spread out the earliest number, the date at the top of the page entered into his consciousness like a key slipping into a lock. It was the seventeenth of December: the date of the day after his arrival at Northridge. He glanced at the first page and read in blazing characters: "Reported Failure of Opal Cement Company. Lavington's Name Involved. Gigantic Exposure of Corruption Shakes Wall Street to Its Foundations."

He read on, and when he had finished the first paper he turned to the next. There was a gap of three days, but the Opal Cement "Investigation" still held the center of the stage. From its complex revelations of greed and ruin his eye wandered to the death notices, and he read: "Rainer. Suddenly, at Northridge, New Hampshire, Francis John, only son of the late . . . "

His eyes clouded, and he dropped the newspaper and sat for a long time with his face in his hands. When he looked up again he noticed that his gesture had pushed the other papers from the table and scattered them at his feet. The uppermost lay spread out before him, and heavily his eyes began their search again. "John Lavington comes forward with plan for reconstructing company. Offers to put in ten millions of his own — The proposal under consideration by the District Attorney."

Ten millions . . . ten millions of his own. But if John Lavington was ruined? . . . Faxon stood up with a cry. That was it, then — that was what the warning meant! And if he had not fled from it, dashed wildly away from it into the night, he might have broken the spell of iniquity, the powers of darkness might not have prevailed! He caught up the pile of newspapers and began to glance through each in turn for the headline: "Wills Admitted to Probate." In the last of all he found the paragraph he sought, and it stared up at him as if with Rainer's dying eyes.

That — *that* was what he had done! The powers of pity had singled him out to warn and save, and he had closed his ears to their call, and washed his hands of it, and fled. Washed his hands of it! That was the word. It caught him back to the dreadful moment in the lodge when, raising himself up from Rainer's side, he had looked at his hands and seen that they were red. . . .

*Conrad Aiken*

# MR. ARCULARIS

MR. ARCULARIS stood at the window of his room in the hospital and looked down at the street. There had been a light shower, which had patterned the sidewalks with large drops, but now again the sun was out, blue sky was showing here and there between the swift white clouds, a cold wind was blowing the poplar trees. An itinerant band had stopped before the building and was playing, with violin, harp, and flute, the finale of *Cavalleria Rusticana*. Leaning against the window-sill — for he felt extraordinarily weak after his operation — Mr. Arcularis suddenly, listening to the wretched music, felt like crying. He rested the palm of one hand against a cold window-pane and stared down at the old man who was blowing the flute, and blinked his eyes. It seemed absurd that he should be so weak, so emotional, so like a child — and especially now that everything was over at last. In spite of all their predictions, in spite, too, of his own dreadful certainty that he was going to die, here he was, as fit as a fiddle — but what a fiddle it was, so out of tune! — with a long life before him. And to begin with, a voyage to England ordered by the doctor. What could be more delightful? Why should he feel sad about it and want to cry like a baby? In a few minutes Harry would arrive with his car to take him to the wharf; in an hour he would be on the sea, in two hours he would see the sunset behind him, where Boston had been, and his new life would be opening before him. It was many years since he had been abroad. June, the best of the year to come — England, France, the Rhine — how ridiculous that he should already be homesick!

There was a light footstep outside the door, a knock, the door opened, and Harry came in.

"Well, old man, I've come to get you. The old bus actually got here. Are you ready? Here, let me take your arm. You're tottering like an octogenarian!"

Mr. Arcularis submitted gratefully, laughing, and they made the journey slowly along the bleak corridor and down the stairs to the entrance hall. Miss Hoyle, his nurse, was there, and the Matron, and the charming little assistant with freckles who had helped to prepare him for the operation. Miss Hoyle put out her hand.

"Good-bye, Mr. Arcularis," she said, "and *bon voyage.*"

"Good-bye, Miss Hoyle, and thank you for everything. You were very kind to me. And I fear I was a nuisance."

The girl with the freckles, too, gave him her hand, smiling. She was very pretty, and it would have been easy to fall in love with her. She reminded him of someone. Who was it? He tried in vain to remember while he said good-bye to her and turned to the Matron.

"And not too many latitudes with the young ladies, Mr. Arcularis!" she was saying.

Mr. Arcularis was pleased, flattered, by all this attention to a middle-aged invalid, and felt a joke taking shape in his mind, and no sooner in his mind than on his tongue.

"Oh, no latitudes," he said laughing. "I'll leave the latitudes to the ship!"

"Oh, come now," said the Matron, "we don't seem to have hurt him much, do we?"

"I think we'll have to operate on him again and *really* cure him," said Miss Hoyle.

He was going down the front steps, between the potted palmettos, and they all laughed and waved. The wind was cold, very cold for June, and he was glad he had put on his coat. He shivered.

"Damned cold for June!" he said. "Why should it be so cold?"

"East wind," Harry said, arranging the rug over his knees. "Sorry it's an open car, but I believe in fresh air and all that sort of thing. I'll drive slowly. We've got plenty of time."

They coasted gently down the long hill towards Beacon Street, but the road was badly surfaced, and despite Harry's care Mr. Arcularis felt his pain again. He found that he could alleviate it a little by leaning to the right, against the arm-rest, and not breathing too deeply. But how glorious to be out again! How strange and vivid the world looked! The trees had innumerable green fresh leaves — they were all blowing and shifting and turning and flashing in the wind; drops of rainwater fell downward sparkling; the robins were singing their absurd, delicious little four-noted songs; even the street cars looked unusually bright and beautiful, just as they used to look when he was a child and had wanted above all things to be a motorman. He found himself smiling foolishly at everything, foolishly and weakly, and wanted to say something about it to Harry. It was no use, though — he had no strength, and the mere finding of words would be almost more than he could manage. And even if he should succeed in saying it, he would then most likely burst into tears. He shook his head slowly from side to side.

"Ain't it grand?" he said.

"I'll bet it looks good," said Harry.

"Words fail me."

"You wait till you get out to sea. You'll have a swell time."

"Oh, swell! . . . I hope not. I hope it'll be calm."

"Tut tut."

When they passed the Harvard Club Mr. Arcularis made a slow and somewhat painful effort to turn in his seat and look at it. It might be the last chance to see it for a long time. Why this sentimental longing to stare at it, though? There it was, with the great flag blowing in the wind, the Harvard seal now concealed by the swift folds and now revealed, and there were the windows in the library, where he had spent so many delightful hours reading — Plato, and Kipling, and the Lord knows what — and the balconies from which for so many years he had watched the finish of the Marathon. Old Talbot might be in there now, sleeping with a book on his knee, hoping forlornly to be interrupted by anyone, for anything.

"Good-bye to the old club," he said.

"The bar will miss you," said Harry, smiling with friendly irony and looking straight ahead.

"But let there be no moaning," said Mr. Arcularis.

"What's *that* a quotation from?"

"The *Odyssey.*"

In spite of the cold, he was glad of the wind on his face, for it helped to dissipate the feeling of vagueness and dizziness that came over him in a sickening wave from time to time. All of a sudden everything would begin to swim and dissolve, the houses would lean their heads together, he had to close his eyes, and there would be a curious and dreadful humming noise, which at regular intervals rose to a crescendo and then drawlingly subsided again. It was disconcerting. Perhaps he still had a trace of fever. When he got on the ship he would have a glass of whisky. . . . From one of these spells he opened his eyes and found that they were on the ferry, crossing to East Boston. It must have been the ferry's engines that he had heard. From another spell he woke to find himself on the wharf, the car at a standstill beside a pile of yellow packing-cases.

"We're here because we're here because we're here," said Harry.

"Because we're here," added Mr. Arcularis.

He dozed in the car while Harry — and what a good friend Harry was! — attended to all the details. He went and came with tickets and passports and baggage checks and porters. And at last he unwrapped Mr. Arcularis from the rugs and led him up the steep gangplank to the deck, and thence by devious windings to a small cold stateroom with a solitary porthole like the eye of a cyclops.

"Here you are," he said, "and now I've got to go. Did you hear the whistle?"

"No."

"Well, you're half asleep. It's sounded the all-ashore. Good-bye, old fellow, and take care of yourself. Bring me back a spray of edelweiss. And send me a picture post card from the Absolute."

"Will you have it finite or infinite?"

"Oh, infinite. But with your signature on it. Now you'd better turn in for a while and have a nap. Cheerio!"

Mr. Arcularis took his hand and pressed it hard, and once more felt like crying. Absurd! Had he become a child again?

"Good-bye," he said.

He sat down in the little wicker chair, with his overcoat still on, closed his eyes, and listened to the humming of the air in the ventilator. Hurried footsteps ran up and down the corridor. The chair was not too comfortable, and his pain began to bother him again, so he moved, with his coat still on, to the narrow berth and fell asleep. When he woke up, it was dark, and the porthole had been partly opened. He groped for the switch and turned on the light. Then he rang for the steward.

"It's cold in here," he said. "Would you mind closing the port?"

THE GIRL who sat opposite him at dinner was charming. Who was it she reminded him of? Why, of course, the girl at the hospital, the girl with the freckles. Her hair was beautiful, not quite red, not quite gold, nor had it been bobbed; arranged with a sort of graceful untidiness, it made him think of a Melozzo da Forli angel. Her face was freckled, she had a mouth which was both humorous and voluptuous. And she seemed to be alone.

He frowned at the bill of fare and ordered the thick soup.

"No hors d'oeuvres?" asked the steward.

"I think not," said Mr. Arcularis. "They might kill me."

The steward permitted himself to be amused and deposited the menu card on the table against the water-bottle. His eyebrows were lifted. As he moved away, the girl followed him with her eyes and smiled.

"I'm afraid you shocked him," she said.

"Impossible," said Mr. Arcularis. "These stewards, they're dead souls. How could they be stewards otherwise? And they think they've seen and known everything. They suffer terribly from the *déjà vu*. Personally, I don't blame them."

"It must be a dreadful sort of life."

"It's because they're dead that they accept it."

"Do you think so?"

"I'm sure of it. I'm enough of a dead soul myself to know the signs!"

"Well, I don't know what you mean by that!"

"But nothing mysterious! I'm just out of hospital, after an operation. I was given up for dead. For six months I had given *myself* up for dead. If you've ever been seriously ill you know the feeling. You have a posthumous feeling — a mild, cynical tolerance for everything and everyone. What is there you haven't seen or done or understood? Nothing."

Mr. Arcularis waved his hands and smiled.

"I wish I could understand you," said the girl, "but I've never been ill in my life."

"Never?"

"Never."

"Good God!"

The torrent of the unexpressed and inexpressible paralyzed him and rendered him speechless. He stared at the girl, wondering who she was and then, realizing that he had perhaps stared too fixedly, averted his gaze, gave a little laugh, rolled a pill of bread between his fingers. After a second or two he allowed himself to look at her again and found her smiling.

"Never pay any attention to invalids," he said, "or they'll drag you to the hospital."

She examined him critically, with her head tilted a little to one side, but with friendliness.

"You don't *look* like an invalid," she said.

Mr. Arcularis thought her charming. His pain ceased to bother him, the disagreeable humming disappeared, or rather, it was dissociated from himself and became merely, as it should be, the sound of the ship's engines, and he began to think the voyage was going to be really delightful. The parson on his right passed him the salt.

"I fear you will need this in your soup," he said.

"Thank you. Is it as bad as that?"

The steward, overhearing, was immediately apologetic and solicitous. He explained that on the first day everything was at sixes and sevens. The girl looked up at him and asked him a question.

"Do you think we'll have a good voyage?" she said.

He was passing the hot rolls to the parson, removing the napkins from them with a deprecatory finger.

"Well, madam, I don't like to be a Jeremiah, but — "

"Oh, come," said the parson, "I hope we have no Jeremiahs."

"What do you mean?" said the girl.

Mr. Arcularis ate his soup with gusto — it was nice and hot.

"Well, maybe I shouldn't say it, but there's a corpse on board, going to Ireland; and I never yet knew a voyage with a corpse on board that we didn't have bad weather."

"Why, steward, you're just superstitious! What nonsense."

"That's a very ancient superstition," said Mr. Arcularis. "I've heard it many times. Maybe it's true. Maybe we'll be wrecked. And what does it matter, after all?" He was very bland.

"Then let's be wrecked," said the parson coldly.

Nevertheless, Mr. Arcularis felt a shudder go through him on hearing the steward's remark. A corpse in the hold — a coffin? Perhaps it was true. Perhaps some disaster would befall them. There might be fogs. There might be icebergs. He thought of all the wrecks of which he had read. There was the *Titanic,* which he had read about in the warm newspaper room at the Harvard Club — it had seemed dreadfully real, even there. That band, playing "Nearer My God to Thee" on the after-deck while the ship sank! It was one of the darkest of his memories. And the *Empress of Ireland* — all those poor people trapped in the smoking-room, with only one door between them and life, and that door locked for the night by the deck-steward, and the deck-steward nowhere to be found! He shivered, feeling a draft, and turned to the parson.

"How do these strange delusions arise?" he said.

The parson looked at him searchingly, appraisingly — from chin to forehead, from forehead to chin — and Mr. Arcularis, feeling uncomfortable, straightened his tie.

"From nothing but fear," said the parson. "Nothing on earth but fear."

"How strange!" said the girl.

Mr. Arcularis again looked at her — she had lowered her face — and again tried to think of whom she reminded him. It wasn't only the little freckle-faced girl at the hospital — both of them had reminded him of someone else. Someone far back in his life: remote, beautiful, lovely. But he couldn't think. The meal came to an end, they all rose, the ship's orchestra played a feeble fox-trot, and Mr. Arcularis, once more alone, went to the bar to have his whisky. The room was stuffy, and the ship's engines were both audible and palpable. The humming and throbbing oppressed him, the rhythm seemed to be the rhythm of his own pain, and after a short time he found his way, with slow steps, holding on to the walls in his moments of weakness and dizziness, to his forlorn and white little room. The port had been — thank God! — closed for the night: it was cold enough anyway. The white and blue ribbons fluttered from the ventilator, the bottle and glasses clicked and clucked as the ship swayed gently to the long, slow motion of the sea. It was all very peculiar — it was all like something he had experienced somewhere before. What was it? Where was it? . . . He untied his tie, looking at his face in the glass, and wondered, and from time to time put his hand to his side to hold in the pain. It wasn't at Portsmouth, in his childhood, nor at Salem, nor in the rose-garden at his Aunt Julia's, nor in the schoolroom at Cambridge. It was something very queer, very intimate, very precious. The jackstones, the Sunday-School cards which he had loved when he was a child. . . . He fell asleep.

THE SENSE of time was already hopelessly confused. One hour was like another, the sea looked always the same, morning was indistinguishable from afternoon — and was it Tuesday or Wednesday? Mr. Arcularis was sitting in the smoking-room in his favorite corner, watching the parson teach Miss Dean to play chess. On the deck outside he could see the people passing and repassing in their restless round of the ship. The red jacket went by, then the black hat with the white feather, then the purple scarf, the brown tweed coat, the Bulgarian mustache, the monocle, the Scotch cap with fluttering ribbons, and in no time at all the red jacket again, dipping past the windows with its own peculiar rhythm, followed once more by the black hat and the purple scarf. How odd to reflect on the fixed little orbits of these things — as definite and profound, perhaps, as the orbits of the stars, and as important to God or the Absolute. There was a kind of tyranny in this fixedness, too — to think of it too much made one uncomfortable. He closed his eyes for a moment, to avoid seeing for the fortieth time the Bulgarian mustache and the pursuing monocle. The parson was explaining the movements of knights. Two forward and one to the side. Eight possible moves, always to the opposite color from that on which the piece stands. Two forward and one to the side: Miss Dean repeated the words several times with reflective emphasis. Here, too, was the terrifying fixed curve of the infinite, the creeping curve of logic which at last must become the final signpost at the edge of nothing. After that — the deluge. The great white light of annihilation. The bright flash of death. ... Was it merely the sea which made these abstractions so insistent, so intrusive? The mere notion of *orbit* had somehow become extraordinarily naked; and to rid himself of the discomfort and also to forget a little the pain which bothered his side whenever he sat down, he walked slowly and carefully into the writing-room, and examined a pile of super-annuated magazines and catalogues of travel. The bright colors amused him, the photographs of remote islands and mountains, savages in sampans or sarongs or both — it was all very far off and delightful, like something in a dream or a fever. But he found that he was too tired to read and was incapable of concentration. Dreams! Yes, that reminded him. That rather alarming business — sleep-walking!

Later in the evening — at what hour he didn't know — he was telling Miss Dean about it, as he had intended to do. They were sitting in deck-chairs on the sheltered side. The sea was black, and there was a cold wind. He wished they had chosen to sit in the lounge.

Miss Dean was extremely pretty — no, beautiful. She looked at him, too, in a very strange and lovely way, with something of inquiry, something of sympathy, something of affection. It seemed as if, between the question and the answer, they had sat thus for a very long time, exchanging an unspoken secret, simply looking at each other quietly and kindly. Had an hour or two passed? And was it at all necessary to speak?

"No," she said, "I never have."

She breathed into the low words a note of interrogation and gave him a slow smile.

"That's the funny part of it. I never had either until last night. Never in my life. I hardly ever even dream. And it really rather frightens me."

"Tell me about it, Mr. Arcularis."

"I dreamed at first that I was walking, alone, in a wide plain covered with snow. It was growing dark, I was very cold, my feet were frozen and numb, and I was lost. I came then to a signpost — at first it seemed to me there was nothing on it. Nothing but ice. Just before it grew finally dark, however, I made out on it the one word 'Polaris.' "

"The Pole Star."

"Yes — and you see, I didn't myself know that. I looked it up only this morning. I suppose I must have seen it somewhere? And of course it rhymes with my name."

"Why, so it does!"

"Anyway, it gave me — in the dream — an awful feeling of despair, and the dream changed. This time, I dreamed I was standing *outside* my stateroom in the little dark corridor, or *cul-de-sac,* and trying to find the door-handle to let myself in. I was in my pajamas, and again I was very cold. And at this point I woke up. . . . The extraordinary thing is that's exactly where I was!"

"Good heavens. How strange!"

"Yes. And now the question is, *where had I been?* I was frightened, when I came to — not unnaturally. For among other things I *did* have, quite definitely, the feeling that I *had been* somewhere. Somewhere where it was very cold. It doesn't sound very proper. Suppose I had been seen!"

"That might have been awkward," said Miss Dean.

"Awkward! It might indeed. It's very singular. I've never done such a thing before. It's this sort of thing that reminds one — rather wholesomely, perhaps, don't you think?" — and Mr. Arcularis gave a nervous little laugh — "how extraordinarily little we know about the workings of our own minds or souls. After all, what *do* we know?"

"Nothing — nothing — nothing — nothing," said Miss Dean slowly. "*Absolutely* nothing."

Their voices had dropped, and again they were silent; and again they looked at each other gently and sympathetically, as if for the exchange of something unspoken and perhaps unspeakable. Time ceased. The orbit — so it seemed to Mr. Arcularis — once more became pure, became absolute. And once more he found himself wondering who it was that Miss Dean — Clarice Dean — reminded him of. Long ago and far away. Like those pictures of the islands and mountains. The little freckle-faced girl at the hospital was merely, as it were, the stepping-stone, the signpost, or, as in algebra, the "equals" sign. But what was it they both "equalled"? The jackstones came again into his mind and his Aunt Julia's rose-garden — at sunset; but this was ridiculous. It couldn't be simply that they reminded him of his childhood! And yet why not?

They went into the lounge. The ship's orchestra, in the oval-shaped balcony among faded palms, was playing the finale of *Cavalleria Rusti-cana,* playing it badly.

"Good God!" said Mr. Arcularis, "can't I ever escape from that damned sentimental tune? It's the last thing I heard in America, and the last thing I *want* to hear."

"But don't you like it?"

"As music? No! It moves me too much, but in the wrong way."

"What, exactly, do you mean?"

"Exactly? Nothing. When I heard it at the hospital — when was it? — it made me feel like crying. Three old Italians tootling it in the rain. I suppose, like most people, I'm afraid of my feelings."

"Are they so dangerous?"

"Now then, young woman! Are you pulling my leg?"

The stewards had rolled away the carpets, and the passengers were beginning to dance. Miss Dean accepted the invitation of a young officer, and Mr. Arcularis watched them with envy. Odd, that last exchange of remarks — very odd; in fact, everything was odd. Was it possible that they were falling in love? Was that what it was all about — all these concealed references and recollections? He had read of such things. But at his age! And with a girl of twenty-two!

After an amused look at his old friend Polaris from the open door on the sheltered side, he went to bed.

The rhythm of the ship's engines was positively a persecution. It gave one no rest, it followed one like the Hound of Heaven, it drove one out into space and across the Milky Way and then back home by way of Betelgeuse. It was cold there, too. Mr. Arcularis, making the round trip by way of Betelgeuse and Polaris, sparkled with frost. He felt like a Christmas tree. Icicles on his fingers and icicles on his toes. He tinkled and spangled in the void, hallooed to the waste echoes, rounded the buoy on the verge of the Unknown, and tacked glittering homeward. The wind whistled. He was barefooted. Snowflakes and tinsel blew past him. Next time, by George, he would go farther still — for altogether it was rather a lark. Forward into the untrodden! as somebody said. Some intrepid explorer of his own backyard, probably, some middle-aged professor with an umbrella: those were the fellows for courage! But give us time, thought Mr. Arcularis, give us time, and we will bring back with us the night-rime of the Obsolute. Or was it Absolete? If only there weren't this perpetual throbbing, this iter-ation of sound, like a pain, these circles and repetitions of light — the feeling as of everything coiling inward to a center of misery...

Suddenly it was dark, and he was lost. He was groping, he touched the cold, white, slippery woodwork with his fingernails, looking for an electric switch. The throbbing, of course, was the throbbing of the ship. But he was almost home — almost home. Another corner to round, a door to be opened, and there he would be. Safe and sound. Safe in his father's home.

It was at this point that he woke up: in the corridor that led to the dining saloon. Such pure terror, such horror, seized him as he had never known. His heart felt as if it would stop beating. His back was towards the dining saloon; apparently he had just come from it. He was in his pajamas. The corridor was dim, all but two lights having been turned out for the night, and — thank God! — deserted. Not a soul, not a sound. He was perhaps fifty yards from his room. With luck he could get to it unseen. Holding tremulously to the rail that ran along the wall, a brown, greasy rail, he began to creep his way forward. He felt very weak, very dizzy, and his thoughts refused to concentrate. Vaguely he remembered Miss Dean — Clarice — and the freckled girl, as if they were one and the same person. But he wasn't in the hospital, he was on the ship. Of course. How absurd. The Great Circle. Here we are, old fellow . . . steady round the corner . . . hold hard to your umbrella . . .

In his room, with the door safely shut behind him, Mr. Arcularis broke into a cold sweat. He had no sooner got into his bunk, shivering, than he heard the night watchman pass.

"But where" – he thought, closing his eyes in agony – "have I been?"

A dreadful idea had occurred to him.

"IT'S NOTHING serious — how could it be anything serious? Of course, it's nothing serious," said Mr. Arcularis.

"No, it's nothing serious," said the ship's doctor urbanely.

"I knew you'd think so. But just the same — "

"Such a condition is the result of worry," said the doctor. "Are you worried — do you mind telling me — about something? Just try to think."

"Worried?"

Mr. Arcularis knitted his brows. *Was* there something? Some little mosquito of a cloud disappearing into the southwest, the northeast? Some little gnat-song of despair? But no, that was all over. All over.

"Nothing," he said, "nothing whatever."

"It's very strange," said the doctor.

"Strange! I should say so. I've come to sea for a rest, not for a nightmare! What about a bromide?"

"Well, I can give you a bromide, Mr. Arcularis — "

"Then, please, if you don't mind, give me a bromide."

He carried the little phial hopefully to his stateroom, and took a dose at once. He could see the sun through his porthole. It looked northern and pale and small, like a little peppermint, which was only natural enough, for the latitude was changing with every hour. But why was it that doctors were all alike? and all, for that matter, like his father, or that other fellow at the hospital? Smythe, his name was. Doctor Smythe. A nice, dry little fellow, and they said he was a writer. Wrote poetry, or something like that. Poor fellow — disappointed. Like everybody else. Crouched in there, in his cabin, night after night, writing blank verse or something — all about the stars and flowers and love and death; ice and the sea and the infinite; time and tide — well, every man to his own taste.

"But it's nothing serious," said Mr. Arcularis, later, to the parson. "How could it be?"

"Why of course not, my dear fellow," said the parson, patting his back. "How could it be?"

"I know it isn't and yet I worry about it."

"It would be ridiculous to think it serious," said the parson.

Mr. Arcularis shivered: it was colder than ever. It was said that they were near icebergs. For a few hours in the morning there had been a fog, and the siren had blown — devastatingly — at three-minute intervals. Icebergs caused fog — he knew that.

"These things always come," said the parson, "from a sense of guilt. You feel guilty about something. I won't be so rude as to inquire what it is. But if you could rid yourself of the sense of guilt — "

And later still, when the sky was pink:

"But is it anything to worry about?" said Miss Dean. "Really?"

"No, I suppose not."

"Then don't worry. We aren't children any longer!"

"Aren't we? I wonder!"

They leaned, shoulders touching, on the deck-rail, and looked at the sea, which was multitudinously incarnadined. Mr. Arcularis scanned the horizon in vain for an iceberg.

"Anyway," he said, "the colder we are the less we feel!"

"I hope that's no reflection on *you*," said Miss Dean.

"Here . . . feel my hand," said Mr. Arcularis.

"Heaven knows it's cold!"

"It's been to Polaris and back! No wonder."

"Poor thing, poor thing!"

"Warm it."

"May I?"

"You can."

"I'll try."

Laughing, she took his hand between both of hers, one palm under and one palm over, and began rubbing it briskly. The decks were deserted, no one was near them, everyone was dressing for dinner. The sea grew darker, the wind blew colder.

"I wish I could remember who you are," he said.

"And you — who are you?"

"Myself."

"Then perhaps *I* am yourself."

"Don't be metaphysical!"

"But I *am* metaphysical!"

She laughed, withdrew, pulled the light coat about her shoulders.

The bugle blew the summons for dinner — "The Roast Beef of Old England" — and they walked together along the darkening deck toward the door, from which a shaft of soft light fell across the deck-rail. As they stepped over the brass door-sill Mr. Arcularis felt the throb of the engines again; he put his hand quickly to his side.

*"Auf wiedersehen,"* he said. *"Tomorrow and tomorrow and tomorrow."*

MR. ARCULARIS was finding it impossible, absolutely impossible, to keep warm. A cold fog surrounded the ship, had done so, it seemed, for days. The sun had all but disappeared, the transition from day to night was almost unnoticeable. The ship, too, seemed scarcely to be moving — it was as if anchored among walls of ice and rime. Monstrous, that merely because it was June, and supposed, therefore, to be warm, the ship's authorities should consider it unnecessary to turn on the heat! By day, he wore his heavy coat and sat shivering in the corner of the smoking-room. His teeth chattered, his hands were blue. By night, he heaped blankets on his bed, closed the porthole's black eye against the sea, and drew the yellow curtains across it, but in vain. Somehow, despite everything, the fog crept in, and the icy fingers touched his throat. The steward, questioned about it, merely said, "Icebergs." Of course — any fool knew that. But how long, in God's name, was it going to last? They surely ought to be past the Grand Banks by this time! And surely it wasn't necessary to sail to England by way of Greenland and Iceland!

Miss Dean — Clarice — was sympathetic.

"It's simply because," she said, "your vitality has been lowered by your illness. You can't expect to be your normal self so soon after an operation! When *was* your operation, by the way?"

Mr. Arcularis considered. Strange — he couldn't be quite sure. It was all a little vague — his sense of time had disappeared.

"Heaven knows!" he said. "Centuries ago. When I was a tadpole and you were a fish. I should think it must have been at about the time of the Battle of Teutoburg Forest. Or perhaps when I was a Neanderthal man with a club!"

"Are you sure it wasn't farther back still?"

What did she mean by that?

"Not at all. Obviously, we've been on this damned ship for ages — for eras — for aeons. And even on this ship, you must remember, I've had plenty of time, in my nocturnal wanderings, to go several times to Orion and back. I'm thinking, by the way, of going farther still. There's a nice little star off to the left, as you round Betelgeuse, which looks as if it might be right at the edge. The last outpost of the finite. I think I'll have a look at it and bring you back a frozen rime-feather."

"It would melt when you got it back."

"Oh, no, it wouldn't — not on *this* ship!"

Clarice laughed.

"I wish I could go with you," she said.

"If only you would! If only — "

He broke off his sentence and looked hard at her — how lovely she was, and how desirable! No such woman had ever before come into his life; there had been no one with whom he had at once felt so profound a sympathy and understanding. It was a miracle, simply — a miracle. No need to put his arm around her or to kiss her — delightful as such small vulgarities would be. He had only to look at her, and to feel, gazing into those extraordinary eyes, that she knew him, had always known him. It was as if, indeed, she might be his own soul.

But as he looked thus at her, reflecting, he noticed that she was frowning.

"What is it?" he said.

She shook her head, slowly.

"I don't know."

"Tell me."

"Nothing. It just occurred to me that perhaps you weren't looking quite so well."

Mr. Arcularis was startled. He straightened himself up.

"What nonsense! Of course this pain bothers me — and I feel astonishingly weak — "

"It's more than that — much more than that. Something is worrying you horribly." She paused, and then with an air of challenging him, added, "Tell me, did you?"

Her eyes were suddenly asking him blazingly the question he had been afraid of. He flinched, caught his breath, looked away. But it was no use, as he knew: he would have to tell her. He had known all along that he would have to tell her.

"Clarice," he said — and his voice broke in spite of his effort to control it — "It's killing me, it's ghastly! Yes, I did."

His eyes filled with tears, he saw that her own had done so also. She put her hand on his arm.

"I knew," she said. "I knew. But tell me."

"It's happened twice again — *twice* — and each time I was farther away. The same dream of going round a star, the same terrible coldness and helplessness. That awful whistling curve . . . " He shuddered.

"And when you woke up" — she spoke quietly — "where were you when you woke up? Don't be afraid!"

"The first time I was at the farther end of the dining saloon. I had my hand on the door that leads into the pantry."

"I see. Yes. And the next time?"

Mr. Arcularis wanted to close his eyes in terror — he felt as if he were going mad. His lips moved before he could speak, and when at last he did speak it was in a voice so low as to be almost a whisper.

"I was at the bottom of the stairway that leads down from the pantry to the hold, past the refrigerating-plant. It was dark, and I was crawling on my hands and knees . . . *Crawling on my hands and knees!* . . . "

"Oh!" she said, and again, "Oh!"

He began to tremble violently; he felt the hand on his arm trembling also. And then he watched a look of unmistakable horror come slowly into Clarice's eyes, and a look of understanding, as if she saw . . . She tightened her hold on his arm.

"Do you think . . ." she whispered.

They stared at each other.

"I know," he said. "And so do you . . . Twice more — three times — and I'll be looking down into an empty . . . "

It was then that they first embraced — then, at the edge of the infinite, at the last signpost of the finite. They clung together desperately, forlornly, weeping as they kissed each other, staring hard one moment and closing their eyes the next. Passionately, passionately, she kissed him, as if she were indeed trying to give him her warmth, her life.

"But what nonsense!" she cried, leaning back, and holding his face between her hands which were wet with his tears. "What nonsense! It can't be!"

"It is," said Mr. Arcularis slowly.

"But how do you know? . . . How do you know where the — "

For the first time Mr. Arcularis smiled.

"Don't be afraid, darling — you mean the coffin?"

"How could you know where it is?"

"I don't need to," said Mr. Arcularis . . . "I'm already almost there."

BEFORE they separated for the night, in the smoking-room, they had several whisky cocktails.

"We must make it gay!" Mr. Arcularis said. "Above all, we must make it gay. Perhaps even now it will turn out to be nothing but a nightmare from which both of us will wake! And even at the worst, at my present rate of travel, I ought to need two more nights! It's a long way, still, to that little star."

The parson passed them at the door.

"What! Turning in so soon?" he said. "I was hoping for a game of chess."

"Yes, both turning in. But tomorrow?"

"Tomorrow, then, Miss Dean! And good night!"

"Good night."

They walked once round the deck, then leaned on the railing and stared into the fog. It was thicker and whiter than ever. The ship was moving barely perceptibly, the rhythm of the engines was slower, more subdued and remote, and at regular intervals, mournfully, came the long reverberating cry of the foghorn. The sea was calm, and lapped only very tenderly against the side of the ship, the sound coming up to them clearly, however, because of the profound stillness.

" 'On such a night as this —' " quoted Mr. Arcularis grimly.

" 'On such a night as this —' "

Their voices hung suspended in the night, time ceased for them, for an eternal instant they were happy. When at last they parted it was by tacit agreement on a note of the ridiculous.

"Be a good boy and take your bromide!" she said.

"Yes, mother, I'll take my medicine!"

In his stateroom, he mixed himself a strong potion of bromide, a very strong one, and got into bed. He would have no trouble in falling asleep: he felt more tired, more supremely exhausted, than he had ever been in his life; nor had bed ever seemed so delicious. And that long, magnificent, delirious swoop of dizziness . . . the Great Circle . . . the swift pathway to Arcturus . . .

It was all as before, but infinitely more rapid. Never had Mr. Arcularis achieved such phenomenal, such supernatural, speed. In no time at all he was beyond the moon, shot past the North Star as if it were standing still (which perhaps it was?), swooped in a long, bright curve round the Pleiades, shouted his frosty greetings to Betelgeuse, and was off to the little blue star which pointed the way to the unknown. Forward into the untrodden! Courage, old man, and hold on to your umbrella! Have you got your garters on? Mind your hat! In no time at all we'll be back to Clarice with the frozen time-feather, the rime-feather, the snowflake of the Absolute, the Obsolete. If only we don't wake . . . if only we needn't wake . . . if only we don't wake in that — in that — time and space . . . somewhere or nowhere . . . cold and dark . . . *Cavalleria Rusticana* sobbing among the palms; if a lonely . . . if only . . . the coffers of the poor — not coffers, not coffers, not coffers, Oh, God, not coffers, but light, delight, supreme white and brightness, and above all whirling lightness, whirling lightness above all — and freezing — freezing — freezing . . .

At this point in the void the surgeon's last effort to save Mr. Arcularis's life had failed. He stood back from the operating table and made a tired gesture with a rubber-gloved hand.

"It's all over," he said. "As I expected."

He looked at Miss Hoyle, whose gaze was downward, at the basin she held. There was a moment's stillness, a pause, a brief flight of unexchanged comment, and then the ordered life of the hospital was resumed.

*Oliver La Farge*

# HAUNTED GROUND

G EORGE WATERSON stood up uncertainly. He was shaky and bitterly cold; the nor'wester blew clear through him; by the last
faint daylight he could see sparse dry snowflakes driven under
the leaden sky. Well, that had failed, too, and the immediate business was,
apparently, to continue living. He looked around. By God, with the whole
bay to choose from, he had to go ashore on the beach of the Hales' place —
Haunted Ground, the country people's byname for it, said itself in his
mind. Under his dominant consciousness of cold and misery was a conviction that his luck had irrevocably turned, that now every least chance
was viciously leveled against him.

For the moment, at least, he must continue living. This was too cold.
There was nothing for it but to go up to the Hales', to Haunted Ground.
Wouldn't you know something like that would happen? He climbed the
familiar path up the steep bluff behind the beach, and at the top, where
locust trees broke the wind, stopped to look back. The *Lucy* was just bits
of wood and spars twisting on the rocks, mouthed by the breakers; there
was no longer even the shape of a boat. He didn't want to look. He faced
inland.

He heard his heart beating clearly, almost thunderously, and very
slow. Exhaustion, he thought. There was a good half mile of ascending

road before him, leading up to the crest of the hill topped by the big, high-shouldered old Hale house against the last gray of the western sky, with the elms on one side that always bent away from it, shaped by sea winds. It never did make a cheerful picture. But there were lighted windows.

He supposed Sue would be laid out in one of those rooms — Sue, Sue! Each fresh recollection of her death struck him with the force of the first impact. That damned old house so packed with death! Old Jasper Summers with a mouth full of broken teeth eagerly and bluntly telling him, "Did ye hear abaout Susan Hale? A burglar come into their haouse, first one's ben in the taownship in twenty years, last night and shot her dead." He saw again the triumphant gossip's face in a mist of horror, and heard the calm voice continuing about Mrs. Hale being sick from the shock, and so on, and on, and on.

Sue and John and himself having a snowball fight with hydrangeas. Mrs. Hale would probably have her in the sitting room. In a coffin — oh! Sue riding his pony while he led and John envied. That must have been one of the few times when his money gave him an advantage over the country boy. A still picture and a remembered pain when Sue told him that she was engaged to John. Sue sobbing and clinging to him when John was lost with his boat off Brenton's reef. He had been shocked and ashamed then at a fierce joy that mingled with his sorrow for his friend and for her sorrow. She had said, "Anyway, living in Haunted Ground, I'll see him again when I'm old, the way Granny used to do."

That quiet assumption had made him feel chilly.

He heard his heartbeats again, clear and slow. Vaguely he thought that he had left something of great importance on the beach. It was terribly cold. The high wind had blown his clothes dry.

It hit him again. Sue was dead — dead — dead. He would have won her in time, and she was dead. The first burglar in Quonochaug in twenty years had shot her through the heart. An unknown man casually in the course of his trade blotted out the sun and disappeared. A hole over her heart, spreading red. Sue, Sue! Oh, God!

The house loomed gaunt and dark above the two lighted windows; the wind swooped around it, and the bare trees, twisting away, complained. He knocked and waited, shivering, then knocked again. His heartbeats sounded very loud and he resisted an almost overwhelming impulse to turn and race back to the beach. He had left something vital there. Still no one answered him.

He turned the knob and entered. The sitting-room door was open, letting grateful warmth into the hall. Just as he had thought, the coffin was in the center of the sitting room. Mrs. Hale sat in a rocker opposite. It was unusual to see her with idle hands, not knitting or sewing.

"Please excuse me for coming in like this, Mrs. Hale — "

"That's all right, George; if I'd known what you were I'd have let you in. Sit down."

Odd way of putting it. She looked pale and weak, and her speech, for all its New England precision, had a quality of vagueness. George moved toward the coffin.

"Don't disturb her."

What on earth did she think he was going to do?

"I figured she was tired, and she's laid out so pretty I'm just letting her rest awhile. She's to be buried Thursday."

An unpleasant feeling came over George that the shock had unbalanced the old lady. He gazed at the girl's uncovered face, the rich golden-brown hair, long lashes making shadows on the cheeks, delicate, warm mouth. He thought in trite adjectives, chiefly repeating "lovely." He was glad for the macabre skill of an undertaker who had touched her mouth with lipstick. She had never been a pale person, Sue. The plants of winter were about her, bittersweet, pine branches, even thorny barberry that she loved.

He stood looking for some minutes, not really thinking. His heart-beats seemed yet slower, and again he was troubled about something forgotten on the beach. At length he sat down.

"How did you come here?" Mrs. Hale emphasized the "you."

"When I heard, I — I didn't want to live any longer. I took the *Lucy* out and cracked on sail till she went. We were driven aground here, I was cast up on the beach, and — and here I am." He said the last words dully. "I hated it when I saw I was on your shore, but I'm glad I came now."

"It's hard for you, George. She'll be seeing John after church on Thursday."

"I know." Curious way she had of talking about it.

"It'd 'a' been better . . ." Her voice became inaudible, although her mouth continued in the motions of speech.

The shock had undoubtedly harmed her. He was in none too good shape himself. Those couldn't be heartbeats he heard, they were too slow, and they seemed to come from outside, or from something in his ears from being knocked around so. They were both of them unwell.

Mrs. Hale became audible again. "I don't know what will come of the house when we're all gone. People won't buy it. I tried to sell it before, just after Mr. Hale died. It's got a bad name. The Hales've always been too friendly with their dead. And this — this holocaust it is, really — all centered round the house will make it worse. My cousins will get it, the Warwick Hales, you know. They'll subdivide, I guess. I thought you . . ." Her voice died again.

Decidedly, she needed rest and distraction. So did he. He was being positively haunted.

"Mrs. Hale, please don't think me officious, but I'm sure you need rest; we both do. I'm nervous, and I feel badly, and I'm sure you're overtired."

"I'm not tired. I feel spryer than in a long time, now it's over."

"Well, you know, at moments when you're talking your voice fades into actual silence, although you go on speaking."

"What?"

"Don't be offended. You become inaudible. I'm sure it's fatigue. I know I'm hearing things, so many that I'm frightened. I can hear something like very, very slow heartbeats, and just now I've started hearing footsteps, and I have a strange idea that someone is pulling at my shoulder."

The old lady was sitting bolt upright, staring at him. "My Lord! Then you aren't . . ." Her voice died out again; he could see that she was doing her utmost to tell him something, to make herself heard. She became clear. "Get back to the beach, get back to the beach, you still have time!"

It made his hair rise. And his shoulder *was* being shaken. The beats were very slow. "I don't understand."

She made another desperate attempt to penetrate the silence that shut down between them. At last, with a tremendous effort, she rose and flung open the door to her bedroom. "Look."

"Oh, God!"

Mrs. Hale's body lay, serene and pale, on the bed.

Now very faintly he heard her voice.

"They've found you on the beach, that's what you hear, what's shaking your shoulder. Your heart's still beating. You've got time to go back, to live, to find someone else than Sue. Sue's meeting John on Thursday. Go back to the beach."

Now he knew what he had left behind on the shore, half in and half out of the water. Panic and black horror seized him. He turned blindly toward the outer door, and found himself against Sue's coffin. He could see her sleeping face, clear, through a surrounding darkness.

"Hurry! You'll live and forget and find someone to take her place. Hurry!"

"She's in there?" He pointed to Sue's body.

"Yes, but don't stop to wake her. Hurry."

He stared at the dead girl. He stared into an infinite future. Someone to take her place.

"You know, Mrs. Hale, John was my best friend." He sat down. "Those heartbeats are very slow; they'll be over in a minute."

*Sarah Orne Jewett*

# LADY FERRY

WHEN I WAS A child, it was necessary that my father and mother should take a long sea-voyage. I never had been separated from them before; but at this time they thought it best to leave me behind, as I was not strong, and the life on board ship did not suit me. When I was told of this decision, I was very sorry, and at once thought I should be miserable without my mother; besides, I pitied myself exceedingly for losing the sights I had hoped to see in the country which they were to visit. I had an uncontrollable dislike to being sent to school, having in some way been frightened by a maid of my mother's, who had put many ideas and aversions into my head which I was many years in outgrowing. Having dreaded this possibility, it was a great relief to know that I was not to be sent to school at all, but to be put under the charge of two elderly cousins of my father, — a gentleman and his wife whom I had once seen, and liked dearly. I knew that their home was at a fine old-fashioned country-place, far from town, and close beside a river, and I was pleased with this prospect, and at once began to make charming plans for the new life.

I had lived always with grown people, and seldom had had anything to do with children. I was very small for my age, and a strange mixture of childishness and maturity; and, having the appearance of being absorbed in my own affairs, no one ever noticed me much, or seemed to think it better that I should not listen to the conversation. In spite of considerable curiosity, I followed an instinct which directed me never to ask questions at these times: so I often heard stray sentences which puzzled me, and which really would have been made simple and commonplace at once, if I had only asked their meaning. I was, for the most of the time, in a world of my own. I had a great deal of imagination, and was always telling myself stories; and my mind was adrift in these so much, that my real absent-mindedness was mistaken for childish unconcern. Yet I was a thoroughly simple, unaffected child. My dreams and thoughtfulness gave me a certain tact and perception unusual in a child; but my pleasures were as deep in simple things as heart could wish.

It happened that our cousin Matthew was to come to the city on business the week that the ship was to sail, and that I could stay with my father and mother to the very last day, and then go home with him. This was much pleasanter than leaving sooner under the care of an utter stranger, as was at first planned. My cousin Agnes wrote a kind letter about my coming which seemed to give her much pleasure. She remembered me very well, and sent me a message which made me feel of consequence; and I was delighted with the plan of making her so long a visit.

One evening I was reading a story-book, and I heard my father say in an undertone, "How long has madam been at the ferry this last time? Eight or ten years, has she not? I suppose she is there yet?" — "Oh, yes!" said my mother, "or Agnes would have told us. She spoke of her in the last letter you had, while we were in Sweden."

"I should think she would be glad to have a home at last, after her years of wandering about. Not that I should be surprised now to hear that she had disappeared again. When I was staying there while I was young, we thought she had drowned herself, and even had the men search for her along the shore of the river; but after a time cousin Matthew heard of her alive and well in Salem; and I believe she appeared again this last time as suddenly as she went away."

"I suppose she will never die," said my mother gravely. "She must be terribly old," said my father. "When I saw her last, she had scarcely changed at all from the way she looked when I was a boy. She is even more quiet and gentle than she used to be. There is no danger that the child will have any fear of her; do you think so?" — "Oh, no! but I think I will tell her that madam is a very old woman, and that I hope she will be very kind, and try not to annoy her; and that she must not be frightened at her strange notions. I doubt if she knows what craziness is." — "She would be wise if she could define it," said my father with a smile. "Perhaps we had better say nothing about the old lady. It is probable that she stays altogether in her own room, and that the child will rarely see her. I never have realized until lately the horror of such a long life as hers, living on and on, with one's friends gone long ago: such an endless life in this world!"

The days went quickly by. My mother, who was somewhat of an invalid, grew sad as the time drew near for saying good-by to me, and was more tender and kind than ever before, and more indulgent of every wish and fancy of mine. We had been together all my life, and now it was to be long months before she could possibly see my face again, and perhaps she was leaving me forever. Her time was all spent, I believe, in thoughts for me, and in making arrangements for my comfort. I did see my mother again; but the tears fill my eyes when I think how dear we became to each other before that first parting, and with what a lingering, loving touch, she herself packed my boxes, and made sure, over and over again, that I had whatever I should need; and I remember how close she used to hold me when I sat in her lap in the evening, saying that she was afraid I should have grown too large to be held when she came back again. We had more to say to each other than ever before, and I think, until then, that my mother never had suspected how much I observed of life and of older people in a certain way; that I was something more than a little child who went from one interest to another carelessly. I have known since that my mother's childhood was much like mine. She, however, was timid, while I had inherited from my father his fearlessness, and lack of suspicion; and these qualities, like a fresh wind, swept away any cobwebs of nervous anticipation and sensitiveness. Every one was kind to me, partly, I think because I interfered with no one. I was glad of the kindness, and, with my unsuspected dreaming and my happy childishness, I had gone through life with almost perfect contentment, until this pain of my first real loneliness came into my heart.

It was a day's journey to cousin Matthew's house, mostly by rail; though, toward the end, we had to travel a considerable distance by stage, and at last were left on the river-bank opposite my new home, and I saw a boat waiting to take us across. It was just at sunset, and I remember wondering if my father and mother were out of sight of land, and if they were watching the sky; if my father would remember that only the evening before we had gone out for a walk together, and there had been a sunset so much like this. It somehow seemed long ago. Cousin Matthew was busy talking with the ferryman; and indeed he had found acquaintances at almost every part of the journey, and had not been much with me, though he was kind and attentive in his courteous, old-fashioned way, treating me with the same ceremonious politeness which he had shown my mother. He pointed out the house to me: it was but a little way from the edge of the river. It was very large and irregular, with great white chimneys; and, while the river was all in shadow, the upper windows of two high gables were catching the last red glow of the sun. On the opposite side of a green from the house were the farm-house and buildings; and the green sloped down to the water, where there was a wharf and an ancient-looking storehouse. There were some old boats and long sticks of timber lying on the shore; and I saw a flock of white geese march solemnly up toward the barns. From the open green I could see that a road went up the hill beyond. The trees in the garden and orchard were the richest green; their round tops were clustered thick together; and there were some royal great elms near the house. The fiery red faded from the high windows as we came near the shore, and cousin Agnes was ready to meet me; and when she put her arms round me as kindly as my mother would have done, and kissed me twice in my father's fashion, I was sure that I loved her, and would be contented. Her hair was very gray; but she did not look, after all, so very old. Her face was a grave one, as if she had had many cares; yet they had all made her stronger, and there had been some sweetness, and something to be glad about, and to thank God for, in every sorrow. I had a feeling always that she was my sure defence and guard. I was safe and comfortable with her: it was the same feeling which one learns to have toward God more and more, as one grows older.

We went in through a wide hall, and up stairs, through a long passage, to my room, which was in a corner of one of the gables. Two windows looked on the garden and the river: another looked across to the other gable, and into the square, grassy court between. It was a rambling, great house, and seemed like some English houses I had seen. It would be great fun to go into all the rooms some day soon.

"How much you are like your father!" said cousin Agnes, stooping to kiss me again, with her hand on my shoulder. I had a sudden consciousness of my bravery in having behaved so well all day; then I remembered that my father and mother were at every instant being carried farther and farther away. I could almost hear the waves dash about the ship; and I could not help crying a little. "Poor little girl!" said cousin Agnes: "I am very sorry." And she sat down, and took me in her lap for a few minutes. She was tall, and held me so comfortably, and I soon was almost happy again; for she hoped I would not be lonely with her, and that I would not think she was a stranger, for she had known and loved my father so well;

and it would make cousin Matthew so disappointed and uneasy if I were discontented; and would I like some bread and milk with my supper, in the same blue china bowl, with the dragon on it, which my father used to have when he was a boy? These arguments were by no means lost upon me, and I was ready to smile presently; and then we went down to the dining-room, which had some solemn-looking portraits on the walls, and heavy, stiff furniture; and there was an old-fashioned woman standing ready to wait, whom cousin Agnes called Deborah, and who smiled at me graciously.

Cousin Matthew talked with his wife for a time about what had happened to him and to her during his absence; and then he said, "And how is madam today? You have not spoken of her." — "She is not so well as usual," said cousin Agnes. "She has had one of her sorrowful times since you went away. I have sat with her for several hours today; but she has hardly spoken to me." And then cousin Matthew looked at me, and cousin Agnes hesitated for a minute. Deborah had left the room.

"We speak of a member of our family whom you have not seen, although you may have heard your father speak of her. She is called Lady Ferry by most people who know of her; but you may say madam when you speak to her. She is very old, and her mind wanders, so that she has many strange fancies; but you must not be afraid, for she is very gentle and harmless. She is not used to children; but I know you will not annoy her, and I dare say you can give her much pleasure." This was all that was said; but I wished to know more. It seemed to me that there was a reserve about this person, and the old house itself was the very place for a mystery. As I went through some of the other rooms with cousin Agnes in the summer twilight, I half expected to meet Lady Ferry in every shadowy corner; but I did not dare to ask a question. My father's words came to me, — "Such an endless life," and "living on and on." And why had he and my mother never spoken to me afterward of my seeing her? They had talked about it again, perhaps, and did not mean to tell me, after all.

I saw something of the house that night, the great kitchen, with its huge fireplace, and other rooms up stairs and down; and cousin Agnes told me, that by daylight I should go everywhere, except to Madam's rooms: I must wait for an invitation there.

The house had been built a hundred and fifty years before, by Colonel Haverford, an Englishman, whom no one knew much about, except that he lived like a prince, and would never tell his history. He and his sons died; and after the Revolution the house was used for a tavern for many years, — the Ferry Tavern, — and the place was busy enough. Then there was a bridge built down the river, and the old ferry fell into disuse; and the owner of the house died, and his family also died, or went away; and then the old place, for a long time, was either vacant, or in the hands of different owners. It was going to ruin at length, when cousin Matthew bought it, and came there from the city to live years before. He was a strange man; indeed, I know now that all the possessors of the Ferry farm must have been strange men. One often hears of the influence of climate upon character; there is a strong influence of place; and the inanimate things which surround us indoors and out make us follow out in our lives their own silent characteristics. We unconsciously catch the tone of every house in which we live, and of every view of the outward, material world which grows familiar to us, and we are influenced by surroundings nearer and closer still than the climate or the country which we inhabit. At the old Haverford house it was mystery which one felt when one entered the door; and when one came away, after cordiality, and days of sunshine and pleasant hospitality, it was still with a sense of this mystery; and of something unseen and unexplained. Not that there was anything covered and hidden necessarily; but it was the quiet undertone in the house which had grown to be so old, and had known the magnificent living of Colonel Haverford's time, and afterward the struggles of poor gentlemen and women, who had hardly warmed its walls with their pitiful fires, and shivering, hungry lives; then the long procession of travelers who had been sheltered there in its old tavern days; finally, my cousin Matthew and his wife, who had made it their home, when, with all their fortune, they felt empty-handed, and as if their lives were ended, because their only son had died. Here they had learned to be happy again in a quiet sort of way, and had become older and serener, loving this lovable place by the river, and keepers of its secret — whatever that might be.

I was wide awake that first evening: I was afraid of being sent to bed, and, to show cousin Agnes that I was not sleepy, I chattered far more than usual. It was warm, and the windows of the parlor where we sat looked upon the garden. The moon had risen, and it was light out of doors. I caught every now and then the faint smell of honeysuckle, and presently I asked if I might go into the garden a while; and cousin Agnes gave me leave, adding that I must soon go to bed, else I would be very tired next day. She noticed that I looked grave, and said that I must not dread being alone in the strange room, for it was so near her own. This was a great consolation; and after I had been told that the tide was in, and I must be careful not to go too near the river wall, I went out through the tall glass door, and slowly down the wide garden-walk, from which now and then narrower walks branched off at right angles. It was the pride of the place, this garden; and the box-borders especially were kept with great care. They had partly been trimmed that day; and the evening dampness brought out the faint, solemn odor of the leaves, which I never have noticed since without thinking of that night. The roses were in bloom, and the snowball-bushes were startlingly white, and there was a long border filled with lilies-of-the-valley. The other flowers of the season were all there and in blossom; yet I could see none well but the white ones, which looked like bits of snow and ice in the summer shadows, — ghostly flowers which one could see at night.

It was still in the garden, except once I heard a bird twitter sleepily, and once or twice a breeze came across the river, rustling the leaves a little. The small-paned windows glistened in the moonlight, and seemed like the eyes of the house watching me, the unknown new-comer.

For a while I wandered about, exploring the different paths, some of which were arched over by the tall lilacs, or by arbors where the grape-leaves did not seem fully grown. I wondered if my mother would miss me. It seemed impossible that I should have seen her only that morning; and suddenly I had a consciousness that she was thinking of me, and she seemed so close to me, that it would not be strange if she could hear what I said. And I called her twice softly; but the sound of my unanswered voice frightened me. I saw some round white flowers at my feet, looking up mockingly. The smell of the earth and the new grass seemed to smother me. I was afraid to be there all alone in the wide open air; and all the tall bushes that were so still around me took strange shapes, and seemed to be alive. I was so terribly far away from the mother whom I had called; the pleasure of my journey, and my coming to cousin Agnes, faded from my mind, and that indescribable feeling of hopelessness and dread, and of having made an irreparable mistake, came in its place. The thorns of a straying slender branch of a rose-bush caught my sleeve maliciously as I turned to hurry away, and then I caught sight of a person in the path just before me. It was such a relief to see some one, that I was not frightened when I saw that it must be Lady Ferry.

She was bent, but very tall and slender, and was walking slowly with a cane. Her head was covered with a great hood or wrapping of some kind, which she pushed back when she saw me. Some faint whitish figures on her dress looked like frost in the moonlight; and the dress itself was made of some strange stiff silk, which rustled softly like dry rushes and grasses in the autumn, — a rustling noise that carries a chill with it. She came close to me, a sorrowful little figure very dreary at heart, standing still as the flowers themselves; and for several minutes she did not speak, but watched me, until I began to be afraid of her. Then she held out her hand, which trembled as if it were trying to shake off its rings. "My dear," said she, "I bid you welcome: I have known your father. I was told of your coming. Perhaps you will walk with me? I did not think to find you here alone." There was a fascinating sweetness in Madam's voice, and I at once turned to walk beside her, holding her hand fast, and keeping pace with her feeble steps. "Then you are not afraid of me?" asked the old lady, with a strange quiver in her voice. "It is a long time since I have seen a child." — "No," said I, "I am not afraid of you. I was frightened before I saw you, because I was all alone, and I wished I could see my father and mother;" and I hung my head so that my new friend could not see the tears in my eyes, for she watched me curiously. "All alone: that is like me," said she to herself. "All alone? A child is not all alone, but there is no one like me. I am something alone: there is nothing else of my fashion, a creature who lives forever!" and Lady Ferry sighed pitifully. Did she mean that she never was going to die like other people? But she was silent, and I did not dare to ask for any explanation as we walked back and forward. Her fingers kept moving round my wrist, smoothing it as if she liked to feel it, and to keep my hand in hers. It seemed to give her pleasure to have me with her, and I felt quite at my ease presently, and began to talk a little, assuring her that I did not mind having taken the journey of that day. I had taken some long journeys: I had been to China once, and it took a great while to get there; but London was the nicest place I had ever seen; had Lady Ferry ever been in London? And I was surprised to hear her say drearily that she had been in London; she had been everywhere.

"Did you go to Westminster Abbey?" I asked, going on with the conversation childishly. "And did you see where Queen Elizabeth and Mary Queen of Scots are buried? Mamma had told me all about them."

"Buried, did you say? Are they dead too?" asked Madam eagerly. "Yes, indeed!" said I: "they have been dead a long time." — "Ah! I had forgotten," answered my strange companion. "Do you know of any one else who has died beside them? I have not heard of any one's dying and going home for so long! Once every one died but me — except some young people; and I do not know them." — "Why, every one must die," said I wonderingly. "There is a funeral somewhere every day, I suppose." — "Every one but me," Madam repeated sadly, — "everyone but me, and I am alone."

Just now cousin Agnes came to the door, and called me. "Go in now, child," said Lady Ferry. "You may come and sit with me tomorrow if you choose." And I said good-night, while she turned, and went down the walk with feeble, lingering steps. She paced to and fro, as I often saw her afterwards, on the flag-stones; and some bats flew that way like ragged bits of darkness, holding somehow a spark of life. I watched her for a minute: she was like a ghost, I thought, but not a fearful ghost, — poor Lady Ferry!

"Have you had a pleasant walk?" asked cousin Matthew politely. "Tomorrow I will give you a border for your own, and some plants for it, if you like gardening." I joyfully answered that I should like it very much, and so I began to feel already the pleasure of being in a real home, after the wandering life to which I had become used. I went close to cousin Agnes's chair to tell her confidentially that I had been walking with Madam in the garden, and she was very good to me, and asked me to come to sit with her the next day; but she said very odd things.

"You must not mind what she says," said cousin Agnes; "and I would never dispute with her, or even seem surprised, if I were you. It hurts and annoys her, and she soon forgets her strange fancies. I think you seem a very sensible little girl, and I have told you about this poor friend of ours as if you were older. But you understand, do you not?" And then she kissed me good-night, and I went up stairs, contented with her assurance that she would come to me before I went to sleep.

I found a pleasant-faced young girl busy putting away some of my clothing. I had seen her just after supper, and had fancied her very much, partly because she was not so old as the rest of the servants. We were friendly at once, and I found her very talkative; so finally I asked the question which was uppermost in my mind, — Did she know any thing about Madam?

"Lady Ferry, folks call her," said Martha, much interested. "I never have seen her close to, only from the other side of the garden, where she walks at night. She never goes out by day. Deborah waits upon her. I haven't been here long; but I have always heard about Madam, bless you! Folks tell all kinds of strange stories. She's fearful old, and there's many believes she never will die; and where she came from nobody knows. I've heard that her folks used to live here; but nobody can remember them, and she used to wander about; and once before she was here, — a good while ago; but this last time she come was nine years ago; one stormy night she came across the ferry, and scared them to death, looking in at the window like a ghost. She said she used to live here in Colonel Haverford's time. They saw she wasn't right in her head — the ferry-men did. But she came up to the house, and they let her in, and she went straight to the rooms in the north gable, and she never has gone away; it was in an awful storm she come, I've heard, and she looked just the same as she does now. There! I can't tell half the stories I've heard, and Deborah she most took my head off," said Martha, "because, when I first came, I was asking about her; and she said it was a sin to gossip about a harmless old creature whose mind was broke, but I guess most everybody thinks there's something mysterious. There's my grandmother — her mind is failing her; but she never had such ways! And then those clothes that my lady in the gable wears: they're unearthly looking; and I heard a woman say once, that they come out of a chest in the big garret, and they belonged to a Mistress Haverford who was hung for a witch, but there's no knowing that there is any truth in it." And Martha would have gone on with her stories, if just then we had not heard cousin Agnes's step on the stairway, and I hurried into bed.

But my bright eyes and excited look betrayed me. Cousin Agnes said she had hoped I would be asleep. And Martha said perhaps it was her fault; but I seemed wakeful, and she had talked with me a bit, to keep my spirits up, coming to a new, strange place. The apology was accepted, but Martha evidently had orders before I next saw her; for I never could get her to discuss Lady Ferry again; and she carefully told me that she should not have told those foolish stories, which were not true: but I knew that she still had her thoughts and suspicions as well as I. Once, when I asked her if Lady Ferry were Madam's real name, she answered with a guilty flush, "That's what the folks hereabout called her, because they didn't know any other at first." And this to me was another mystery. It was strongly impressed upon my mind that I must ask no questions, and that Madam was not to be discussed. No one distinctly forbade this; but I felt that it would not do. In every other way I was sure that I was allowed perfect liberty, so I soon ceased to puzzle myself or other people, and accepted Madam's presence as being perfectly explainable and natural, — just as the rest of the household did, — except once in a while something would set me at work romancing and wondering; and I read some stories in one of the books in the library, — of Peter Rugg the missing man, whom one may always meet riding from Salem to Boston in every storm, and of the Flying Dutchman and the Wandering Jew, and some terrible German stories of doomed people, and curses that were fulfilled. These made a great impression upon me; still I was not afraid, for all such things were far outside the boundaries of my safe little world; and I played by myself along the shore of the river and in the garden; and I had my lessons with cousin Agnes, and drives with cousin Matthew who was nearly always silent, but very kind to me. The house itself was an unfailing entertainment, with its many rooms, most of which were never occupied, and its quaint, sober furnishings, some of which were as old as the house itself. It was like a story-book; and no one minded my going where I pleased.

I missed my father and mother; but the only time I was really unhappy was the first morning after my arrival. Cousin Agnes was ill with a severe headache; cousin Matthew had ridden away to attend to some business; and, being left to myself, I had a most decided re-action from my unnaturally bright feelings of the day before. I began to write a letter to my mother; but unluckily I knew how many weeks must pass before she saw it, and it was useless to try to go on. I was lonely and homesick. The rain fell heavily, and the garden looked forlorn, and so unlike the enchanting moonlighted place where I had been in the evening! The walks were like little canals; and the rose-bushes looked wet and chilly, like some gay young lady who had been caught in the rain in party-dress. It was low-tide in the middle of the day; and the river-flats looked dismal. I fed cousin Agnes' flock of tame sparrows which came around the windows, and afterward some robins. I found some books and some candy which had come in my trunk, but my heart was very sad; and just after noon I was overjoyed when one of the servants told me that cousin Agnes would like to have me come to her room.

She was even kinder to me than she had been the night before; but she looked very ill, and at first I felt awkward, and did not know what to say. "I am afraid you have been very dull, dearie," said she, reaching out her hand to me. "I am sorry, and my headache hardly lets me think at all yet. But we will have better times tomorrow — both of us. You must ask for what you want; and you may come and spend this evening with me, for I shall be getting well then. It does me good to see your kind little face. Suppose you make Madam a call this afternoon. She told me last night that she wished for you, and I was so glad. Deborah will show you the way."

Deborah talked to me softly, out of deference to her mistress's headache, as we went along the crooked passages. "Don't you mind what Madam says, leastways don't you dispute her. She's got a funeral going on to-day;" and the grave woman smiled grimly at me. "It's curious she's taken to you so; for she never will see any strange folks. Nobody speaks to her about new folks lately," she added warningly, as she tapped at the door, and Madam asked, "Is it the child?" And Deborah lifted the latch. When I was fairly inside, my interest in life came back redoubled, and I was no longer sad, but looked round eagerly. Madam spoke to me, with her sweet old voice, in her courtly, quiet way, and stood looking out of the window.

There were two tall chests of drawers in the room, with shining brass handles and ornaments; and at one side, near the door, was a heavy mahogany table, on which I saw a large leather-covered Bible, a decanter of wine and some glasses, beside some cakes in a queer old tray. And there was no other furniture but a great number of chairs which seemed to have been collected from different parts of the house.

With these the room was almost filled, except an open space in the centre, toward which they all faced. One window was darkened; but Madam had pushed back the shutter of the other, and stood looking down at the garden. I waited for her to speak again after the first salutation, and presently she said I might be seated; and I took the nearest chair, and again waited her pleasure. It was gloomy enough, with the silence and the twilight in the room; and the rain and wind out of doors sounded louder than they had in cousin Agnes's room; but soon Lady Ferry came toward me.

"So you did not forget the old woman," said she, with a strange emphasis on the word old, as if that were her title and her chief characteristic. "And were not you afraid? I am glad it seemed worth while; for to-morrow would have been too late. You may like to remember by and by that you came. And my funeral is to be to-morrow, at last. You see the room is in readiness. You will care to be here, I hope. I would have ordered you some gloves if I had known; but these are all too large for your little hands. You shall have a ring; I will leave a command for that;" and Madam seated herself near me in a curious, high-backed chair. She was dressed that day in a maroon brocade, figured with bunches of dim pink flowers; and some of these flowers looked to me like wicked little faces. It was a mocking, silly creature that I saw at the side of every prim bouquet, and I looked at the faded little imps, until they seemed as much alive as Lady Ferry herself.

Her head nodded continually, as if it were keeping time to an inaudible tune, as she sat there stiffly erect. Her skin was pale and withered; and her cheeks were wrinkled in fine lines, like the crossings of a cobweb. Her eyes might once have been blue; but they had become nearly colorless, and, looking at her, one might easily imagine that she was blind. She had a singularly sweet smile, and a musical voice, which, though sad, had no trace of whining. If it had not been for her smile and her voice, I think Madam would have been a terror to me. I noticed to-day, for the first time, a curious fragrance, which seemed to come from her old brocades and silks. It was very sweet, but unlike any thing I had ever known before; and it was by reason of this that afterward I often knew, with a little flutter at my heart, she had been in some other rooms of the great house beside her own. This perfume seemed to linger for a little while wherever she had been, and yet it was so faint! I used to go into the darkened chambers often, or even stay for a while by myself in the unoccupied lower rooms, and I would find this fragrance, and wonder if she were one of the oldtime fairies, who could vanish at their own will and pleasure, and wonder, too, why she had come to the room. But I never met her at all.

That first visit to her and the strange fancy she had about the funeral I have always remembered distinctly.

"I am glad you came," Madam repeated: "I was finding the day long. I am all ready, you see. I shall place a little chair which is in the next room, beside your cousin's seat for you. Mrs. Agnes is ill, I hear; but I think she will come to-morrow. Have you heard any one say if many guests are expected?" — "No, Madam," I answered, "no one has told me;" and just then the thought flitted through my head that she had said the evening before that all her friends were gone. Perhaps she expected their ghosts: that would not be stranger than all the rest.

The open space where Lady Ferry had left room for her coffin began to be a horror to me, and I wished Deborah would come back, or that my hostess would open the shutters; and it was a great relief when she rose and went into the adjoining room, bidding me follow her, and there opened a drawer containing some old jewelry; there were also some queer Chinese carvings, yellow with age, — just the things a child would enjoy. I looked at them delightedly. This was coming back to more familiar life; and I soon felt more at ease, and chattered to Lady Ferry of my own possessions, and some coveted treasures of my mother's, which were to be mine when I grew older.

Madam stood beside me patiently, and listened with a half smile to my whispered admiration. In the clearer light I could see her better, and she seemed older, — so old, so old! And my father's words came to me again. She had not changed since he was a boy; living on and on, and 'the horror of an endless life in this world!' And I remembered what Martha had said to me, and the consciousness of this mystery was a great weight upon me of a sudden. Why was she living so long? and what had happened to her? and how long could it be since she was a child?

There was something in her manner which made me behave, even in my pleasure, as if her imagined funeral were there in reality, and as if, in spite of my being amused and tearless, the solemn company of funeral guests already sat in the next room to us with bowed heads, and all the shadows in the world had assembled there materialized into the tangible form of crape. I opened and closed the boxes gently, and, when I had seen everything, I looked up with a sigh to think that such a pleasure was ended, and asked if I might see them again some day. But the look in her face made me recollect myself, and my own grew crimson, for it seemed at that moment as real to me as to Lady Ferry herself that this was her last day of mortal life. She walked away, but presently came back, while I was wondering if I might not go, and opened the drawer again. It creaked, and the brass handles clacked in a startling way, and she took out a little case, and said I might keep it to remember her by. It held a little vinaigrette, — a tiny silver box with a gold one inside, in which I found a bit of fine sponge, dark brown with age, and still giving a faint, musty perfume and spiciness. The outside was rudely chased, and was worn as if it had been carried for years in somebody's pocket. It had a spring, the secret of which Lady Ferry showed me. I was delighted, and instinctively lifted my face to kiss her. She bent over me, and waited an instant for me to kiss her again. "Oh!" said she softly, "it is so long since a child has kissed me! I pray God not to leave you lingering like me, apart from all your kindred, and your life so long that you forget you ever were a child." — "I will kiss you every day," said I, and then again remembered that there were to be no more days according to her plan; but she did not seem to notice my mistake.

And after this I used to go to see Madam often. For a time there was always the same gloom and hushed way of speaking, and the funeral services were to be on the morrow; but at last one day I found Deborah sedately putting the room in order, and Lady Ferry apologized for its being in such confusion; the idea of the funeral had utterly vanished, and I hurried to tell cousin Agnes with great satisfaction. I think that both she and cousin Matthew had a dislike for my being too much with Madam. I was kept out of doors as much as possible because it was much better for my health; and through the long summer days I strayed about wherever I chose. The country life was new and delightful to me. At home, Lady Ferry's vagaries were carelessly spoken of, and often smiled at; but I gained the idea that they disguised the truth, and were afraid of my being frightened. She often talked about persons who had been dead a very long time, — familiar characters in history, and, though cousin Agnes had said that she used to be fond of reading, it seemed to me that Madam might have known these men and women after all.

Once a middle-aged gentleman, an acquaintance of cousin Matthew's, came to pass a day and night at the ferry, and something happened then which seemed wonderful to me. It was early in the evening after tea, and we were in the parlor; from my seat by cousin Agnes I could look out into the garden, and presently, with the gathering darkness, came Lady Ferry, silent as a shadow herself, to walk to and fro on the flagstones. The windows were all open, and the guest had a clear, loud voice, and pleasant hearty laugh; and, as he talked earnestly with cousin Matthew, I noticed that Lady Ferry stood still, as if she were listening. Then I was attracted by some story which was being told, and forgot her, but afterward turned with a start, feeling that there was some one watching; and, to my astonishment, Madam had come to the long window by which one went out to the garden. She stood there a moment, looking puzzled and wild; then she smiled, and, entering, walked in most stately fashion down the long room, toward the gentlemen, before whom she courtsied with great elegance, while the stranger stopped speaking, and looked at her with amazement, as he rose, and returned her greeting.

"My dear Captain Jack McAllister!" said she; "what a surprise! and are you not home soon from your voyage? This is indeed a pleasure." And Lady Ferry seated herself, motioning to him to take the chair beside her. She looked younger than I had ever seen her; a bright color came into her cheeks; and she talked so gayly, in such a different manner from her usual mournful gentleness. She must have been a beautiful woman; indeed she was that still.

"And did the good ship Starlight make a prosperous voyage? and had you many perils? — do you bring much news to us from the Spanish Main? We have missed you sadly at the assemblies; but there must be a dance in your honor. And your wife; is she not overjoyed at the sight of you? I think you have grown old and sedate since you went away. You do not look the gay sailor, or seem so light-hearted."

"I do not understand you, madam," said the stranger. "I am certainly John McAllister; but I am no captain, neither have I been at sea. Good God! is it my grandfather whom you confuse me with?" cried he. "He was Jack McAllister, and was lost at sea more than seventy years ago, while my own father was a baby. I am told that I am wonderfully like his portrait; but he was a younger man than I when he died. This is some masquerade."

Lady Ferry looked at him intently, but the light in her face was fast fading out. "Lost at sea, — lost at sea, were you, Jack McAllister, seventy years ago? I know nothing of years; one of my days is like another, and they are gray days, they creep away and hide, and sometimes one comes back to mock me. I have lived a thousand years; do you know it? Lost at sea — captain of the ship Starlight? Whom did you say? — Jack McAllister, yes, I knew him well — pardon me; good-evening;" and my lady rose, and with her head nodding and drooping, with a sorrowful, hunted look in her eyes, went out again into the shadows. She had had a flash of youth, the candle had blazed up brilliantly; but it went out again as suddenly, with flickering and smoke.

"I was startled when I saw her beside me," said Mr. McAllister. "Pray, who is she? she is like no one I have ever seen. I have been told that I am like my grandfather in looks and in voice; but it is years since I have seen any one who knew him well. And did you hear her speak of dancing? It is like seeing one who has risen from the dead. How old can she be?" — "I do not know," said cousin Matthew, "one can only guess at her age." — "Would not she come back? I should like to question her," asked the other. But cousin Matthew answered that she always refused to see strangers, and it would be no use to urge her, she would not answer him.

"Who is she? Is she any kin of yours?" asked Mr. McAllister.

"Oh, no!" said my cousin Agnes: "she has had no relatives since I have known her, and I think she has no friends now but ourselves. She has been with us a long time, and once before this house was her home for a time, — many years since. I suppose no one will ever know the whole history of her life; I wish often that she had power to tell it. We are glad to give shelter, and the little care she will accept, to the poor soul, God only knows where she has strayed and what she has seen. It is an enormous burden, — so long a life, and such a weight of memories; but I think it is seldom now that she feels its heaviness. — Go out to her, Marcia my dear, and see if she seems troubled. She always has a welcome for the child," cousin Agnes added, as I unwillingly went away.

I found Lady Ferry in the garden; I stole my hand into hers, and, after a few minutes of silence, I was not surprised to hear her say that they had killed the Queen of France, poor Marie Antoinette! she had known her well in her childhood, before she was a queen at all — "a sad fate, a sad fate," said Lady Ferry. We went far down the gardens and by the river-wall, and when we were again near the house, and could hear Mr. McAllister's voice as cheery as ever, Madam took no notice of it. I had hoped she would go into the parlor again, and I wished over and over that I could have waited to hear the secrets which I was sure must have been told after cousin Agnes had sent me away.

One day I thought I had made a wonderful discovery. I was fond of reading, and found many books which interested me in cousin Matthew's fine library; but I took great pleasure also in hunting through a collection of old volumes which had been cast aside, either by him, or by some former owner of the house, and which were piled in a corner of the great garret. They were mostly yellow with age, and had dark brown leather or shabby paper bindings; the pictures in some were very amusing to me. I used often to find one which I appropriated and carried down stairs; and on this day I came upon a dusty, odd-shaped little book for which I at once felt an affection. I looked at it a little. It seemed to be a journal, there were some stories of the Indians, and next I saw some reminiscences of the town of Boston, where, among other things, the author was told the marvelous story of one Mistress Honor Warburton, who was cursed, and doomed to live in this world forever. This was startling. I at once thought of Madam, and was reading on further to know the rest of the story, when some one called me, and I foolishly did not dare to carry my book with me. I was afraid I should not find it if I left it in sight; I saw an opening near me at the edge of the floor by the eaves, and I carefully laid my treasure inside. But, alas! I was not to be sure of its safe hiding-place in a way that I fancied, for the book fell down between the boarding of the thick walls, and I heard it knock as it fell, and knew by the sound that it must be out of reach. I grieved over this loss for a long time; and I felt that it had been most unkindly taken out of my hand. I wished heartily that I could know the rest of the story; and I tried to summon courage to ask Madam, when we were by ourselves, if she had heard of Honor Warburton, but something held me back.

There were two other events just at this time which made this strange old friend of mine seem stranger than ever to me. I had a dream one night, which I took for a vision and a reality at the time. I thought I looked out of my window in the night, and there was bright moonlight, and I could see the other gable plainly; and I looked in at the windows of an unoccupied parlor which I never had seen open before, under Lady Ferry's own rooms. The shutters were pushed back, and there were candles burning; and I heard voices, and presently some tinkling music, like that of a harpsichord I had once heard in a very old house where I had been in England with my mother. I saw several couples go through with a slow, stately dance; and, when they stopped and seated themselves, I could hear their voices; but they spoke low, these midnight guests. I watched until the door was opened which led into the garden, and the company came out and stood for a few minutes on the little lawn, making their adieus, bowing low, and behaving with astonishing courtesy and elegance: finally the last good-nights were said, and they went away. Lady Ferry stood under the pointed porch, looking after them, and I could see her plainly in her brocade gown, with the impish flowers, a tall quaint cap, and a high lace frill at her throat, whiter than any lace I had ever seen, with a glitter on it; and there was a glitter on her face too. One of the other ladies was dressed in velvet, and I thought she looked beautiful: their eyes were all like sparks of fire. The gentlemen wore cloaks and ruffs, and high-peaked hats with wide brims, such as I had seen in some very old pictures which hung on the walls of the long west room. These were not pilgrims or Puritans, but gay gentlemen; and soon I heard the noise of their boats on the pebbles as they pushed off shore, and the splash of the oars in the water. Lady Ferry waved her hand, and went in at the door; and I found myself standing by the window in the chilly, cloudy night: the opposite gable, the garden, and the river were indistinguishable in the darkness. I stole back to bed in an agony of fear; for it had been very real, that dream. I surely was at the window, for my hand had been on the sill when I waked; and I heard a church-bell ring two o'clock in a town far up the river. I never had heard this solemn bell before, and it seemed frightful; but I knew afterward that in the silence of a misty night the sound of it came down along the water.

In the morning I found that there had been a gale in the night; and cousin Matthew said at breakfast time that the tide had risen so that it had carried off two old boats that had been left on the shore to go to pieces. I sprang to the window, and sure enough they had disappeared. I had played in one of them the day before. Should I tell cousin Matthew what I had seen or dreamed? But I was too sure that he would only laugh at me; and yet I was none the less sure that those boats had carried passengers.

When I went out to the garden, I hurried to the porch, and saw, to my disappointment, that there were great spiders' webs in the corners of the door, and around the latch, and that it had not been opened since I was there before. But I saw something shining in the grass, and found it was a silver knee-buckle. It must have belonged to one of the ghostly guests, and my faith in them came back for a while, in spite of the cobwebs. By and by I bravely carried it up to Madam, and asked if it were hers. Sometimes she would not answer for a long time, when one rudely broke in upon her reveries, and she hesitated now, looking at me with singular earnestness. Deborah was in the room; and, when she saw the buckle, she quietly said that it had been on the window-ledge the day before, and must have slipped out. "I found it down by the doorstep in the grass," said I humbly; and then I offered Lady Ferry some strawberries which I had picked for her on a broad green leaf, and came away again.

A day or two after this, while my dream was still fresh in my mind, I went with Martha to her own home, which was a mile or two distant, — a comfortable farmhouse for those days, where I was always made welcome. The servants were all very kind to me: as I recall it now, they seemed to have a pity for me, because I was the only child perhaps. I was very happy, that is certain, and I enjoyed my childish amusements as heartily as if there were no unfathomable mysteries or perplexities or sorrows anywhere in the world.

I was sitting by the fireplace at Martha's, and her grandmother, who was very old, and who was fast losing her wits, had been talking to me about Madam. I do not remember what she said, at least, it made little impression; but her grandson, a worthless fellow, sauntered in, and began to tell a story of his own, hearing of whom we spoke. "I was coming home late last night," said he, "and, as I was in that dark place along by the Norway pines, old Lady Ferry she went by me, and I was near scared to death. She looked fearful tall —towered way up above me. Her face was all lit up with blue light, and her feet didn't touch the ground. She wasn't taking steps, she wasn't walking, but movin' along like a sail-boat before the wind. I dodged behind some little birches, and I was scared she'd see me; but she went right out o' sight up the road. She ain't mortal."

"Don't scare the child with such foolishness," said his aunt disdainfully. "you'll be seein' worse things a-dancin' before your eyes than that poor, harmless old creatur' if you don't quit the ways you've been following lately. If that was last night, you were too drunk to see anything;" and the fellow muttered, and went out, banging the door. But the story had been told, and I was stiffened and chilled with fright; and all the way home I was in terror, looking fearfully behind me again and again.

When I saw cousin Agnes, I felt safer, and since cousin Matthew was not at home, and we were alone, I could not resist telling her what I had heard. She listened to me kindly, and seemed so confident that my story was idle nonsense, that my fears were quieted. She talked to me until I no longer was a believer in there being any unhappy mystery or harmfulness; but I could not get over the fright, and I dreaded my lonely room, and I was glad enough when cousin Agnes, with her unfailing thoughtfulness, asked if I would like to have her come to sleep with me, and even went up stairs with me at my own early bedtime, saying that she should find it dull to sit all alone in the parlor. So I went to sleep, thinking of what I had heard, it is true, but no longer unhappy, because her dear arm was over me, and I was perfectly safe. I waked up for a little while in the night, and it was light in the room, so that I could see her face, fearless and sweet and sad, and I wondered, in my blessed sense of security, if she were ever afraid of any thing, and why I myself had been afraid of Lady Ferry.

I will not tell other stories: they are much alike, all my memories of those weeks and months at the ferry, and I have no wish to be wearisome. The last time I saw Madam she was standing in the garden door at dusk. I was going away before daylight in the morning. It was in the autumn: some dry leaves flittered about on the stone at her feet, and she was watching them. I said good-by again, and she did not answer me; but I think she knew I was going away, and I am sure she was sorry, for we had been a great deal together; and, child as I was, I thought to how many friends she must have had to say farewell.

Although I wished to see my father and mother, I cried as if my heart would break because I had to leave the ferry. The time spent there had been the happiest time of all my life, I think. I was old enough to enjoy, but not to suffer much, and there was singularly little to trouble one. I did not know that my life was ever to be different. I have learned, since those childish days, that one must battle against storms if one would reach the calm which is to follow them. I have learned also that anxiety, sorrow, and regret fall to the lot of every one, and that there is always underlying our lives, this mysterious and frightful element of existence; an uncertainty at times, though we do trust every thing to God. Under the best-loved and most beautiful face we know, there is hidden a skull as ghastly as that from which we turn aside with a shudder in the anatomist's cabinet. We smile, and are gay enough; God pity us! We try to forget our heartaches and remorse. We even call our lives commonplace, and, bearing our own heaviest burdens silently, we try to keep the commandment, and to bear one another's also. There is One who knows: we look forward, as he means we shall, and there is always a hand ready to help us, though we reach out for it doubtfully in the dark.

FOR MANY years after this summer was over, I lived in a distant, foreign country; at last my father and I were to go back to America. Cousin Agnes and cousin Matthew, and my mother, were all long since dead, and I rarely thought of my childhood, for in an eventful and hurried life the present claims one almost wholly. We were travelling in Europe, and it happened that one day I was in a bookshop in Amsterdam, waiting for an acquaintance whom I was to meet, and who was behind time.

The shop was a quaint place, and I amused myself by looking over an armful of old English books which a boy had thrown down near me, raising a cloud of dust which was plain evidence of their antiquity. I came to one, almost the last, which had a strangely familiar look, and I found that it was a copy of the same book which I had lost in the wall at the ferry. I bought it for a few coppers with the greatest satisfaction, and began at once to read it. It had been published in England early in the eighteenth century, and was written by one Mr. Thomas Highward of Chester, — a journal of his travels among some of the English colonists of North America, containing much curious and desirable knowledge, with some useful advice to those persons having intentions of emigrating. I looked at the prosy pages here and there, and finally found again those reminiscences of the town of Boston and the story of Mistress Honor Warburton, who was cursed, and doomed to live in this world to the end of time. She had lately been in Boston, but had disappeared again; she endeavored to disguise herself, and would not stay long in one place if she feared that her story was known, and that she was recognized. One Mr. Fleming, a man of good standing and repute, and an officer of Her Majesty Queen Anne, had sworn to Mr. Thomas Highward that his father, a person of great age, had once seen Mistress Warburton in his youth; that she then bore another name, but had the same appearance. "Not wishing to seem unduly credulous," said Mr. Highward, "I disputed this tale; but there was some considerable evidence in its favour, and at least this woman was of vast age, and was spoken of with extreme wonder by the town's folk."

I could not help thinking of my old childish suspicions of Lady Ferry, though I smiled at the folly of them and of this story more than once. I tried to remember if I had heard of her death; but I was still a child when my cousin Agnes had died. Had poor Lady Ferry survived her? and what could have become of her? I asked my father, but he could remember nothing, if indeed he ever had heard of her death at all. He spoke of our cousins' kindness to this forlorn soul, and that, learning her desolation and her piteous history (and being the more pitiful because of her shattered mind), when she had last wandered to their door, they had cared for the old gentlewoman to the end of her days — "for I do not think she can be living yet," said my father, with a merry twinkle in his eyes: "she must have been nearly a hundred years old when you saw her. She belonged to a fine old family which had gone to wreck and ruin. She strayed about for years, and it was a godsend to her to have found such a home in her last days."

THAT same summer we reached America, and for the first time since I had left it I went to the ferry. The house was still imposing, the prestige of the Haverford grandeur still lingered; but it looked forlorn and uncared for. It seemed very familiar; but the months I had spent there were so long ago, that they seemed almost to belong to another life. I sat alone on the doorstep for a long time, where I used often to watch for Lady Ferry; and forgotten thoughts and dreams of my childhood came back to me. The river was the only thing that seemed as young as ever. I looked in at some of the windows where the shutters were pushed back, and I walked about the garden, where I could hardly trace the walks, all overgrown with thick, short grass, though there were a few ragged lines of box, and some old rose-bushes; and I saw the very last of the flowers, — a bright red poppy, which had bloomed under a lilac tree among the weeds.

Out beyond the garden, on a slope by the river, I saw the family burying-ground, and it was with a comfortable warmth at my heart that I stood inside the familiar old enclosure. There was my Lady Ferry's grave; there could be no mistake about it, and she was dead. I smiled at my satisfaction and at my foolish childish thoughts, and thanked God that there could be no truth in them, and that death comes surely, — say, rather, that the better life comes surely, — though it comes late.

The sad-looking, yellow-topped cypress, which only seems to feel quite at home in country burying-grounds, had kindly spread itself like a coverlet over the grave, which already looked like a very old grave; and the headstone was leaning a little, not to be out of the fashion of the rest. I traced again the words of old Colonel Haverford's pompous epitaph, and idly read some others. I remembered the old days so vividly there; I thought of my cousin Agnes, and wished that I could see her; and at last, as the daylight faded, I came away. When I crossed the river, the ferry-man looked at me wonderingly, for my eyes were filled with tears. Although we were in shadow on the water, the last red glow of the sun blazed on the high gable-windows, just as it did the first time I crossed over, — only a child then, with my life before me.

I asked the ferry-man some questions, but he could tell me nothing; he was a new-comer to that part of the country. He was sorry that the boat was not in better order; but there were almost never any passengers. The great house was out of repair: people would not live there, for they said it was haunted. Oh, yes! he had heard of Lady Ferry. She had lived to be very ancient; but she was dead.

"Yes," said I, "she is dead."

*Jack Finney*

# WHERE THE CLUETTS ARE

W E HAD OPEN books and magazines lying on every flat surface in the room. They stood propped in a row along the fireplace mantel and lay face up on the seat cushions of the upholstered chairs. They hung like little tents on the chair arms and backs, were piled in layers on the big round coffee table, and lay scattered all over the carpeted floor. Every one of them was opened to a photograph, sketch, floor plan, or architect's elevation of a house. Ellie Cluett sat on the top of the ladder I used to reach the highest of the bookshelves. She was wearing a gray sweater and slacks and was slowly leafing through an *Architectural Forum*. Sam, her husband, sat on the floor, his back against the book-shelves, and now he held up his book for us to look at. This was the big room I worked in and I was at my drafting table watching them.

"How about something like this?" Sam said. It was a color photo-graph of the Taj Mahal.

Ellie said, "Great. The big dome in the center is just right for a television aerial. Okay with you, Harry?"

"Sure. All I have to do is design the place. You'll have to live in it." I smiled at Ellie. She was about twenty-three, intelligent and likable.

Sam said, "Well, I wish you *would* design it and quit pestering us about it." He grinned to show he didn't mean it, though he did. Sam was wearing slacks and a sports shirt and was about my age — somewhere just over thirty.

Ellie said, "Yes, Harry, please. Have it built, and phone us in New York when it's finished. Surprise us! Honestly" — she gestured at the roomful of opened books and magazines — "I know we promised to look through all this, but it's driving me crazy."

"I'll have the rooms padded, then. In tasteful decorator colors."

"Damn it, Harry, I think you're being pointlessly stubborn," Sam said. "There are only two things that matter to me about this house, and you know what they are."

I nodded. Sam owned a big boatyard on the Sound. He wanted a house here in Darley, Connecticut, because it was only thirty minutes from the yard. He sold his boats by demonstration and entertainment, so he wanted an impressive house to take his prospects to.

Sam said, "That's all I care about, and you won't change it if you lock me up in here."

"It isn't as though we'd really be living here," Ellie said gently. "We'll keep our apartment in New York, you can be sure. Except for the boat season, we'll hardly be in Darley."

I didn't want to lose this job. Just before the boat craze began, Sam Cluett started his boat works on nothing; now he was rich and offering me a free hand in designing a showplace with nothing skimped. I wanted to do it and needed the money but I said, "I can't do it alone. If this house doesn't mean enough to you to give it some time and work and to develop some opinions and enthusiasms about it, then I don't want to design it. Because it would never be much of a house. It wouldn't be yours, mine, or anyone's. It would be a house without life or soul — or, even worse, the wrong kind of soul."

Absolutely identical looks came to their faces: brows raised in polite question, eyes alertly interested in and amused by the notion of a house with a soul.

I suspected that I was about to become an anecdote back in New York but I was going to save this job if I could and I smiled and said, "It's true, or close to it. A house can have a life and soul of its own. There's a house here in Darley, twelve years old and it's had nineteen owners. No one ever lives in it long. There are houses like it in every town in the world." I stood up and began walking around the room, hands shoved into my back pockets, picking my way through the scattered books.

Sam sat watching me from the floor, arms folded. Ellie sat on top of the ladder staring down at me, her chin on her fist. There was a faint smile of interest on each face and they looked like a couple of sophisticated kids waiting for the rest of a story.

I said, "It's an ordinary enough house but I prowled through it between tenants, once, and began to understand why it never kept an owner. Everywhere you look the proportions are just faintly unpleasant. There's a feeling of harshness to the place. There's even something wrong in the very way the light slants in through the windows. It wasn't the designer's fault; the house simply developed an ugly life and soul of its own. It's filled with unpleasant associations and after you're in it awhile it becomes downright repelling. I don't really understand why, and I'm an architect." I glanced at Sam, then at Ellie, smiling so as not to seem too deadly serious. Ellie's eyes were bright with interest. I said, "There's another house in Darley that no one has ever willingly left. Those who've left it, the husbands were transferred or something of that sort, and I've heard that each wife cried when she had to give up that house. And that a child in one family said and has continued to say that when he grows up, he's going to buy that house back and live in it. I don't doubt these stories because I've been in that house, too, and I swear it welcomes you as you step through the front door."

I looked at the Cluetts again, and began to hope. I said, "You've been in that kind of house; everyone has. For no reason you can explain you feel a joy at just being in it. I almost think that kind of house *knows* you're in it and puts its best foot forward. There's a kind of felicity about it, everything in it just right. It's something more and better than any designer could consciously plan. It's the occasional rare and wonderful house that somehow acquires a life and soul of its own, and a fine one. Personally, I believe that kind of house comes out of the feelings and attitude and actual love for it of the people who plan it and bring it to life. And that has to be the people who are going to live in it, not just the architect. When I design a house I want it to have a chance of turning out to be that kind. But you're not giving yours any chance at all."

It didn't work. For half an hour, the Cluetts were contrite and industrious, searching through my books and magazines, pointing out to me and each other houses, rooms, windows, doors, roof styles, bathrooms, and gardens they liked or said they did. I sat at my table again, listening, but I knew that interest was synthetic and I added no more notes to the pad in my clip board. I had only one: "Enormous master bdrm w. fireplace." But every client says that; I could have it printed on my note pads. And the Cluetts had nothing more to add; they really didn't care.

Finally, Ellie put a book back on the shelf beside her, then stood up on the ladder and began scanning the top shelf boredly. She reminded me of a child reluctantly doing homework, ready to welcome any diversion, and now she found one. Pulling out a book, she dislodged a thick wadding of paper crammed onto the shelf beside it and caught it as it fell. She unfolded it, opening it up finally to half a dozen big sheets of linen drawing paper each the size of a newspaper page. When she saw what was on the top sheet she slowly sat down on the ladder top, staring and murmuring, "For heaven's sake." After a moment she looked at me, saying, "Harry! What in the world is this?"

"Just what it looks like." I heard the tired irritation in my voice and forced it out before I continued. I wasn't going to take their job, but I liked the Cluetts just the same. "Those are drawings for a house, architectural drawings," I said more pleasantly. "That top sheet is a perspective showing what it would look like finished. The sheets underneath are the working drawings for building it. They've always been up there; belonged to my grandfather. Most of the stuff on that top shelf was his. He was an architect and so was my father."

Sam was getting to his feet, pleased with the diversion, too, and Ellie quickly turned on the ladder, hurried down it, then dropped, kneeling, to the floor and smoothed the big top sheet flat on the rug. "Look!" she said excitedly.

Sam and I went to stand beside her, staring. The edges of the paper were yellowed but the rest was bone-white still and I remembered that I'd once meant to frame this and hang it in my office downtown. It was an India-ink drawing, the lines thin, sharp, and black in the scribed and ruled precision architects once favored. It was an incredible sight — I'd almost forgotten — but there lay the clear sharp-etched architectural rendering for a house of the early 1880s just as its designer had conceived it in every gabled, turreted, dormered, bay-windowed and gingerbreaded detail.

"Imagine," Ellie murmured, her voice incredulous and delighted. "Why, it never entered my head that these houses were actually built!"

"What do you mean?" Sam said.

She turned to look up at him, eyes shining. "Why, they've always *been* here — forever! Since long before any of us was born. They're old, shabby, half tumbling down. It simply never occurred to me that they could ever have been new! Or not even *built* yet, like this one!" Quickly, she began spreading out the other sheets in a half circle.

I knew what she meant and so did Sam, and he nodded. It was strange to see at our feet the actual floor by floor plans — the framing plans and sections, full-sized profiles, every last detail, all precisely dimensioned ready for construction — of what had to seem to our eyes like an old old house. And for some moments, then, silent and bemused, we looked at the careful old drawings thinking the wordless thoughts you often think looking at a relic of other earlier lives than your own.

It seems to me that it's usually impossible to get hold of another time. You look at a pair of high-button shoes, the leather dry and cracked, buttons missing, the cloth uppers nearly drained of color by the years, and it just isn't possible to get into the mind of some long-gone woman who once saw them new. How could they ever have been new and shining, something a woman might actually covet?

But these old drawings lying on the floor beside us weren't quite like any other relic of the past I'd ever before encountered. Because these were the house before it was built; old though they were, these were still the plans for a house-yet-to-be. And so at one and the same time they were quaint and old-fashioned, yet new and fresh, still untouched by the years. And it was possible to see in them, and feel, not merely quaintness but something of the fresh beauty the architect must have seen and felt the day he finished them a lifetime ago.

Ellie was getting to her feet and I turned to look at her. Her jaw actually hung open a little and her eyes were wide and almost stunned in a kind of incredulous awe at what she'd just thought of. "Sam!" she said, and grabbed his forearm. "Let's build it!"

"What?"

"Yes! I mean it! Let's built it! And I'll furnish it! In the style of those days! Why, good lord," she murmured, turning to stare at nothing, eyes shining with excitement, "there's not a woman I know who won't envy me green."

Sam is bright and used to making decisions, I suppose. His eyes narrowed and he stared at Ellie's face as though testing or absorbing her feelings through her eyes as she stared back at him, elated. Then he stepped forward abruptly and looked down at the drawings again for half a minute. He took a few paces around the room, then turned to me. "Is it possible, Harry? Could we live in it and have it make any kind of sense?" Suddenly he grinned, delighted at the notion.

I shrugged and said, "Sure. Why not? If you're willing to pay the cost. The plans are there and can be followed today as well as in the eighteen eighties." Both started to speak but I held up a hand, cutting them off. "But to build even a contemporary house with that much floor space would be very expensive, Sam. And with this house, every foot of that space would cost twice as much, three times as much, maybe more. Who can say? You might not even get a bid on a job like that."

"Oh? Why not?"

I touched the plans with the toe of my shoe. "Look at the lumber specifications. Half of it different from anything milled today — heavier, thicker, longer. You'd pay a fortune in special milling costs alone. Look at the fancy trim all over the house inside and out. When those plans were drawn I suppose it could be bought from stock. Today it doesn't exist. All of it would have to be special order, lathed and jig-sawed out and by people not used to it. Lot of errors and spoilage. What's more, the entire construction method is different from today's. No contractor has had any experience at it, or his men, either. He might not even bid; you'd have to pay cost plus. And the final price?" I shook my head. "It would be fantastic, and if you ever wanted to sell you'd have the world's biggest white elephant on your hands, a brand-new antique that no bank in the world would ever lend you a dime . . . "

Sam shut me off with a hand on my arm, smiling. He said gently, "Everything you're telling me, Harry, can be said in one word — money. Well, I've got the money and whatever it costs to build this house I guarantee you it'll be worth it." He saw I didn't know what he meant, and said, "Harry, boats are sold just like anything else — in a variety of ways. And one of the best ways is publicity. Think of the *talk* this'll make!" He grinned tensely. "Every customer I bring into that house will go home full of it. Why, Sam Cluett's new place will be talked about at cocktail parties, in restaurants, on boat decks, and in living rooms all over the Eastern seaboard. And who is Sam Cluett? Why, he makes boats! Harry, I could blow the place up two years after it's finished and it'll have paid for itself three times over." He turned to Ellie, saying, "Baby, you've picked yourself a house," then he swung back to me. "You know the contractors here. Hire one, Harry, and follow through for me, will you? Don't even ask for a bid; just have him follow the plans and send me his bills as he gets them, adding — what? Twenty per cent? Work it out with him." Sam glanced at his watch. "Now, let's get out of here and go look for a site!"

He was right about the talk. He and Ellie picked a building site that same afternoon, Sunday, and Monday morning I bought it for them — a three-and-a-half-acre plot over three hundred feet deep in the best residential section of town. It had been held for years in the hope of a fat price, and now Sam paid it. And less than seventy-two hours after Ellie Cluett dislodged the papers that were the forgotten plans for a forgotten house, its foundation was being laid — of brick, just as the old plans specified.

At first the new house attracted no attention; the wood frame of one house looks just about like any other at the beginning. Then the roof framing began and before it was finished it was plain to everyone passing that these were remarkably steep and complex gables. They intersected in dozens of places; they were pierced by innumerable dormers; at corners, they rose into sharp, narrow peaks, and they projected over — it was suddenly obvious — what were going to become bay windows and an enormous porch. And now all day every day cars crept past and clusters stood on the sidewalk as people watched the steady, skeletal growth in fresh white pine of a brand-new Victorian mansion.

I was just as fascinated. I had plenty of work. Specifying, ordering, and checking up on all the special milling were a job in themselves and I had much more to do. But still I spent more time at the new house than I really had to. Even at night, as though I were the actual architect, I'd sometimes drive over and prowl around and through it. One night I found Ellie standing on the walk, the big collar of her camel's-hair coat turned up, hands deep in her pockets, looking at the half-finished house.

The house was set far back from the street, and from the sidewalk the eye could take it all in. There was a three-quarter moon; we could see clearly. The new wood looked pale against the night sky and the door and window openings were narrow black rectangles, for the house was no longer skeletal. Most of the exterior sheathing was on, and the external shape of the house was complete. For the first time we could see, rising from the bare wood-littered earth, the beginning reality of what had been only architectural drawings.

Ellie murmured, "Isn't it astonishing?"

"Yeah." I was enjoying the almost ghostly sight of this strange unfinished house in the moonlight and I began fooling, playing with words. "We're looking at a vanished sight. This is a commonplace sight of a world long gone and we've reached back and brought it to life again. Maybe we should have let it alone."

Ellie smiled. "I don't think so. I feel good about it."

The work went fast; the men liked this job. Several had grown mustaches or sideburns in styles they thought appropriate to the house. One of the carpenters had just finished a year in New Jersey doing nothing but hanging doors in over nine hundred identical tract houses. He told me this job was the first time carpentering actually was what, as a boy, he'd imagined it to be. Now the siding was on, and the big veranda was complete. All windows were in. Everything was finished outside, in fact, except the eave ornamentation, not yet delivered, and some special-patterned shingle work on the gable ends.

Inside the hammering was constant — inlaid hardwood floors going down on the third floor, interior trim on the first and second. Plastering was finished, complete with old-style wood lathing, and on the first floor, doors were being hung — inches wider, two feet taller, and far heavier and more solid than any ordinarily made today. Their surfaces were beautifully paneled with fine moldings, and they, too, were new-minted and fresh-sanded, not even drilled yet for lock sets. Walking through the house, I'd stop when no one could see me, close my eyes, and sniff the familiar damp-plaster, new-wood fragrance of a just-finished house. Then I'd open my eyes and wonder at the magnificent brand-new old mansion in which, incredibly, I stood.

Sam wanted speed, and got it. When the completed house was still wet with paint, new grass was showing on the landscaped grounds, and transplanted bushes almost surrounded it. He'd had a dozen fir trees trucked to and planted on the grounds at whatever enormous cost — full-grown trees taller than the roof. And five stone masons, all I'd been able to round up, were building a wall clear around the grounds using old gray stone from a dismantled church. And now, the activity of building over and the house painted — entirely white — it lost its visual novelty and took its place in the town. People pausing on the walk dwindled to an occasional one or two.

The day Ellie finished furnishing it she stopped at my office downtown and invited me to see it. We drove in her car, and when we reached the house the great wrought-iron gates stood open in the wall and we swung through them onto a snow-white gravel driveway that curved up to the shaded veranda.

Ellie stopped halfway, giving me a chance to look around. All trace of raw newness was gone; the grounds were lush. This was June and the immense lawns were a flawless, fresh-mowed, brilliant summer green. The hedges were perfectly trimmed and flower beds stood in full bloom.

The house itself was immaculate; it sparkled. It stood there in the splendor of its grounds like a new-cut jewel in a just-finished setting — solid and vigorous, in the very prime of its youth — the living and finished reality of drawings that had lain dustily on my shelves for years.

I had only an impression of the interior when we'd finished — of large-patterned wallpaper suggesting the nineteenth century but colorful, gay, wonderfully cheerful; of last-century furniture intricately but beautifully carved, ornately but gracefully curved, finished to perfection and upholstered in tufted velvets of emerald green, canary yellow, scarlet, coral, and sky blue. I remember a little dressing room carpeted in pink. All doors were dull white, with polished brass hardware. The house sang.

I was out of town on a job the night of the Cluetts' big party a week later, the housewarming. But I drove back late in the evening and, while I wasn't dressed to go inside, I stopped my car by the big iron gates and what I saw was the most haunting sight I've ever seen.

The house was equipped with two lighting systems. One, which I designed, was electric with concealed outlets and almost unnoticeable flush ceiling lights. The other was gas, the lines following the original plans and with ornate fixtures which Ellie had searched out and bought, in all the principal rooms. Tonight as I sat looking in through the big gates, only the gas system was in use. And on all three floors of the big, rambling house, every window — tall and arched at the tops, looking like rows of great slender candles — glowed against the blue summer night with the yellowy, wonderfully warm light electricity has never equaled.

Dancing couples moved across those rectangles of light and music from a live orchestra moved out through the open windows across the lawns into the darkness. Sam had bought a horse and carriage to meet his New York guests at the railroad station. Tonight he'd hired three more and now they all stood on the white gravel of the curved driveway. Any guest who'd come by car had parked in the street. This was one of the last June nights and the air was balmy and alive with the drone of insects, the very sound of summer; and the lawns, strung with candlelit Japanese lanterns, flickered with fireflies. From the veranda I could hear laughter and the murmur of voices softened by distance and people stood outlined on the glowing candle shapes of the windows. Over and enclosing it all, the backdrop for everything, stood the great dark silhouette of the turreted, dormered, many-gabled house. It was a scene lost to the world, a glimpse of another time and manner of living, and I sat there for a long time before I drove home.

You lose touch with clients fairly quickly once a house is finished. For a time you're in each other's company and minds every day, more intimate than friends. Then suddenly you're busy with someone else. I didn't see the Cluetts again till well after Labor Day. Then one afternoon on impulse, I stopped in, not sure if they were still there. But they were. Sam met me on the porch in shirt sleeves — it was warm yet — calling to Ellie that I was there. He led me to the end of the veranda. There was a wooden porch swing, and we sat down, lifting our feet to the porch railing.

I said, "No work today, Sam?"

He smiled. "No. Lately I've been taking more time off than I used to."

From the window behind me, I heard steps in the kitchen, and the sound of glassware. Then Ellie appeared in the doorway.

I stared in open astonishment. Ellie — smiling mischievously as she bent forward to set a tray on a little wicker table — was wearing a dress that began high at the neck and snug around it and ended well below her ankles, brushing the porch floor. It was a soft leaf green and the long sleeves ended at the wrists in lace cuffs. The upper arms weren't actually puffed but they were full, peaking up a little at the shoulders. It was a dress of the last century and as Ellie sat down I saw that her hair was long now. It was parted in the center and braided and coiled at the back into a flat disk covering the nape of her neck.

Sam was grinning. He said, "You wouldn't want us to be the only things in the house that weren't appropriate, would you, Harry? Ellie and I decided we ought to be dressed for the place." With his fingers he flicked one of his cream-colored pants legs, and I saw that they were patterned with a light-blue stripe, a kind of trousers last worn decades ago. Then I realized that his hair wasn't just overdue for cutting; he was wearing it in a style outmoded when my father was born.

I grinned, too, then. Ellie was pouring from a brown stoneware pitcher beaded with tight little drops, the ice clinking as it slid into the glasses. I said, "You look wonderful, both of you; absolutely right for this house. Your guests must get a kick out of it."

"Well, as a matter of fact," Sam said, "we've pretty well quit entertaining my customers here. Not many of them really appreciated the place."

Ellie handed me a filled glass, and I tasted the drink; it was fresh-squeezed lemonade, and delicious. I said, "You must like the house for its own sake, then."

"I can't tell you how much," Ellie said softly. "We've moved here permanently, you know. We don't go to New York any more."

For half an hour, then, we talked about the house. Ellie told me she even sewed here in a little room at the top of a turret. It was something she'd never before had patience for but she'd actually made the dress she was wearing. She said the pattern for it and even the exact shade just came drifting into her mind one day and she wanted to have it and made it herself.

Presently she said, "I always assumed that the plans for this house had never been used, didn't you, Harry?" I nodded, and she said, "But it's just as possible that they *were* used, isn't it?"

"I suppose so."

She smiled wonderingly. "Strange, isn't it, to think that this house existed before? Right here in Darley, undoubtedly, maybe in sight of this one."

"If it existed."

She looked at me for a moment, her face dead serious. Then, with such quiet certainty that I smiled in surprise, she said, "It did."

"Oh? How do you know?"

Ellie looked at Sam. He hesitated, then nodded slightly, and Ellie turned back to me. She said, "You know how associations slowly form in a house you've lived in for a long time. The way the sun strikes the ceiling of a certain room may remind you forever of how it felt when you were a child getting dressed for school. Do you know what I mean?"

I said, "Sure. After a hot day, the beams of my house cool off and contract; make a lot of noise. Every time it happens I remember the first time I tasted strawberries as a kid. With some of the other old associations in my house, the memories are gone, only the emotions left, and I can't remember why they began."

"Yes!" Ellie leaned forward, excited. "This house is full of them! Turn a corner in the front hallway, and the way the stairs rise toward the second floor gives me a feeling of peace. And when the back screen door slams, just the sound of it makes me happy for no reason I know." She hesitated, then said, "And there are other more specific things. One morning I walked into the library. Sam was sitting there reading. The windowpanes are divided into quarters, and the sun came through at an angle, and four diamond-shaped patches of sunlight lay across the bindings of the books on the shelves. Harry, I saw them, smiled, and said to Sam, 'Well, the Pelliers arrive tomorrow for a week. Won't we have fun!' And Sam looked up and nodded. He knew it, too! Then we just stared at each other. Because we don't know anyone named Pellier; we never have. And no one was coming next day."

Sam said, "I thought she was nuts, too, Harry, till that happened. But from then on, things happened to me, too. There's an upstairs window, and when you open it, it squeals and the sash weight rattles. All I can tell you is that whenever that happens I'm just glad to be alive. And a couple of months ago I opened the front door to see if the morning paper had arrived. My hand touched the doorknob and the instant I felt it — it's porcelain and oval; feels like a china egg — I thought, *Today's the parade!*

At the same time, I knew there wasn't any parade, hadn't been a parade in Darley for years." He turned to Ellie. "Tell him about the skating."

She said, "Night before last we were reading in the living room. I looked up from my book at the fireplace, then thought, *In a couple of months, we'll be lighting that. And when we do, there'll be skating on Sikermann's Slough.* Yet I don't even know what that means."

I felt the hair on the back of my neck prickle as I said, "I do. It's been filled in and forgotten for years but it was still there when my father was a boy — a slough that used to freeze over every winter. It was on a corner of what was once the Sikermann farm, sometime in the eighteen eighties."

In Darley, as elsewhere, building slacks off during the winter; and whenever I had time, I tried to learn where or when the old house existed before but I never did. The title block of the original plans tells for whom they were drawn but I found nothing about him or the plans in town records, which isn't particularly surprising. I poked through back files of the old Darley *Intelligencer,* too, but found out very little; they're incomplete with gaps of days, weeks, months, and even years. All I learned was how many more fires there were back in the days of largely wood construction and of gas and kerosene lighting and wood stoves.

But I have no doubt that that house existed — sometime in the eighties, I should think. And that it was a happy house — one of the occasional rare and wonderful houses that acquire souls and lives of their own; the kind of house that seems to know you're in it and puts its best foot forward; a house born of the feelings and love of the lost and forgotten people who planned, built, lived in, and gave it life. I think that like many another house of the times this one burned and that maybe my granddad produced the plans for a fire-insurance claim agent, then stuck them on his shelves. I don't know.

But in one way or another its life was cut suddenly short. And then, miraculously, it found itself in being again. Room for room, in every least detail — exactly as it had been in the far-off moment when fire flared along the edge of a curtain, perhaps — the old house existed once more. And it simply resumed its life; the kind of life and times, of course, that it knew.

I've never gone back to it. I suppose I'd be welcome but I don't feel that I belong there any more, not in the life the Cluetts lead now. They leave the grounds only when necessary, Sam driving his buggy. No one goes in; the big gates are kept closed. Sam sold his boatyard this spring — for enough money, I've heard, so that he need never work again. They no longer take a newspaper and whether they read their mail no one knows; they never send any.

But every night the lights are on, the wonderfully warm yellow-orange gas lights, and all last winter they used the fireplaces. This summer people have had glimpses of them. They've been seen playing croquet on the lawn, Ellie in a long white dress. And just this week twin hammocks, the kind with long fringe at the sides, appeared on the shaded veranda. And the two of them lie there reading the lazy afternoons away. I know what they read. The books they'd bought had arrived when I last visited the Cluetts, and along with other fine leather-bound old volumes there were the complete works of Dickens and Sir Walter Scott, just the thing for long summer afternoons far back in the past.

For that's where the Cluetts are, of course. I don't quite believe stories I've heard — that one night last winter it snowed on their property and nowhere else; and that occasionally sun has shone or rain has fallen on their roof but not on the rest of the town, as though the house existed in some other year. Just the same, Ellie and Sam are living far back in the past; that's where they are. For their new house is haunted by its old self. And its ghost has captured the Cluetts — rather easily, for I think they were glad to surrender.

# THE AUTHORS

CONRAD AIKEN ("Mr. Arcularis")
Born in Savannah, Georgia, and a graduate of Harvard (1911), Conrad Potter Aiken (1889–1973) was a prominent poet, essayist, novelist, and short-story writer. His many literary awards included the Pulitzer Prize (1930) for *Selected Poems*. Recommended works are *Collected Poems* (1953, 1970) and *The Collected Short Stories of Conrad Aiken* (1966). His daughter, Joan Aiken, is a well-known fantasy writer. "Mr. Arcularis" first appeared in *Criterion,* Apr., 1932.

DANA BURNET ("Fog")
Born in Cincinnati, Ohio, Dana Burnet (1888–1962) graduated from Cornell Law School (1911) and worked seven years as a reporter for *The New York Evening Sun* before becoming a full-time writer. Several of his plays were produced on Broadway, including *Four Walls,* which was made into a movie with Gilbert Roland and Joan Crawford. His short stories were highly regarded and "Fog" was included in *The Best Stories of 1916.* The story first appeared in *McBride's Magazine,* Feb., 1916.

HORTENSE CALISHER ("The Summer Rebellion")
Born in New York City, Hortense Calisher (1911– ) graduated from Barnard College (1932), and spent much of her career teaching at various

colleges and universities. Her work has appeared in many prestigious magazines and journals and won four O. Henry Prize story awards. Recommended works include *Journal from Ellipsia* (1965) and *The Collected Stories of Hortense Calisher* (1975). "The Summer Rebellion" first appeared (in a different form) as "The Summer Psychosis" in *Harper's Bazaar,* Sept., 1967.

ROBERT M. COATES ("The Hour After Westerly")
Born in New Haven, Connecticut, Robert Myron Coates (1897–1973) graduated from Yale University (1919). An art critic and writer, his works include *The Eater of Darkness* (1929), *The Hour After Westerly and Other Stories* (1957), and *The View from Here* (1960), an autobiography. His short stories appeared in both the *O. Henry Memorial Award Prize Stories* (1937) and O'Brien's *Best Short Stories* (1939). "The Hour After Westerly" first appeared in *The New Yorker,* Nov., 1947.

THOMAS A. EASTON ("Roll Them Bones")
Born in Bangor, Maine, Thomas A. Easton (1944– ) earned a Ph.D. in theoretical biology from the University of Chicago. He is an adjunct assistant professor of biology at Thomas College in Waterville, Maine. The book reviewer for *Analog Science Fiction Magazine,* he is the author of approximately thirty science fiction stories, and has written twelve books, including texts such as *Bioscope* (1979, 1984) and *Careers in Science* (1984). "Roll them Bones" is an original story published here for the first time.

JACK FINNEY ("Where the Cluetts Are")
Born in Milwaukee, Wisconsin, Walter Braden "Jack" Finney (1911– ) was educated at Knox College. He is a full-time writer whose fantasy works include two novels, *The Body Snatchers* (1955) and *Marion's Wall* (1973), both of which were filmed. Another fantasy novel, *Time and Again* (1970), has been called one of the five best mystery novels ever written. His fantasy short stories appear in three collections: *The Third Level* (1957), *I Love Galesburg in the Springtime* (1963), and *About Time.* "Where the Cluetts Are" first appeared in *McCall's,* Jan., 1962.

RICHARD FREDE ("Mr. Murdoch's Ghost")
Born in Albany, New York, Richard Frede (1934– ) graduated from Yale University and presently resides in New Hampshire. A full-time writer, he has appeared in most of the leading magazines and has published more

than a dozen novels under his own name and several suspense novels under a pseudonym. His most widely known work is *The Interns* (1961), which served as the basis of two films. "Mr. Murdoch's Ghost" first appeared in *The Magazine of Fantasy and Science Fiction,* May, 1977.

SARAH ORNE JEWETT ("Lady Ferry")
Born in South Berwick, Maine, Sarah Orne Jewett (1849–1909) graduated from Berwick Academy (1866) and received an honorary doctorate from Bowdoin College (1901). She appeared in most of the leading magazines of her day, primarily writing short stories about small-town New England life. Recommended works are *The Country of the Pointed Firs* (1896) and *The Best Short Stories of Sarah Orne Jewett* (1988). "Lady Ferry" first appeared in her collection *Old Friends and New* (1879).

OLIVER LA FARGE ("Haunted Ground")
Born in New York City, Oliver Hazard Perry La Farge (1901–1963), received a baccalaureate (1924) and master's degree (1929) from Harvard University. He spent much of his career as an anthropologist studying Indians of the Southwest. The author of many novels and short stories, he received the Pulitzer Prize for fiction (1929) for *Laughing Boy* and the O. Henry Special Prize for short short stories for "Haunted Ground" in 1931. The latter story first appeared in *Ladies Home Journal,* Aug., 1930.

H. P. LOVECRAFT ("The Shunned House")
Born in Providence, Rhode Island, Howard Phillips Lovecraft (1890–1937) was primarily self-educated due to poor health and bizarre family circumstances. An extremely important and influential figure in horror fiction, he spent most of his time corresponding with, and rewriting the manuscripts of other, aspiring writers, such as Robert Bloch. Several of his works, including "The Colour out of Space" (1927), "From Beyond" (1934), and "Herbert West — Reanimator" (1922), have been filmed. "The Shunned House" first appeared as a privately printed book (The Recluse Press) in 1928.

ELIZABETH A. LYNN ("The Island")
Born in New York City, Elizabeth A. Lynn (1946– )received a baccalaureate from Case Western Reserve University (1967) and a master's degree from the University of Chicago (1968). A feminist and an expert in Aikido, she taught and worked in hospital settings before becoming a full-time fantasy and science fiction writer. A winner of two World Fantasy

Awards, her works include the Tornor Trilogy (1979, 1979, 1981) and a collection *The Woman Who Loved the Moon and Other Stories* (1981). "The Island" first appeared in *The Magazine of Fantasy and Science Fiction,* Nov., 1977.

J. A. POLLARD ("Old Woman")
Born in Waterville, Maine, Jean Ann Pollard is a graduate of the University of Massachusetts. The author and illustrator of *The New Maine Cooking* (1987) and *The Ice Ladder* (1987), a children's book, she has recently turned to fantasy and science fiction. "Old Woman" is an original story, appearing here for the first time.

WILBUR DANIEL STEELE ("The Woman at Seven Brothers")
Born in Greensboro, North Carolina, Wilbur Daniel Steele (1886–1970) graduated from the University of Denver in 1907 and received an honorary doctorate from that school (1932). He was noted for his short stories and is the only person to win three first prizes ("The Man Who Saw Through Heaven" [1925], "Bubbles" [1926], and " 'Can't Cross Jordan by Myself' " [1931]) from the O. Henry Award Committee. Many of his finest stories are collected in *The Best Stories of Wilbur Daniel Steele* (1946, 1970). "The Woman at Seven Brothers" first appeared in *Harper's Magazine,* Dec., 1917.

JOHN W. VANDERCOOK ("The Challenge")
Born in London, England, John W. Vandercook (1902–1963) dropped out of Yale to become an actor and reporter. The author of fourteen books, he became a radio commentator by chance in 1940 when he happened to be visiting the NBC studio as a story about the West Indies, on which he was an expert, began to break. Pressed into service as a commentator, he was hired and retained that position until retiring in 1960. "The Challenge" first appeared in *Ellery Queen's Mystery Magazine,* July, 1952.

EDITH WHARTON ("The Triumph of Night")
Born in New York City, Edith Newbold Jones Wharton (1862–1937) became the first woman to be awarded an honorary doctorate from Yale University (1923). The author of 47 books — one of which (*The Age of Innocence*) won the Pulitzer Prize (1921) — she spent much of her life in France, and was a close friend of Henry James. Recommended works include *Ethan Frome* (1911), *The Ghost Stories of Edith Wharton* (1937),

and her autobiography, *A Backward Glance* (1934). "The Triumph of Night" first appeared in *Scribner's Magazine,* Aug., 1914.

HENRY S. WHITEHEAD ("The Trap")
Born in Elizabeth, New Jersey, Henry S. Whitehead (1882–1932) graduated from Harvard University and Berkeley Divinity School. He became an Episcopal priest, was appointed a deacon in 1912, and an archdeacon to the Virgin Islands in 1921. After discovering *Weird Tales* magazine, he began writing horror stories, many with a Caribbean background. Two collections of his fantastic stories are *Jumbee and Other Uncanny Tales* (1944) and *West India Lights* (1946). "The Trap" was first published in *Strange Tales of Mystery and Terror,* Mar., 1932.

LEROY YERXA ("Carrion Crypt")
Leroy Yerxa (1915–1946) was born in Old Town, Maine. His father, a woolen goods finisher, moved to New York and then Michigan. After graduating from Eaton Rapids High School, Leroy started a career in journalism and public relations, but gradually turned to writing short stories. For several years before his untimely death due to a stroke, he worked as a staff writer for the Ziff-Davis Publishing Company, producing more than fifty science fiction and fantasy stories in his own name and under various pseudonyms. "Carrion Crypt" first appeared in *Fantastic Adventures,* July, 1947, under the pseudonym Richard Casey.

Detroit City Ordinance 29-85, Section
29-2-2(b) provides: "Any person who
retains any library material or any part
thereof for more than fifty (50) calendar days beyond the due date shall be
guilty of a misdemeanor."